Belinda Seaward

Belinda Seaward was born in Cornwall to a British mother and Polish father. She began her career as a journalist and worked on national newspapers including the *Daily Mail* and *Sunday Times*. She has lived and worked in the Arabian Gulf and also spent time on a coffee plantation in Zambia, where her acclaimed second novel *Hotel Juliet* is set. She now lives in Devon, where she teaches philosophy and in her spare time works with her Arabian horses.

Praise for Belinda Seaward

'Moving and insightful . . . Young, courageous and frightened Krystyna in 1939 seems just as alive as confused, middle-aged Catherine in the present day. Though the two never met, how their stories intertwine reveals the tragic yet beautiful truth of secret pasts' *Press Association*

'A thrillingly observant writer and crafter of highly sensual prose, Seaward employs language and lore . . . to considerable metaphorical effect . . . its richly descriptive escapism is seductive' *Daily Mail*

'A breathtaking work and a deeply moving elegy to the transitory nature of family life' *Scotland on Sunday*

'A gripping evocation of love and passion' *Sainsbury's Magazine*

'This poignant epic is a real page-turner . . . a mesmerising, well-crafted novel' *Birmingham Evening Mail*

'A cinematic novel of breadth and beauty . . . Superbly written, the author's descriptions . . . are possessed of an almost ineffable resonance' *Argus*

'Well-researched and engrossing narrative . . . beautifully written' *www.bookbag.co.uk*

'Very quietly binds a spell on the reader . . . unusual and absorbing' *Shropshire Star*

D0262686

Also by Belinda Seaward

The Avalanche
Hotel Juliet

The Beautiful Truth

Belinda Seaward

JOHN MURRAY

First published in Great Britain in 2012 by John Murray (Publishers)
An Hachette UK Company

First published in paperback in 2013

1

© Belinda Seaward 2012

The right of Belinda Seaward to be identified as the Author of the
Work has been asserted by her in accordance with the Copyright,
Designs and Patents Act 1988.

All rights reserved. Apart from any use permitted under UK copyright law no part
of this publication may be reproduced, stored in a retrieval system, or transmitted, in any
form or by any means without the prior written permission of the publisher, nor be
otherwise circulated in any form of binding or cover other than that in which it is
published and without a similar condition being imposed on the subsequent purchaser.

All characters in this publication are fictitious – other than a few historical figures –
and any resemblance to real persons, living or dead, is purely coincidental.

A CIP catalogue record for this title is available from the British Library

ISBN 978-0-7195-2131-7
Ebook ISBN 978-1-84854-671-4

Typeset in Bembo by Hewer Text UK Ltd, Edinburgh

Printed and bound by Clays Ltd, St Ives plc

John Murray policy is to use papers that are natural, renewable and recyclable
products and made from wood grown in sustainable forests. The logging and
manufacturing processes are expected to conform to the environmental
regulations of the country of origin.

John Murray (Publishers)
338 Euston Road
London NW1 3BH

www.johnmurray.co.uk

Dedicated to Krystyna of Kraków, who understood love

1

The man's face is familiar, eerily familiar, a face from a thousand dreams to come. He uses his familiarity to his advantage, smiling, placing his pudgy hands on the table in front of him as if this were an ordinary friendly conversation between equals. He has a sweet smell; there's a mildness about his eyes, which remain soft as he asks his questions, patiently laying them out neatly one by one. He wears an immaculate uniform with a starched collar; the colours of his decorations bring almost a touch of warmth to the cell. There is something priestly about him. Of course there is, he is after extracting a confession.

'You were a sergeant in the Home Army, weren't you a perfect patriot, my friend?' His voice is seductive. His eyes say that they are sorry that he has no choice other than to continue.

'I have already said that I was a member of the resistance. What more do you want?'

He smiles and leans forward. 'The truth, my friend, I want you to tell me the truth.'

'I have already told you the truth.'

The interrogator looks at his watch and yawns. It's four

Leabharlanna Poibli Chathair Baile Átha Cliath

Dublin City Public Libraries

in the morning, breaking hour. They have been talking like this since midday. It is extraordinary how words can stretch to fill any length of time. These people are masters at pulling language into shapes that seem impossible. When they have finished with words, you believe everything they say, for that is the game; the end point of the investigation is not to make you confess, but to make you doubt. To doubt all that makes you human.

There have been days like this. Too many to count. Janek knows that the interrogators sleep in the prison. The UB are not allowed homes or personal lives. They are captives, just as he is. When he first arrived he thought of scratching a calendar on the cell walls to record his time as others had done before him. Etched into the hard shell around him were initials, names, dates, a few complete messages to wives and husbands, to children, to life itself. There were words of hope and there were words of desperation. He considered leaving his mark, but after the sixth day that seemed futile.

'Do you understand what we do here?' the interrogator continues. His round face shines in the bare light. It's almost a holy light, pure, untainted. It fills the cell with radiance.

Janek shifts on his stool. 'You ask questions.'

The interrogator is irritated by the response. He nods to a young officer standing behind Janek. At a sign from the interrogator, the officer aims his boot at Janek's buttocks and kicks him off the stool. The floor is gritty. He can feel it under his cheek. At some point sand has been sprinkled in here. The young officer's boots grind the minute glass particles into even finer sand as they kick steadily at Janek's ribs, his stomach, his kidneys, his genitals. The sound reminds Janek of feed sacks dropping one after another from a hay loft.

'That's enough,' says the interrogator. Blowing from his efforts, the officer picks up the stool and turns it with its legs pointing upwards. Janek lies on the cement floor with his knees drawn up to his chest, listening to the sound of his own blood pounding in his ears. His body is a bag of hot pulp, but the floor is cool, almost soothing. His eyelids flutter. A violet light pulses on the edge of his vision. For a second he thinks he can smell fresh water. The interrogator's voice slices through the hallucinations, breaking his fall into oblivion. 'Perhaps now you would like a more comfortable seat?'

Trying to balance on a stool leg with his thighs outstretched is even more excruciating than the kicks and blows. The interrogator's expression is one of compassion. 'Who do you know?' he asks gently. 'What are the names and addresses of your Home Army friends?'

'I've given you names.' There is blood in his mouth again. It is strange how you can get used to the taste of it and even find it a relief. Its salt is sustaining him.

The interrogator nods to the officer. He takes a step forward. He is perhaps the same age as Janek, twenty-five or thereabouts: white-skinned with a narrow, closed face; unblinking, dry eyes and pale, almost invisible lips. The interrogator raises his finger, indicating the officer should wait. He bites his lip. He shakes his head and smiles a slow, sad smile. It is unfortunate, but he has caught Janek out in a lie. He has no other option than to punish him. He leans forward with his elbows on his desk. He speaks slowly and with regret. 'My friend, I'm afraid those names are the names of the dead.'

The stool cracks against the cell wall. Shoved down on the floor for another pummelling, Janek is gratified to see that one of stool legs has split off from the base. The punches and kicks are not so bad this time. His officer is getting tired. He is losing his appetite. His tight breathing suggests he might be asthmatic. In a while another officer will come to take over and they will drag Janek back into his cell.

Blood and shit cake the back of his pants and he is shaking like a dog. At least he isn't crawling. Sometimes they did that: brought in prisoners on their hands and knees as examples of their work. He is still just about standing. He isn't screaming or moaning either. There are others all the way down the corridor doing that for him. He has made it a point of honour that he won't call out. No matter how bad the pain, he will maintain a vow of silence. The interrogator has told him that he is trained in the art of breaking down a man, stripping him to his essential components like an aircraft engine, each piece of him disassembled, reconfigured, reordered into a blueprint of the interrogator's choosing. 'I can play God,' he'd said in his silky voice. 'I can create new men: I can start them afresh. Just like Adam.' In another part of the prison there were other brutes engaged in refashioning their version of Eve. It is ugly work. Their methods are crude. Most of them are poor mechanics. Janek's refusal to acknowledge their effortful labour is his protection. Silence keeps him intact.

The guard shoves him through the door of cell number twelve. Something is different. The air smells cleaner somehow. He staggers inside and the door sinks shut behind him. Now he sees what they have done: the glass has been removed from the high window. The blanket has been taken from the bed. Icy air blasts through the barred portal. Outside, dawn is breaking. He can see clouds, edged with rose, the morning star. He takes a deep breath.

The door opens. 'Face the window. Stand to attention!' He stands. Another order is shouted at him. 'Strip off your clothes!' He strips. His clothes are snatched out from behind him, as if they are valuable booty. Naked, he stands before the open window. 'You are forbidden to move!' He remains still. He watches the sky. There are no birds. No signs of life except for the clouds. For hours he stands to attention, lost in the grey sky, waiting for release. Every so often the cell door opens and a guard comes in with a bucket of water which is hurled at his back. The cold makes his teeth chatter. His lips, ears and nose are numb. He longs to throw his arms around himself, but he knows that they will be watching from the spy-hole. They will have posted someone out there to see if he cheats.

By the fifth hour the cold has made him desperate to urinate. He calls out to the guard asking to use the bucket in the corner of the cell. The guard shouts that he is not to move. In defiance Janek takes a single step towards the bucket. The cell door is wrenched open. Two guards rush in and grab him. One holds him under the arms from behind while the other kicks him repeatedly in the groin. He feels the breath of the guard behind him, thick and heavy and warm on his neck. The guard stops kicking. He goes over to the bucket in the corner and drags it across the cement floor, slopping its contents over the side. The bucket has not been emptied in days and the smell makes Janek want to retch. He swallows his nausea, chewing with his teeth, as if digesting a particularly tough piece of gristle.

For nine hours he stands naked, frozen, immobile. His

mind roams in loops across fields and forests and lakes. At one point he is convinced he can taste mushrooms. He hears someone laughing, a girl, whose face keeps fading in and out of focus. She has pale hair and sapphire eyes, but he cannot be certain that she is a girl because sometimes she has the appearance of a horse: a white horse galloping through snow. He can feel her pulse, her animal pulse.

'Did you enjoy your session of winter sports?' The interrogator is back in business again. He wears a fresh white shirt and his hair is clean. He smells of spicy cologne. Janek, who is still naked and filthy, wonders whether this form of one-upmanship is listed in the UB handbook of methods to break a man. How to dehumanize a prisoner: taunt him with your scrupulous personal hygiene. In other words: rub his face in his own shit.

'Is that what you call it?' The broken stool has been replaced and he is allowed to sit on this one the right way up.

The interrogator feigns a convivial mood and his fat little hands play with a brass inkwell and blotter on the centre of his desk. He leans his head back and laughs. 'Obviously we haven't frozen out your sense of humour.'

'Not yet.' He doesn't know why he is speaking this way because if he continues the middle-aged officer seated at the interrogator's right will be given the nudge to begin. Maybe that is why he is sounding insolent: maybe he wants no more than to get it over with. The waiting is worse than the actual fact of a beating. Janek understands that he is already becoming accustomed to the brutality. Soon they will have to find other methods with which to torture him, or shoot him.

The interrogator toys with the inkwell. 'Tell me the name of the woman you call your sister, the one who was the colonel's messenger girl.'

'I've told you.'

'But you haven't been very helpful. You haven't told us where she lives.'

'I don't know where she lives.'

The nudge is given. The officer shunts his bottom out of his seat. He lifts the inkwell and blotter from the middle of the desk and places them on the edge closest to Janek. Then he takes Janek's hands in both of his and rests them palm down on the blotter.

'Where does she live?' the interrogator asks.

'I've told you. I don't know.'

With all the force in his slack middle-aged body, the officer slams the brass inkwell down across Janek's finger-nails. All three men watch as the blood sprays across the blotter like fine red ink.

'Perhaps your memory has been jogged?' The interrogator shifts his chair closer to the desk and peers into Janek's eyes.

Make no sound. Betray no pain. If you give them your pain, they own you. Once they have you, they have the right to snap you into pieces ready to be remade. Always remember that their object is not the truth, but conformity.

'I don't know where she lives.'

2

Kraków, present day

When Catherine was twelve, her father gave her a pair of binoculars. Bulky with a leather strap, they bashed her breastbone as she tried them on, twiddling the focus dials to magnify the white rabbit in the garden. His pink eye zoomed bright, frightening her with its limpid, bloody intensity. 'For night-time,' her father said, watching her, his legs straight in narrow black trousers with a double seam from waist to ankle, his clean white shirt billowing at the small of his back. He nipped one end of a limp black bow tie between his teeth, making his next words difficult to decipher. 'Good for washing starts.' Released from knotting, the teeth slipped into a smile. 'Watching stars,' he repeated. 'You can follow eclipse.'

It was the beginning of July and the days smelled of cut grass, creosote and sun lotion. At night huge gold moths blundered into her bedroom where she lay reading astronomy books under the yellow glass lamp. Because he was always working at the hotel, her father rarely kissed her goodnight. The binoculars in their blocky box with their faint smell of cigars were some consolation. Every evening she waited until she could hear the television singing downstairs, and then, bunching her nightdress under her knees, she climbed on to her windowsill and lifted the barium crown glass lens to her eyes. Once her pupils had adjusted, she opened her heart to the skies.

A month after he gave her the binoculars, her father vanished from her life. He left no trace, no afterglow, no signs that he might return. There was an odd, achy space in the wardrobe where his shirts and hotel clothes had hung. A smell of Aramis, laundry and betrayal.

The television stayed on downstairs more or less permanently. In the cool of her room Catherine lay on her bed reading about the planets. She kept her curtains open and lifted her eyes from her book to the mute white face that hovered there, full and unafraid. The moon moved tides, caused swells and pulls; it shifted directions in people, too, turned them restless or mad, its cycles female, intimately linked to blood and birth. Brimming with feeling, her mind spinning from reading, she scanned the sky with her binoculars. The bright summer stars Vega, Altair and Deneb welcomed her and she noted them with joy. The sky was a treasure trove, a sea chest of delights, and like the sea it never stopped moving; it ebbed and flowed, grew light and dark and it was free. When she left the window open to sleep it blew a soft breath on to her face.

At first she believed that her father would return. He would come back with another gift, perhaps a telescope this time. He would reappear when the tides changed, when the weather in the house grew less stormy. She waited all summer. There were no letters. Weeks rolled past and winter slipped into view with sharp, clear skies that quickened her pulse. Orion straddled the space through her window, his belt gleaming in the darkness.

In crowds she scanned faces half hoping, half fearing she would find some feature she recognized: a pale pocked forehead, a jaw with the taut exactness of the heel of her own hand, a piece missing from the rim of his right ear. She listened for his walk, looked for his laugh; she followed one or two people home, not because they looked like him, but because something in the way they carried themselves showed they understood what she lacked. She went after them because they would have known what to do.

She found solace in study and her teachers saw to it that she got the support she needed when her mother was in hospital. She took sciences and mathematics. She was selected as one of the school superstars, those few who were shooting towards bright futures. On the morning she sat her Cambridge entrance examination, her mother collapsed with two broken ribs, a fractured collarbone and a sprained ligament in her ankle. She had fallen down the steps in the garden while trying to peg out washing. A neighbour found her, bruised and weepy, and drove her to Accident and Emergency. Catherine visited her after school with a clean nightdress and her washing things. She sat by her mother's hospital bed and held her hand. Her mother's face was puffy and under her right eye there was a storm-coloured bruise.

'I'm sorry,' her mother said. She turned her head into the hospital pillow. 'I keep getting it wrong.' Her skin felt cold and clammy and when she tried to fasten the buttons on the nightdress her hand shook.

Catherine was in her second year at Cambridge when her mother died following another fall that led to a punctured lung and then pneumonia. The hospital helped Catherine to arrange the funeral. 'What about your father?'

the Irish nurse, Doreen, a friend of her mother's, asked. 'How shall we contact him?'

'I don't think we can – he hasn't been in touch since he left,' Catherine said. Doreen nodded. She didn't pursue it. For a month or two afterwards, Doreen called her once a week to see how she was coping. Catherine took the calls in a chilly high-ceilinged room overlooking a lawn; in the distance she could see the Bridge of Sighs. Eventually Doreen's calls dropped away and Catherine was left alone. She fell into her studies. Work swallowed her whole.

Her father lost magnitude and became distant, a nebulous part of her dreams. She forgot to think about him. But sometimes she was caught off-guard. A hissing sharp smell was enough to make her stop and examine amber fingers cupped around a petrol lighter hovering over a cigarette. Smoke. It had kept him busy, preoccupied by nervy tobacco-driven rituals, his form blanketed in blue, as if he'd wrapped a cloud around himself. He didn't talk when he smoked. He was utterly absorbed in smoking, protected by it. She began to recognize that there was some part of him, perhaps even all of him, that wanted to remain lost.

She was in the midst of her doctorate on Cecilia Payne, the pioneering English astronomer who discovered in 1925 that hydrogen was the most abundant element in the sun and stars, when, overwhelmed and daunted, her core collapsed. Her supervisor at Cambridge, Jonathan, a windswept, tousled, terribly kind man who kept his bicycle leaned under the window in his tiny office, advised a complete rest from reading. 'Nothing, not even a shopping list. You need to percolate for a bit.'

She slept. She drove out to the Fens, the binoculars bumping on the passenger seat of her old Renault, and tried to free her mind from the logjam of words and ideas. She watched whooper swans build huge loose nests and settle down on clutches of palm-sized eggs. They raised their young with haughty tenderness, chaperoning them along the long green V of water, like kings and queens, a flotilla of young royals in their wake. Their honking calls and brash take-offs contrasted absurdly with their effortless grace in flight. She spent hours watching them through the binoculars. When it rained she retreated to her car and drank coffee from her flask. Often she wept in sorrowful relief.

By the spring of that year – it must have been 1985 – she was cured, enough at least to contemplate a return to the discoveries of Miss Payne. Her supervisor made little comment other than advising her to take early nights and drink hot chocolate. On no account must she give up her visits to the Fens. She promised him she would look after herself and after a few months her doctorate took flight. Jonathan took her out for high tea and told her that she was back on track. Newly rejuvenated, her curiosity began to pull her by the hand, like an insistent child, to cupboards and drawers she had not opened since her mother's death.

One evening after she returned home from the library she pulled out the small blue leather suitcase from under her bed and went through it, sorting out the letters and photographs from things like her mother's passport, one corner snipped across, her birth certificate, qualifications and certificate of marriage. She transferred this to the second pile. Her mother had kept only one photograph of her wedding day. It showed a curvy young woman in a close-fitting cream suit with big cloth buttons and a neat hat with a veil, lifted off her face for the picture. She was smiling radiantly into the camera. Her new husband, older, dazed, his eyes half closed against the sun, wore a dark wool suit that was immaculate, but slightly too big for him. The photograph had been taken outside a register office in north London where the newly-weds had lived until she was born. They moved, a year or so later, to Devon so that her mother could be close to her parents. Catherine searched the suitcase for more, but there was nothing.

A few nights later she went through her mother's clothes, and found deep in the inner pocket of a man's raincoat a wallet. It smelled of old leaves. The satin lining was in holes and the leather had been eaten away at the corners. Inside were złoty notes, soft as blotting paper, a red and white Solidarity badge with its flaring flag insignia, and a scrap of yellow paper on which someone, perhaps her father, had scrawled: Paradise Hotel, Brighton.

She handed in a draft chapter to Jonathan, who told her to take the weekend off. She travelled from Cambridge to London and then to Brighton by train from Victoria. It was early May. The sky was full of movement. The trees were new brides catching fresh skirts. Catherine found she could not lean back in her seat. Perching forward as the train leapt down the line, she gulped the unfolding view of houses and office blocks, knowing that she was getting closer.

She wasn't surprised that he had come to the sea. She remembered how he had loved Torquay. Its mild bright air, its palms, its hotel villas and careless charm brought out his exuberance. He loved ice cream and flicking through the waves with his trousers rolled to the knee, his hand warm in hers. He loved throwing small wet pebbles, bouncing them and curving them on the water with astonishing speed and precision, drawing admiring glances from other less dexterous fathers.

One summer he taught her to swim. They were paddling, and she already knew how to tread water, but swimming was another level. She was ready, he said. Then without waiting for her reply he lifted her up and threw her in, the little skirt around her costume flipped up her legs. The water smacked her hard. She pushed through her own frantic bubbles and surfaced shocked and thrilled. He waved at her and held out his arms and then they both saw her mother standing, her magazine forgotten on the blanket, sunglasses pushed back on her head.

She drank warm squash to take away the taste of the salt while her father went to buy them all an ice cream. She was allowed two scoops, for being so brave. She lay on the blanket in the sun while her mother rubbed off the wet sand and massaged suncream into her back. Her father returned with ice creams sticking out of a red bucket which came with a flat spade. They spent the rest of the afternoon kneeling in the damp sand at the shore and he showed her how to make a castle with a moat and drawbridge and turrets laced with pretty shells. Further up the beach, her mother watched, arms drawn across her tanned knees, smoking cigarette after cigarette which she ground into the sand.

It was his day off, a woman with hair dyed to a deep shade of plum told her at the Paradise Hotel. He went out early that morning. The woman folded her fingers into her palm and squinted at her lacquered nails. It was lunchtime and from the grill room came the sound of scraping plates and sizzling meat. 'Stay if you want, love, have a drink.'

'I've come from Cambridge.' Catherine heard the wobble of tears in her voice. 'I need to see him.'

'But I think you've missed him, love. Did he know you were coming?'

'No, I phoned yesterday to see if he was here and someone said he was.'

'You should have come sooner. On his day off he goes out early.' The woman looked as if she wanted to add something more, but decided against it. 'What was it that you wanted?'

Catherine gulped. She glanced at the woman framed in a square hatch. From this porthole she had seen him come and go daily, and Catherine's stomach twisted with jealousy. 'What was he wearing?'

The woman narrowed her eyes and pretended to think. After a moment she gave in and frowned. 'I don't know. I didn't notice.'

Catherine closed her eyes. Her plan to search for him on the beach evaporated. Without some sort of clue, he would remain lost. She could come back, of course, find out when he was working next, but she knew that she wouldn't. She couldn't do this twice.

'Can I see his room?'

The woman's nails shot into view; the colour of orange crush, the lacquer was eerily perfect. Behind her a switchboard plugged with different tubes, like those screwed in to the end of old-fashioned bicycle pumps, winked and hummed. A red light flashed. The woman flicked a switch and the light went off. 'I don't think so, dear. I don't know who you are.'

Catherine was amazed. 'I'm his daughter.'

The woman leaned back against her swivel chair and scanned Catherine's face as if she did not believe her. Then she leaned down and scratched her calf with her nails, which squeaked against heavy-duty nylon. When she came up again her face was flushed. With deliberate slowness she swung her chair round and swept her eyes across a great board of keys that covered half of the office wall. Most of the keys had coloured plastic tags: red, green and yellow. On the far right of the board was a section of keys with no tags. The woman hooked one of these down and passed it across the hatch. She looked Catherine full in the face for what seemed like a minute, her expression shrewd.

'Don't lose it, will you? We need all the keys in case there's a fire.'

The room was at the top of a fire escape. The door was so thin she could have pushed it in with her shoulder. Inside, purple nylon curtains were drawn against the daylight casting a hazy gloom. There was a faint smell of fried food and stale cigarette smoke. The bed filled most of the space. With her heart thudding in her chest she stepped over to it and laid her hand on the pillow. She turned back the sheet and stood for a moment looking at the naked place where he had slept. Then she kicked off her shoes and lay down with her face to the pillow, which smelled sweet as if it did not belong to this tawdry cell, but somewhere more generous. A travel alarm clock ticked by her ear. Beyond the fire escape she could see the outline of seagulls circling on huge white wings. The clock ticked away. She felt her breathing slow.

When she woke he was standing over her with a patient look on his face as if he had been there for a while. She sprang up immediately and ran her hands through her hair, which fell in hot spirals down her shoulders. He glanced away. His eyes were heavy.

'I shouldn't have done it like this,' she said. 'I should have warned you.'

He sat down on the bed and brought his knuckles up to his mouth. She could see that it was taking all his effort not to cry. He could not look at her. She felt appalled. She gabbled at him for a few minutes, but there was too much to say and eventually her words stopped. He remained sitting on the edge of the bed with his head bowed. She noticed his hair was thinning at the crown. 'I'm so sorry,' he said after a minute, his accent soft, emphasizing the long 'o' sounds. He sounded to her more Polish than she remembered, as though he were out of practice with his English. He lifted his eyes and slowly turned his head as if to disperse something that shamed him. He tried to speak again, but no words came. There was just the dry sound of his tongue clicking against the unfamiliar language on his palate.

Her hands shook as she put on her shoes and smoothed her shirt. 'I didn't come looking for apologies. I came . . .' She paused, wondering now why she had come. 'To find out where you were.' She'd almost said 'who', but stopped herself.

He swallowed and with difficulty he spoke again. 'As you can see' – he dragged his arm across the room which had grown hot and tight – 'I am here.'

'I've disturbed you.' She didn't know what else to say.

He stood up and looked at the paper-thin door. They both knew that when she went through it for a second time they would never see each other again. She felt her throat thicken as she took in the whole of him. He was thin and pale, the freckles showing through the fine red hairs at the base of his throat and on his arms. A cheap gold watch dangled loosely from one wrist. 'I still have the binoculars,' she blurted out.

He nodded and brought his hand up to his mouth again.

His green eyes flooded. Then she was outside in the weak sunshine, holding on to the arm of the fire escape as she half ran, half fell down to the gravel path below.

On the train journey home she tried not to think about him. There was nothing more she could do. She had found him and that was that, perhaps it was enough; it certainly seemed more than he could bear. She would leave him to live in his own private way. The visit had answered something, though. It confirmed what she had always suspected: that her father had no ordinary explanation for why he left. It was as though he had done what he could in one life and then slipped into another.

It was enough for her to settle down into academic life at Cambridge and to try to build a life with someone who loved her. The memory of the thin room faded and sometimes she wondered whether she had dreamed it. Sometimes the old longing emerged, especially when things were going well. Every time she achieved some success in astronomy she had to suppress the urge to make another trip to the Paradise Hotel. But then there were other times, usually when colleagues asked about her father in the past tense – 'did he ever go back to Poland?' – that she shamefully allowed them to think that he was dead.

And now, in a sense, he has reappeared. Catherine looks around her at the audience gathered in the eerie beauty of the salt chamber. They have come to hear a concert, a requiem by Zbigniew Preisner, one of Poland's revered film composers. There are several here tonight who might be her father had he been given the chance to become someone else: graceful men in well-cut suits, freshly shaved necks dovetailing cleanly against laundered shirts; polished crocodile shoes with a little gleaming chain across the instep. Her heart skitters at the sight of an orange polka-dot silk tie. The men seem patient, almost docile next to their women, who wear textured woven jackets and carry glossy handbags, gold and silver earrings glimmering in the bare underground light. Blithely confident in their swathe of scent, it's the women who are talking, mostly to each other, using hands and eyes, touching a shoulder or upper arm for emphasis, leaning in close for the reply. The chamber reverberates with their muted, yet animated sound, like birds at dusk: a mellifluous stream of Polish mixed in with French, Spanish and Dutch. A few Americans and British, fussing over seats and programmes.

The chapel, carved entirely from a grey-green block of salt, is lit by five long-stemmed chandeliers, each one hung with individually carved salt crystals, the pale pewter light appearing to Catherine like slow streaming starlight. Her eye sweeps around the chamber, taking in the statues, one of Pope John Paul II in still, salt-bound perfection with a basket of yellow roses at his feet. On the salt walls are carved reliefs, lit by hooded lamps, chisel marks etched in the rock turning it into elephant hide. The largest relief, inspired by Leonardo da Vinci's *Last Supper*, shows the disciples leaning like blown trees in a salty coast wind around the central figure of Jesus, who sits with his arms outstretched across a long dining table. Her glance hovers over the figure on the right, his arm in its rock-salt sleeve projecting violence of movement as he turns away to whisper to the disciples at the end of the supper table. It took miners sixty-eight years to carve the figures. Most of them were self-taught and worked in dim lamplight, fingers stiff in the bone-chilling air. *The Last Supper* has a three-dimensional quality; she feels she could almost slip inside it. 'This is Polish history,' mutters an elderly woman next to her. 'Betrayal and resurrection.' She glances at Catherine as if they have met previously and is trying to place her. Then she shakes her head and moves away to take her seat.

Rows of wooden chairs sit on the carved honeycombed floor facing the high altar decked in white candles to illuminate the rock-salt statue of St Kinga, the forward-thinking thirteenth-century Hungarian princess, who instead of a dowry asked her father for a business venture and received a salt mine. Konrad had told her the story on the way down to the chamber.

Now she joins him, slipping into the seat he has saved for her, finding the wood surprisingly warm. She looks at his knees spread slightly apart under the thick clean cream of his American chinos. He inclines his head towards her and speaks out of the side of his mouth. 'Is this okay?'

He's being gracious and is referring to the seats and possibly the occasion, which was his idea, but there is a hint, revealed by a note of hectic glitter in his eyes, that he might be referring to their meeting itself.

'It's great. Wonderful. Thank you.' She feels shivery, close to exhaustion.

He looks at her for a moment and then turns his attention to the high altar where the choir enters, the singers arranging themselves in height order. Most of the women are short and bosomy with weathered peasant faces; the few tall and slender ones soar at the back. The men, grey and crumpled, seem daunted and bunch close together. The orchestra is already seated, the women violinists in black velvet gowns, the men younger than their choir counterparts, one or two tanned and relaxed, chatting across their instruments, which rest easily on their knees.

The conductor walks with brisk steps to the front and pauses to endure a ripple of applause, the tension in his neck indicating a need to be inside the music. He turns his back on the audience and faces his choir. They quiver and then with one intake of breath begin.

The music is a low hum. It has a subterranean quality, ancient and proud and solemn. It oozes into the chamber, quiet at first, and then note by note grows louder and clearer, filling the spaces between the ranked rows of audience, flowing over them like a deep, soft breath. Whole sweet voices soar into the chamber. The music builds in delicate geological layers; thin as slate a solo violin slips into place to be accompanied a beat later by a solitary bell. The women sing. *Lacrimosa*. The salty stone pours with sound. At the final movement she looks across and sees Konrad rumpled in tears.

Afterwards they take a train back to the city centre and then go for dinner in Kazimierz even though it is late. When they arrive at the Ariel most of the customers are drinking coffee at the end of their meal. The waiter seats them in a corner and lights the white candle on their table with a snap from a heavy cigarette lighter. Smiling politely in spite of the late hour, he indicates their menus and then withdraws to an archway near a stone fountain; the water illuminated green and rose reminds her of the pools in the mine.

Konrad picks up a menu and dips into it, raking the choices. His knee jiggers under the table, setting the water glasses tinkling.

'Shall we order? Are you ready?' His expression is pensive.

She would like more time, but is afraid to ask for a moment. The waiter hovers and she points to something that doesn't sound too daunting. He takes their orders and glides to the door of the unseen kitchen. She is aware that she is clenching her knuckles.

Konrad looks at her and then glances away. She considers asking him what he thought of the concert and almost immediately rejects the thought. 'I'm sorry. I'm still a little shell-shocked,' she says.

'We don't need to talk any more if you feel too tired. We could just finish here quickly.'

She wishes she had spoken to him on the train. Then they wouldn't have to start all over again. A basket of rolls sits on the table. Suddenly hungry, she reaches over and takes one.

'It must feel overwhelming,' he says, watching her break open the bread. 'Everything I've told you. Of course, I've been thinking about all this for a while.' He looks at her over the candle flame. His eyes are soft grey with flecks of amber drifting in the irises.

She chews on her bread and looks at him. 'It's strange to be here,' she says. 'I never imagined that I would come.' She puts the roll down on her side plate. 'You know all this was closed to me, like a sealed book.'

'You mean Poland, or your father?'

'Well, both, I suppose. There was the mystery of the man and a lot of that was bound up with the mystery of the place.' She pauses, trying to collect her thoughts in spite of her dizzying tiredness. 'I didn't know anything. While he was alive that was somehow part of the secret bargain I made with myself after I tried to see him: that I wouldn't try to know.' She runs a hand across her brow. 'I'm sorry, I've just realized how opaque that sounds.'

Konrad frowns. 'Not at all. I mean it's understandable. You had nothing to go on.'

She exhales. 'Well, now I do. Thanks to you.'

He rakes his hands through his hair. 'I'm not sure that I'm prepared to take the full blame.' He gives her a lopsided smile. 'He was quite adamant that I find you. He wanted you to know. I'm just passing on what he told me.'

She fiddles with her napkin. 'I'm grateful. You didn't have to get in touch with me, and it's very good of you to give up your time like this now. I mean I don't want to put you out.'

He grimaces. 'What a strange English expression.'

She feels hot and uses the napkin to fan her face. She takes a sip of water and feels calmer. 'Thank you: that's all I'm really trying to say.'

He smiles at her.

'My father never really got to grips with English, at least that's what I remember.'

'But he didn't speak Polish with you either?'

'No. Not a word. His English sounded . . .' She pauses and tries to remember. 'Well, translated, I suppose. Now that I think of it, the Polish was there and he was nudging it away with English that sounded Polish.' She brings her fingertips to her temples. 'I'm sorry, that doesn't really make much sense, does it?'

He balls his hands together and rests his chin on them. 'When he came back, Janek had trouble at first speaking Polish. He had to relearn his own language.'

Janek. It is strangely thrilling to hear his name. She glances around the restaurant. Over at the bar a young man in a long white apron holds glasses up to the light to check for smears. She looks down at her large white plate. She has ordered pork which she never normally eats.

'Is it all right?' Konrad asks.

'I really prefer meat well done.' She is hot with embarrassment.

Konrad calls the waiter from his sentry position at the fountain. Her plate is discreetly lifted away and returned to the kitchen.

'Don't worry, they're used to it. He'll bring it back cooked.' Konrad looks with slight dismay at his own plate of chicken and potatoes. He lifts his fork and then puts it down again.

'Please. Don't wait for me, it will get cold.'

He lifts his fork doubtfully and begins to eat in furtive bites, taking his time. His lips are as pale as the underside of a mushroom.

'Did it take you long to find me?' she says when he rests his fork again. 'I mean my father had no information. The last time I saw him was in Brighton in 1985. I didn't leave an address.'

He dabs at his mouth with his napkin. He takes a swift drink of water. 'The binoculars. He told me he had given you binoculars. I just put that into the search engine, your name and binoculars. I found you in one hit. I couldn't believe it. It was almost too easy.' He smiles at her. 'When I saw your field of work it made sense.'

She relaxes. 'I was always going to be an astronomer. I mean I never really thought about anything else. Was it like that for you, with films?'

'I suppose it was. It just took me a long time to get round to admitting it. I made movies in my head at law school and when I failed it was easier to tell my father that I'd fouled up my studies than say I wanted to go in an entirely different direction.'

'Why couldn't you tell him?'

He sighs and opens his hands and looks down at his palms. 'You're not the only one who made a secret bargain not to probe,' he says. 'I wanted to know my father, too.' He lifts his eyes and looks at her, frankly, a little ruefully, and it is her turn to glance away. 'But he wouldn't let me.'

They are both silent for a moment. Then to get over the awkwardness, he attempts a joke by mentioning the photograph of her on the Institute of Astronomy website where she is Dr Catherine Jasinski, whose research interests include the formation of galaxies, most particularly the birth of new planets, comets, light curves and stellar winds. The photograph had been taken by the river one autumn afternoon. She remembers it was windy that day and her hair had blown in auburn waves across her face. 'Push it back, so that I can see your eyes,' Dominic had said. 'Your lovely blue eyes. You look very Polish right now.'

Dominic. She wonders what he is doing back at their home in Cambridge. The usual summer break routine, which he pursued with the same vehemence he gave to his research in mathematics. Reading, gardening, cooking; a little fishing if he could find the stillness required. She ought to let him know that she has arrived, but it would seem odd to telephone now, too late for checking in. Better to wait until the morning after a good night's sleep.

Her pork arrives, drenched in red sauce cooked to treacle. She spears a piece and puts it in her mouth, working her cheeks against the searing heat. They eat in bursts, attempting conversation, but finding it tricky to begin another thread. They clear their plates at the same time. She looks at their knives and forks resting on the smeared white china and her head swims with fatigue. The waiter returns. He puts a hand on her shoulder. 'Was it okay for you?' His eyes are kind, the hand on her shoulder unexpectedly warm and comforting.

'Yes, thank you.' Absurdly, she feels close to tears.

They are not offered dessert. It is clearly too late, not that she wants anything more to eat, even so it feels as if there is something missing.

Konrad calls the waiter and orders a shot of honey vodka. 'Catherine?' He says her name carefully, breaking it into its three parts, his tongue slipping over the 't'.

Her instinct is to refuse, but she finds herself smiling at the waiter as he persuades her to 'try', his eyes softly locking on to hers as if her acceptance is the only thing he requires at this precise moment in time to be forever blessed, never mind that it is close to one in the morning and he has been on his feet possibly since dawn with little sleep the night before evidenced by the dark pouches under his eyes and the smell of weariness in his clothes. Was this what it was like for her father at the Paradise Hotel? Now she understands what patience he must have had to endure such a working life. She sips the vodka. Its fiery sweetness lifts her spirits and clears some of the exhaustion from her mind.

After dinner they walk through the narrow cobbled streets of the Jewish Quarter, passing the synagogue and floodlit churches, stone carved faces of the Virgin Mary glowing like lamps to light their way. At the corner of Grodzka Street music thumps from bars and cafés where groups of young people are still drinking under red and white umbrellas. Elegant stone buildings in cameo colours: mint green, melon, peach and pink pose against a sky of deep blue. Looking up, Catherine locates Zeta, the brightest star in Orion's belt, whose blazing light is thirty-five thousand times brighter than the sun. Close to Zeta is the nebula, the mysterious coil of gas and dust with its sculpted head, dished nose, small ears and long flowing mane emulating the fine lines of an Arabian. There were horses in the field behind their home in Devon. One morning she'd woken earlier than usual, a strange quiet in the room. The fields were drenched in snow. She could see the horses sheltering under a huge oak tree. There was someone with them. Her skin prickles at the memory. She hadn't realized it until now. The man with his hand on the neck of the grey horse was her father. She turns back to Konrad. His attention is firmly on the terrestrial, his eye drawn to the young couples enjoying the warm air, the light on their skin a rich, butter gold. The night is heavy with perfume. Even the ancient stone smells of it.

'Kraków thinks it wants to be Prague, but it isn't quite so sure of itself. Sometimes everywhere is deserted at this time,' he says as they cross the main market square, dominated by the Cloth Hall with its long colonnaded arcade and the Gothic twin towers of St Mary's.

Catherine glances at the great church porch. Her guidebook advised looking at the details of the decorative work through binoculars. 'I've never been to Prague. I suppose it's something you do when young.'

'Hey.' Konrad squeezes her elbow. The gesture is playful, almost brotherly, but it still sends a shock wave through her to the roots of her hair. 'We're not that old!'

We. They have already established that they are the same age, born in the same year, 1962, a month apart. She is the elder. Forty-nine is an interesting age. By now we have become who we are. At forty-nine we have established an identity. But what if she isn't quite who she thinks she is? What if she must now reconsider?

Konrad accompanies her into the lobby of the Europolski Hotel. The concierge jerks up from his newspaper and pushes her key across the desk. She turns it over in her palm. It's made of wood and looks heavier than it actually is, which sums up the hotel itself. The thought of her room with its lightweight wooden furniture and thin, glossy bed-throws raises gooseflesh on her arms. She becomes aware of Konrad looking at her.

'Thank you for the concert.' She had almost forgotten it. How could this be? Wrapped in the warmth of those pure voices she had thought that she would carry them with her for ever.

Konrad takes her hand and brings it up to his lips in an ironic imitation of the old courtly Polish greeting. 'It's been a pleasure.' He drops her hand. His expression is now serious. 'Do you want to meet again tomorrow? We could talk some more.'

She turns the key over in her palm and looks at the number of her room. Number twelve. She nods. 'Yes.' Then quickly adds, 'I want to know everything.'

He dips his head, takes a step back, allowing her room.

She feels flustered. 'Do you have far to go?'

He seems puzzled by her question. 'No, not at all. The apartment is just off Kopernika, ten minutes' walk away.'

For some reason this satisfies her. She takes the stairs to her room on the first floor.

Inside, she locks the door and walks over to one of the twin beds, places her hand on the cold silken cover and then peels it off, flinging it on to the other bed. She runs a bath and soaks for a while, idly studying her toes – freshly varnished with rose-pink polish, like a girl's feet – cradling the slope of the deep bath. Steam clouds the mirror and she cannot see her face when she brushes her teeth. She pulls on a cotton dressing gown and returns to the bedroom where her large brown leather travel bag is slumped on the floor at the foot of the bed. Inside is a padded envelope containing Konrad's notes for the outline of his film: 'I've also put some other stuff in there that might interest you.' He'd handed her the package before she went back to the hotel to change for the evening. She ought to wait until the morning. She'd be able to concentrate better then, but curiosity and a strange kind of urgency overwhelm her. With trembling hands she tears open the padded envelope and finds a stack of smooth typed pages that she puts aside for one moment. Instead she picks up a yellowed bundle of papers, and, her heart thudding, a collection of photographs. One shows a boy wearing a wool cap, his face pressed against the cheek blade of a fine chestnut horse. The photograph is worn and soft as if it has been looked at a thousand times and the boy's face is blurred, but there is no mistaking the expression in his eyes. She props the photograph by the bedside lamp and sinks back into the pillows with her arms behind her head. She knows she will not sleep. She wants to remember this expression, this look of complete trust and joy. She wants to know why she had never seen such a light in her father's eyes, why it had been extinguished.

3

Eastern Poland, March 1939

In the early morning Krystyna went across to the stables to feed the horses. Janek was there already, head bent over a feed sack from which he was filling a row of pails. She picked up the first pail and swung it, testing its weight for a moment before moving on down to the stalls.

'Hey.'

She turned. Janek was staring at her, his eyes two gleaming green slits in the smoky dawn light.

She realized now that she hadn't greeted him good morning. Her mind had been on her mare who had been suffering from colic.

'*Dzień dobry.*'

He inclined his head, his eyes softening, and then with swift, efficient movements he continued filling the rest of the pails.

The stable block was divided into roomy stalls with low whitewashed walls so that the horses could look over and see each other, mothers and daughters occupying neighbouring spaces once the foals were weaned. Her mare Izabela, a pearl-grey Arabian with twilight eyes, slipped back from the stable door. Sometimes on scenting her morning feed, she would mutter her appreciation, but today she greeted the pail silently, arching her neck, her liquid eye glimmering. Leaving the pail outside, Krystyna went in. A warm draught emanated from the mare's low-slung belly. It was less distended than it had been in previous days. Krystyna ran her hand over it and the mare sighed; her musky chestnut and mushroom scent filled the stall. Krystyna collected the pail, set it down and then, using the telepathic language she had learned to offer to horses, gave the mare the signal to come forward. Izabela hesitated for a moment, one curved ear pivoting in the direction of the dwór. Krystyna listened, but there was no sound coming from the house; there was only the immediate noise of horses mumbling their mix of oats and bran, the dry switch of tails and the occasional click of an equine hip. She opened her hand and the mare stepped out of her trance and dropped her head into the pail.

She went back and collected more pails and fed the other horses. Janek brushed by, his arms filled with hay. The winter had eaten up nearly all their hay stock and the few remaining bales in the barn were rationed by Krystyna's father. Only the thin white mare Celestyna was allowed unlimited forage. Krystyna stood with her for a few moments and stroked her neck. The mare's teeth were so worn she sucked her hay into pellets that she rolled around her mouth before dropping them out into her bedding. In the past few days her breathing had become laboured, her eye glassy with pain. She had bred many fine colts and fillies, including Krystyna's own mare, but she now appeared like a ghost horse. Her father had talked of shooting the mare; it would be kinder than letting her suffer another harsh winter when temperatures fell as low as minus twenty, but he could not bring himself to do it.

The males of her family were cavalry officers, a tradition that stretched back to the fifteenth century when her ancestors fought on horseback for Polish kings. At one time her grandfather had kept more than a hundred horses on the estate, prized grey or chestnut mares with satin-fine coats and long manes and tails and stallions with compact bodies composed of oiled muscle, ice-white stars and nostrils that fired with blood when they danced across the fields. Their home-bred Arabians were highly sought after, renowned not only for their beauty, but also for their intelligence, stamina and courage, qualities that Krystyna, who had grown up hearing stories of the cavalry horses, determined that she would cultivate for herself.

For a short, golden season the horses had attracted buyers from across Europe and America, and her father had planned a trip to Arabia to expand the stud. She would travel with him as his assistant and rider. A battle injury meant that he was no longer able to ride himself; she would be his representative. He seduced her with exotic plans, showing her maps of the desert regions they would need to cross to find tribes who guarded their exquisite horses like secret daughters. They would camp under the stars and drink camel's milk. She would ride the horses in the early mornings when it was cool. Their Arab hosts would find it strange that a girl could ride so well, but they would respect her and treat her like an honorary boy. 'I know these people,' he said to her one night when they talked in the library. 'I understand what matters to their hearts. They are not unlike us Poles in that once they make a friend it is for life.'

Her father heaved himself up from his chair to put more logs on the fire. His damaged right leg was much thinner than the left. He was part of a small force of Polish officers who fought the formidable Red Cossacks in the battle for Komarów during the Polish–Soviet War in 1920. The Cossacks were known for their daring and skill in the saddle, but on that day the Polish lancers on their quick-thinking, light-footed Arabians outran them, pushing the Cossack riders to their limits until they defeated them. Pierced by a lance in the thigh, her father had fought on until the end, his saddle slippery with blood. Once when she surprised her father changing into work overalls in one of the outbuildings she had glimpsed the injury. The whiteness of his legs had startled her and the hole, deep in the top of his diminished thigh, was perfectly smooth as if someone had taken a serving spoon to his marrow.

That evening in the library she glanced at the paintings of Polish cavalry officers set up high against the dark wood panelled walls. One of the paintings showed her great-grandfather leading a charge on a white stallion. The colours of earth and blood were slick against the flaring darkness. Her father followed her gaze and his expression became thoughtful. Years ago he had shown her the double-breasted tunic, clustered with badges and medals, and riding boots, mummified around their wooden lasts, that had been worn by her great-grandfather Juliusz. These musty relics were stored in a gnarled chest in one of the dwór's many attics. When her father opened the lid the sour smell made her cough; the uniform was stiff with sweat and age. There were stains on the cuffs, the hem was frayed and the brass buttons were dull and tarnished. Nonetheless there was something deliciously intoxicating about lifting a sleeve and pushing her fingers inside the fluted breast pockets. Later that night, Krystyna lay awake in her room under the attic imagining the spirit of Juliusz presiding over the household, an angelic winged hussar defending them all with his lance.

She thought of Juliusz now as she glanced through the stable window and out to the yard where her father, still in his pyjamas, over which he had thrown his old army coat, his hair standing up at the back of his head in grey tufts, was crossing the cobbles on his way to raise the Polish flag. He used to put up the flag only for special occasions, but since Hitler had come to power in Germany he had made it a daily habit. Unaware that she was watching him, he stopped and looked across the yard to the stables and his shoulders straightened under the coat. He drew one hand up and saluted the flag and put his other hand on his chest. His breath clouded his expression. She turned from the window, her throat tightening.

She finished her chores. It was easier now she didn't have to wear the heavy gloves and padding of winter. In between her other duties at home and school, she and Janek had spent most of the past few months up in the barn mending tools, oiling and repairing leather and making a space in the hayloft for the harvest to come.

Summer. It was what they dreamed of and carried within them like another layer, a lighter, easier version of who they were during the hard frozen months. In the summer they loved to spend afternoons fishing for crayfish in the deep, cold waters of the lake where the sand was as cool as opal under the damp soles of their feet. Their legs would grow suntanned and iridescent with tiny gleaming hairs. In the summer, Krystyna felt herself sleeken, become satiny, irresistibly touchable; she loved the sensuous feel of her own young body in summer: the sweet sting of grass under her back, the hot hand of sun on the crown of her head, the swooning scent of shady pine branches. She loved the silvery-silt taste of lake water on her tongue, the heavy saltiness of stones she would balance on her stomach just to feel something tangible, something gripping from the ground.

The region of lakes and meadows where they lived was known as the place where God had lost his shoes, a paradise, she imagined, that God had created for his own blissful enjoyment, slipping off his muddy work boots when he was done with creating, wading up to his thighs in water so shockingly alive and clear and miraculous it reflected back an image of the creator as a young and beautiful man, a Greek sculpture with perfect limbs. Such were her daydreams and fantasies: an intense theatre of fragments, thoughts, half-remembered stories, myths, readings, wishes and desires. In the waters of the lakes there was Narcissus. Echo's voice carried by the wind through forests of elm, larch and oak, trees that grew so free they formed impenetrable inky canopies where deer, elk and wolves foraged or hunted and settled down at night in dry hollows filled with autumn leaves of amber and ruby and gold. From these richly jewelled nests they observed their immaculate world.

She never spoiled her dream, but she had learned enough hard facts about her country to understand that it had struggled even to exist. One of the very first things her father had told her about her own country's history was that Poland had vanished from the map completely for more than one hundred years. For a century Poland had no name and lived only in memory. It took the First World War to resurrect it. Three times in its history Poland had been torn apart and divided, portioned by its greedy

35

neighbours. It had been crushed and crumpled and squashed, like a piece of bread trodden underfoot: first partition, second partition, third partition, treaty, death and rising; the maulings were endless. But in spite of all attempts to smother it, Poland refused to disappear. When challenged or oppressed, it rose; it reared and kicked its feet in the teeth of its enemy. If war came again, and many people were convinced that it was inevitable, her father declared that they would face up to their oppressors. It was what Poles did best.

'Hey.' Janek interrupted her thoughts and leaned over Izabela's stable door. Now that he had her attention he rested his head on his arms. They were the same age, fifteen, born in the same year, but Janek was younger by six months. She looked at his hair, the colour of firelight, fine electric strands rising by some invisible magic. His shoulders were hunched under his work overalls, twin nubs of bone moving as he breathed. Even tired, as he was now, he seemed to coil within himself, stoking himself with concentrated vitality. Sometimes he was grumpy and sullen, sometimes ravenously hungry, sometimes sad, but always he was relieved to see her. Late one afternoon when they were lying in the hayloft sharing confidences, one of which was at her insistence the very worst that they could imagine, he confessed his fear. And it was simple: that she would not be there in the morning. The very worst that he could imagine was that she should vanish.

Krystyna pulled a straw from the stable bed and touched Janek's cheek. His eyes fluttered. A few weeks ago his father Lorenz, who managed the estate, had fallen ill with a lung complaint and Janek had been given his duties on top of his own.

'Don't sleep. Come riding with me.'

Janek rolled his shoulders and flexed his elbows as if testing his body. From the corner of the stall his horse Gazela blew a plume of breath through her nostrils.

'See, even she is tired. She agrees that it is better to sleep.'

'We won't stay out long. You can sleep after.'

'Father said he saw a hare last night in the meadow.'

He lifted his head and Krystyna knew that she would not have to persuade him because his eyes had changed. She went to fetch saddles and bridles from the house. Irena was eating breakfast at the kitchen table with the cook Anastazia, who along with Lorenz now made up the entire estate staff.

'What are you doing?' her stepmother called out. 'Don't you want to eat something?' Irena half rose from her seat, flicking crumbs from a narrow wool skirt that accentuated the swell of her belly. Her dark hair was awry, and she pushed it behind her ears, showing the milky pearl earrings Aleksander had given her on their wedding day two years ago. Seeing Krystyna with saddle and sheepskin already in her arms, bridles slung across the pommel in a tumble of oily leather, Irena sank back into her place and pulled her chair closer to the table. In the silence that followed Krystyna heard the measured ticking of the kitchen clock.

Anastazia met her eyes. Before she had joined them as cook, gardener, needlewoman and general estate worker (mostly because she could drive) she had been a nun at a Franciscan convent. Her hair had not been cut since she left the convent twenty-one years ago in 1918, the same year Poland regained independence. Now as a fifty-five-year-old woman she wore it in a long chestnut plait down her back. There was no grey in her hair, unlike Irena's.

Despite being twenty-five years younger, her stepmother had a white flash at her temple.

Anastazia took a couple of fresh plum cakes from a plate and wrapped them in a cloth for Krystyna to take to the stables, patting her arm as she did so.

Her stepmother fiddled with her watch. 'Tell me, Anastazia' – Irena's voice was weary and stretched – 'do we have dried mushrooms left in the store?'

Walking across the yard to the stables with the still warm cakes in her pocket, Krystyna felt her spirits lift. The feeling of caution that had covered her all winter rose and flapped its bat-black wings to the trees. She glanced up and saw that the branches were studded with tiny green shoots. The biting cold was beginning to leave and the air felt soft on her face.

A high whistle caught her attention. Janek was out in the yard throwing spruce cones to the wolfhounds. At his command, they tumbled over each other to be first, dropping their scraggy hindquarters down to the cobbles. They waited for the next signal, their rough muzzles resting between their paws, their eyes fixed on Janek's left arm. He drew it back, arcing through the air until it reached shoulder height. His wrist opened and the enclosed cone burst free, sailing in a high crescent over the cobbles. At the next whistle the dogs scrambled up and leapt for the prize. The winner was the one who caught the cone in mid-air, and he got to keep it and chew it to pieces while the others watched, plotting like thwarted emperors.

Leaving him to finish his game, Krystyna carried the saddles into the stable block. Her mare was resting, one hind leg cocked. She went into her stall and spent a few minutes grooming her before she drew on the bridle, adjusting the leather straps so that they sat flush against the mare's broad cheekbones. She placed the sheepskin and then the saddle on next, buckling the girth loosely, and then led her mare down through the stalls. Janek, his cheeks flushed, was now rubbing a brush over his mare. 'See you outside,' he said as she went past.

There was a stone mounting block in the yard. She lined up her mare, taking her time. Her father had taught her how to move around horses, without resistance, as if drawing a feather through ink. Izabela stood breathing in the fresh morning air, the fine hairs of her swan-white winter coat plumped up. A few tufts had come out in the grooming brush and once it started to get warmer, she would rapidly shed the rest. Krystyna drew her leg over the saddle. As she sank into the seat, she felt at once the strange intoxicating mixture of familiarity and glimmering excitement that came over her each time she connected with her horse.

Janek came out with Gazela. He mounted her and led the way. Her tail was high and she moved her quarters in a four-time swinging gait, hind feet tracking into the indents left by her fore feet. Krystyna tried to bring Izabela along-side, but she preferred on this morning to fall back into the groove made by the other mare. Krystyna did not try to urge her forward. Sometimes it was like that with horses; they walked out with moods and feelings that were differ-ent to what you expected. If you wanted a fast, exciting ride and they were in a dreamy, following sort of mood, it upset them when you asked them to do more than they felt like offering; they would do what you asked, but reluc-tantly and in an offended way. At some point in the ride something would go wrong: the horse would slip on ice and fall or scrape a leg; or a fir tree bough, weighed down by a platter of snow, would shear off from a trunk and crash into the track; or a blizzard would suddenly whip up from nowhere. These were not accidents, Krystyna had come to understand: they were foreshadowings, warning glimpses, tears in the fabric. All the horses had an uncanny ability to know when such events were about to happen. They would shy or take a turning for no apparent reason, or they would stop. It was as though they could remember things that had not yet occurred.

Gazela surged ahead. Krystyna could see the top of Janek's head, his red wool cap bobbing as he rode. His eyes, she knew, would be restlessly searching the fringes of the meadow for white hares. She allowed Izabela to take her time. The track was mostly clear, but under the trees pools of soft snowmelt glinted in the sun, and the mare chose to pick her way carefully. The leather saddle creaked beneath her as they traversed the meadow, their combined breath coming in short puffs in the clean air. Krystyna felt the cakes jostle in her pocket and saliva flooded her mouth. If she stopped now, she could eat them both and Janek would never know.

Guilt got the better of her and she asked Izabela for a trot and then a canter, sitting deep in the saddle as the mare pushed forward, her ears two perfectly carved stencils against the glassy blue sky. Janek had rounded a corner so that now he was out of sight. As they moved faster, Izabela's breathing increased in tempo to an excited yip, yip, yip and Krystyna felt the blood from the mare's neck warm her hands. They turned the corner and the other mare came into sight. With a jolt Krystyna saw that she was riderless. Gazela's neck was dipped, her nostrils exploring something that lay on the ground.

She eased Izabela to a halt. The mare snorted and arched her neck and Krystyna smoothed her withers to calm her. She looked over to where Janek's mare was feeling the wet grass. A white hare was sprawled almost lazily in a pool of blood. In the space where its head had been was a slick, naked pink cord. Janek was crouched some distance away, his face gluey with tears. His red cap lay in the grass. 'Are you hurt?' she called out.

He jerked his head, but did not look at her.

A cry overhead made them lift their faces to the sky and there they saw the answer (her father would not allow traps or wires or shooting of hares on his estate): a hawk hovered above them on perfectly balanced tawny wings. She could see its bullet head and innocent eye. Janek rubbed his hand across his face. A thin stream of snot danced for a moment from the joint of his thumb before dropping into the grass. His mare nudged his knee and Krystyna watched his fingers rake through her forelock.

After a moment he stood up and brushed his knees. The back of his riding trousers was damp with dew. He moved towards the hare but did not look at it. He lifted his cap and put it on his head, pulling the brim low over his eyes. His mare followed him and stood at his side. He wiped one cheek with the back of his hand before he pulled the stirrup towards his foot and remounted his horse.

At the edge of the meadow there was a line of oak trees. Janek turned his horse towards their craggy trunks. The blood had returned to his face and he seemed on the point of saying something, perhaps looking for a way to free his mind from feelings that took him to a place she could not reach. The sight of blood or intestines was commonplace on a country estate, but Janek was made of some porous substance that offered no protection from the gruesome or even the merely sad. When one of the dogs died, he was sick for three days. Sometimes he had difficulty eating meat and would push his supper around his plate until his father ordered him to stop. Remarkably, Janek was able to assist when the mares foaled, staying in the stalls until the early hours, waiting for the placenta to drop, watching the quivering newborns wobble on their soft hooves to the udder. Sometimes the weaker ones died and he laid them out in the straw and left them alone with the mares.

He waited for her to draw level. Under the trees was a mile-long gallop they had not raced all winter because the snow had been too deep. Now the sandy track was mostly clear except for a few white patches at the edges. She felt Izabela quiver under her. They both rode to win, but never gloated or paraded their victories. Winning seemed hollow and futile if the race was not even, if either horse stumbled, or was startled by a pheasant or deer. When held up by unforeseen events, they were inclined to start the race afresh. Once they ran alongside a fox. Krystyna remembered how noiseless it had been in comparison to the horses with their great pounding hearts and powerful pushing lungs. The fox had seemed to fly past on its quiet red and white paws, an earthbound bushy comet. Across the meadow she could see the prints of their tracks outlined in the dew.

Janek turned to her. His eyes were bright. 'Ready?'

They released their horses together and there was a moment, almost of shock, when the mares gathered energy and held it to themselves before launching their hindquarters into full flight. Krystyna felt the wind break in waves over her ears. She leaned forward, her hands high, grazing the taut muscle on Izabela's neck. The mare collected under her. For a moment she seemed content to move in a graceful rhythm, but then as Gazela surged forward, she shifted her weight on to her hindquarters and pounded her way down the track. They were neck and neck. Krystyna could see Gazela's eye glowing, her white mane flipping and Janek crouched forward, his skin stretched over his cheekbones, his ears raw and tight. The trees flashed past and she leaned lower as Izabela took the lead. Her throat swelled with joy as the mare opened up and seemed to fly. Then there was a blur at her side and Janek's mare shot into view, snaking past, grit and snow flying up from her hooves. Conceding the race, Izabela uttered a short grunt and shifted her gait from gallop to relaxed canter. She slowed to a walk as they neared the end of the track where Janek waited, his head bowed on his horse. He glanced up at Krystyna and nodded. His eyes had lost their shock from discovering the dead hare and were bright and clear. He dismounted and let his mare stand for a few moments to catch her breath before walking her back to the stable yard.

After they had rubbed the horses down and replenished their hay racks, they went up to the hayloft. It was only when they were lying down that Krystyna remembered about the plum cakes. She reached into her pocket. They were a little squashed and, still, amazingly warm. But when she passed one over to Janek, his fingers stayed curled on his chest. She left the cake on his hand and let him sleep.

4

Kraków, present day

Catherine leaves the hotel and walks to the square. It is early morning, but already warm. She can smell lily of the valley from the flower stalls where women in nylon overalls perch under sun umbrellas, arranging apricot and cream rosebuds into tightly packed posies. Seeking custom, one or two call out to her. It embarrasses her that she does not have enough Polish to reply. At the very least she ought to have brought a phrase book, but somehow in the urgency of leaving Cambridge it hadn't occurred to her that she was going somewhere she wouldn't be understood. Smiling at the women, she tells herself that she will buy some roses later; their fragrance will bring something fresh and vital to the hotel room.

The square is subdued, a vast, sunlit space swimming with lime blossom. The few pedestrians look as if they belong on a film set. There's a man in a long red brocade dress – a priest or an actor, Catherine cannot decide – who is dangling a rubber snake, and a girl, around thirteen years old, in a shimmering white gown, ruby ringlets bouncing on her shoulders. In contrast to the weather-bleached stone and faded, near-invisible charm of the ancient buildings, the modern street signs shout their bright allure: *Hotel Columbus, Kosmetyki, Drzwi Gerda, Restaurant Galicia, the English Football Club Bar.* At one end of the square, a vast stage is under construction, scaffolding poles clanking and chiming, providing percussive accompaniment to a middle-aged man in black jeans and silver trainers who sings a soulful lullaby in Polish. In a trance, she stops to listen, and hears the singer's words in English: '*Wept today, wept today, wept today, yeah, wept today, wept today, wept today, yeah, yeah.*' She ends up having to rush down Floriańska Street to reach the coffee shop on time.

Konrad is already settled into one of the booths, his face hidden by a thick leather menu. He glances over the top as she sits down in a tumble of apologies. 'Relax. I only just got here myself.' His face reddens as he realizes that the pocket-sized notebook and pencil next to his elbow give him away.

Watching him whisk the book out of sight, she wonders what his handwriting looks like.

'I really can't decide whether to have the fillet of goose or baked quail.' He hands over the menu.

'You can't be serious. It's breakfast time.'

'You didn't have breakfast at the hotel?'

'Just coffee.' She meets his eyes. She hadn't stayed for breakfast. In the dining room, an argument had been going on between a couple at the table next to her and a persistent taxi driver.

'Well, you'll need something pretty substantial because I'm going to keep you for ages.' In the dim light his eyes are the colour of warm slate.

She scans the menu, but the words swim together. The roof of her mouth has gone dry. She snaps the menu shut. 'I'm sorry – I'm not really that hungry yet.'

He has noticed her tension, but chooses to ignore it. He rolls his eyes down his own menu as if he has all the time in the world. She feels her stomach tighten and then release into a betraying growl; she is really quite hungry, but it would seem odd to change her mind. She doesn't want him to think that she is inconsistent. He lifts his eyes. 'The cakes here are great. The best in Kraków. I used to come here a lot with Krystyna and she always would have cake. She adored it and it was impossible to resist following her. I never really had a sweet tooth until I met her.' He smiles at the memory. 'It's strange, isn't it, I mean how some people can do that, change your mind about what you like, you know, even in a small way?'

Catherine thinks of Dominic's attempts to educate her about food. He was always raving about some new dish, something she had to try. Oysters. The last time they went out to dinner he had commanded her to try the oysters that he bought as a dozen to share. She had tipped the shell the wrong way, trying to suck the slippery grey flesh from the narrow point and Dominic had sighed and rolled his eyes as if she had somehow let him down. She's conscious that Konrad is staring at her with mild amusement again. 'Yes,' she says. 'There are some people who seem to have some sort of magnetic ability to change your mind.' She now remembers the scene that put her off her breakfast. 'But there are others you absolutely want to run from.' She tells him about the breakfast taxi driver. 'He was touting Auschwitz, and this couple, you could tell they were really embarrassed, but he just kept on pushing it. Eventually they had to call the manager to get him to leave.'

Konrad winces. He presses the points of his fingers to his temples. 'I just hate seeing those cheerful little yellow buggies everywhere, you know, advertising it like just another tourist destination, an interesting museum to be crossed off the list of hot spots or something.' He pauses, aware of the edge of scorn in his voice. 'Sorry.'

'Isn't it a museum?' she asks.

He lifts his fingers from his forehead and glances at them. 'I don't know,' he says. 'Really I don't know. I've been here almost a year now and something tells me that I should go, but I just can't. I just can't bear to go.'

She expects him to ask her for her views, but he doesn't; he seems too caught up in his own confusion about it, and she is relieved. She picks up a menu and runs her eyes over the drink selection; her face breaks into a smile as she reads aloud. 'Tea with lemon, tea with cream, *tea with jam?*'

Konrad smiles, but there's a bite of tension around his mouth. She reads out, 'Tea with rum, coffee *expresson* (big one), coffee fantasy.' She lifts her eyes. She feels a little giddy. 'This is so delicious.' Now he catches on to the joke and surreptitiously, with an eye to the waitress hovering in the background, he reaches across to another table and plucks off a second menu. They hold the serious leather-bound books to their chests and look at each other. His eyes are gleeful.

'Now this you really *must* try,' he says, keeping his expression grave. 'Rabbit by Polish art.' He pauses for effect. 'In cream and herb sauce *sprinkled* with white wine.'

She is crying with laughter by the time they have finished, to the bafflement of the young waitress, who hovers by the kitchen door, order book and pencil tucked snugly into the pocket of her white apron. 'Yes, please,' she says, anxiously searching their faces during a gap in their mirth, which feels in this darkly respectable establishment with its amber glass lamps and aquarium gloom to be some kind of infringement. Konrad orders coffee, hazelnut cake and a large glass of water. Catherine does the same. She feels her giddiness subside and a fluttery apprehension take its place. The coffee arrives. It tastes like liquid smoke.

'I don't know about Auschwitz either.' She pauses and looks at her cake fork. 'I just hope that it hasn't been turned into some sort of hideous theme park.'

He takes a sip of coffee and dabs at his mouth with a napkin before replying. 'The Poles wouldn't do that. It's too sensitive. Of any nation in Europe, the Poles have a sense of history.' He spears some cake with his fork. 'Krystyna took me to a church once. People had been executed in this church, but it still felt like a church. We stood and watched the light pouring through the stained-glass windows. There was no sense of horror, only peace. That experience made me understand something about consecration. A consecrated church remains a sacred building no matter what occurs there; you could feel that as soon as you entered. There was a beautiful sadness about that church. I think that's what I dread about Auschwitz, the total lack of consecration.' He rests his fork on his plate for a moment.

She drinks some coffee. The image of a light-filled church hangs in her mind, still as a lake. Konrad rests his hands on the table. He catches her looking at his wedding ring and a muscle at the corner of his mouth twitches. His eyes fade out. She becomes aware of how parched she is. The heat in her hotel room made it difficult for her to sleep after reading. 'You are married.' She doesn't intend this to be a question, merely an observation, but he looks at her as if she has somehow caught him out, as if he had been trying to hide the fact.

He plays with the cake fork. 'I'm married.' He smiles a downward smile. He removes his hand from the fork and splays his fingers. She looks at the creases on his knuckles, the veins under his skin. He meets her eyes. 'Catherine, I've been married for twenty-five years.'

She's not sure how to respond. They have too quickly shifted from the conversational to the confessional. She realizes that she doesn't really want to know about his marriage or his life in America, but understands also that he thinks he has a duty to tell her.

'I suppose I'm on a kind of sabbatical,' he says, looking down at the table. 'For a long time, Angela and I have been leading what you could call separate lives.' He glances at her, checking her reaction. Catherine tries to keep her expression neutral, but she is aware of a tightness over her face. Konrad continues: 'She's a lawyer, she's involved in humanitarian work, takes on big cases and she needs a lot of headroom.' He pulls at his hair. 'She's brilliant.'

Catherine watches him finish his cake. There's something touching about the concentration he gives it.

He pushes his plate away and wipes his mouth. 'You're not married?'

'No.' She pauses. 'But I live with someone.' He nods once and pushes his plate more firmly to one side. She feels a flutter of apprehension. Now she asks him. 'Do you have children?'

'Yes, two boys, and they are both at college now. The elder is in his final year studying law at Harvard. The younger is travelling through Asia before he starts med school.'

'Such a high-flying family!' She doesn't intend this as a reproach and is sorry to see him flinch.

'Yes, there they are working their asses off while I'm having a holiday from responsibility.'

She senses that these are someone else's words. Picking up her fork, she slices off a morsel of hazelnut cake. Its salty sweetness melts in her mouth. She wonders what his wife looks like. She finds herself imagining the layout of his home; she sees stripped wooden floors, clear windows, light and space and air; his wife, in a smart jacket, bent over a silver laptop. Interestingly, she cannot imagine him in his own home. Instead she sees him sitting on a beach, a car parked up on the headland; behind him pale sand dunes, dry grasses rasping in a breeze. She knows that he drives to the beach to avoid going home; she knows this as if he had just told her and it makes her feel slightly afraid.

Konrad orders more coffee. She declines and sips some water instead.

'Why a sabbatical?' she asks.

His glance is intense. 'So many reasons, but mostly I wanted time to think. I needed to slow everything down and stop moving – for a long time I suffered from an almost pathological dissatisfaction.'

'That sounds painful.'

'It drove me to make films so all was not lost.'

She laughs. 'Go on.'

'I got interested in this idea of real work and made documentaries about people who had found their calling. I filmed cowboys, astronauts and beauty queens; I went to rodeos, prairie farms, prisons, mines, athletics tracks, ball parks, hotels. Each time I set out with my small crew I had the idea that I would return with something whole and perfect, something almost sacred.' His eyes glitter at her across the table.

'I've felt that way,' she says. 'At certain times, when I've been alone in the observatory.'

'Just you and heaven?'

She grins at him. 'Something like that.'

'I loved being on the road. I had my crew, my travelling family, so I never felt alone. Before we started on each film, I would get this rush, thinking about the workers we'd meet in Arizona or Detroit or Chicago, all the dust and dazzle of these incredible places. It was a great way of getting to know my own country. America is an entire planet: mountains, plains, desert, big sky, the ocean; we would just roll through it all in our truck.'

'It all sounds very . . .' She wants to say 'romantic', but hesitates over the word. 'Fascinating,' she finishes.

Konrad's expression is pensive. 'It was. At first I thought I would keep going. But after a while I began to notice that the interior all smells and tastes the same: the roads, the hotel rooms, the malls, the studios; a few days in a new place and it would all begin to feel – I don't know – some-how *dense* and familiar, and that disturbed me because I'd started out on this journey wanting to find something defining about America, I guess as a kind of response to the pernicious idea that it was losing its identity. What started to happen was that each city, each state, each landscape seemed to slide effortlessly into another. We kept on travelling, but I no longer felt anything; I was no longer excited. I'd become jaded. I moved through it all behind sealed glass – and it was easy, so terribly easy. I was getting a name for myself, I was getting accolades; I was getting a lot of attention for my work.' He runs his hands through his hair. 'That bothered me and I had to stop.'

'So you came to Europe?'

'Poland is not Europe. It's a place all by itself.' He sips his coffee and looks at her over the rim of his cup.

His glance is encouraging, but she hesitates. For some reason she feels that her own story will be disappointing. 'I haven't travelled, not properly. I've pretty much stayed in Cambridge.'

He puts down his coffee cup. 'What I most love about living in Kraków is that I can walk everywhere.' He runs his fingers across his face. 'Part of this whole *life experiment* is about claiming time, allowing my days to find their natural rhythm and routine. I watch people. I write. I take photographs. I wait. I have no deadlines. It's a good cure for an over-achiever.'

Catherine recalls her meetings with her supervisor Jonathan, who understood the pressures of the overwhelmed. He would have approved of Konrad's experiment. 'You haven't decided when you're going back?'

'No.' He meets her eyes. 'I haven't decided.'

She glances around the coffee shop. An elderly Polish couple sit side by side in the next booth. Occasionally the woman speaks and the man seems grateful not to have to fill the silence. He sits slumped into his suit. His eyes are pale and tired. 'Did you come here with my father?'

'Once. After Krystyna died.' His eyes flick over at the couple in the next booth. 'It was difficult, though. The cold brought him down. Towards the end he lost a lot of weight.'

She bites her lip.

Konrad continues: 'He became ill with pneumonia in February. I would go to his apartment most days to make sure he was eating. He usually made a big pot of vegetable soup and lived on it for a week at a time. I'd take him some fruit or fresh bread and he would serve me some of his soup and we'd sit together for a while. He didn't talk much.

One day I suggested we go for a walk to the park. He started coughing as soon as his chest hit the cold air and so we came in here for a hot drink. He knew that this was where I used to meet Krystyna, but he didn't say anything about it.'

Her palms feel damp. 'They didn't live together?'

'No, he had his own apartment. He was always self-sufficient. Krystyna invited him to stay with her, but he refused. He wouldn't have wanted people to think that she was looking after him. It was the other way round, of course, he looked after her until I came along and then he stepped aside. He let me have my time with her.'

Her eyes prickle. She excuses herself and goes to the bathroom where she splashes cold water on her face. Drying her eyes, a rush of tears floods the green paper towel. She stands for a few moments weeping in gulps.

Konrad stands at her approach and waits until she has settled back into the booth before he sits down again. She can't remember the last time a man stood for her. She sips some water. Her eyes still feel sore. Konrad keeps his gaze averted.

'I'm not ready today, but will you show me where Janek is buried?'

'Of course, Catherine.' His voice is low. 'It's not far. We can walk there one afternoon.'

'Thank you.' She hesitates. 'I mean for inviting me here.' She fans her face. 'Sorry, it's strange to be able to talk about him. I'm not used to it.'

'I wondered whether I had done the right thing. I mean you might not have wanted to know. Some people wouldn't.'

She considers this. 'For years my father was an

unanswered question, a puzzle, a conundrum. He was utterly closed to me.'

Konrad leans forward, his eyes vivid: 'And now I've opened him up?'

She hesitates. Her heart thumps. 'I told people he was dead.'

Konrad exhales. 'Catherine, I know how it feels to have a stranger for a father.' His voice is thick.

'I read some of your writing last night.'

Their eyes meet for a second. 'What happened to your father still haunts me,' he says. He hesitates. 'I think right now I need to order something a little stronger than coffee.'

He calls the waitress over and speaks to her in Polish, a swift exchange. The soft cadence of the language makes it sound intimate.

'Do you feel as if you belong here now?' she asks him.

'It's easy for me to live here, much easier than I thought it would be. People assume I'm Polish because I speak the language.'

'I envy you.'

'I guess your father never spoke Polish to you?'

'No.'

The waitress returns to the table and sets down two small glasses of vodka. 'It's sadly common among fathers. I had to bully my father to teach me, and then he only managed a few words. I mostly taught myself through conversation classes. I now understand the meaning of mother tongue. If the mother doesn't speak a language, it's easily forgotten. My sons don't have Polish.' He reaches over and chinks his vodka glass against hers. '*Na zdrowie!*'

She laughs and takes a sip of vodka. It warms her stomach. She glances around. The coffee shop is now filled with people ordering lunch. From the kitchen comes a rich smell of simmering meat. 'I can see why you like it here.'

'It's a bit of an institution. Every day you see the same people.'

'You come here every day?'

He takes a sip of vodka and grins at her. 'Yes, I'm afraid I do. But I blame Krystyna. She never could cook. She used to bring me here.'

'I wish I could have met her.'

He nods. 'She had this way of speaking that made you give her your complete and utter attention. Time dissolved with her; it was like being immersed in water. Once she started with her memories, it was like a stream that needed to flow. She made her own film story. I just recorded it.'

'And my father stayed in the background all this time?'

'Very much so. He would sometimes come to meet her afterwards and they would go for a walk in the park together or go shopping, but it was clear that her time with me was her own. It wasn't until I spoke with him after she had died that I realized what he was carrying in his memory.'

She leans towards him, needing to hear more. 'Was it a relief to him, do you think, to speak about what happened?'

Konrad's face is thoughtful. 'I wondered about that myself. It was difficult, you know, to prise the lid off the box. It wasn't easy for him. But in the end I think it was a relief to break his silence.' He takes a sip of vodka. 'He said that I could use what he told me. Not for his own sake, but for all the people who didn't make it out alive; for all the people who screamed into the night. Those were his exact words.'

She feels a chill run down her arms. An image of the hotel room in Brighton comes into her mind. Now thinking about it, the tightness of the room had reminded her back then of a cell. She ought to have stayed, or returned another time. The bargain she made not to probe now seems cowardly.

'What about your father? It sounds as though you didn't really know him when you were growing up,' she says.

'No, and that must seem strange to you because at least we shared the same house.' He looks at her, his eyes steady. 'Like you I stopped asking questions when I got no response. I learned to live with silence. Maybe that's why I went off in pursuit of noise. All the men I filmed had dirty, crazy jobs.'

He takes a sip of vodka. 'You know I think we find what we need even if we don't know what it is at the time. We create a way to fill in the gaps.'

'Unless we're traumatized,' she offers.

'That's true. The traumatized don't know where to look.' He smiles and exhales. 'But maybe this is getting a bit too intense. I don't know, shall we take a break, get the bill, go and see if there's still life out there?'

Konrad peels off a few złoty notes from his wallet. Before he puts it in his back pocket she catches a glimpse of a photograph of two young fair-haired boys. Behind her the waitresses talk in Polish. As they get up from their seats, Catherine feels a nip of loneliness. It's been years since she spent a morning talking like this, deep, nourishing talk; she misses it already, and how strange that is. How new and unexpected.

They leave the coffee shop and walk down Floriańska Street, which Konrad tells her formed part of the ceremonial Royal Road leading up to the castle. 'Everything that has happened in this city, this street has witnessed it.'

They walk side by side, elbows occasionally jogging, as they step aside to let a horse omnibus go on its way. The immaculate pair of grey horses, hooves clamped in thick iron shoe bars, harnessed to a gleaming open wooden carriage, slip down the street, and it's as if a cloth has been lifted, giving a glimpse of another era. The smell of new paint and horse sweat lingers as they continue walking towards the square.

She thinks they might go their separate ways after he has seen her to the hotel, and the thought of a bath and then an early supper in one of the Italian restaurants tucked away in a side street followed by a quiet evening reading alone is appealing, but instead he asks her if she would like to see the Czartoryski Collection; there is just enough time before closing. As they climb a set of creaking wooden stairs, lined by lead-mullioned windows, open to let in a breeze, she wonders whether he had thought of coming to the museum because he wanted to prolong the time with her, or whether he had in fact intended to come alone and was simply asking her to join him out of politeness.

The stairs lead up to a large and airy gallery filled with marble sculptures from the first and second centuries. They pause at a statue of Bacchante Ariadne astride a panther. Catherine is struck by the intensity of Ariadne's expression radiating from the perfect oval of her face, the size of a child's hand. The room has something of the feel of a beautiful graveyard in moonlight. The marble is strangely fleshy and she cannot resist touching the next sculpture: a beheaded Venus with two dimples in her back, just above the buttocks. When she withdraws her hand she sees Konrad watching her from across the other side of the gallery, letting his eyes linger on her. She is nervous when he comes over, thinking that he might say something, but he acts as if nothing had occurred, and tells her that they should look at the Leonardo da Vinci painting before the museum closes.

She is sure that they are the only visitors. On duty at the gallery entrance is a heavily built Polish woman, who displays little emotion and seems to be benignly passing the minutes until closing time. There are no folded arms or pursed lips, only a heady scent of lilies from an arrangement in a window alcove at the foot of the stairs, and a strange, slow calm. If this were London, Catherine thinks, there would be bustling by now, possibly even irritation. Her mind slips over visits she has made to galleries and she wonders whether Dominic is planning to go on his own to art shows or the theatre. Their summer break always began with a few days at home, sleeping in and eating more elaborate meals than usual, out in the tiny walled garden where they had a couple of old cane chairs, inherited from Dominic's mother, and a round glass table that was furred with moss because they always forgot in autumn to put it into their small shed along with the chairs, which were by now rotten, the canes too brittle to hold any weight. She remembers their conversation a few nights before she left for Kraków was interrupted by the sound of the wood splitting under their tension. Dominic had wanted to come with her to Poland and he had asked her what she thought he was going to do for a week all on his own.

'Go fishing. Do what we normally do after we've recovered from work. Go up to London, there's lots of art you said you wanted to see.'

'But you'll miss out.'

'Then we'll go together when I come back.' But he refused to be placated and hunched his shoulders and puffed out his bulk against the disintegrating chair. His sleeves were rolled up and his arms were dark with thick black hairs. His face was a dull red and his mouth was very wet. When he sat up, too abruptly, he knocked over a glass of wine on the table; it didn't smash. It rolled on its belly and spilled its contents across the glass surface, dripping over the side in a thin stream that splattered her bare feet. 'Sorry, sorry. I'll clear it up.' But he hadn't and in the morning she looked at the chairs as she drank her tea and saw that the seat of his had finally collapsed and felt relieved and strangely elated.

They come upon the painting almost unexpectedly, as if they hadn't gone there to find it, but had discovered it by accident. Konrad draws in his breath. The painting has a beauty that is almost audible. It radiates from the work in soft waves. The woman's face is turned to the right, in line with her shoulder, and her expression is watchful and poised, as if someone has called her name and she is deciding whether or not to respond. The silver ermine, coiled in the crook of her arm, has an ear cocked in the same direction, a tiny muscular paw lifted against the pleat of a sleeve. The smooth pelmet of the young woman's hair, slender bands around her forehead and the strand of jet at her neck give the painting a geometrical precision.

'Look at her hand,' Konrad whispers. 'The long, strong fingers. It's so powerful, almost masculine.' He brings his hand up to his chin and kneads at his jaw. His fingers are long, too, and pale-skinned. His eyes flicker over the painting.

In the silence of the gallery Catherine becomes aware of their breathing, the soft rustle of their clothes. She can smell the soap he washed with. Each time he exhales the edge of his linen jacket brushes against her shoulder. Then she becomes aware of a shuffling behind them and when she turns, stretching and blinking as if she has just woken from a dream, she sees that the woman attendant is waiting for them. The woman lets them look at the painting for a minute longer and then starts to turn off the lights.

They walk out into the warm street, passing tourist shops selling crystal figurines, vodka glasses in wine-gum colours, wooden toys, pottery and puppet dragons. They stop at an ice-cream parlour and she orders a lime sherbet. Konrad has another coffee. They sit outside on metal chairs. In the bright light she notices lines of weariness around his eyes. She wonders whether he slept much the night before.

He watches the street for a few moments. 'For a long time I couldn't understand why my father never wanted to return to Poland,' he says as if in response to a question. 'I thought it was a kind of stubbornness or misguided pride. I would have thought that after the end of communism he might have wanted to come and see for himself what had happened to his country, but he never even talked about it. My mother tried to persuade him, but he acted as if Poland didn't exist; it was of no interest to him.'

'You sound angry with him.'

'I was angry, especially when I was growing up. Later, after I left home, I mostly felt frustrated. He made me feel irrelevant.'

She dips her spoon into the ice cream. It creaks and breaks off in a thin shaving. Lime fizzes on her tongue. 'What was his profession?'

'He managed an accountancy company. After he'd retired he used to sit with his American newspaper and his Italian coffee and read about what was happening in the world.

Sometimes he would take an entire day to read the *New York Times* from cover to cover, but when I tried to engage him in conversation about politics or current affairs, he would make some sad, flippant remark such as: "It will all be forgotten about tomorrow; you'll see, every trash can will be filled with yesterday's news, what does any of it matter?" And that would make me want to goad him, but when I did, when I forced him to argue with me, he would clam up for days afterwards and we wouldn't hear a word from him, not at mealtimes or when he went out; there would just be this terrible silence around him that was like – I don't know – it felt like death.'

'It sounds like depression.'

Konrad looks thoughtful. 'He probably was depressed all his adult life. When I think of him, I see a late summer lake with dust on the top, a faint stirring under the surface – it must have been tough for him having such a querulous, pushy, arrogant American son who thought he knew everything. It made him sadder, I think.'

'You were an only child?'

'No, I have a sister, Olenka.' His expression softens for a moment. His eyes flick over a group of students queuing to buy ice cream. He watches them laughing and adjusting rucksacks, lazy and indulgent with each other. 'She's a history lecturer at Columbia.'

'Is she as challenging?'

He pushes his coffee cup away and rubs at his eyes before he replies. 'She is, but not in the same way. She's always been more rational about these things, less emotional. She quietly got on and read books while I kicked up dust. In the early years she tried to protect me from myself.' He nods his head. 'She got me out of trouble a few times. She was always standing up for me at school.'

'So you were a bit of a rebel?'

He shrugs. 'I need something to care about, something that isn't me. You know the film profession is crammed with people who don't fully believe in themselves.'

She considers this for a moment and realizes that it is true also of academia. She wonders whether it is not true of most institutions. 'If you fully believe in yourself, you're not going to be working for an organization, you're going to be self-reliant,' she says.

He looks squarely at her. 'Olenka believes in herself. She told me once that she never doubted that she would study history. Her life was all ready and waiting for her. She just had to qualify for it; that was the word she used: *qualify*. She had to get herself fit for the life she would inhabit and she went about it systematically, meticulously and courageously. She put herself through college by waitressing and working in a library, she worked her way up the university hierarchy and she is now a professor. She married a linguist and they have two children, a son and daughter, and they are well-balanced and poised to continue the good work passed on by their parents. She makes bringing up a family seem so simple and so natural whereas I . . .' He looks at her. 'For a long time I dreaded every day. I felt buried by the responsibility.'

'So that's really why you ran away?' Catherine finishes her ice cream.

'I've been talking way too much, sorry.' He slides his hand across the table and for one alarming moment she thinks he is going to take hers, but he decides against it and stands up awkwardly, bashing his knee on the metal table leg and wincing as he looks round for someone to pay.

They fall silent as they walk back to her hotel. Her feet

feel swollen from the heat. After seeing her to the lobby Konrad walks back across the square and she finds herself wondering what he will do for the rest of the evening. She takes the stairs to her room, which is stuffy. She opens the window a notch and lies on the bed and kicks off her shoes. After a moment she reaches over to the bedside table for the stack of pages in the padded envelope. Then with the sound of Polish voices buzzing in her head, she begins once more to read.

5

Eastern Poland, November 1939

The mares were restless, calling in low ruffles of sound that drifted across from the yard and up to the window in Krystyna's room. She lay with her face turned in the direction of the stables, listening, preparing to leave the warm huddle of her child's narrow bed and go out into the cold to see what was disturbing the horses. Sometimes wolves came down from the forests at night to scavenge, especially hungry during the winter months, their howls ringing around the dwór. Her father usually left them alone, but he had shot one a few mornings ago. A big shaggy sable creature, caught with a bronze chicken between its jaws. At the shot, the wolf slumped into the snow and the bird tumbled out unharmed, indignantly scattering feathers. 'Go for your ride, both of you,' her father called to them. His face was flushed and the saved chicken was struggling to free itself from where he had pinned it under his left arm. She started towards the stables. But when she looked back she saw Janek had remained rooted to the spot, his face hidden under his clouded breath.

Krystyna had got both horses ready. They had snorted when she led them from the stables and skittered at the

64

sight of the wolf. It lay on its side, its coat hairs standing up in a stiff, thick pelt, the clefts between its clean, slim paws as dark as rain. It had a hole, the size of a fingertip, on its bony brow. The air around it smelled dry and wild. Her father had put the unharmed chicken back in the coop and collected a few eggs in a basket that he put down in the snow for a few moments. He scooped up the corpse and slung it across his shoulders; the wolf's fawn legs fell loose around his neck and its amber eyes were wide open as he carried it to the barn. They both mounted and sat silently on their horses looking down at the trail of blood beading the snow. Eventually the horses became impatient and began to paw the snow, eager to be released into the clear, cold air. That day they had taken a shorter route than usual, keeping their horses to a walk all the way.

It was bright outside. Moon glare swept across her clothes tumbled into a heap at the foot of her bed along with her books and the diary she had been keeping since the first day of September when the Germans had invaded Poland followed, seventeen days later, by the Russians. She wrote down everything that she heard, especially the things that her stepmother and father spoke about in their room in the early hours of the morning when they believed she was asleep. Her mind burned with images: Polish cavalry officers riding their horses into enemy lines, the city of Warsaw smoking from Luftwaffe attacks, the Polish government leaving the country with suitcases packed with reserves of gold.

At home mundane, ordinary activities had taken on aspects of the forbidden. Reading at night with the light on was no longer allowed, nor using too much water to wash, nor eating until she felt full, nor asking too many questions. School was closed. In spite of the arrival of the new baby, there was a quiet in the house, all the attention drawn to what was happening in the world outside. Occasionally Irena appeared with the baby clamped to her shoulder and urged Krystyna to tidy her room, but mostly she was left alone. To keep her mind active Krystyna read in the library; she also wrote daily, tremulously throwing her thoughts and feelings on to the page. She had not written at such length before and it was strangely exciting. When she read her words back to herself they sounded as if they had been written by someone else.

Her country had been torn in half again, split between the Germans in the west and Russians in the east who had carved out new territories on Polish soil. One night in October her father took her into the library and showed her the divide on a map. 'Here.' He jabbed his finger into a jagged space marked out in the middle of the map with Warsaw at one end and Kraków at the other. 'This is what is left of Poland, the so-called General Government.' His eyes glittered in the firelight.

She peered at the map. The dwór hovered in a spot that appeared midway between the new boundaries. 'So where are we?' she asked her father. 'Are we west or east, German or Russian?'

Her father folded up the map and then took her by the shoulders. He steered her towards the fireplace where flames vaulted up the vast chimney. 'We are at home,' her father said. His fingers dug into her shoulders and she tried not to flinch. 'We are still in Poland.'

She stared at the gobbling flames and said nothing.

A week or so later, some friends of Irena's, an actor and his scarlet-haired wife, arrived at the dwór, numb with exhaustion after a long journey from the west by train and on foot. They talked of masses of people being moved into the central area, filling the trains to bursting point as the Germans brought in families from the Reich, installing them in Polish apartments and houses. At the same time, they said, vast numbers of Polish families were being forced to leave for those newly evacuated cities and towns.

'It is chaos,' the actress said at breakfast on her first morning. 'People are just crawling all over each other to either get in or out.' Her face clouded. 'The Germans are even taking Polish children from orphanages, the young and beautiful blonde girls especially.'

'But why?' Krystyna had asked. 'What harm have the children caused?'

'None,' the actress replied, her face a slim oval moon between the long red curtains of her hair. 'They want them to be brought up as Germans.'

'That's terrible.'

'It's unfortunately true,' the actress sighed and glanced towards Irena who sat a little apart from them on a low chair rocking the baby, Henryk, to sleep. 'I'm sorry, but it makes me glad that I don't have children.'

Her husband, a small, vividly intelligent man who moved with the grace of a dancer, reached over and covered her hand with his own. His dark eyes hesitated and then searched around the breakfast table where they sat, plates pushed to one side after their meal of toast with jam and hot milky coffee. Outside, the trees reached skeletal arms against a dove-grey sky. 'You must know that the Germans are targeting Jews. They are shooting people like dogs.' The actor swallowed. 'They are burning synagogues with people inside.'

From Irena there came a gasp, and she covered her mouth with her hand. Her eyes were two wide, liquid pools.

Her father stared at the actor, his jawbone rigid. In recent weeks he had lost a lot of weight and his eyes seemed to have fallen deeper into their sockets. 'The Germans are too soft to make it this far,' he said in a tight voice. 'Not when the snow comes.'

There was a silence. The actor looked down at his hand which still covered his wife's. She leaned her chin on her other hand and glanced over at Henryk who had remained asleep while they talked, his cheeks rosy with heat, little fists curled like tiny ferns in an arc over his head. Her father, too, swept his gaze over his new son who was due to be christened in a few days. No one mentioned the threat from the east.

The priest did not appear as arranged on the day of the baptism. Her father, fearing that he had been arrested, sent Anastazia to the church to look for him. She found it cold and empty. There were used red glass holders for votive candles near the altar. On her way out of the church she took one of these glasses and filled it with holy water. She carried it back to the dwór, her eyes balancing on the horizon so as not to spill a drop.

Later that evening Henryk, bathed in lace, was baptized in the library. No one mentioned the absence of the priest. All their attention was concentrated on the child, who lay on his back on a new wolf skin, his face turned so that one clear dark eye was visible, his gaze drawn to the ring of red candles burning with a small, fierce light around him.

Krystyna remembered how Anastazia wetted her fingers and made the sign of the cross on Henryk's forehead, smoothing a few strands of his dark hair. She remembered the words of the prayer that asked Mary to protect the child from harm. She remembered how Henryk looked up at Anastazia with absolute trust in his eyes, as if she were the entire universe. She remembered the sound of Irena sobbing. She also remembered kissing the cold cheek of her own mother as she lay with her hands crossed over her chest in her coffin and the swooning scent of the lilies piled around her. Born with a weak heart, her mother had died when Krystyna was five years old. Anastazia looked after her until her father met Irena.

Everything was allowed the night of the baptism. A fire was lit in the massive stone grate. The flames made shadows on the ceiling and the gold lettering from the shelves of books gleamed in the warm light. High on the panelled wall over the fireplace Juliusz shone from his white horse. The actor and his wife joined them. He had slicked back his hair and wore a white shirt with a stiff collar; his wife was wrapped in a lavender shawl that smelled of scent. Dishes of pork and vegetables Krystyna believed she would never taste again miraculously materialized from the larder, and there was honey tea and beer and wine and abundant logs for the fire, and in the midst of this sense of fullness everybody was animated and kind to one another. No one spoke of war. It was as if they had all agreed not to so that Henryk could be named without fear. At one point Krystyna looked round to see her stepmother and father embracing each other under the chandelier in the centre of the library; her father's lips were touching the white streak of Irena's hair, and she seemed to come alive in his arms, pulled from a trance, two high spots of pink colouring her cheeks. Just behind them, the baby lay on his wolf pelt, peacefully asleep.

But towards the end of the evening the atmosphere changed. Her father called everyone together and waited for a moment. Anastazia lifted the sleeping Henryk into her arms and took him off to feed him in the kitchen. Irena's face paled as her husband took his position at the fireplace, one elbow propped on the stone mantelpiece to take the weight off his damaged leg. Earlier he had been laughing and drinking with the actor and his wife, but now his expression was composed. He shifted his weight on to his good leg and spoke in a calm and confident voice reminding them of the honour of the Polish nation, the right to property and land, the right to live in peace. 'I call on all of you to remember this one important thing: it is better to die free than be forced into slavery. We Poles have fought many battles and we have learned courage, honour and dignity. We have learned to stand up for what we believe in. We have learned how to love our country, and want to defend it as we would defend a sister or a brother, a mother or a father. Our country is our family. It is the place where we belong, where our children belong. No one, not even the worst aggressor, can take this from us. The fight begins and ends in our hearts.'

At this everyone cheered and embraced each other with tears streaming down their faces. After feeding Henryk, Anastazia came in from the kitchen and Irena took the baby from her, standing apart from the celebrations, her face a tight, bone mask. Eventually her father went over to where Irena stood and lifted his new son aloft, the lace train rumpled like paper, and everyone crowded round him again.

Now, outside her window, the spruce tree was creaking in the wind. Krystyna wondered whether an ice storm was coming. That would explain why the horses were calling. She sat up and listened. The horses fell quiet. Obviously whatever danger they sensed had passed. There were only two horses left now, her mare and Janek's. Celestyna, the old mare, had died in her sleep the day before. Krystyna had found her lying on her side at the back of her stall. Her neck felt slack and warm and she might have been asleep except that her legs were stiff and her eye was no longer clear, but clouded over. After running to the house to tell her father, Krystyna was surprised to find Lorenz in the kitchen twisting his cap in his hands. Her father's shirt was half unbuttoned and his hair stood up in tufts. They stopped talking when they saw her.

'Celestyna has gone,' she told her father.

He had not spoken immediately. His skin had a blue tinge. She wondered why he had not bothered to dress properly. Alarm gripped her throat as she realized that Lorenz had come to deliver bad news.

'Where's Janek?' she blurted out.

Lorenz looked at her. His throat was bundled with scarves. His voice was hoarse as he spoke. 'He's at home asleep.'

There was a strange tension in the kitchen that she had never felt before. 'Father, what's happening?'

Her father had run his hands through his hair. His voice was thick. 'Wait for me outside. I will come to bury her.'

A cold gust rattled the windowpane, interrupting her thoughts. Krystyna shuddered and pulled her blanket around her shoulders. She blew on her fingers and then took out her diary from under her pillow and began to write. When she couldn't sleep, she wrote down what was on her mind and it seemed to help. She recalled the image of her father pulling the sleigh that carried Celestyna to her burial in the forest at the back of the house. The mare's hooves had been very yellow against the snow. On the way they had startled a deer which leapt between the birch trees with a sideways zipping motion, looking back at them once before disappearing into the whiteness. Krystyna had carried the shovel. When they reached the spot, she and her father had between them eased the old mare off the sleigh and laid her down on the frozen ground. Celestyna's eyes were now closed. Her white lashes were the same colour as the snow. Her body was cold bones. Krystyna's father took the shovel and began to clear a hollow in the snow. The ground was too frozen to dig a grave, and they would have to bury the horse not in soil but in ice. When he was finished he was sweating. He had to lean against a tree for a few moments to regain his strength. Krystyna felt her stomach twist with fear. She helped him drag the mare to the hollow. Then she took the shovel from him. 'I want to finish this.'

'Are you sure?' His face was grey with exertion.

She nodded and lifted the shovel, but something in her father's expression made her hesitate. He was looking down at the snow where Celestyna now lay with her forelegs and hindlegs curved into a crescent. The mare had chosen her own moment to die and for that she knew her father was grateful. He closed his eyes for a moment and she did the same. The forest was silent save for the sound of their breathing. When they opened their eyes again her father turned to her and laid his hand on her arm.

'We don't have much time,' he said.

She glanced up at the sky where full snow clouds hung like heavy bags of laundry. Her throat was thick and she felt a tightening across her chest. 'I'll be quick,' she said.

Her father's eyes were two dark points of light that now searched her face. 'You must promise me that you will escape if you can.' His voice was low and urgent. 'If the soldiers come, you must try to get out through the forest and head for the Lithuanian border. Take the horses.'

She stared at him, her heart beating hard. Her father glanced over his shoulder through the copse of birch trees, each one of which wore a napkin of fresh snow. She took a few deep breaths of the thin air. 'I promise,' she said. 'I won't let you down.'

His eyes leapt. He nodded once and then looked down at the mare. There were a few wisps of straw caught in her mane. He bent and plucked them out and then coiled a few long white strands of hair around his fingers. He snapped the hair from the mane and put it in his overcoat pocket. When he had finished, she lifted the shovel and dug it into the snow.

She stopped writing. Outside the horses were calling again. She wondered whether Janek was awake. The cottage he shared with his father, the old gamekeeper's place secluded in the wood, was about a quarter-mile away from the house. But he knew when the horses were unsettled. Often he had dressed in the dark and, taking care not to wake his father, put on his boots and heavy coat and gone to the stables. When the mares were foaling he slept in the straw beside them. Sometimes during his quiet periods when he needed to be free from people he sat in the stall with Gazela's head in his lap.

She glanced across her room, thinking now that she would get up and get dressed. Janek's cap was hanging on the back of a wooden chair. If it had been her favourite cap she would have searched every room for it, even rooms she rarely entered; shuttered dark spaces with cold fireplaces and foggy mirrors, damp curtains and cobwebs as big as bird nests, places that she thought of as the ghost rooms of the dwór. But not Janek. He didn't mind about things in the way she minded. He was not attached to things. A mirror was just a mirror, a wardrobe held no interest, a collection of books was exactly that. Clothing was to him just something to keep him warm. It would have been a nuisance to lose his cap, nothing more. It was how boys were, she understood: unconcerned, careless, except that he was not like that. He was the opposite; almost too concerned, and that was why he forgot small things. That was why he was not interested in furniture. He would have lived outside all year round if he could. No, bigger things crowded his mind; he had explained it to her once when they were out riding: 'When something happens, something that makes me feel, it's as if I'm drowning. I have to go away and let everything calm down.'

'So at least you have feelings.' She'd regretted the words as soon as she'd said them. Janek had not responded. He'd ridden on with his eyes cast down to the snow, pretending to search for wolf or elk tracks, and she'd felt a gap open up between them, like a space in an ill-fitting window frame. It pushed her back into herself. It was awful. It felt like a denial. In all the time they had grown up together she'd believed that Janek was following her. She'd laid down a trail for him and she was confident that he would never leave her. She'd always known that she was going somewhere, that instinct she had been born with and, of course, it had been encouraged by her father who had wanted her to carry herself with honour. 'You know what you want,' her stepmother said to her one day shortly after the actor and his wife left for Lithuania. 'You know what to aim for.' Her head was held to one side and there was a look of regret in her eyes. Her friends had offered to take Henryk to safety and her father had tried to encourage Irena to leave with them, but she had dithered and in the end her friends had left without her. For days after her father had been unusually quiet, and spent long periods closeted in the library with his books and maps.

Over the past few weeks they had sold off the most valuable paintings, except the family ones, and silver and furniture. In spite of her father's insistence that they should continue living as if Poland were still free, the house had gradually surrendered its treasure. Things that had remained in place in certain rooms and spots for years vanished overnight. Krystyna recalled running down the stairs and feeling a chill from the arched window on the first landing, and a sense that something was out of place. She had stood on the landing, unable to continue until she knew what was missing. At first she could not remember and paused with her hand on the empty windowsill, her mind straining to think of what had been there, partially blocking the light, for it was that sense of a gap unplugged that had caught her attention, but the harder she tried to remember it, the more elusive the missing object became, as if by the very act of trying to recall it she was instead pushing it further away. Frustrated, she had been forced to tear herself away from the window not knowing what it was. The thought of the missing object disturbed her and for the rest of the day she kept returning to it, working and worrying at it like a toothache, but then eventually she forgot all about it.

A few days later, coming down the stairs in the morning

light she saw that the tall space flush against the lower pane was once again occupied by a Chinese vase. Hovering, uncertain, she had needed to confirm its reality with her fingertips. The porcelain glaze was cool to the touch. In a daze Krystyna had gone to the kitchen where Irena was feeding Henryk. Between spooning mouthfuls of warm porridge into the baby's mouth, Irena solved the mystery of the Chinese vase's reappearance. It had been sold, she said, but the person who had bought it had not arrived to collect it. Irena's hand was shaking as she returned her attention to the baby's wetly alive mouth.

Every morning since the vase had returned Krystyna stopped by the window on the first landing to touch it because of all the things in the house it seemed to belong so perfectly. It fully inhabited its space and that was why when it had gone missing she couldn't remember it; some things were not supposed to disappear.

She looked at Janek's cap again. He would not suspect that she had it. She had picked it up from the snow one morning when she had gone out riding alone because sometimes she just liked the feeling of having the sky to herself. On solitary rides such as this one she made plans for the life she intended to live when the war was over. Her stepmother was right: she had a very clear sense of her own destiny. She wanted to live in a city, an old city such as Kraków or Lublin, where she would study history. She needed to know more about the world and how it had come to be this way rather than another; why had the Germans chosen to invade Poland, was it simply because Poland was so easy to flatten? Poland's army had been outnumbered by the Germans, but the cavalry had put up a fight. She had heard her father talk about the officers who had charged the German supply lines on horseback, refusing to give up, turning their brave horses towards the enemy intent on defending their country. Her father had told the story with pride, as if he had taken part in the charge, rather than hearing about it from others who had in turn been told of it, so that it became like a legend, a story that was intended to give people hope, but it had made Krystyna worry. If the cavalry on their fearless horses could be crushed, what hope was there for the ordinary people of the country? Surely Britain would not leave Poland to fight it out alone? Countries depended on each other. There were treaties and agreements, historical and political links, and there were promises, too.

She should give the cap back to Janek, but for some reason she kept putting it off. But this morning she would make an effort to remember. This morning she would wear it to the stables and see how long it took him to notice . . .

She lifted her head. There were footsteps on the stairs. Her heart skittered as the door opened. The soldier stood framed in the doorway, his breath forming a white cloud. When it dispersed, she saw a sharp chin, glinting with bristles, like the snout of a young fox, a pinched nose and electric-blue eyes that registered surprise at finding someone sitting up and awake. He paused and seemed to check himself as he entered her room almost apologetically. He was dressed in an olive-grey uniform and carried in one hand a fur cap. She noticed his fingers clenching into the fibres. His rifle was slung across his body and he brought with him a smell of cold metal and petrol. As he advanced across the room he glanced at his boots, carefully stepping over her clothes and books that still lay tumbled together on the rug. He came right up to the foot of her bed and hovered for a moment, his eyes averted, but just when she thought it might not be as bad as it appeared, he lifted his chin in one swift, savage movement and the moonlight illuminated his skin, which was smooth and deadly, as if it had never felt the warmth of blood.

'Get up.' He spoke in Polish.

This time he failed to lower his eyes as she slipped her bare knees from the covers and went over to her clothes to dress. She shivered, pulling on her lower things first, relieved when he turned his back as she lifted her night-dress over her head. Almost immediately the icy eyes snapped back to her and then in a strained, high-pitched Russian-accented voice he began to issue instructions, pointing at the chest of drawers, demanding that she find a bag and stuff it with as many outdoor clothes as she could carry.

On the dresser there was a photograph of Janek with Gazela's chestnut dam taken six years ago soon after she gave birth to the filly that would become his own. The soldier kept looking at it. She wanted to put it in her bag, along with the red cap, but felt that this might disturb something and cause him to break out of the tension that was holding him in her room so intimately that she could smell the onion in the white vapour of his breath. He moved over to her window and looked down into the yard. She wondered whether there were more soldiers. Perhaps this scene was being repeated in the largest bedroom on the other side of the house. To give Irena a rest, Anastazia had that night offered to take Henryk into her own room under the eaves, a small, quiet chapel at the top of the dwór that she had peacefully and stubbornly inhabited ever since coming to the house despite Irena's insistence that she take a larger, warmer room on the first floor where everybody else slept.

The soldier had his back to her. She whisked the photograph from the dresser and shoved it inside the red cap, pushing it deep into the pit of the bag. A strap on her duffel bag was rotten and snapped as she pulled it tight. She looked at the worn piece of leather. There were soft scrapes and tiny indentations in the grain which had whitened with age. These had come from when she was a baby. For some reason the only thing that would console her when she could not sleep was sucking on a leather strap. She threw the strap down on the rug, but then changed her mind and put it inside the bag with her clothes. The soldier looked around as she pulled the remaining strap tight and buckled it.

'Go downstairs. I will carry bag.' His voice was lower now, but still stuttered over the unfamiliar Polish.

She was about to leave when she noticed her diary and pen lying partly concealed under her bed. They must have fallen when she jumped out of bed. 'One moment . . .'

The soldier's eyes seemed to crackle. 'I said, go.'

'I just asked for a moment.' She spoke quietly and rapidly, hoping that he wouldn't understand, and then, gulping down her fear, she reached towards the diary and put her hand on its familiar hard blue cover.

The soldier crossed the room in one stride. His boot hovered over her hand. She tried to push the diary further under the bed, but it was too late. She felt the pieces of grit in the sole of his boot scratch her skin as the boot came down, lightly at first, almost as if he were having a joke with her, but then she felt his foot and with a sickening feeling in her stomach, the full weight of his body clamp her hand.

Holding her bruised hand to her chest and resisting a temptation to whimper, she went downstairs. The soldier followed behind her, close enough for her to feel his warmth and hear the sound of his rifle strap snagging at the metal buttons on his coat. The kitchen was dark and chilly. He dropped her bag on the flagstones and ordered her to sit. He left her and returned upstairs. She pulled out a chair. Its wooden back felt frozen to the touch. She rested her throbbing knuckles against it for a moment and then sat down.

Only a few hours ago her family had eaten supper together in this kitchen. The smell of soup still lingered. Anastazia had used the last of the dried mushrooms along with some chopped onion and shreds of cabbage and dried dill to stuff the *pierogi* parcels, small succulent morsels of mushroomy deliciousness that burst in the mouth and made Krystyna feel warm and safe. She heard voices upstairs. She could not tell who was speaking, or how many voices there were, but it sounded like a lot. It also sounded as if furniture was being thrown around. There was a thump and then a thud and then silence. She held her breath. Her chest burned and there was the accompanying sensation of something hard and gristly stuck in her throat, making her want to gag. Upstairs Irena was sobbing: a long, dry cry that reminded Krystyna of the night Henryk was born. The commotion in their room – her father was now shouting – along with the thought of the soldiers going out to the landing where they would surely find the wooden door that hid the narrow stairs leading up to Anastazia's room made her shudder all over.

A sound from outside the house pulled her attention from what was happening upstairs. She went to the window and through a crack in the shutters saw four men with guns pointing straight ahead. There was no flicker of life in their eyes. They stood in a hard frozen line like lead soldiers. She pulled away from the window and returned to the table. Fear trickled over her. They were surrounded and there was nothing she could do except wait for her father and Irena to be marched down the stairs at gunpoint. There was more shouting from her father. His voice sounded stretched, as if at any minute he would tear holes in it. Irena was still weeping. The soldiers talked in Russian over the protests, as if to drown them out, and that, at least, was a relief because if they kept talking it meant they were not preparing to shoot.

Crouching low, she peered through the shutters again. The soldiers had moved around to the back of the house where there was a terrace looking out across the meadow that sloped down towards the river. At the start of the summer her father and Irena had sat drinking wine and watching the horses, talking about the ones they would have to sell and those that they could perhaps keep, if things improved. But things, of course, had steadily got worse.

The shouts upstairs had subsided into a babble, her father's voice just detectable under a thick blanket of Russian. It sounded as if he were negotiating with the soldiers. She sat for a while longer with her eyes on her bag and then as the voices began to climb once more she recalled her father's words in the forest. With her heart pounding, she rose to her feet.

In the dark hallway she felt her way to the saddle racks. She identified Izabela's bridle by its smell and the suppleness of the reins and lifted it from its hook. The saddle slid from its post and on to the crook of her arm. Taking care not to jingle stirrup irons, bit rings and buckles, she moved to the main door and heaved it open. Outside she gulped down the blue night air, but then realized that she had left her bag in the kitchen. If she went back for it she might meet the soldiers coming down the stairs.

She listened for the soldiers outside. They were on the far side of the house. She could hear faint voices and the sound of boots crunching snow. Putting down the saddle and bridle, she paused, bent double by a stab of pain in her gut that brought tears to her eyes. She would not get far without warm clothing or food, but to return might slam the door on her tiny opportunity. She hovered, unable to decide, but then the same taut feeling that had pushed her out of the house in the first place took over, and she went back, her heart lurching into her throat at each retraced step. The kitchen was how she had left it. She went into the larder and pulled down two jars of plum jam from the top shelf. The bread that was being saved for breakfast rested on a board under a cloth. Hesitating, she heard heavy footsteps above her head. Outside one of the wolfhounds began to howl. Her hands shook as she pushed the jam and bread into her bag and then swung it on to her back.

The dogs came forward as she crossed the yard and licked her hand. Their eyes were alert at the prospect of an outing. She gestured to them to stay in the barn, making them lie down in the straw. They watched her as she went to the feed sacks and scooped some oats into an old sack that she folded over and tied up before putting it into her duffel bag.

She went to the mares. They stood close in their stalls,

their eyes huge and wary. Krystyna knew that she would not be able to take Izabela and leave Gazela behind because the mares would call to each other. She would have to take them both. Izabela dipped her head into the bridle and stood motionless as Krystyna laid the saddle on her back. She pulled up the girth, allowing her hand to linger in the velvet hollow behind the mare's front legs for a moment, her cold, scared fingers seeking the warmth and the soft rise of her horse's belly. 'We're going to warn Janek,' she whispered as Gazela looked over at her saddled companion. 'Don't worry, I'm not going to leave you behind, but you must follow quietly.'

The horses seemed to hold their breath as Krystyna led them out into the snow. There was no sign of the soldiers. Her throat tightened as she imagined them all inside the house. She bit her lip. As she climbed up to mount Izabela, she caught a glimpse of the stars poised in their remote beauty, each one distinct and unassailable. She settled into the saddle and, checking that Gazela was following, she lifted her reins and pointed Izabela towards the track that led down to the cottage in the woods.

Izabela's ears flicked back and forth, testing the night for sounds of danger. Usually owls called or foxes barked and fought, but tonight the snowy meadows were silent, smooth stretches gleaming under metallic moonlight. The banks were stripped of life and the trees drooped solemnly under their weight of snow. The only sound was of hooves crumpling the frozen ground.

Krystyna stroked Izabela's neck. She must not panic. She must just ride calmly to the end of the track. Under her, the mare relaxed and lengthened her stride, pushing her breath through her nostrils.

The snow around the gateway to the cottage was undisturbed. Krystyna laid her face against the mare's neck for a moment in relief. She had in her fright half thought that the soldiers might have gone to the cottage first. She dismounted, sinking up to her knees in fresh snow. Izabela lowered her head and blew at the white powder through her nostrils. Gazela's nose came level, ice-beaded whiskers brushing against her companion's. Krystyna touched their ears. They felt cold and hard. 'Wait here. I won't be long.'

The cottage was empty. Krystyna went from room to room, her breath snagging, expecting at any moment to find Janek and his father slumped together, already dealt with by the soldiers. It was impossible that they should not be there. She could not believe that Lorenz had saved himself without considering her family. She could not imagine Janek packing his bag with his father standing over him, looking on as the soldier had looked at her in her room only a short while ago. Janek would not have agreed to flee without trying to warn them first. This was true, but it was also true that in both their rooms the drawers storing their warm clothes were empty.

The horses lifted their heads as she ploughed back through the snow towards them, tears streaming down her face. Her ears were blocked, submerging her for a moment deep into her own shocked bewilderment. Gasping for air, she led Izabela out of the fresh snow to a flatter place so that she could mount. She put her foot up to the stirrup ready to leap when a sound, like a slap or a cracking dry branch, exploded into the night. The mare shifted sideways and Krystyna lost her grip on the stirrup and fell backwards into the snow. She saw the mare's ears flatten as the second shot slammed out, clearer and sharper than the first as if the shooter was now properly taking aim. Her tears froze on her face. She lay in the snow wide-eyed with terror, a strange dry knocking feeling hammering at the space underneath her ribs. When she eventually pulled herself up and hauled her body into the saddle she was unable to choose the direction in which she wanted to ride and sat with her arms crossed tight under her ribs which continued to pulse and ache. It was the mare who made the decision to move, backing away from the cottage and stepping out towards the meadow where the line of oak trees, full crowns mounded with snow, stretched away into the distance.

6

Kraków, present day

'Catherine?' His voice is close. She breathes in the warmth
of it. 'Catherine, are you okay?' The note of concern
pulls her properly awake. She sits up in bed and blinks into
the musty darkness of the hotel room. There is a hot, sweet
smell that she realizes is coming from her own body.

'I'm sorry.' The telephone receiver is wet with her sleepy
breath. 'I've overslept.' She swallows. Her throat feels thick.
The room is airless. She needs orange juice, a large coffee,
a roll, something dry to settle her stomach. She shifts
position and the twisted phone cord shunts over a crowd
of miniatures jostling for space on the bedside table.
Instinctively she reaches out to catch them, but misses,
fingers fumbling as the bottles tumble on to the carpet.

'You sure everything's okay?'

The morning seems an unwelcome, blaring intrusion,
too keen and inquisitive for her frame of mind. Catherine
untwists the telephone cord and leans back against the
pillow and sighs. 'I'm exhausted,' she tells him honestly. 'I
need to sleep for a bit.' A crack of light noses between the
gap in the curtains. Fat, buttery, late morning light. How
long had she sat in her robe by the window with Krystyna's

story cradled in her lap? Her tongue feels heavy in her mouth and she can still taste the sweetness from the tiny, potent bottles that had helped to keep her awake.

'Sure. How about you get some more rest and I call you later?' His voice is soothing, sweet and whole. No ifs or buts or pauses or maybes. Relief washes over her.

'Thank you.'

There's a pause on the other end of the line. She can hear him breathing as he considers what to say.

'Okay.' He doesn't put down the phone.

She stretches her legs in the bed, luxuriating in the prospect of a few more hours of rest. But perversely she now feels awake. Maybe she need not sleep. She could take a long bath. Read. It is years since she surrendered herself to the voluptuous pleasure of solitary reading.

Konrad's voice drifts across her thoughts. 'How about we meet for a late lunch?' There's a hesitant note in the suggestion, as if he's worried she might refuse.

'That sounds good.' She could still take her time. She could choose what to wear, perhaps her spotted sleeveless linen dress that skims her thighs and shows her waist. She runs her hand across her pelvis where her hip bones thrust out. She has lost weight, which is a surprise.

'I'll call you later.' A pause as he catches his breath. It sounds as if there is something else he meant to say, but he goes without voicing it.

She puts down the phone and then carries his words with her into a full, cleansing and dreamless sleep from which she is woken by the sound of a trolley with a squeaking wheel in the corridor outside her room.

She showers, washes her hair, lathering on more conditioner than usual, and puts on her dress and a pair of bronze strappy sandals she bought in London one rare Saturday without Dominic. She glances at her reflection in the full-length mirror. Her arms and neck are freckled and tanned a pinky brown. Her hair smells fresh and shimmers with gold and auburn lights. Her eyes seem bluer. She makes a face and then goes over to the phone and dials her number in Cambridge. She listens to the sound of it ringing. It's a habit of Dominic's to take a long bath late morning if he has no lectures. He ought to be there. The automated message service that they have never personalized cuts in. She leaves a message for Dominic saying that she forgot to bring her mobile charger and that she will call again later. She puts down the phone. Almost immediately it rings again. Expecting it to be Dominic, she answers and receives a message from reception that Konrad is waiting for her downstairs. Smiling to herself she picks up her room key and leather bag and hesitates outside the lift, which groans on its ropes somewhere in the bowels of the basement, and instead takes the stairs down to the lobby.

'Hi. I'm over here.' Konrad looks up from one of the dark brown leather couches in the lobby. He's reading a Polish newspaper. A coffee cup rests on the smoked glass table in front of him.

'Hello.' Suddenly she feels shy. He stands up. She notices how elegant his feet are: bare and brown inside robust leather sandals.

'Did you get some rest?' He sweeps his eyes over her dress and damp hair, a quick, furtive appraisal.

'Slept like a log.' She catches herself: 'Do you have that expression in America?'

'My son used to say: slept like a bear.' He glances at her, gauging her reaction.

She laughs. The tone of her voice surprises her. It's a different kind of laugh. Normally she comes across a little strained and breathless. Uptight. Dominic once told her he hated her nervous laugh. It was inauthentic, he said. It bothered him. To appease him she spent a few weeks trying not to laugh. Her colleagues asked her if she was ill. Then she became ill. For months she felt as if someone were following her. The anxiety and fear stopped her sleeping. Dominic's response was to say that he preferred her fake than depressed. She feels a surge of anger at the memory.

'I prefer your son's version – logs are sort of dead,' she replies in a bright voice.

Konrad's eyes soften. 'I've spent many years trying to *be* that log.' He wears clean creased cotton, which contributes to the feeling around him of poise and readiness. But he also looks tired. She wonders then if he left the hotel after first calling her. Perhaps he stayed reading his newspaper from cover to cover while she slept. The thought makes her feel odd, as if she is pretending to be someone else, the kind of sophisticated woman who might meet an attractive stranger in a hotel bar.

His hand hovers over the small of her back as they walk out into the sun-drenched square. Red flags advertising the Kraków Film Festival flap and jink on white metal poles, the canvas material buffeting and curling, like mast sails. The sky is a deep flawless blue.

Konrad stops in front of a film poster. John Malkovich's blunt, handsome face stares back at them. 'Could I drag you along to a film while you're here?' His voice is casual, relaxed. 'A selfish request, of course. I really want to see Malkovich playing a professor in disgrace.'

'In Polish?'

'In English with Polish subtitles.' His eyes gleam at her.

Her throat tightens. 'It's ages since I went to the cinema. Years, I think.'

He pantomimes a shocked, eyes-rolling expression. 'Telescopes have a lot to answer for. You have some catching up to do.'

'I do.' She glances at the poster once more before they pull away.

As they stroll around the square, Konrad tells her about the films he has loved. His voice is animated, rapid, his expression boyish, unselfconscious, and he uses his hands to punctuate his talk. She finds that she has to speed up her steps to keep pace with him. 'Ever since I was a kid I've loved the cinema. There's just such a thrill in sitting down to watch the curtains lift and the screen rise like the inside of a great clean egg, and then all those powerful studio images, the names, they were like promises to me back then: Paramount, Universal, Twentieth Century Fox. I was always the first to arrive at the Saturday cinema and the last to leave. I dreamed of the cinema, yearned for it.' His voice warms as he shares the memory.

She marvels at how it is that words can contain such joy. It reminds her of when she was a teenager, spending nights on the beach in Devon sitting around a driftwood fire shooting sparks into the night, everyone's eyes bright and clear as they surrendered to the need to talk, an instinct so vital and urgent it superseded sex. The sound of other voices from other fires fused together into the night. When eventually the babble subsided, everyone lay down and looked up at the stars swimming across the night sky. She remembers the hush, the sound of people breathing around her, the pull and draw of the surf across the shingle. The descending cries of cormorants. There would be a moment of silence, but then after a while someone would make a drowsy comment and the talk would start all over again, but softer this time, almost sleep talk, and it would still be going in the morning when she woke.

Konrad takes her to an Italian restaurant tucked away down one of the side streets. Inside the restaurant is small, but there's a spacious courtyard at the back with tables placed at discreet intervals. White linen lifts in the hot breeze. She can smell the flowers and the dusty trees and the water fountain. Behind their table is an old yellow stone wall, crumbling as soft as flour. In the air there's a murmur of garlic and thyme. They settle in deep wicker chairs. She finds that she is hungry and orders antipasto and sea bass. They eat their first course silently, but comfortably. Every now and again Konrad looks up from his tumble of parma ham and smiles.

A middle-aged waiter, full-bellied with sun-browned arms, brings scooped white plates heavy with salted fish, steaming tender inside roasted silver foil parcels. Pink sweet half-moons of flesh melt on her tongue. The wine is very cold; its colour reminds her of gooseberries, which in turn reminds her of her grandmother: her mother's mother, a doctor who worked in Nigeria following her training as a maxillofacial surgeon in London. A small woman with grave and generous hands that grafted slim pockets of skin on to the ravaged faces of leprosy victims, stitching as neat as a baby's teeth. Catherine, who had helped her mother to go through things after her grandmother's death, had found a book of tiny crinkled black and white photographs of Africans waiting under the trees outside a field hospital. Several pictures showed her grandmother, petite in a summer dress protected by a white apron. 'Could I keep these?' she'd asked.

'What for? You don't know any of the people in them.' Without looking at the photographs, her mother had pushed a pile of sweaters into a plastic bag.

'I knew Cynthia.' They had always called her grandmother by her first name.

Her mother paused, her arms filled with tiny shoes destined for the ranks of black plastic sacks heaped on the bed. These were already stuffed with immaculately conserved narrow-waisted dresses, dainty jackets, kid gloves and veiled hats dispatched with an efficiency that pierced Catherine's heart. Her grandmother had been no larger than a ten-year-old child.

Her mother had dropped the shoes into the mouth of the nearest sack. Her face was flushed. 'We can't keep everything.'

'I know. I'd still like something.'

Her mother pushed the photographs across the bed towards Catherine, a tight smile on her lips. 'Take the whole album, then.'

On her return from Africa, her grandmother had settled in Devon where she married a botanist and together the couple grew rare English fruit in a sprawling garden composed of old railway sleepers, raised beds, compost heaps, warm espaliered walls, pruned white stumpy branches and mysterious black nets. The house had flaking white-painted shutters, flagstones in the kitchen, worn smooth with age, glass cold in winter. In the beamed bedrooms there were narrow beds humped with candlewick, cobwebs with perpetual spiders caught in their safety nets like fatally plump trapeze artists; the place smelled of rotting wood and, one night when they stayed after her mother had drunk too much to drive them home, Catherine remembered hearing the companionable gnawing of mice and rats. That night an eye, sequin bright, had peered down at her from a rafter, enquiring what she was doing there. Who was she? And how did she get to find out?

'Would you like dessert or coffee?' Konrad's voice lengthens into a drawl as he stretches in the sun. His short shirt sleeves press against the veined pale underskin of his forearm. An image of the nude statues in the Czartoryski Collection swims into her mind.

'I'll leave dessert, the fish was just perfect, but I could I suppose have an espresso.'

'You *could you suppose*?' His eyes crinkle at her.

'I'm sorry, that sounded impossibly prim.'

'Hey, I'm just teasing you.'

She recalls their laughter over the menu in the Floriańska coffee shop. How long ago that now seems. Time has stretched. It feels as if she has been in Kraków for weeks instead of days.

'But no jam.' Her attempt at teasing him back sounds stiff and she flushes with embarrassment.

'We only drink tea with jam.'

'*We*? So you think of yourself as Polish rather than American?' Her question comes out bolder than she intends. She watches him straighten his posture as he considers how to respond.

'I guess I do now; well, since I've been here. I speak Polish and that makes me feel Polish. I feel more relaxed as a Pole than I do as an American. So I'm morphing maybe.' He scrunches his hair. She wonders how it feels in his hand: dry, a little rough on the ends. He continues: 'So, do you consider yourself English through and through?'

'That's a difficult question. I mean before I came here I would have said yes, absolutely. I'm your archetypal English woman. Pale, awkward, a little bit too clever, something of a social misfit because of my job. Stubborn. Difficult to live with. Remote.' She realizes that she has just described Cecilia Payne.

The waiter whisks their plates away and Konrad orders two double espressos before turning his attention back to her. 'You should have squeezed self-deprecating in there somewhere.'

'Oh, we English definitely *do* self-deprecating, although in my case it's more like self-assassination.' She trails off, wondering whether she's said too much.

'Hey, go easy.' His eyes are gentle. 'There's a fine line, don't you think, between self-deprecating and self-defeating?' He sits back in his chair and folds his arms.

'I suppose so.'

'We can't bear being thought arrogant. Krystyna was always very clear about these things. She believed it was essential to know our own worth. It was lazy not to.'

She wonders whether he is mocking her. She looks into the garden. Willow branches snagged by purple blooms of clematis, a little tatty and dusty like once glamorous curtains, screen off the rear part of the garden, leaving the courtyard open like a stage, now flooded with ripe afternoon light.

Eventually she says, 'Perhaps your aunt was born self-assured, like one of my astronomer women: absolutely bloody indestructible.'

He smiles faintly. She intended some irony in her

assessment, some levity, but it appears she has misjudged his sensitivity. 'Catherine' – his grey eyes fix on hers – 'she was the most real woman I have ever met.' He drains his espresso cup and calls for the bill.

She wonders whether she has spoiled something.

They return to the square; the street bars and cafés are packed with animated young people enjoying some unannounced celebration. She looks at the lazy sprawl of tanned healthy limbs, rumpled clothes and sun-bleached hair and feels momentarily bereft. The heat clatters down on the centre of her head. She excuses herself for a few minutes and scans the stalls, looking for a sun hat, but the striped booths offer only toys and confectionery sweating under cellophane. Her eyes feel tight and her feet are beginning to swell in her new sandals. A crowd of schoolchildren intent on the sweet stalls jostles past her. Now she feels a pang for the cool quiet of winter Cambridge with its empty greens and chill stone. She buys a bottle of mineral water from a small supermarket in a dark street off the square and carries it back to where she left Konrad outside the film festival booth. He has disappeared. She tries not to appear concerned and opens the water and splashes some on her wrists and around the back of her neck. As she lifts her hair, she catches him staring at her from a stall opposite.

They have half an hour before the Malkovich film. He suggests a cold drink. They settle on plastic chairs at one of the outdoor bars. They sit opposite each other. He drinks a Polish beer. She orders a white wine spritzer. It tastes acidic and the alcohol goes immediately to her head. They talk in disconnected bursts, asking polite questions of each other. Silences well. She feels afraid. Each question is a coin dropped down a shaft. After another attempt to find the join, the frayed end of conversation left dangling at lunch, Konrad leans in his seat, the corners of his mouth slumped in defeat. She feels a pulse of anxiety. You're not very good at this, she berates herself. You can't keep it up. Perhaps the morning is all she will have: one bright burst of possibility; perhaps there is nothing more. She wishes she could find the courage to break the impasse, but she is now lost. She shouldn't have come. She'd thought naively that Kraków, the city of myth and legend, might have some kind of magical power of drawing out her thoughts and feelings – somehow it would give her the confidence she lacks, but it has instead pushed her deeper into herself. She feels herself retreating, closing over, mouthing platitudes to Konrad. All the delight that she had felt in him just a short while ago seems to have vanished. She experiences a throb of misery. Konrad sits in the shade and sips his beer. One leg is crossed over his knee in a pose that seems relaxed, but she can see the tension corked in his ankle. She reaches for her drink. The ice-cold glass is now warm and the spritzer has gone flat.

The cinema is a relief. Cool and dark. And the film is good, painfully good. Watching Malkovich's performance of a bleakly charismatic South African professor who comes unstuck over an affair with a young student, she feels as if she's reviewing part of her own life. Konrad angles his body away from her in his seat and she is grateful. When the film is over, they will separate, and that will be that: an interesting interlude, nothing more. She will ask if she can take home the film notes; she might be able to borrow the papers for a short while. She could post it all back to him. It really isn't necessary to stay.

It is still early evening when they step out of the cinema and into the air again, yawning and blinking as if they have just woken from a deep dream. Konrad suggests a drink. Her thoughts of flight fade. Perhaps another few days would do no harm. She's supposed to leave on Saturday. It's only Monday. It would be a waste not to use up her hotel booking. She would also have to explain to Dominic why she had come home early.

Konrad heads for a table at one of the quieter bars. After they have settled, he orders vodka. 'How about you?'

'I think I'll be reckless and have vodka too.'

'Careful now.' His shoulders relax as he relays their orders to a young waitress, choosing to speak in English, this time, perhaps in deference to her. Catherine feels her head clear.

Konrad leans forward. 'I'm interested – what's academia in Britain like?'

'You mean – do seedy old professors get off with their students?'

He puts his head back and laughs. The sight of his Adam's apple exposed against his throat causes a stir in her. 'That's exactly what I mean.'

'There are a few who think it's a professional perk.' She tries to keep her voice neutral. 'I suppose I should confess that I was a student of my current partner.' She sits back and considers the awkwardness of what she's just said. *My current partner*, as if there has been a series of them, a long line of professors waiting in line to be disgraced by her. 'Dominic,' she adds, hastily. Instantly she regrets speaking his name; in this situation it feels almost as if she has just crossed an invisible line.

'Tell me about him. How did you two meet?' Konrad's tone is intrigued.

She feels her stomach turn over. She takes a sip of vodka, aware of Konrad's eyes watching her. 'He's not the kind of person you actually *meet*.' She laughs. The vodka warms her insides. It loosens her. 'We collided at Cambridge when I was an undergraduate. Dominic was well known. He was everywhere. He just radiated, I don't know, something extraordinary. He was large, no, actually I mean huge. He filled lecture rooms. I remember him coming in and beginning to speak as he took his coat off. He was brilliant. Charismatic. Passionate. Everyone had an opinion about him and everyone talked about him. Wherever you were, you could *feel* him.'

'Pretty irresistible, then.' His expression is inscrutable.

'I was bowled over.' Inwardly she recalls the night. Dinner in an old candlelit restaurant with lead-mullioned windows. Wine the colour of clerical velvet. Smoke-scented male skin. Deep brown sorrowful childlike eyes. The walk across the lawns to St John's. The olive waters of the Cam flowing under the Bridge of Sighs, named, he told her, with his lips on her neck, after the original in Venice that led to a prison. Her soaring excitement at his nearness, his insistent heat, his dense bulk. His obvious attraction to her. The moon seemed swollen with beauty as he kissed her and then, shockingly, drove his huge heavy hand between her thighs.

'Is he an astronomer like you?'

'No, a mathematician.' She finds that she cannot say more.

She expects Konrad to pursue her with questions about her life with Dominic and she braces herself. Instead he remarks, 'My least favourite subject at school.' His eyes are wry and there is a hint of mockery. 'I was an utter numbskull. If you'd known me then you wouldn't be sitting here drinking with me now.'

'I wouldn't?' She feels breathless that she has so easily escaped the question of Dominic.

'Believe me, you wouldn't. I couldn't wait to get out of school. I remember the last day I didn't even show up. I went to see a movie on my own and afterwards wanted to tell my friends about it – that's how stupid I was – and of course I was caught strolling back in and they fined me an extra day.'

She laughs. 'I can't believe this now, but I looked up to rebels like you. I was terribly impressed by people who didn't seem to care.'

He rests his chin in his hand and looks at her. 'And I was secretly envious of all the clever people like you.'

They fall silent as all around the square church bells strike the hour led by the solo bugle trumpeter of St Mary's. The air is cooler now and the sky has deepened in colour to a plush dark aubergine. She catches sight of Sirius sparkling with a clean, steady brightness, and a short distance away, hanging as if from a coat peg, a spare crescent of moon.

Konrad follows her gaze. 'I can't imagine what it must be like to be able to read all of that. So beautiful. So mysteriously abstract.' She watches his throat as he scans the sky. When his gaze returns his expression is amused, as if he has just caught himself out. 'One of my kids wanted to be an astronaut when he grew up.'

'Is that the doctor?'

'Yes, Josh – the one who's travelling.' His expression falters for a moment.

'When will you see him again?'

'I don't know. We email. He's currently in Sumatra. He said he'd make his way here some time before he goes home.' He picks up his empty vodka glass and twirls it.

She is silent for a while. 'I often wondered whether my father missed me.'

Konrad looks down at the table. 'He didn't think he was entitled to miss you. He felt that your mother would have been relieved that he had left.'

Catherine rests her chin in her hand. 'Well, he was right about that. She was relieved, but only because it meant that there were no obvious witnesses. No one around to watch her self-destruct.'

'Except you.'

'I didn't count. I just did the clearing up.' She pauses, appalled at the note of bitterness in her voice. 'I'm sorry, that didn't come out right. What I mean is that he left us in a mess.'

'Catherine.' His voice is soft. 'There was no way that he could stay. He said he had no choice, but to go. He would have taken you with him, but he had no means of looking after you.'

She stares at him for a moment. A memory comes into her mind of her mother picking up a glass bowl and admiring the air bubbles trapped inside, and then, a separate memory of shards strewn across the kitchen floor. The kitchen door was open and it was raining. The strap of her school bag had dug into her shoulder as she knelt down with a piece of kitchen roll to pick up the pieces.

'When I went to see him in Brighton that time, he seemed afraid. I don't know, it was as if there was something he wanted to confess; does that make sense?'

Konrad exhales. He picks up his empty vodka glass and

calls the waitress over and orders another. 'Like so many others he kept his memories to himself. He felt deeply ashamed even though it was not his fault that he was arrested. The system did that to him, made him doubt who he was. Imagine that for more than two years he woke every morning expecting to die. Imagine what that would do to a person.'

Catherine bites her lip. 'Did he think I would judge him for being in prison?'

'His silence was his way of protecting you and everyone who knew him. In later years he never even discussed it with Krystyna, and she, being a historian, at least would have understood. I was the first person he told.'

She twists her nails against her lip. 'I almost can't bear to hear about it, and yet I want to know.'

'He was interrogated for eight hours every day for the first two months of his arrest. He had no contact at all with the outside world for two years. He was not allowed one shower or wash in that time. He told me that was worse than some of the tortures.'

She looks at him. 'How did he get out?'

'They released him when they had done their work. He told me a priest who had been brought in to administer last rites to some soldiers before they were executed, helped him get to hospital in another part of Poland.' The waitress returns with Konrad's vodka and sets it down on the table. He lifts the glass and takes a mouthful. 'There were thousands like your father. They are known as the doomed or cursed soldiers.'

'Because they were a target after the war?'

'Exactly; the Soviets wanted to crush all possible opposition. The Home Army represented the spirit of resistance.

That had to be annihilated. The Soviets tried to break the country from within. People were encouraged to inform on each other.' He runs his hand down his face.

She feels her throat tighten. 'I wish . . .' She falters. 'I was going to say that I wish I'd known, but maybe it was better that I didn't. Maybe he was right to remain silent all those years. I'm now thinking that maybe he was even right to leave us. We were always strangers to him. Maybe he just needed to come home.' She looks at Konrad across the table. Gently and firmly he reaches over and cups her hand in his. She looks down at his fingers and glances up at the stars which swim through a blur of tears.

'Would you like something else to drink?' His look is open and frank. 'Some coffee?'

'No, I'm all right.' She hears the habitual note of defensiveness creep into her voice. His openness wavers and he removes his hand from hers. In a moment it will close over. 'On second thoughts, maybe I'll have a glass of wine.'

Instead of calling the waitress, he gets up and, ducking under the beer umbrellas, goes inside the bar. Left on her own for a moment, Catherine feels relief. Heat pulses from the cobbles, but the air is now distinctly chill. She pulls her cardigan from her bag and puts it across her shoulders. She is shivery and has the beginning glimmers of a migraine. She must have caught the sun on her bare arms at lunch. She had no idea it would be so hot. But then thinking about Kraków's position on the map, right in the centre, midway between east and west, the very heart of Europe, she should have known that it would be warmer than Cambridge. An image of the small paved garden at home flicks into her mind and she wonders if Dominic is out there now, sitting with his wine glass, which will not be the first of his day, papers strewn at his feet, an exasperated, wounded look in his eyes, as if he is perpetually in search of something that eludes him. She'll call him again later. Let him know how things are.

Konrad returns and slides into his seat. As he arranges his legs his ankle grazes hers and he shifts it away carefully. She feels the heat in the space between them. A bottle of red wine arrives, swaddled in a white napkin, which for some reason makes them both smile. The glasses shine in the amber light from the street lamps. He lifts the bottle and weighs it under his hand for a moment before he pours out the wine. It is the colour of garnet and smells of wood smoke.

He takes a sniff before drinking. 'It's Austrian Pinot Noir. I only pretend to know about wine. Someone recommended this once and I never forgot the taste of it. I look for it wherever I go. I guess I should be a little more adventurous.'

She laughs and some of the tension from earlier melts. She considers telling an anecdote about her own ignorance of wine when she failed to appreciate the solemnity of a rare bottle presented at a dinner party she attended with Dominic. She recalls a hot room in Cambridge, the walls carpeted with books, clever people around an oval dining table, the women sharper than the men. A pungent smell of sweat and the fruity must of old wool and personal neglect. There was the usual idiotic hilarity, the slight displacement from normality that accompanied parties of academics, at least those that she had attended, when all the guests were so much older than she was. There were twelve years between her and Dominic. Up until that night she hadn't felt it mattered. That night had gone on too long, reaching a crescendo with strident voices, interrupted opinions, someone at her elbow being persistently rude. What she remembers most was the lack of kindness in the room. At some point she knocked over her full glass. There was silence, in which one or two people pointedly looked at the dusty bottle in the centre of the table, and she recalled to her shame a speech about its vintage to which she had not listened. She could hear them all breathe in and then a mass of concealing voices which pretended not to notice what she had done. As she stared at the wine spreading its wings across an expanse of white damask, she'd felt a terrible relief.

'I don't know anything about wine either,' is all she reveals. Konrad watches her as she sips from her glass. She feels under no pressure to say that she likes it. There is nothing greedy about Konrad. He has no *designs* on her, Dominic's word, his way of expressing his jealousy when she captured the attention of another man. There was a period when he accused her of courting interest, a dark period, when she retreated into her work. Those were the nights she slept in the observatory dome in a sleeping bag, the hood open, the light of Antares striking out singular and strong from the cluttered sky.

She lowers her glass. 'It's good.'

He nods and takes a deep mouthful. She watches him wrap his fingers under his chin and lean on them to rest for a moment. She wonders if he slept much last night. His skin looks a little grey.

He lifts his head and looks at her. 'You're not too tired?'

'I was wondering the same about you.'

He shakes his head and crinkles his eyes. 'I'm not tired, just relaxed.' He glances at her again. 'It feels good to relax.'

He stretches his legs under the table and leans his head back to look at the sky. 'It feels good to be here.'

She sips her wine. A few more people arrive and settle into the plastic chairs, talking in low confessional voices. Occasionally English words escape the embrace of the soft velvet Polish and shine bright as steel pins: 'he', 'live', 'fight'. She runs her eyes over Konrad's face. The sharp clean line of his jaw is in contrast to the softness of his eyes which answer her look.

Konrad's fingers spread on the table between them. 'But I prefer the winter. Kraków feels older in winter. You get more of a sense of history. I used to walk around the square sometimes with Krystyna. She had a stick to stop her falling into the snow. It belonged to her father and the top was carved into the head of a wolf. Sometimes she would let me take her arm, but not often. It was clear that she preferred to lean on her stick.' His eyes slip back to the present. 'We talked a lot, as we walked. It was easier for her than face to face. She was never very good at being interviewed.'

She nods. 'So when did you write it all down?'

'As soon as I could. I would take my notebook and go and settle in a coffee shop and let it pour out while it was still fresh in my memory. What I've given you is a distillation of that.'

'She remembered it so well.'

'She faced her memories. She believed that the worst thing for anyone was to deny their own life: to pretend or cover up. So many people did. Some even changed their names because it was too difficult to live with who they were or what they had been.'

'Under the Soviets?'

'Yes, under communism. The Poles have made real attempts to bring that period of history out into the open. They even have a name for it: Lustration. Krystyna approved. She left nothing unsaid. She wanted it all out of her.'

'While my father did the opposite?'

He nods and sips some wine. 'It was harder for him. He hadn't lived through as much – she taught all the way through those intense Soviet years, often giving lectures in secret – he felt tremendous guilt about that.'

'He felt he should have stayed?'

'If he had known that she was still alive, I'm sure he would have done.'

'Krystyna didn't have much contact with you when you were growing up in America?'

He bites his lip. 'You know, my father never made any attempt to contact her. He just assumed she was dead.'

'So how did you find out that she was still alive?'

He smiles. 'It's simple. She saw one of my films on television. Our surname is pretty rare in Polish. She wrote to the studio.'

'When did you first come over?'

'Pretty soon after I got the letter I made a short visit. I was filming in Montana at the time and had only a few days with her. I met your father then, briefly. I had no idea who he was. But I knew he was from that time during the resistance. I could tell by the way they looked at each other that they had been through something important together.'

He leans over and pours her another glass of wine and as she reaches out to steady the stem their hands graze each other. A ripple of feeling courses down her arm. Her lips tingle when she brings the wine glass up to her mouth.

'I came a few more times, always on short visits. Then I moved over last July. Krystyna died the following spring.' His eyes slide away from her and up to the sky again. 'In March. It was raining. She was looking at the rain when I called to see her. Together we watched the drops sliding down the balcony window and they were beautiful, thick and silvery and heavy. I'd never seen rain like it. We went out to the Planty just so she could walk in the rain . . .' He breaks off.

Catherine sips some wine and waits for him to continue. Konrad folds his hands on the table. 'She had a heart attack that night.'

'Did you find her?' Her voice is almost a whisper.

'No, Janek did. When I got there he was sitting on the bathroom floor with her. She must have had her heart attack in the bath because her hair was still wet. He'd wrapped a robe around her and was drying her hair with a towel.' He comes to a halt.

Catherine imagines the two of them together in a chilly tiled bathroom with high ceilings. She sees her father sitting with his back against the bath in which the water has turned cool. He is exhausted from the effort of pulling Krystyna from the bath. She lies across his lap: frail, quiet, dignified. Outside rain spatters on the windows. 'There's another reason why I wrote everything down,' Konrad says after a moment. 'I want to show what I've written to my father. I have this crazy, romantic idea that when I go back I will offer him his past, like a gift. It's a terrible risk, of course.'

'You mean he might reject it?'

'I've thought about how I might approach it; you know, maybe give it to him in slices so that he doesn't have to take all of it in at once. I started to write him a letter, but I didn't send it. My father is an old man now and I'm not sure that he is robust enough to learn what happened to his sister.' He pauses and takes a deep breath. 'But I don't know. I'm still working out what to do.'

Catherine reaches across the table and takes his hand. It surprises her how easily this happens. He dips his head and then brings her hand up to his lips, which feel warm and heavy. He murmurs something in Polish as he kisses her on the flat part of her wrist. He lowers her hand, but with no trace of guilt or anxiety. Her heart strikes in her chest. She looks at him.

They are silent for a moment. She speaks first. 'When I read Krystyna's story last night, I just kept wishing that I could have met her. I envy you that.'

Konrad looks into her eyes. 'You know you remind me of her a little.'

'What?' She laughs with incredulity. 'Now you're just trying to flatter me.'

He holds her eyes. 'She inspired me to want to make more of my life, to unveil it, to look at everything without flinching.' He rests his cheek on his hand.

Catherine leans back in her seat. Now she is trembling. They have said too much.

Konrad sips some wine. Catherine feels her breath catch in her chest. Konrad inclines his head. 'I often think that she found me just in time to tell me her story.' He glances at her. 'And Janek's story, too, of course.'

'Was she still beautiful?'

'There was an extraordinary lightness about her. She moved without resistance. One afternoon shortly before she died I went to her apartment and she was sitting by the window. She had on a pale dress and her hair was down. She had just washed it, and she turned to me and I had the strangest feeling that I was looking straight through her.'

Catherine notices the tiredness has slid from his eyes.

'She would sit by the window and wait for Janek to arrive. It was the high point of her day. He usually came around midday and they would take lunch together and then go for an afternoon walk in the Planty. Afterwards he would sit with her while she read or dozed, and his eyes would stay on her face. He could not stop looking at her.' Konrad meets her eyes.

Looking at him now she feels a surge of longing so tender it takes her breath away. 'I'm sorry,' she says, pushing back her chair and knocking the umbrella as she stands up. 'I ought to go.'

He catches her hand. She releases a long breath as he rises to meet her.

'You don't need to go, Catherine.' His face is very close to hers.

'I know, but I'm afraid.'

'I'm afraid, too. I'm afraid of all the things I've said and all the things I'm going to say and can't take back. I'm afraid just to stand here and look at you.'

She pulls her hand away and clenches her fingertips against the edge of the table. 'I don't know,' she says. 'I don't know if I can.'

'Catherine' – his voice is low – 'you don't need to worry. I'm not even going to ask.'

7

Eastern Poland, January 1940

Krystyna rocked in the saddle and let the mare pick her way through the forest. The tracks were those the horses had taken many times before, and their steps were light and confident, their tails lifted as they wound their way through birch trees they had known as saplings, crossing streams they had drunk from many times, now flecked with snow, the water frozen at the margins into clear panes. Halting at a frozen bank, she noticed sealed into the ice compressed fern fronds, seed keys and hard, bright berries: perfectly preserved moments of a floating autumn.

At dawn she needed to dismount to pee. Crouching in the snow, her spread knees shaking with fatigue, she smelled wood smoke. Stiff with alarm, she decided against mounting immediately and instead led the horses to a clearing where there was a black patch in the snow. She knelt down, flicked off her gloves and trailed her fingers through the remains of a fire. It was difficult to tell how old it was because the ashes were black and cold. She wondered whether this was where Janek and his father had camped on their way out. The idea that they had gone before her and that she was following in their tracks gave her some measure of comfort. Soon she would see them, resting, leaning their backs against the trees, their knapsacks open on the snowy ground. Their faces would brighten with relief when they saw her come to find them with the horses.

She remounted, blowing on her fingers before she put on her gloves. She would need to make a plan. It was too dangerous to ride aimlessly in the daylight. There were bound to be soldiers prowling the area in their grey coats and she would be easy prey. Until she had decided what to do she would ride only in the thickest part of the forest and follow a direction which she judged to be north, using the stars to point her in the right direction.

She rode for hours, moving deeper into the forest, stopping only to pee and drink, cupping the icy stream water in her palms, gasping at the cold of it. The sky was white and heavy with more snow. The horses moved slowly to preserve heat. While she rode Izabela, the other horse carried the duffel bag. When Gazela pushed ahead, Krystyna could see the outlines of the things she had packed at home and her throat ached. Into her mind came an image of her father leaning against the tree the day they had buried the old mare. She had done as he asked. But she had abandoned them all.

They came to a river and she let the horses stand in the rush of water while she stayed on the bank. The smell of leaves and cold sky squeezed her heart. The horses drank deeply, slurping the water, their soft mushroomy lower lips trembling with pleasure. She lay on her chest and cupped her hands into the icy stream and drank too, wiping the stickiness from her eyes. She reached into the duffel bag and pulled out a hunk of bread and a jar of jam. She tore off small pieces of bread and dipped them into the jam, licking the syrup from her fingers. The horses watched her, their eyes dark. From the duffel bag she pulled out the bundle of oats and fed the horses, who released long sighs.

Packing the provisions into the duffel bag, she felt the fierce cold drop away for a moment. Warmth radiated from her chest and down her arms; she could feel her skin, the blood circulating in her fingers and toes. She led the horses to a clearing and decided to walk with them for a while. Ahead the forest track was lined by young fir trees. Sunlight touched their branches and lit the snow with an inner glow. She walked between her horses, her eyes on the end of the track. As the sun rose higher there were occasional flashes of fire from the firs, and then stronger flares until it seemed as if entire trees were on the cusp of bursting into icy flames.

After a while hunger began to gnaw at her insides. They reached the end of the track and she looked around for somewhere to rest for a while. There was a parting through the dense trees, a deer track, too narrow for them all to slip through, but it might just give her somewhere to sleep unexposed. She led the horses to a spruce tree and slipped off their bridles and loosened their girths. Their breath warmed her fingers as she fed them each another small handful of oats. She took off her coat and laid it over Izabela's neck. Inside the duffel bag she found a red jersey, an old one of Janek's for Gazela. The mare grazed her knuckles with her pale whiskers when she pulled the jersey around her neck. It smelled of apples. She ate some more bread and jam, trying to chew slowly so as to make it last. She looked at the horses resting now with their necks low, hind legs tipped against the snow, and a sob escaped her throat.

Between the trees she found a fox den, the ground scraped clear of snow at the entrance. There was no sign of the foxes, but their acid smell pierced her nostrils. After dressing in another layer of clothes from the duffel bag she found a place to lie down. The bag made an awkward pillow under her neck and she slept with the dull pain of something pressing against the bone behind her ear.

She woke in darkness to the sound of a snap, like something hard hitting leather. Her chest hammered with fear as she leapt up from the den. Between the trees she saw Izabela jerk her head, the white of her eye swimming in the darkness. Gazela ducked her neck and scurried backwards and then Krystyna heard the sound again: the crack of leather. Someone was trying to lasso the horses. She stood shaking between the trees. Now she could see the outline of a Russian soldier, bulky, short-legged with a heavy wind-roughened face. He was lunging at Gazela, but it was not a rope he was using, but the belt from his army coat. He grunted with each breath and his steps were unsteady as he took aim with the belt, trying to fling it around the mare's neck. She sidestepped him and stood snorting with her eyes wide. The soldier lurched through the snow to Izabela, who dodged his attempts with deft steps. Infuriated, the soldier yanked the belt around his coat and pulled it tight. Breathing heavily, he reached inside his coat pocket and took out a small cloudy bottle. He drank in gasping gulps and after he had finished gave a soft belch. The horses scuttled out of his way as he approached them, wiping his wet mouth on the back his hand, his small eyes fixing on them. They backed away from him, shielding each other with their flanks. Their tails were high, ready to take flight. He lumbered towards them and they took off through the snow until they had reached a point where they felt they could turn and face their pursuer. The Russian swayed, unsteady on his feet. He took another savage pull on his bottle. The horses watched him from a distance. He dropped the bottle in the snow and staggered backwards. She thought he was going to fall, but he shoved his hand inside his coat and pulled out a pistol.

A scream flared and guttered out in her throat. She clapped her hands over her mouth and rocked her body backward and forward as she watched the soldier take aim. Her eyes felt like two frozen marbles in her face. He fired. She heard the soft almost gentle sound of the bullet whisking through the air, like a whirring of wings, and heard her own blood roar in reply. A second shot followed the first. This time she could not bear to look. She sank down in the snow and clutched her arms around her, rocking, stuffing her fist into her mouth to stop the storm of moans.

It was dawn when she finally crept out of the den. Between the trees the sky was the colour of a pale summer rose. A new skin of frost glittered on the ground. The air felt very clear and still. She pushed aside snowy branches, her fingers rigid with tension. A fir branch swung back, its needles biting into her ear. She ducked through the gap and stood up. Her knees trembled. The neck of the bottle was sticking out of the snow. Next to it was a circular yellow patch that smelled of urine. The snow was churned with broken hoof prints. She knelt down and put her hand inside one perfectly formed print and looked out along the deer track where a fox, startled by her scent, stopped and lifted its head; its eyes fixed on her for a moment, bright, enquiring, curious, and then in a fine mist of snow it was gone.

With the duffel bag clamped to her back, she walked. When the sun burst through the trees, she took off her second layer of clothes and packed them in the bag. She had no idea of the direction in which she was heading. All she could do was to follow the hoof prints snaking across the forest in a glittering trail.

The sun was high in the sky when she stopped. She relieved herself and covered the stain with fresh snow. Fastening her belt, she stiffened as she smelled wood smoke. Through the trees a small wooden chalet crouched in the snow, shutters closed like palms held to a face. Outside a woman in a faded headscarf scattered potato peelings to a few russet-coloured chickens. As Krystyna approached they jerked their bony heads and paused in their pecking, suspicious eyes swivelling all in the same direction, feathered ribs heaving the frail air. The woman flung her offerings in the snow and waited, her expression neither welcoming nor hostile. At her feet her hens grouped closer together and crooned anxiously.

Krystyna hesitated outside a low gate in front of the chalet. The woman looked her up and down, her eyes betraying nothing. Her hens ruffled their feathers.

'Have you seen any horses?' Krystyna asked. Her mouth was thick with thirst and her legs and lower back ached with cold and fatigue. 'Two greys, one with blue eyes?'

The woman stared at her. Her skin was scribbled with fine dry lines as if someone had drawn across it with a grey pencil. Her eyes, though, were as bright as a child's and sapphire blue. She glanced towards a barn leaning up against the side of the chalet. Krystyna followed her gaze and understood.

The horses did not look up as she went into the barn.

They carried on pulling at a mound of hay, their eyes heavy with contentment. In an ecstasy of relief Krystyna ran her hand down their necks, stroked their bellies and their haunches. The mares blew air through their nostrils and continued to chew. The woman brought in a bucket of fresh water. She offered it to Krystyna to drink from first, dipping into the cold water with a chipped metal mug. The water tasted of iron and moss and river melt. Krystyna took the bucket to the mares and as the horses sucked up the water, the old woman watched, her top lip moving, head nodding as if keeping time to a stream of music inside her head.

She beckoned to Krystyna to follow her inside the chalet where a fire of newly split logs hissed in the grate. A narrow bed made up with a quilted patchwork cover stood in front of the fire. Immediately the woman turned back the covers and patted the pillow, indicating that Krystyna should sleep. She felt her body melt at the prospect of a few hours of rest. Now that she knew the horses were safe she could drift off without fear.

The old woman's gemstone eyes watched as Krystyna took off her boots and pushed them under the bed. Her lips muttered as before. Then, satisfied that her guest was taken care of, she picked up a basket and went outside. The sudden bright slice of light reminded Krystyna that it was still only morning. She took off her trousers and sweater and lay down on the bed. The fire crackled bedside her. The room was warm and dark. She pulled the quilt over her and sank into sleep.

She woke at twilight to the smells of cooking. The old woman was bent over a pot in the kitchen, stirring soup with a wooden spoon. Her eyes flared when she saw her guest. She pulled out a wooden chair from a small table. 'Sit down, I've made you some soup.' She took a wooden ladle and filled a huge fragrant bowl of potato and onion broth from the saucepan and set it down on the table in front of Krystyna. The soup was thick and rich. Krystyna gulped down the first couple of spoonfuls, scalding her lips and tongue. The woman watched, her eyes thoughtful. When Krystyna had finished, she took the bowl to a black pot on her stove and ladled out another helping. Krystyna tried to protest. 'Please, save some for yourself.'

The woman twitched her lips. She placed the second bowl down, pushing it close to Krystyna's chest. She folded her arms and lifted her chin. Chastened, Krystyna felt the steam rise from the soup and warm her face. She lifted her spoon. The old woman nodded.

After Krystyna had finished the second bowl, the woman moved towards the door. She announced that she was going to chop some more wood and look at the horses. She indicated the pot on the stove. 'Take some more if you're hungry.'

'What about you?' she asked the old woman. 'Aren't you having any?'

The woman pulled on her headscarf. Her eyes were warm. 'I have eaten already.' She picked up a short axe by the front door and went out.

Krystyna leaned back in her chair and put her hand over her stomach, which gurgled and growled and felt tight. Sleep tugged at her again and she closed her eyes. From outside came the sound of an owl calling for its mate. The woman returned with a basket of logs and bustled around the chalet, sweeping the grate and pushing more wood on the fire, which crackled and hissed. When she had a good blaze going, she went to a battered old chest at the foot of the bed and lifted out an armful of heavy grey wool blankets. 'Take them to the barn, for your horses.'

Krystyna was embarrassed. 'No, it's all right. They won't need them.' But the woman insisted, pushing the blankets into Krystyna's tired arms where they hung voluptuous and heavy, dense with wood smoke.

She carried the blankets outside to the barn. It was just dark. The first stars gave a thin, pure light that slipped into the barn through slits in the cladding. The rafters were crumbly with dirty webs. In the corner a pair of lamp-coloured eyes, bird or cat, impossible to tell, peered down at her. Moored in dust were pieces of farm machinery, including a chain harrow and plough, blades still crumbed with earth. Bloated bags of seed and corn slumped in a corner along with a pile of dry rotten apples. Hanging on a nail was a pair of man's overalls, dark with grease stains, knees worn through into holes. Krystyna wondered whether these had belonged to the old woman's husband, but she knew that she would not be able to return to the chalet with questions. She was beginning to understand that all the old ways of being with people had gone.

The horses lifted their heads from their mound of hay, curving their ears towards her in enquiry. She showed the blankets to them, allowing them to sniff the unfamiliar embedded scents before she slid the covers over their backs. Izabela exhaled and rested her hind foot; her crystal eyes half closed in drowsy contentment. Gazela brushed her hand with her damp nostrils. Her eyes were huge dark pools of knowing. Krystyna put her face against the mare's neck and breathed in her warm walnut smell. 'Everything will be all right now,' she said. The mare stood still and listened while she sobbed.

The old woman stood as Krystyna came in, her lips muttering their silent prayer. She indicated the bed. 'I'm not tired, but you must sleep.'

The quilt rolled around her, ripe with the old woman's smell. She closed her eyes thinking that she would simply doze for a while and they could then exchange places. But when she woke it was light and she realized that she had slept through until morning. In a fright, she sat up and looked around the chalet, wondering where the old woman had spent the night, horrified that she might have been forced out to the cold barn. Her gaze was drawn to an upright chair behind the bed. The old woman's headscarf was there, resting on the back of the chair, its threadbare material carefully smoothed as if it were a favourite fine shawl. A fresh fire was in the process of being laid with split logs, clean white bellies uppermost; she could hear the clump of an axe outside.

Pushing the covers back, Krystyna swung her legs on to a cold wooden floor. Under the bed was a pair of felt slippers. She put these on and padded over to her clothes which like the headscarf had been carefully folded and smoothed. A pool of light spread under the window. Here she dressed, taking her time to shake out her socks, which were dry again. The smells from her sweater and riding trousers rose in a wave of homesickness and she stood for a moment, her mind tumbling through images of the dwór with its corridors, its chandeliers, its empty rooms. Already it seemed like a palace of ghosts, but she tried to push this thought away. The old woman came into the chalet carrying a small basket in which there were three brown hen's eggs. 'I hope you slept well,' the woman said, smiling, showing teeth worn to the colour of amber. 'I looked at the horses. They're still lying down. I have never seen a horse with such unusual eyes.'

Krystyna looked through the window where there was a patch of pale sky, the same watery glass blue as Izabela's eyes. Her father had delivered the filly six years ago. She had needed turning before she would come out with her head between her soft hooves; he'd been the first person to hold the new horse in his warm hands and in the weeks that followed she had not needed to learn to trust humans. Whenever Krystyna or her father went into the stable to check on the mare and foal, Izabela would bounce over to them and lick the salt from their hands. Gazela was born a few weeks later and after they were weaned, the two fillies shared a stall, curling against each other as they lay down at night like a pair of cats in a basket. She remembered how she and Janek spent hours leaning over the stall wall, watching them feed and stretch out their long legs, for these were the horses that had been promised to them, and they did not want to miss a moment of their growing.

The old woman gestured to her to sit at the table while she went to the stove to boil the eggs. As Krystyna waited for breakfast she was suddenly overwhelmed by a wave of fear. Soon she would have to continue her journey through vast stretches of forest that she did not know. The idea that Janek and his father were ahead, somehow carving the way for her, now seemed foolish, a simple wish that had kept her going. Now she realized that she was truly alone. She didn't know what she could do. She couldn't return to the dwór. She looked at the old woman as she carried their steaming eggs, placed in bright painted wooden cups on a tray, to the table. 'I don't know where I'm going,' she blurted out. 'I don't know where is safe.'

The old woman raised her eyes and looked at the chalet's wooden beams. 'Nothing is safe any more, nowhere is safe.' There was no distress in her voice; she spoke as if calmly enunciating a fact.

'Then I have nowhere to go,' Krystyna said.

The woman lowered her voice as if she did not want to be overheard. 'You must not give up. Whatever happens to you, you should protect your courage and feed your hope. Go slowly, but go forward and learn to live in your heart.'

'What if I have lost my heart?'

'You will find it again. It's waiting for you.' The woman brought her fist to her own chest. She thumped herself against her breastbone and held Krystyna's gaze in a challenge that started the blood pumping faster in her own chest. She looked down at the egg and then lifted her spoon to crack the shell. The yolk burst out engorged with ripe colour that held her for a moment before she dipped in her spoon to eat. The old woman cackled with delight as if she had won some minor victory. She dipped into her own egg. In between hot sweet-salty mouthfuls Krystyna studied the woman's face. Its maze of wrinkles reminded her of the cracked glaze on the porcelain vase on the stairs at home. She pushed the thought away: she must not think of home. She finished her eggs and the old woman sighed. 'Now go and see your horses.'

She entered the barn and the mares greeted her by rippling their nostrils. They were on their feet, rhythmically working their way through a thick pile of fresh hay. Krystyna lifted a handful and inhaled deeply. In her mind she saw a meadow of sun-ripened grass. A boy and a girl ran through it, both laughing. Her throat filled up. Izabela turned her mild eyes to her and puttered her soft lips into the crook of her neck. Krystyna stroked her mane, picking out the few strands of straw that had become ensnared in the fall of white hair. In the next stall Gazela swiped a tuft of hay and chewed dreamily, content in the way that only horses can be when they melt and give themselves over to wherever they are.

She returned to the chalet. On the table were two glasses of linden tea and a collection of waxed paper parcels. Krystyna sat down. She knew it was useless to argue against hospitality. As was the way with the old Polish people, kindness would if challenged become fierce. Krystyna nodded her appreciation at the parcels. 'Thank you.'

Afterwards Krystyna tried to help with the chores, but the old woman pushed her into a chair and bustled about, clearing the dishes, twitching blankets, shoving logs deeper into the fire with an urgency that made it seem as if it were she and not Krystyna who would soon be leaving. When the woman finally finished she stood with her eyes on the door, her expression poised. Her lips ceased moving. Krystyna saw that she was waiting for her. She hesitated for a moment, but the woman's narrowed eyes and folded arms warned against expressions of gratitude or tearful farewells. There was nothing for Krystyna to do except nod her head. It was enough. In that moment she felt something still in her heart, her child's clamour finally silenced, replaced by a new sensation of strength. She was going to ride across a country occupied by two armies and she was going to do it alone. Escape was possible. The actor and his wife had made it to Lithuania and she had studied enough maps with her father to know that if she followed the line of the River Bug north she would eventually reach the border. As she strode across to the barn the glare of sunlit snow tore tears from her eyes. She drew the back of her hand across her cheekbones and wiped it dry on the inside of her arm, her mind focused on what she must next do. She lifted her saddle from the straw and brushed it clear of chaff and dust before placing it on Gazela's back. Noting the shift in the sequence of things, Izabela glanced over. 'It's okay, you'll get your turn later,' she said, pulling up a leather strap. 'I'm going to share the riding between you so that you won't get too tired.' The mare blinked and blew through her nostrils. She let Gazela take the lead as she moved the horses from the barn and out into the snow where the woman stood at the doorway of the chalet, a blanket thrown over her shoulders, the bulging duffel bag at her feet.

Krystyna mounted Janek's mare. The old woman came forward and stroked the other horse down her neck. In that moment Krystyna saw what she must do. She turned to face the woman. 'I can't take them both. I haven't got enough food for the two of them.' The woman nodded. She took hold of Izabela's halter. Krystyna felt her mouth go dry with fear and longing. Why had she saddled Gazela? Perhaps it wasn't too late to tell the old woman that she had made a mistake, but already she knew that it was Gazela she needed with her. Janek's horse would draw him to her. She understood this clearly and perfectly as if a cold part of her brain had switched on in order to prevent her from making wrong decisions. She knew the old woman had meant well when she said that she should follow her heart, but at that moment she could not. At that moment, the moment she gave up her horse, she had to forget her heart.

The woman took the lead rope and led Izabela towards the barn. The mare followed the woman into the barn as if this had been her intention, to return to the pile of sweet-scented hay. Krystyna kept her eyes fixed on Gazela's ears, which were now alert, scanning her surroundings for approaching danger, and tried to breathe away the pain between her ribs. She rode into the forest, heading for a group of birch trees bunched together, lean white ghosts offering brittle armfuls of snow to an immaculate blue sky. The duffel bag thumped at her back, its unfamiliar parcels knocking against the ridges of her spine. Almost unbelievably, she could smell bread.

It was late afternoon when she stopped riding. She drew Gazela to a halt in soft snow and dismounted. Snow fell across her boots with the feathery lightness of ash. She stood for a moment rubbing her ears, which felt wooden with the cold. In the stillness she became aware of a piercing hissing in her head as if gritty sand were being shaken around inside the shell of her skull. She pinched her fingers across the bone between her eyes. Normally the skin there felt greasy, but now it was dry. Cold and stiff, not like skin, more like linen sheets that had stayed out too long on a line. She was desperately thirsty.

She did not know if she had the strength to ride on to find a stream. Instead she knelt down and clawed a handful of powder snow. It disintegrated against her fingers, leaving a soapy residue. Her chest ached with disappointment and fatigue. She could not stay and drink dry snow. She had no choice but to ride on.

After a while she noticed a cluster of pine trees in the distance. The snowbound branches with islands of evergreen showing through were clamped close as if the trees were hunching their shoulders. She lifted her reins and clicked to Gazela to walk on faster. The tired mare hesitated, flicking her ear backward. She stumbled. Krystyna knew her hooves were packed hard with ice. Later she would have to dig them out with a hoof pick. The mare recovered her footing and picked up her pace, her ears now curving towards the trees, trying to hear or sense what waited for them there.

Water. At the foot of the pines was a silver knife of a stream, the water glinting sharp, the taste of it thrilling in her mouth. She lay gasping on the bank, stupefied by the smell of water and a sense of lazy relief that she would not have to force her legs into the saddle again, at least not until the morning.

Under the pine branches she found cones, dozens of them, light and warm in her hand, leaving on her skin the ghost of a smell of mushrooms and aromatic oils. She built a fire and arranged the cones on the base, choosing the biggest ones. The old woman had stuffed candles and a lighter into the base of the duffel bag and when Krystyna lit the first of the cones she felt sorry when the flames scorched their honeycomb perfection. She watched them shrivel and then, aware that the fire would soon burn out if she did not feed it, went off in search of more fuel. On the upper bank of the stream she found some dry branches and dragged these to the fire where she sat cross-legged, her hair stiff around her face, holding out her hands to the flickering well of heat as she fell into an exhausted trance.

She woke to the feeling of cold clutching at the small of her back, dread rising in her, a taste of ashes in her mouth. Her hair was lank on her shoulders, heavy with the stink of smoke. She swung her head to look for the mare. She was resting near the pines, her neck lowered, nostrils billowing softly. Overhead the stars were fine points of light. She got up to look, leaning far back so that she could take in a whole vast stretch of sky and find the square of Pegasus, the Delta star and the Pole Star, right at the tail of Ursa Minor, the little bear. At New Year Janek had taught her the names of the constellations. He'd only just learned them himself from an astronomy book his father had given him at Christmas. But instead of saving up his knowledge and polishing it to flaunt to her, he admitted that he was unsure which constellation was which. She remembered the waver in his voice and his pinched, white face, his green eyes anxiously scanning the sky.

On New Year's night the whole family wrapped in coats and fur hats and boots and harnessed the horses to the sleigh. They went to pray at the wooden church at the top of the hill. When they came out with the other families all talking over the top of each other Janek drew her to one side. He stood behind her and placed his hands on her shoulders, as if to balance himself, and told her to look up at the sky. She lifted her head. The sky was thick with stars, so many clusters and disconnected shapes it was bewildering, but he said you could trace a route through them; it was an ancient form of navigation. With the stars no one could ever be lost. As they both looked she held her breath, aware of his heart beating behind her, fast as a bird's. 'There, the square!' he'd gasped, unaware that the adults were standing smoking near the sleighs, watching them and chuckling at the sight of their inno-cent embrace. He dropped a kiss, light as a raindrop, on to the top of her head and urged her to look. 'Follow my arm!' She swivelled her head, her crown still tingling from his touch. 'Do you see it?' he said, his voice raw with excitement. 'Do you see Pegasus?'

There were stars reflected in the stream she saw now as she knelt to drink. She rubbed her eyes with her cold fingers, knowing that it would be dangerous for her to slip into another doze. She needed to eat and find somewhere to make her bed for the night. Hunger pains tugged at her stomach and her head felt as if it had been released from her body to float wearily above her shoulders. Slapping the back of her hand against her cheek, she got up from the stream. Under the snow-laden branches of the pines something caught her eye. It was the duffel bag, doubled over, as if it had been kicked.

Her mouth was wet with anticipation as she tore open its canvas neck and stuffed her hands inside. Her fingers closed around a waxed packet, tied with string, which she pulled into her lap. Inside the paper she found a round of rye bread, its smell honey-sweet and dense, a pale disc of ripe smoked cheese, a small pot of jam, blue-jewelled, and two hard-boiled eggs, shells as cold as icy stones. The old woman had even thought to include a knife and this Krystyna used to smear gouts of jam on to a fistful of bread, cramming it too fast and too greedily into her mouth, ashamed of what she was doing, knowing that it was too much, knowing that she should break the bread into smaller pieces, but unable in the urgent grip of her need to stop. High in the sky above the pine trees, branches weighted with snow like the white robes of priests, the huge cold eye of the moon swam in its amber aura.

8

Kraków, present day

The next evening they go for supper in the Jewish Quarter. Konrad chooses one of the older restaurants with a few rickety tables set up on the cobbles. Wind tugs at the tablecloths, the starched white linen straining for freedom. An unruly gust almost topples their table as Catherine goes to sit down. Konrad catches her elbow and pulls out her chair. 'Hey, we better get anchored fast.' He sits down and reaches for his napkin. A breeze grabs it from his hands and sends it sailing across the street. He gets up and goes in pursuit of it, taking long steps, and when he returns his expression is triumphant.

A couple at the next table smile with complicity. They are both in their mid forties, stylish, relaxed; they look well in themselves with full-of-health limbs and glowing complexions. Everything about them seems right. The man suggests to Konrad that they put their flyaway tables together and join forces. His accent sounds Dutch. Catherine watches Konrad search for a reason to decline. His expression is eager to please, open and friendly, but there is a mild panic in his eyes, a little frantic twitch that secretly delights her.

'Thank you, that's kind of you, but we haven't much time.' He is awkward; the social excuse embarrasses him and he seems equally flustered by what she guesses is the habitual use of the word 'we'.

The Dutchman opens his hands, his manner casual, unconcerned. He's not going to take Konrad's refusal personally.

His partner, an elegant woman wearing mint green, smiles at them. 'We're celebrating, that's why. He wants someone else to join in.'

Konrad can't help himself. 'What are you celebrating?'

The Dutch couple look across the table at each other. They have the comfortable ease of a long-standing partnership, no sharp edges, as if they have been poured from the same mould. Catherine thinks of Plato's *Symposium*, the idea that all couples were originally one and had been cleaved apart. These two have returned to each other.

'Our divorce!' The woman's eyes shine. She reaches across the table and takes her companion's hand.

Catherine can tell that Konrad is startled. He looks at them holding hands across the rippling linen. 'Congratulations.' His voice is a little uncertain.

The Dutchman gives a loud guffaw which echoes across the street, causing the other diners to glance round. 'Not *our* divorce, my sweet.'

'I'm sorry.' The woman brings her hand up to her mouth as she realizes her mistake. 'We were married to other people, but now we aren't.'

Catherine feels her throat tighten. Konrad nods at the couple. 'Enjoy your evening.'

'You, too.' The man lifts a glass of champagne in their direction. 'Enjoy life.'

'We will.' Konrad's eyes are again filled with mild panic. She wants to reassure him, but somehow she feels frozen. The couple bend their heads together and laugh.

A waiter comes to their table. Konrad translates the menu for her. She orders chicken. A coal-black cat with cool green eyes picks its way through the tables. She feels the electric needles of its coat brush against her ankle. There's a smell of drains.

Konrad notices the cat. 'There's someone who dines out every night – just like us.' His eyes are warm and immediate.

Dominic would *hate* this place, she thinks.

'I'm already getting used to it,' she tells Konrad. 'Fatal.' An image of their kitchen in Cambridge, with its crammed pine cupboards, its sticky floor with a flap of lino that catches on the bottom of the fridge door every time it is opened, springs into her mind. Periodically she and Dominic would talk about updating the house, a 1930s semi-detached with bay windows and room upstairs for an office each, but their conversations never led to them taking steps towards either taking out the old units or looking through catalogues to find something that suited them better, something that they actually liked. They shared ownership of the house, but had not taken responsibility for it. In the absence of a formal marriage between them, it united them. It also acted as a silent barrier.

For a long time Catherine had wondered what it was that prevented them from making any changes. Lack of money was no longer an adequate excuse, for Dominic had inherited a substantial sum on the death of his father, a former navy captain, who had been well provided for during his long retirement. In their twenty-eight years together, it had seemed as if they were waiting for permission to fully inhabit the house. At some point what had been provisional had become permanent. And that, of course, didn't merely apply to the house.

The waiter brings their order. Konrad turns his attention to his steak. She starts on her chicken. It is rich and savoury. While she eats, she covertly watches the Dutch couple.

They lean their elbows on the table, body postures mirroring each other, right down to the way their ankles curl around each other so that one right foot is pivoting on the cobbles. They touch each other frequently, light presses of the hand on the top of the wrist, sometimes lacing their fingers together and then breaking apart, their movements smooth and swift as they enact their affectionate grammar. They begin to talk and shift their chairs to make this more comfortable, lifting them up over the uneven cobbles, laughing as they do so because it is awkward, not easy with such raised cobbles to find stability. In the centre of their table a candle flame leaps for oxygen under a tall glass jar. The woman's gold bracelet gleams in the light as she takes her partner's hand and fondly turns it over with her own, and the gesture is so loving and so appreciated it creates a long, fluid pause in the talk. Aware that she is staring perhaps too closely, Catherine finishes her meal, scraping every last morsel from her plate.

Konrad lays his knife and fork down at the same time. 'You look as if you enjoyed that.'

'I was starving. I have to admit I didn't stop for lunch as I was just too engrossed in reading some more of your story.'

'Have you looked at Krystyna's war diary yet?'

'I read some of it last night before I went to sleep.'

He holds her eyes for a moment. Catherine takes a sip of water. The breeze has subsided and the street now feels cool and still. She reaches down into her shoulder bag for her cardigan and pulls it across her shoulders. The wine has made her feel drowsy and she tries to suppress a yawn.

'Hey.' Konrad's grey eyes are puckered with concern. 'Do you want to call it a night?'

She blinks. 'I'm fine – could we just walk for a bit?'

As they get up to leave, the Dutchman calls out a question to Konrad. 'Do you know the Polish word for "light"?'

'If you mean lighter, the word is *zapalniczka*, but all other forms of light are different words.'

The Dutchman catches the waiter's eye to signal that he would like a light for his slim cigar. The waiter, a young man in his twenties, comes over immediately with a cigarette lighter. '*Zapalniczka.*' The Dutchman practises his Polish and the young man smiles and thanks the man. With her fingers held to her lips, the Dutchwoman watches, her eyes gleaming with secret delight.

'Goodnight,' the Dutch couple call out to them as if they are departing friends.

They walk to the Planty, a network of boulevards that frame the city in a great green living chain of chestnut trees. The air is a warm shawl around her neck and shoulders. She shudders with pleasure.

'You're not cold?' Konrad asks.

'No, not at all, how about you?'

'I'm not cold.'

They laugh even though there is nothing particular to laugh at. Against a teal-blue sky the trees shiver. She glances up and there caught in a halo of leaves is the familiar winking eye of Sirius.

'So where are we going?' She looks at their feet stepping out together. He has a long stride, which she likes.
Dominic prefers to stroll. Had he been next to her he
would have been sitting on one of the wrought-iron
benches by now and pretending interest in the constellations that despite patient prompting from her he could
never quite remember.

'We'll take a turn around.'

She moves closer to him. She'd like to feel his hand on
her waist and wonders whether she dares to make a move.
She also feels she has drunk too much. She didn't notice
how much wine she'd had because the young waiter had
kept filling her glass. She shifts away from Konrad. It would
be too easy to get carried away, to become giddy and playful. It's time off for both of us, she reminds herself.

They walk on. The gap between them narrows. Konrad
stops and turns to her. Her stomach lurches. He places his
warm broad hands on her shoulders and looks at her for a
long moment. The chestnut trees creak in the wind. She
breathes in their quick, fresh scent and feels her head spin.
He pulls her into his arms. She feels his heart beat hard
against her breastbone.

The sky is a soft dark bowl sprinkled with starlight. A
delicate new moon glints through the trees, like a secret
smile. They walk through the avenues of the Planty,
wrapped in each other, joined at the shoulder, waist and
hip. Sometimes their knees brush. Sometimes she feels the
drop of his lips into the base of her neck. The sensation is
unexpected, like something cool falling from the trees. She
points out the constellations of Hercules, Ophiuchus, the
serpent-bearer, and the parallelogram of stars marking the
head of Draco, the dragon in the north. At the end of an

avenue they find, to her delight, a statue of Nicholas Copernicus. He appears slight and unselfconscious on his plinth, as if he had just landed there like a delicate bronze starling. His narrow face is averted, his attention fixed on the sheaf of astronomy papers under his arm. Close by is an oak tree.

'The tree of liberty,' Konrad tells her, his arms encircling her from behind. His voice reverberates between her shoulder blades.

'Let's pay our respects,' she says.

They place their hands on the bark and lift their faces under the canopy of oak leaves. Their bodies are now separate, but still linked by the warm current of air that flows between them.

It is nearly two in the morning by the time they reach her hotel, having walked the city in a way that she thinks all cities should be walked, with a feeling of surprise and gratitude in every step. They had found churches still open at midnight, including the Holy Cross, ablaze with candles reflecting the palm vaulting spreading from a single white pillar, and the Jesuit Church where they were mesmerized by the pulsing gold-red ink of the polychromic ceiling, spread open like a giant floating flower petal. In some churches sturdy women in headscarves swept the stone floors and extinguished votive candles, which gave off the prickling scent of molten plastic. They stood by the doors and waited for their late visitors to leave, their expressions blandly submissive as if they did not care whether they would have to wait all night. When she remarked on this, Konrad said that it was years of communism that had made people look like that. 'As if they've stepped out of themselves, which is of course what they did in order to survive.

They shut down. If you've had to hide yourself for years, it takes a long time to find your way back to who you are again and some of them never quite made it. A lot of them were left on the wayside.'

Outside the hotel he takes her hand and brings it up to his lips. His eyes are wry, amused, ironic as he observes himself playing the courteous suitor. She is grateful. It makes their imminent separation easier. He takes a step back and stands for a moment absorbing her with his eyes as if he wants to frame her, put her into one of his films.

'Goodnight,' he says.

'Goodnight.'

Neither of them makes a move.

The idea of him looking at another woman with this full, intense, languorous assessment even through the lens of a camera makes her courage waver. She steps out of the pose. He instantly moves forward and takes her in his arms. She rests her head in the warm groove of his shoulder and sobs once swiftly. When she lifts her head he cups her face in both his hands and gently with his thumbs fans away her tears. 'I don't want to leave you, but I also don't want to make this too much, too soon. I want to go back to the apartment and think about you and hold you in my mind.'

Catherine nods. Something this fragile could be so easily crushed. 'I'm going to be thinking about you as well.' She pauses. 'I suppose I don't have much of a choice, not now.'

His eyes are milky. 'I suppose not. I'm going, but I don't want you to look at me. I'm just going to turn around and walk back to the apartment and maybe it will feel that you're still with me.' He takes a step backward, but does not turn around. 'Damn it, if I come any closer, I won't be able to stop myself. Tell me to go. Break the spell.'

A chill makes her shudder. She wonders whether he is trying to warn her of something. A cool voice intrudes, urging her to take note: you don't know him, don't be fooled by intimacy, don't overlook what is truly happening here. Be careful. Think rationally. This might have happened to him before. A man on a sabbatical from his marriage is not to be trusted.

'Goodnight,' she says. 'I'll see you.' His face falls and she sees that he isn't trying to warn her against falling for him too soon; he is trying to protect himself from her. But now it seems too late to retract what she has just said. It's too late to call him back and explain that she meant something else. It would confuse him or possibly humiliate him, make him feel that she is playing games with his feelings and this is the last thing she wants. 'I mean I'll see you very soon. Perhaps in the morning?'

'Sure, I'll call you in the morning.' He keeps his expression neutral, his tone light and breezy, as if nothing at all is at stake and she is relieved, but also slightly disappointed. 'Don't worry, not too early.' Now he moves forward again and kisses her in the centre of her forehead. She wants him to put his arms around her; she needs some confirmation from him now, but he steps back almost as soon as he has deposited the kiss, which feels like a bright, fizzing point between her temples. It will be fine, she tells herself. Just leave it alone and it will be fine.

Inside the lobby the concierge is watching television with the sound turned down. He gets up from his swivel chair and retrieves her key from one of the wooden cubby holes on the board behind him. 'Number twelve, yes.' He hesitates before he pushes it across the desk and she has the distinct impression that he wants to ask her something. At the very same moment she hears a familiar voice behind her and there standing in the lobby gripping the extended handle of his Antler suitcase is Dominic.

'You're back.' His voice is thick and nasal; he sounds as if he has been crying. She is so shocked her hand contracts and she drops the room key on to the marble lobby floor where it lands with a crack and spins like a dice.

Slowly, as if bowing, Dominic bends down to pick it up for her. His linen suit billows over his bulk like creased-up paper bags and gives off a sickly-sweet smell of tired travel and alcohol. When he hands her the key, his hand is shaking. Somehow he manages to tell her that he arrived several hours ago, four to be precise, and he even looks at his sweaty wristwatch as if to confirm the length of time he has been waiting for her in the hotel bar. She wants to ask him why he has come, but the question seems unnecessarily cruel. The thought of inviting him up to her room is impossible and so she suggests that they order tea and talk in the bar. Dominic looks crestfallen, but acquiesces and perhaps in an attempt to regain some dignity pushes his suitcase in front of her so that she is forced to follow him.

The concierge brings a copper tea tray to the bar. He settles it on a low table between a pair of armchairs and withdraws, raking a heavy velvet curtain across a brass pole to give them some privacy. She pours tea. They look at each other warily as if they have just finished a long conversation or an argument and are already exhausted. The cup in Dominic's hand rattles against the saucer as he lifts it. His eyes have a dull, punched quality. His stomach strains against his linen shirt, a few black hairs sprouting through the gaps in the material. He has lost a button, she sees, and for some reason this makes her feel a rush of tenderness for him.

Dominic glances around the bar as if seeing it for the first time. 'I imagined you would have stayed somewhere more upmarket.' With difficulty he puts down his cup. His knees are spread and he appears awkward in the chair, or perhaps it is his bulk that now feels awkward. He is not good in heat, she remembers, and it is airless in the dark bar, which smells of stale wine and perfume and strong cigarettes.

'It's fine. I'm not here for long.' Her head buzzes with tiredness.

He wipes his sweating forehead with the back of his hand. In recent years he has allowed his hair to grow and it curls around his head in exuberant iron-grey waves. She wonders why he hasn't asked why she is returning to the hotel so late. 'Cath, I'm so sorry for barging in on you like this.' Miserably he looks down at his knees and seems to gather momentum. 'I just couldn't manage at home.' He brings a hand up to his face and holds his jaw for a moment. He makes a sound in the back of his throat. 'Ach.'

'It's okay.' She hears the note of defeat in her voice. He glances at her, puzzled and grateful. His need both touches and repels her. She looks at him slumped forlornly in the chair and feels the full weight of his yearning. He has followed her because he could not be by himself. Her few days of freedom now seem cruel, almost a punishment; for a moment she had believed that things could be otherwise, that she could escape where she is, but his arrival has punctured her bud of hope before she could even fully acknowledge it. So this is the dark matter of her life. This is what she must deal with. What she has found now seems faint in comparison, a remote point of light.

'It's good to see you.' She can't say what she feels. In

truth, it's bewildering and frightening to see him, but also inevitable and predictable; it is what she knows and what she expects. There's a grim rightness to Dominic being in Kraków, reminding her that he is still tightly bound into her life.

'You, too . . .' He hesitates. 'You look well.'

She drops her eyes and drinks her tea. Dominic slumps deeper into his seat and sighs as if he has just resolved something. She feels a weariness settle in her.

'You're exhausted,' she says gently.

'I haven't slept since you left.' His eyes search her face, appealing for release.

She nods, understanding. She's always known that he felt incomplete without her. It was partly why she had stayed with him for so long. She was for him the solution to the eternal problem of solitary existence: at least that was how he had expressed it to her when they first revealed themselves to each other: 'You are my answer.'

'Well, you can get some rest soon,' she croons.

He closes his eyes and his face relaxes into a smile.

'I thought you might be angry.' His eyes suddenly flick open. 'How's it been going anyway? Have you found out much?'

She realizes that he hasn't listened to the message she left. 'I'll tell you in the morning.'

'Cath, I believe it is the morning.'

She stiffens as her mind snaps into defence. 'It was too hot to sleep. I went for a walk.'

'On your own? You're braver than I thought.' His voice is lazy and his eyes droop.

She looks at his hefty thighs spread in the leather seat and has to push down a wave of hostility. Perhaps she should just tell him the truth, get it over with. 'I went out to supper with a few people.' She is surprised at how easily she lies.

'Good for you,' he says. His face slackens and she sees that he lacks energy for a proper fight. Relief washes over her. Then he adds in the same slow drawl: 'We're still okay, aren't we?'

'Of course,' she says, her mouth thick with the taste of betrayal. 'We're still okay.'

Dominic sighs. She has never seen him look so depleted. Despite his sweaty ruddiness his body looks punctured. 'Thank you.'

His meekness alarms her. Usually she has to be so careful, the slightest comment could be misconstrued, perceived as an insult or affront. She has learned not to get too particular, to go for breadth in her way of being with him rather than depth. She has constructed this partly as a bridge for herself, a way of navigating without constantly bumping up against him. Now she understands that this is what he has come in pursuit of: her scaffold. He needs it to hold him together. He needs her still to be his answer.

She finishes her tea. He has let his go cold. She understands that he is holding off calling for alcohol, specifically red wine, which he drinks continuously now as other people drink tea or coffee, an ever-present uncorked bottle on his desk at home. Her eyes are stinging. She needs proper rest; she needs to find a point of stillness so that she can begin to deal with his arrival. 'We'd better get some sleep,' she says, keeping her voice neutral. 'Let's go up to the room.'

He looks at her balefully, a few strands of sweaty grey hair flopping forward into his eyes. 'I could book another room, but' – he pauses, a resigned note in his voice – 'maybe it's too late.'

'It's a twin room. We could sleep for a bit, talk properly in the morning.'

He compresses his lips and nods, but remains wedged in his seat. She gets up first and stretches. He follows her motion, lifting his head slowly, his eyes perplexed, as if examining something in his mind, something stuck, like a great block of stone that he wants to dislodge but does not have the energy to shift. He hauls himself out of his seat. His sweaty clothes smell powerfully of spirits.

Inside the room he takes a shower. She sits on the bed closest to the window with the curtain open a few inches. A line of gold touches the rooftops. It is dawn. She watches Venus rise. She drinks a miniature of brandy and feels it chase away the tension in her gut. Behind the thin bathroom door she hears the groan of Dominic's feet on the plastic shower tray.

The brown padded envelope containing Krystyna's story sits on the bedside table. She picks it up and feels the weight of it in her hands. She has read perhaps a third. She holds it against her chest, wondering when she will be able to return to it. From the bathroom comes the sound of water slapping against the tiles. She longs to read, to wrap herself once more in this story. Before she began her degree and set her course on scientific theory, reading was her secret joy. She read all the novels by Colette and Edith Wharton, spent entire summers in alternate worlds of feeling and sensation, moving back and forth between her home in south-west England and the salons of France and America. By reading she could make her longing disappear. She wonders why she felt she had to give it up. Plenty of her colleagues still read novels and they had tried to persuade her to join book clubs, but she didn't want to talk about the books she read, she wanted to feel them. She looks at the package in her hands. It now seems charged: a delicate treasure; a document of hope.

Abruptly the shower head is turned off. She slides the package under her bed. Dominic wrenches open the door and comes out with a white towel around his waist. His heavy tread makes the mirror on the wardrobe rattle and the water glasses chink against each other. As he pads to the empty single bed, preposterously too narrow for him, the knot in the towel comes untied. He balls it in his hand and holds it close, making her think of a rugby player protecting himself. He rolls across the room, knocking his thigh against the table on which the television sits. He drops the towel; his nestling genitals appear like a dark accusation. The bed squeaks and slides across the floor as he drops his full weight on to it, reaches for the remote from the bedside table and points it at the television screen, his expression passive as he flicks through the channels to find an appropriate narcotic. He settles on a music programme featuring a blonde woman who sings soulfully in Polish. In deference to Catherine, he turns the sound down.

She slips between her single sheets. She lies straight on her back. Restlessly Dominic shifts on the next bed and the springs prong with tension. The passion in the TV singer's voice throbs through the restraining silence. She feels too alert to sleep, too aware of him shifting and grunting. She listens to him swallow. His stomach gives a tight whine. His physical presence is so strong it is as if he is lying on top of her, his stomach, a great bristly bladder, pressing down on her. He flicks the television off and huffs as he arranges his body in the narrow bed. She lies still and stiff, arms by her sides. The ceiling in the room seems very close, thick plaster swirls like a series of overlapping vortexes. This was not how the evening was supposed to end. The avenue of trees now seems like an evaporating dream. Unable to sleep, she rolls and turns. She cannot believe how quickly things have changed. A few hours ago, there had been so much, almost too much, as if she had been given all of her life all at once. Now it seems as if she has missed her moment. She should not have left him. She should have asked him to take her to his apartment. Dominic would not have intruded then. He would not have found her until she had become free.

The phone wakes her a few hours later and groggily she lifts the receiver, aware of Dominic stirring in the next bed, his face muddled, a rumpled mass of hair twisting in different directions.

'Hi.' The anticipation and light warmth in Konrad's voice cut straight through her. Her body feels as if it is made of very fine glass. 'Did you sleep? Did you read any more?' No, she feels like crying out. No. The story has been cruelly interrupted.

'I'm just about to shower,' she tells him, hoping that he will pick up the warning in her voice. 'I need to call you back.'

'Catherine, is everything okay?'

She has to resist the urge to tell him that no, it isn't. Everything is not okay. Everything is uncertain. Things have changed.

'We'll talk a bit later.'

There's a catch in his voice. 'Sure.'

She holds the phone against her chest, feeling as if she

has wounded him. 'Konrad.' Just speaking his name aloud feels dangerous. There's a pause in which she becomes aware of Dominic stirring behind her and then a wave of wet warmth as he passes close to her on his way to the bathroom. He slides the door across and then releases his bladder in a long shuddering stream. She feels afraid that Konrad will hear and draw the wrong conclusions. She must say something. She must let him know. The toilet flushes. She takes her opportunity.

'Dominic has arrived.'

'What?' He is incredulous, but there is also a note of relief in his voice that her anxiety is not directly connected to him. 'Where is he?'

Now she feels ashamed. She should have had the strength last night to insist Dominic took another room. 'He's in the bathroom.'

Konrad is silent.

Her eyes feel stretched in her face. She runs her hand across her forehead. 'He was waiting for me when I got back to the hotel.'

'Oh, God.'

'I'm sorry.' She doesn't intend this to sound like an admission of anything, or a withdrawal, but now that she has said it, she thinks he may take it either way. She's about to tell him that she will try to meet him later when the bathroom door slides open and there is Dominic coming towards her, his naked body, darkly furred, burly and some-how sorrowful in its heaviness. Without saying anything more she puts down the phone.

'So, was that him?' He sits on the bed and pulls the quilt around him.

'Who?' She feels protective of his name.

'The person you were just speaking to. It was him.' He rubs his head. His skin gives off the ripe humid smell of sleep. 'Konrad.'

There is a brutality in the way he pronounces it, hard and angular. It feels invasive. He is treading on something.

'Yes.'

Now it comes, the accusation, she can feel it, like a dark, electric storm. 'You were with him last night?'

'Yes, we went out for dinner. With a Dutch couple we met.' She hears the forced brightness in her own voice. 'Interesting people.' Dominic darts a look at her and she flounders. 'Konrad intends to make a film about his aunt.' She is rambling, giving him facts, trying to offset his interest, but already she sees that she is failing. He has picked up on her nervousness; she will have to offer him something more. She wonders whether to tell Dominic about the story under the bed, but decides not to in case he asks to read it. She couldn't bear his scrutiny. He would have questions. His mathematical mind would want to piece it all together, to make sense of it. Krystyna and Janek. Your father, he would remind her. Now you have the facts. Now you know how it all adds up. Now you can get on with your life.

Dominic rips off a piece of his thumbnail: 'Are you going to meet him today?'

'Well, I suppose not, now that you're here.' She tries to keep her voice neutral with no sense of blame. 'I'm going to shower,' she adds, throwing him a smile. He grunts.

She steps into the hot steam and the feeling of being naked is arousing. Her body feels soft and hair-trigger sensitive. She soaps herself gently across her breasts, brushing her nipples with the palm of her hand, imagining

Konrad there in the glass cubicle with her, his hand between her wet thighs, his mouth on her collarbone. All the time she is aware of Dominic only a few inches away moving about the hotel room, bashing into the furniture as he dresses. She towels herself dry and slowly applies body cream; touching herself in this way feels new and forbidden. Beyond the sliding door she can hear sounds of knocking and the tight squeak of wheels. Her heart deflates like a limp balloon as she hears the scrape of clothes on hangers and the hump of Dominic's suitcase heaved up on to the rack on top of hers.

They are the only guests at breakfast. The concierge from the night before serves them in a room hung with paintings of the Polish cavalry streaming across a snowy landscape on fine-boned horses with long flowing tails. The concierge's expression is dry, his temples twitching as he takes their order for scrambled eggs with bacon. While they wait, they drink flat sweet orange juice from heavy polished glasses. The concierge brings a pot of coffee. Its taste reminds her of Konrad, which makes her throat ache. Her shower has left her feeling raw and vulnerable and nervous of being discovered. When the eggs arrive she looks down at their glistening yellow curded mass and has to push down a wave of revulsion.

Leaving the eggs, she eats a slice of dry toast. Dominic notices, but says nothing. He reaches across the table to the coffee pot and grasps its black handle. His fingers brush hers and she has to resist an urge to jump away in shock. They seem grotesque to her, the long bent hairs on his knuckles almost too personal. He pours for them both and she can tell that it is an effort for him to keep his hand steady.

Cradling his cup in both hands he drinks his coffee in short concentrated sips. 'I suppose quite a lot has happened since you arrived?'

'Yes.' She searches for a way to explain, but the immediacy of the walk in the garden with Konrad is still so compelling that she cannot see a way to move beyond it.

Dominic draws back in his seat, irritation flickering across his eyes like static. 'It's not the same at home without you.' His expression is sullen. 'I don't know what to do with myself. It's just too lonely.'

She feels her chest tighten. 'We talked about this before I left.'

'I know.' He glances down at the table. 'I tried, I really tried, but it just didn't work.' He sighs and runs his hands through his hair. 'You know I don't function on my own. I'm no good.'

'You could have gone to London. You said your sister was going to come up, you were going to go fishing, you wanted to read . . . you were looking forward to some time on your own.'

'Don't blame me, Cath, all right.' His eyes flare at her.

'I'm not blaming you. There's nothing to blame. I'm just saying that's what you were planning.'

'Well, I didn't feel like seeing anyone.' He puts his coffee cup down. His hand is steadier now and he seems stronger, even bullish. He leans over and takes her plate of uneaten egg and wordlessly scrapes it on to his own. She watches him, the small of her back aching with tension. Little globules of egg stick to his lips. She wonders what he has been eating since she left. Their fridge at home was always stocked with cheese, cold meats, salad, olives, pots of dip; he liked onions, garlic, chilli, anchovy, robust flavours, but unless she prepared meals for them he would open the fridge door and complain that there was nothing to eat.

'There was no one I felt like calling. Especially not my sister. I wasn't in the right mood for her.' He leans back in his seat and regards his cleared plate with slight puzzlement as if he cannot recall eating from it.

Catherine drinks her coffee in silence. Nothing will console him. All the activities and plans and discussions they had before she left are now irrelevant. Dominic didn't want to play at being self-reliant. 'So what would you like to do now that you are here?'

He throws her a bemused look. 'You could show me the places you've been.'

She shudders. The idea of revisiting places she has discovered with Konrad, the old coffee shop, the jewelled churches, the square, the Planty, the Jewish Quarter, seems abhorrent, a desecration. In the few trips she had made with Dominic to France, usually the Dordogne because he had friends living there, he would claim restaurants – he liked big, relaxed, vibrant places where the emphasis was on drinking beer or wine outside under large coloured umbrellas; the smaller, darker, older places of her choice he deemed 'suffocating' or 'poky', or 'depressing'. The smell of old stone made him wheeze and the narrow stools were too dainty and made him shift and wriggle like a restless child.

'You wouldn't be interested.'

He jerks his head. 'Why wouldn't I?' His eyes are hard, belligerent.

'Because I know you.' She tries to keep her voice light.

When they first met, his need for roominess had made her think that he was interested in living widely and freely.

He was someone, she'd thought, who would understand her attachment to observation, her devotion to the mystery of solar systems, to vastness and all that was living and dying unseen on earth. She misread his fear of abandonment for generosity. He allowed her space at the beginning. Whatever she needed, it was hers. All he wanted for her was her own happiness. He didn't want children. He was too old. She was released into the capsular world of the observatory. It was somewhere he recognized, not dissimilar to the tight, closed, boxy rooms of mathematics with their flat screens, radiant books and framed fractals. There was beauty and symmetry in mathematics; there was also complexity of thought and discovery. There was Truth. Their academic specialisms overlapped, dovetailed, and for a few years it did seem as if they were a perfect fit. There were no serious disagreements between them, nothing to disturb the calm waters of their learned life together.

They bought their home in their third year together and moved in during the summer when they were both on leave from their university posts. There was a heatwave that year and they worked outside with their papers, sometimes until dusk. She remembers she was working on Type 1 supernovae, developing a theoretical model to explain the enigma of hydrogen-poor explosions using binary star systems, pairs of stars so close together that they exert substantial influence on one another's evolution. The supernovae were thought to begin with two main sequence stars circling a common centre of gravity. Hydrogen flooding from the first star was thought to build up so quickly that the companion's gravity could not hold it all. Then some of the escaping gas formed a cloud that cloaked each of the stars, dragging on them and changing their orbits, eventually bringing them closer together. She remembers showing Dominic a photograph of a collapsing superstar, and the rapture on his face had made her feel as if she had returned to somewhere safe. That night they made love in the garden on newly cut grass, giggling at the thought of the neighbours looking out from their bedroom window at the sight of the professor's naked backside going for it under the strobe light of the moon. She thought she had found all that she needed to be happy.

'Perhaps we could go somewhere new for both of us,' she offers. 'There are plenty of galleries and museums I haven't yet seen.'

'How about Auschwitz? Have you been yet?' Dominic's expression is alert with possibility.

'I don't think I want to go.' She feels shaken at the thought.

'You can't come to Kraków and not see Auschwitz. It's part of history.' His eyes are glinting with challenge. 'You said you were interested in history. Isn't that why you came?'

There is something about his casual glee that is unnerving. 'I know, but maybe not today. Couldn't we just stay here, get used to being with each other again?'

He looks at her perplexed. She can tell that he is thinking about why they might need time to get used to each other after all their years together. Not unreasonably he has assumed familiarity, and although he is aware that he might be interrupting her time with Konrad, time that does not include him, he is not going to concede. He has the benefit of their long association – *their* history together, which cannot be denied or unlived – and he is going to use it to his advantage. He leans his elbows on the table and emits a sigh. She's not making enough of an effort for him, his attitude and expression tell her; she needs to perk up or he will start to wonder and possibly intrude further, and she cannot risk that.

'Well, let's go up to the room and look at the guidebook and decide what to do.'

His shoulders drop as he relaxes for the first time. He smiles at her and reaches for her hand. She lets him take it and fold it inside his damp palm even though it feels strange, as if she doesn't know him at all.

'You go. I'll stay and have another coffee.' He releases her hand.

She unlocks the room with her key and goes to her suitcase and pulls out the guidebook. They could go to the castle, she thinks, or the Jewish museum. She brushes her teeth. Maybe it isn't as bad as she thinks. All she needs to do is just keep Dominic occupied for a few days and then maybe she might be able to persuade him to go home. But the feeling of dread lurching in the bottom of her stomach tells her that this is unlikely. The phone begins to ring in the next room. She hesitates, her heart thudding, toothbrush poised over the sink. She listens to it for a few seconds more and then turns on the tap and rinses out her mouth. By the time she turns it off the phone has stopped ringing.

9

Eastern Poland, February 1940

Every day the duffel bag grew lighter. Krystyna kept it close to her at night, using its crumpled canvas folds as a pillow to rest her head. All the food had gone except for a thin layer of dark jam. She rationed it daily, eating a hazelnut-sized globule from the tip of her knife. The intense sweetness made saliva rush into her mouth and dribble down her chin, startling her with its warmth, its lively greed. Soon the last layer of jam had been scraped from the jar and she used her wet finger to rub out the rest, sucking on it until her skin puckered. She used the jar to carry snow for drinking water.

She knew that if she didn't find food soon she would become sick. At night her chest hurt as if she were breathing through bruised ribs. Hunger and thirst left her feeling tired and dreamy. It was particularly acute during the late afternoons after she had been riding all day, following elk tracks and hare crossings that looped the forest floor in delicate chains. At night she gnawed on the leather strap to keep the hunger pangs at bay. As her energy fell, she lost her grip on time and would slip from the mare and sit in the snow under the sweeping arms of the trees until she recovered. Her will seemed to have shrunk to a small hard frozen bead, no bigger than the size of a pea. She was afraid of losing it altogether. The mare waited patiently, head lowered, her legs slightly splayed as she breathed. Krystyna tried not to look at her belly, the ribs showing through in thick ridges. Gazela's coat had lost its sheen and her eyes were dull. She uncovered bracken for her by the banks of the stream and the mare chewed slowly. Sometimes they were lucky and found young saplings that had escaped the deer and she broke these over her knee and fed them to the horse. Nonetheless as the days went on Gazela grew more listless with fatigue and began to stumble. To encourage her Krystyna held the duffel bag under her nose and let her breathe in the forgotten aroma of oats.

The duffel now flapped against her back like a pair of useless, deflated wings. Krystyna knew that if they didn't find a town or village soon they would both die. Without food she found it difficult to plan her route. There seemed to be no point to anything, no reason to keep going. For several days in a row she ate nothing and sat with the duffel bag between her knees, a pressing feeling around the back of her eyes, as if a thumb were being pushed through her skin from the inside. She was too dry and hollow to weep. She felt bludgeoned by cold and hunger. At night she curled up on the hard-packed snow and groaned herself to sleep.

One morning she woke and found the forest submerged in cloud. She rubbed snow into her eyes but the fog failed to clear. When she got up her knees buckled; hot needles of pain speared the space under her arms. She sat down and breathed, counting up to ten and then down again. She remembered her father telling her how he had survived after the lance ripped open his thigh down to the bone. He rode for miles, his leg bound by his jacket, by concentrating all his thought on the footfalls of his horse. 'I understood that pain only existed when you gave it room,' he had told her one night in the library. 'When I refused to let it come in, it miraculously went away.' His eyes, brimming with life in the firelight, stayed in her mind as she reached behind her for the duffel bag.

Her clothes smelled empty, except for Janek's cap, which still carried traces of his scent deep up inside the brim. She pulled it close to her face for a moment. Her chest contracted with pain. Remembering her father's words, she firmly pushed it away, but it seemed to come back even stronger, taunting her with its bawling need. She swallowed, waiting for the next wave of pain. If she could catch it before it flared like a match she would be able to send it on its way. She began to count to ten. The mare's eyes rested on her face.

After a while her eyes cleared and she felt strong enough to ride. She followed a narrow track and each time the pain sneaked up on her she pretended that she was her father riding his horse from the battleground. In the late afternoon she came across an ancient oak tree with a thick, dry girth. She dismounted under the spreading expanse of branches that for some reason had kept all their leaves. Behind the tree there was a deep fast-flowing stream with shallow sloping banks. She led the mare to drink. After sucking long draughts of water Gazela nosed at the snow and nibbled at frozen leaves, her white breath billowing like pipe smoke.

They camped for the night on a soft patch of ground under the oak tree. In the morning she saw that Gazela had eaten long strips of bark from its rough torso, exposing the green skin underneath. The sound of her crunching was crisp in the cold bright air. Leaving the mare to continue her feed, Krystyna took a track that led deeper into the forest. There were more oak trees and birch and elm. On the forest floor there was plenty of dry firewood. She half thought that here she might make a shelter and wait out her time instead of riding on. But what if Janek found them both starved to death in the snow? If she stayed camping in the forest, she would lose touch with everything that had meant something to her. If she gave up, she would certainly die; even to think of giving up was to invite failure. If her father were with her now, he would remind her of her duty to whatever was left of her family. She had to find Janek and his father.

There was a sharp crack. She whirled round, but saw nothing except for the narrow deer path snaking its way between the snowy trees. Her footprints were soft hollows. She peered ahead to the trees framed against a lavender sky. Along the branches new frost glimmered with a clean light; the air smelled pure. The splintering sound came again, this time to her right, and she whipped her head in its direction, her heart beginning to race as her body prepared to flee.

The sight of a grey-green coat hunkered down in the snow caused her throat to stall. Her eyes jerked with a rush of tears as her heart pumped faster. Here was her end. She had been led to her own death. She stood straight and still. She felt almost calm. In a moment the soldier would turn and he would shoot her like a deer. Then he would shoot her mare. There was no place to hide; the trees here were too slender, too dazzlingly lit. She was caught in a snare of light. She waited. Her breath sounded harsh in her nostrils and she tried to quieten it. The figure in the coat tensed. Then he slowly rose to his feet and turned round.

At the sight of his russet hair she called out, stunned. He stood knee-deep in the snow, the coat in heavy folds around him, like a rumpled stage curtain. He peered at her, his eyes narrowed into glittering slits. She took a step back and her hand hovered over her mouth.

He was not Janek. He was too young, about nine years of age with brittle arms and milky skin, a sprinkle of freckles like rust spots spoiling his cheeks. In one hand he carried a limp white hare, ears flat along the line of its back, the bob of its tail bumping against the snow. He took a step towards her and she caught sight of its eye. Still bright with life, it pierced her like an echo of joy.

They stared at each other across the snow. The boy's eyes kept straying to his catch. She kept her gaze on his face.

'My name is Krystyna,' she called to him.

'Benedykt.' He had a gruff, deep voice. 'From Komarno.' His eyes were fierce.

'Is that near here?'

He acted as if she hadn't spoken and strode up to a tree and slung the hare over a branch. 'I need to collect wood,' he told her in his rough voice. 'You come with me.'

'All right.' She was startled at his assurance.

He set off, trudging through the deep snow, hitching up the long sides of the army coat. He glanced back to check that she was following and his eyes hovered over the hare folded forlornly on its branch, his expression one of mistrust, as if he were afraid it might spring into life again. 'Here,' he said, his gaze snapping back to her. 'You can help me pick up sticks.'

They gathered a pile of firewood from the forest floor, working side by side, bent at the waist like potato pickers, scrabbling at the snow, their bare cold hands sometimes touching as they combed the frozen ground. The boy was faster than she was and put his sticks in a pile, arranging them neatly. She followed him, her eyes blurring once more with exhaustion. At one point she stood up and placed her hand against her side and took a few deep breaths.

'Are you sick?' he called over to her in his man's voice.

She took another few deep breaths. The pain gouged at her side, begging to be let in. She began to count silently. The boy watched her, his eyes flickering over her face. At the corner of his mouth a tiny muscle pulsed like a miniature heartbeat. 'Go back,' he said. 'I will bring the wood.'

She returned to the oak tree. At her approach the mare lifted her head and whickered a low greeting. Krystyna put her arms around the mare's neck and breathed in her warmth. 'I've found someone,' she told the horse. 'He'll be here soon and I'll have something to eat. That will make me strong again.' She stroked the mare's belly. 'I wish I had more for you.' The mare reached forward with her nose and licked the salt from her hand. Then she jerked her head up at the sight of the grey-green coat tramping through the trees.

Benedykt's eyes softened when he saw the horse, but he did not come over immediately. He arranged his armful of sticks into a fire, which he lit with a petrol lighter he pulled from his pocket, handling it deftly. He hunched over the fire, coaxing the flames with his small chapped hands. When the wood was hissing and steaming to his satisfaction he got up and wiped his palms down his coat.

He came up to the tree and looked at the mare, his eyes huge with awe. 'How have you managed to keep her?'

Krystyna understood. It was extraordinary. Even emaciated the horse was almost too much to be real: warm and beautiful, suffused with animal life. 'There were two. I had to leave the other behind.'

Benedykt nodded as if this explained something. He moved his hand towards the mare and let her sniff his knuckles. Her chin hairs moved over his skin as she gently explored him. Enraptured, he ran his hand under the thick warmth of her mane and rocked back on his heels as he kneaded the slack muscle. Then he dipped under her neck and worked on the other side with long strokes. He talked to the mare in a consoling voice as if he were calming her down after a fright. The mare listened and breathed her slow breath, keeping time with him. As he reached her withers, she quivered her bottom lip. He scratched her, drawing her grease into his fingernails, which were rimmed with dirt and bark from his forest trawl. He worked over the mare until he reached the strong rudder of her tail. There he stopped. His eyes clouded over. His chest heaved and he bent his face into the side of her rump. The horse turned her neck to look at him, bending her body so that she could nuzzle at him and draw him to her like a foal. Respecting his need for privacy, Krystyna withdrew to the fire.

On his return, Benedykt stirred the damp smoking branches with the toe of his boot. She noticed that he was wearing men's boots, good thick heavy brown leather boots with metal toecaps and tight clean laces. He looked at her with glistening eyes. 'We had horses,' he said. 'At home. I used to ride in the forest with my father.' His nose puckered and she thought he might cry, but he took a deep breath and gathered himself. 'Is she fast?'

Krystyna remembered the races with Janek along the line of oaks in the meadow. How long ago it seemed, years might have passed in the time. She looked into the flames. 'Like lightning,' she said.

The heat from the fire grew more intense as it burned down. The boy glanced over his shoulder to the hare hanging from a branch. His eyes streamed from the smoke and he drew his sleeve across his face. He bit on the inside of his lip. 'I will help you to skin it, if you like,' Krystyna said. 'I have a knife. It's still sharp.'

He hunched his shoulder and flinched and she realized that she had offended him. He reached into one of the coat's deep pockets and pulled out a bulky package bound with dark oilcloth trussed with string. He unwound it across his knees. She saw a collection of small tools and various knives. He selected one: a heavy blunt short paring knife with a sharp tip and ran his finger down the edge to test it, his breathing concentrated, the tip of his tongue a tiny red newt. Without saying another word he got up and went to the tree where he pulled down the hare and with two or three swift strokes cut it open down its belly and shook out its guts. Blood and intestines tumbled into the snow. Krystyna looked away. There was a faint smell of urine in the air. Saliva filled her mouth and her stomach heaved. She brought her knuckle up to her mouth.

When she turned back she saw that Benedykt had driven a stick through the hare and was now roasting it over the embers, turning it frequently so that it would not catch. Stripped of skin, its flesh was a pale, taut violet. The meat sizzled as it cooked and the scent awoke her hunger which clawed at her stomach. More saliva flooded her mouth. The hare turned on its spit and she caught sight of an eye, now a black slit. Nausea rose in her guts.

They ate side by side on a thick branch, boots scuffing the sooty snow, licking their slick fingers, lips dewy with grease. There was a spot of blood the size of a coin on the toe of one of the boy's boots. He noticed her looking at it and bent down and balled some snow in his fingers to try to rub it off, but it smeared into a stain. 'Don't worry, you can wash it off in the stream,' she said. She wanted to reassure him, but he shrugged off her concern and sat looking at his boots, his face crumpled with pain.

They ate every scrap of the hare, even crunching on the bones. The night fell in black waves around them. Krystyna felt her limbs relax in the warmth from the fire. Her eyelids felt heavy. Tonight she might sleep for more than a couple of hours. Her body, parched from lack of food and rest, seemed to be filling up. She put her hands on her shoulders and stretched her back. She turned to the boy ready to thank him for the hare, but her gratitude froze on her lips.

He was staring at the flames, his lower lip trembling, his eyes glimmering in the dark. 'I jumped from the train,' he said, the roughness in his voice parting for a moment, like the hinged halves of a nut, revealing the child he was.

'The train? Where?' The idea of trains, fumes, noise, platforms, people rushing with suitcases seemed so unreal to her, he might have been recounting a dream.

'I ran along the track and then I found a way into the forest,' he said, his voice wavering. He lifted his arm and drew his sleeve across his face. Now she saw that he was crying. 'My father told me to jump.'

'When was this?' she asked, keeping her voice low, the

voice she used to speak to her horses. 'How long ago?'

He pursed his lips and looked over the top of the fire. There was a silence in which he thought. She waited. Then he turned and looked at her and she saw confusion and fear and the beginnings of despair. 'I don't know. I lost count. I started to count the days, but then I forgot.' He looked down at his feet in shame.

She reached over and patted his knee. He flinched from her touch. She withdrew her hand. Between the trees a yellow moon rose as if on invisible wires. Somewhere in the distance a wolf or a dog howled.

Eventually the boy said, 'My father was the chief of forests.' He looked into the trees, and in that moment an expression of wonder swiftly passed over his face, as if he were imagining his father there, caught in the golden moonlight, in evening dress, conducting the firs, the spruce, the pines and the birch with his chief's baton. His expression changed and the illusion faded. 'The soldiers took him.'

She was silent for a moment as she registered what he was trying to tell her. 'Russians?'

'Yes, Russians.' He rocked his body. His knees poked through his thin trousers, like the sharp points of one of his knives. 'They arrested him and put us all on the train. We had some of our stuff in bags with us.' His eyes strayed to the spot where he had left the hare skin in the snow, not stretched out but curled up so that it looked as if it were sleeping. 'My mother had a baby.' He paused and swallowed. 'My little sister. She died on the train.' He looked down at his boots and dragged the stained toe across the snow where it left a faint smear of pink. 'The other family with us had a baby too, a boy, and he also died.' He lifted his chin and looked at her with incomprehension, his eyes weary. 'They were forced to throw him from the train. After I jumped from the train with my sister, I found him on the track. He was frozen hard. I buried them in the deep snow next to each other.' He closed his eyes and immediately fell into an exhausted sleep.

After a while Krystyna got up from the fire and went over to where the mare stood under the oak, one hind hoof delicately at rest. She smoothed her neck and put her face against her curved cheek and breathed in her warm caramel smell. For a moment she was caught up in the boy's story, imagining him carrying his sister in his arms across the frozen tracks, her body as cold as stone, her eyes popped like a cooked hare. Then more images hurled themselves at her in a shower of brightness. There was her stepmother, packing clothes, her cheeks feverish, her father parading Henryk on his wolf skin, Anastazia making the sign of the cross, the sound of prayer. She remembered the wormy sensation of Henryk, kicking at her with all the force he could muster from his firm, hot little legs, tight as ripe plums; his yell and the way he had commanded all the attention in the house. She remembered, too, the sound of the horses calling and then the crunch of boots on snow, her father shouting, and the crack of rifle shots, one rapidly following another, but now her mind froze and there was nothing more. The mare flexed her neck and sighed. Over at the fire, she saw the boy still sitting as she had left him: a small, hunched silhouette.

In the morning they drank water from the stream and rubbed their faces with their cold hands. As they squatted over the water she asked him if he wanted to ride with her for a while. He flicked his coral hair back from his eyes.

'All right. I'll show you where the village is.' She saw that he needed to feel that he mattered. She said that they would take it in turns to ride Gazela. He could go first if he wanted. His eyes widened and at the corner of his lips there hovered the ghost of a smile.

The stirrup leathers were too long for his legs. She doubled them back over in a loop and placed his feet in the too-big man's boots inside the cold irons. He did not look down at her adjustments. He sat with his chest thrust forward, his sharp chin lifted. He had put on a pair of man's leather working gloves, scraped and scuffed at the finger-tips, and held the reins in one hand, quite high. 'I'll walk alongside,' she said.

In response he slackened the reins and brushed his legs quietly against the mare. She moved off immediately, ears springing forward. Benedykt gave a shy smile of delight. He reached down to smooth the mare's neck. He relaxed his shoulders and rested his buttocks deeper into the saddle and the mare lengthened her stride and lifted her back. Krystyna saw that he knew how to ride; he had perfect balance. 'You're so much lighter than me,' she called up to him. 'I'll have trouble keeping up with you.'

He guided Gazela on to a narrow track. She had seen this path before and had not wanted to take it because it seemed to lead deeper into the forest where the trees competed for light, taking each other around the throat in a stranglehold of frosted ivy. 'You'll just have to walk faster,' he said, his eyes now scanning the track. 'We want to get there before dark.'

She let him ride for several hours, refusing to stop and exchange places when he called down to say that it was her turn. The snow was packed hard on the track and mostly unmarked, except for the filigree tracings of bird prints along the softly ridged edges. Here, it was too narrow for her to walk alongside the horse and so she fell in behind, tucking her chin into her chest for warmth.

They rode and walked all day, following deer tracks between the trees. Gazela, strengthened by her rest, kept up an even pace, her front and hind hooves leaving deep V shapes in the snow, like four cleft hearts. At dusk they stopped and made a camp in an old part of the forest where the trees rose like steeples, branches dark near the top from where they had shrugged off their burden of snow. Lying down near the embers of their fire, she looked at the sky stretching away from her in a skin of inky blue. Stars appeared like droplets of fine rain on a windowpane. She shifted the duffel bag under her neck and tried to get comfortable on the evergreen branches she had laid on the snow. Benedykt lay next to her, stiff in his military coat. The uniform was Russian. He hadn't told her where he had acquired it. She listened to him breathe, his chest wheezing with every in-breath. Her own chest was sore again and she had the familiar pain in the hollow of her armpits near the wing of each breast. Her stomach was a cold disc under her hand, tightly suspended between the knots of her hipbones. Every now and then it would give a whine of protest and raise its fist from within. They had not found anything to eat.

In the morning a fall of fresh snow settled in fine lace across their coats and boots. Even Gazela's eyelashes were coated with a thin rim of white that highlighted the lustrous river darkness of her eyes. There was a fizzing chill in the air. Silent with hunger, they went in opposite directions to relieve themselves. Squatting in the new snow, she watched her urine drill into the fresh snow in a rod of hot, dark amber. Her sweat smelled stronger than usual; yeasty and humid. Because there were no leaves close by, she used the edge of her palm to wipe herself and noticed a slight brownish deposit, like dirty saliva. She rubbed it clear on the snow and returned to their camp.

Benedykt was feeding Gazela snow. The horse dipped her head, lapping at his fingers gratefully, almost guiltily, as if the boy truly had found some delicious hidden morsel buried in a cache under the trees. At Krystyna's approach they stopped their game and then it was her turn to feel guilty for denying them even the imaginary pleasure of food.

'We have to keep going,' she said. He looked at her and smiled. She wondered whether he had forgotten about the village. 'We have to keep moving, at least.'

Benedykt nodded. 'It's not far. One hour and I can get there, but' – he hesitated and flicked his eyes over the mare – 'it is better if I go into the village alone.'

She stiffened. He was right. The horse would attract too much attention. She turned away for a moment to gather her strength. His innocence shamed her. She ought to make him stay with the horse while she went into the village, but she didn't know the area. And because she was slower on foot, it would take her longer to go in and out. She also knew he would fight her rather than allow her to take care of him like a mother, and she understood even in her guilt that if she took the fight away from him, he would have nothing left. 'All right,' she said. 'But don't be long. Don't take risks. Just find food and come straight back here, an hour at most.'

His mouth lifted at the corners and for the first time he appeared almost animated. 'I know how to do this. I can bring food for us: eggs, maybe a chicken, some potatoes.'

The thought made her feel weak. 'You're sure it's safe?' But as soon as she said the words she realized how wrong she was even to mention the idea of danger. She didn't want him to go from her feeling afraid.

He narrowed his eyes. 'In this village there are Germans,' he said. 'Not Russians.' He shrugged his shoulders and pulled the cumbersome coat more tightly around his frail body and bit down on his lip. 'I think maybe this is not so bad.'

'You must be quick, don't be tempted to take more than you can carry.'

He lifted his chin. 'I will take only what is necessary.' He straightened his shoulder and patted the pocket with the package holding the knives. His eyes were restless to be away on his mission.

'Come back before dark.'

His eyes danced. 'Don't worry, you will be seeing me in precisely two hours and five minutes. One hour there, one hour back. Five minutes to grab a nice tasty chicken for tonight.'

She sighed. He started to move away from her. She called him back. 'Benedykt!' He turned, his white face calm and untroubled. She wanted to grab him and hold him close for a moment, but knew that would be too much for him. 'Some oats, if you can find them, for the horse.' It had started to snow. A few flurries whipped his face. He nodded at her and then bent his head, shoved his hands deeper into his pockets, and trudged into the swirling whiteness. Looking at his retreating figure she wanted to call him back and suggest they exchange coats, but he was too far gone for that.

All day she waited for him under the snowy boughs of a pine tree, tending to the mare, watching the forest for signs of his return, biting her fingers to stop them numbing with the cold. As the light fell to a smoky grey she left her post and gathered cones and branches for kindling and lit a fire on the embers of the last one around which they had slept the night before. She remembered how just before she woke she had heard him cry out in his sleep for his father, just once, his voice small and fearful. When he woke his face had a confused look, his eyes glazed, as if he had been travelling in a dark place for many hours.

Dozing by the fire, she dreamed of sitting in the kitchen at the dwór. Anastazia was making apple sauce and scents of cloves and nutmeg drifted through the house. At one point in the dream she was back in her room lying on her bed writing her diary and listening to the owls calling across the trees in tight screeches and long answering hoots. The door opened and her father walked in wearing his riding clothes. He asked her to take the horses from the barn. From the look of urgency in his face, she knew she had to be quick and so she leapt from her bed and hurriedly dressed, but she couldn't find her boots and had to run down the stairs barefoot and out into the snow. As she saddled the horses, one mare each for her and her father, she felt safe and confident. If they rode away immediately, they would escape the Russians.

She woke feeling nauseous and dizzy. Brushing the snow from her clothes, she saw something move in the trees: a dark stout shape with a huge crown of antlers that in the morning light seemed dipped in liquid gold, like a polished church candelabra. The elk turned to look at her. Its muzzle was grey and it studied her without fear. She felt held by its presence, its self-assured power, and it settled something inside her that had been brewing ever since she had left the dwór, threatening to burst and somehow contaminate her. The elk swung its antlers in a playful fashion and she imagined how it would be to have such wonderful horns: an entire casket of gold swords that could be drawn to suit the occasion, which made her think of Benedykt and his oilskin case of knives and the brave tilt of his shoulders as he set off through the forest to the village where there were Germans. The feeling of fear that she thought had gone came back again in an intense dark hum and to clear it she looked at the elk spinning snow from its slim heels, a tight feeling at her throat. She watched until the animal had gone and then went behind a tree and squatted to pee. A gout of plum-coloured blood fell from her into the snow and for a long moment she stared at it aghast, her parted knees quivering with shock, but somewhere there was a vague knowledge that she hadn't remembered until now, like the dawning of some deeply private inner secret.

She spent the rest of the day pacing with her hand pressed to her abdomen to try to relieve the pulsing cramps. They came in waves; some were little more than flutters, ripples of pain, but others were deeper and seemed to wrench her pelvic bones. After her initial fright she had torn some strips of cotton from one of the flannel shirts she had packed to make a pad to staunch the flow. As she did this, securing the rags so they would not slip, she wondered how long she would bleed. She also wondered what she would say to the boy when he returned.

By the end of the day there was no sign of him and she decided that she had no choice but to ride the mare to the village to find out what had happened. She waited until dark and then leaving the saddle hidden under a tree, mounted bareback. Krystyna touched Gazela's sides and they set off in the direction the elk had taken, following a twisting track around the young birch trees, peeling stems like ripped newspaper in the strange ghostly light. After an hour of riding she heard the sound of a dog barking and smelled wood smoke. Under the cover of trees she dismounted and left the reins tied on the mare's neck. Should she need to flee, the mare would instinctively make her way back to the old woman's barn, she was certain of it. Then she continued on foot, crouching low, stopping every now and again to listen to the sounds coming from the village which lay ahead in a cluster of low wooden houses, one or two with yellow lamplight showing through the windows. There might be Polish people there like the old woman who would welcome her with food and warmth, she thought, but there was another part of her, a clear, rational, almost nagging voice that told her to be careful because things were different now and she did not know what to expect.

She edged forward until she could see a row of houses with wooden fences marking the small gardens in the front. In spring and summer these would be flourishing patches of flame-coloured plants: dahlias, begonia and geranium; now they were mounded with snow. She caught a scent of dog. Inside the picket fence of the nearest chalet, a German Shepherd was pacing, marking its square of territory, snaking its sandy quarters back and forth, tail held low. The dog barked as a pair of men wearing long belted coats and caps with shiny peaks walked down the lane in front of the houses. Two deep tracks carved on each side and the smooth hump of snow in the middle told her that the lane had been used by vehicles repeatedly, although there was no sign of anything now, just the men walking down one of the tracks, their boots crunching in time along the gritty snow. One stopped briefly and lit a cigarette; she smelled tobacco and saw the gleam of the buttons on his coat in the light. He was young with a straight jaw so carefully shaved the skin looked like oiled white bone. The men continued down the lane, talking and laughing. They stopped near the dog and one of them said something – it sounded like a dog's name – but the dog ignored them and continued to bark without force or meaning, a weak call for attention, as if it had been barking without a break for many hours. The man shouted an order at the dog, causing it to fall back on its haunches for a moment before starting its bark again. The man leaned over the fence and as the dog sprang forward to greet him with licks and whines, jumping up at him, he casually lifted his elbow. The dog made contact and seemed to hang from the man's arm, its sandy front legs folded neatly as it swung back and forth. Then there was a sound like a crack and it dropped out of sight into the snow. The second man pushed a pistol back into his belt and walked on as if nothing had occurred. Krystyna shoved her knuckles into her mouth and closed her eyes. Her heartbeat surged in her ears. When it subsided she heard the first man shouting after his friend, words that sounded like fingers clawing against the deep substance of the night.

She stumbled back to the horse and put her face against her neck, sobbing freely. What kind of cruelty would make a man shoot a dog for no reason? Her ears were still ringing with the sound of the crack. She saw once more the dog's soft collapse. At least the end had been quick. It had not suffered. It had died in surprise. Her breathing slowed. She wiped her eyes and blew her nose. She would wait for a few minutes and then go in as quickly as she could to find Benedykt. But she knew by now that the chances of coming across him were remote. Something had clearly happened to him.

She left the mare and crept forward, pausing every now and then to hide behind a tree. The village was silent. Moonlight shone on the snow-covered roofs. Now she saw that there was no smoke from the chimneys. The paths leading up to the doors had not been swept. She came to the last house in the row. The shutters were closed, but she could see a chink of light through a crack in the wood, and there was a thin stream of smoke coming from the chimney. She took a deep breath and knocked. She thought she heard a stirring inside, but nobody came. She tried again. Her teeth chattered as she waited, thudding her arms around her body to keep warm, but still no one came. She knocked again and thought she heard a low voice, and something scrape inside, as if a chair was being pushed back. Still nothing. She was about to give up and try the next house when she heard the sound of coughing and shuffling steps.

'I'm Polish and I need your help. I've lost a boy, about nine years old, wearing a Russian coat. He came here earlier looking for food. I need to find him.' Her words tumbled out, stuck together in her haste. She paused to take a breath. 'He's my brother.'

The man looked at her through filmy grey eyes. 'Polish,' he said. He tottered forward and held on to the door and she caught the damp sourness of his old man's scent. He was wearing a stretched pullover and clinging to the wool

fibres were half a dozen tiny brown wrens. 'They are kill-
ing us. There will be no more Poles.' He looked straight at
her. The wrens clung tighter and made a cheeping noise
like animated dried leaves. 'You have come to the wrong
place.' He made as if to close the door.

'Please. Do you have any food?'

The man hesitated. The wrens scurried up to his neck
and nested on his shoulder. He stepped back from the
door and she took that as an invitation to enter. The
hallway led off to a small room which was heated by a
stove next to which the old man had been evidently
sleeping in a chair with stuffing coming out of the seat
and arms. The old man saw her looking; his eyes were
dismissive, as if the chalet no longer had anything to do
with him.

He went off on his felt slippers and returned with some
bread, an onion and three potatoes. She understood that
this was all the food he had left.

'Have you got something to carry it with?'

She shook her head. She had forgotten to bring the
duffel bag. Muttering, he collected a mushroom basket and
piled the provisions into it. The wrens watched her, eyes as
bright as pins. He saw her looking at them.

'I found the nest abandoned,' he said.

She nodded and then picked up the full basket. 'Thank
you for the food.'

'You have to get out of here now,' he said. The wrens
scuttled on his chest. 'This morning the Germans killed
five men in the village square. They shoved us out with
their dogs and made us watch the executions. Women and
children had to look. One of the children who had been
caught stealing chickens was thrown in for good measure.

They wanted to warn us not to resist.' He stared at her. 'You must get out.'

She moved a few paces backwards. Her mouth was dry. She thought of the dog and the casual way it had been shot for barking. 'Why are you still here?'

'I'm too old to waste a bullet on.' He glanced around the chalet. 'If there's anything else you want, take it.' He looked at his birds nesting together near his heart. 'Only leave me my little ones.'

By the fireplace she spotted a shovel. She asked the old man if she could have it.

'Take anything you want.' He took down a tobacco tin from the fireplace and pressed it into her hands. 'Open it.'

She prised off the lid and saw that the tin was stuffed with złoty notes. Underneath the notes were two boxes of matches wrapped in oilskin. 'All the borders are closed,' the old man said. 'Your only hope is to stay in the forest. Or find a way south into the General Government. It is the only place left. Everywhere else is Germany or Russia.' He took a flattish log and pushed it on to the fire. The wrens jittered against him. She thanked him, but he shrugged away her words and shuffled to the door with her. He opened it a crack and without looking back she slipped out into the cold night. She began immediately to search for Benedykt.

It did not take her long to find him. He was lying in the village square with a dark hole, the size of a finger, under his right shoulder blade. He had been shot in the back. Nearby five young men lay crumpled in the flattened snow that was sprayed with blood and pellets of brain; their arms were flung out across each other, fingers clutching at life like the claws of the old man's wrens, and their eyes were open, reflecting the stars. Benedkyt had his mouth open.

His teeth still shone and he seemed about to speak or cry. Pushing down an urge to flee, she disentangled the dead arms and legs, already beginning to freeze, and reached for Benedkyt. His coat was missing. As she pulled at his arms she saw that he had packed newspaper inside his thin shirt. She got him clear of the dead and lifted him on to her shoulder. With her knees buckling in fear she carried him down the lane, passing the garden where the German Shepherd lay like a dark mound of sand, and into the forest where the mare stepped forward from the darkness and stood while Krystyna arranged the limp white body across her back.

Using the old man's fire shovel she buried Benedykt in snow under the oak tree, first twisting off the boots from his small frozen feet. Inside the right boot she found a photograph of a red-bearded man with a broad chest. He looked joyful and vigorous. She put the photograph back inside the boot and then laced both boots together. The newspaper packet showed through his shirt and closing her eyes against the icy feel of his skin she reached in and drew it out. A few flakes of dirty snow drifted out. The mare took a couple of steps forward and dropped her nose to the ground. Krystyna reached into the packet and gasped as her fingers closed on a soft grainy mound. Hot tears spilled down her face as she took a handful of oats and spread it on to the ground. The mare sucked up the feed, licking and chewing her appreciation. She sprinkled another palmful into the snow and then to the sound of the mare's contented munching, she took up the shovel again and began to cover her body with snow.

She carved out a cross and the letter B in the snow mound. Then she said a prayer. The mare stood at her shoulder, her muzzle hairs crumbed with a few flecks of oat dust. Krystyna lifted her head. A shooting star streaked across the sky in a diamond flash. The mare breathed quietly, content now that she had been fed. Her eyes had recovered some of their lustre. Up ahead sparkling in the blackness Krystyna saw the clear outline of Pegasus. Without thinking of what she was doing, she reached up and unfastened Gazela's bridle. She laid her hand on the mare's neck and closed her eyes. She could hear sleigh bells, smell cigar smoke, feel a warm pulse on the top of her head. She held the scene for a few moments and then pushed it away with all her force. 'You're free.' There was a sound of snow squeaking under hooves and the swish of a long tail against a tree. When she opened her eyes again the mare had gone.

10

Kraków, present day

It's hot on the train. They sit in opposing seats in the airless carriage waiting for the other passengers to board. They are a little early. Dominic insisted on leaving plenty of time to reach the central station, his anxiety betraying a lack of trust in the services of other countries. He glances out of the window and taps the heel of his foot rapidly against the floor. His belly pokes out from the tight buttons of his pink linen shirt. She can smell his sweat. He catches her glance and his face darkens. 'Oh, come on,' he says, as if she is responsible for the perceived slowness of the train.

'We're just about to leave,' she says, settling into her usual placatory routine.

Dominic huffs and blows towards the carriage ceiling. He shifts his feet, sweaty inside his heavy sandals, giving off a ripe smell. She rises and nudges down the window. He jabs an aggrieved look at her. Her face is hot when she sits down again. She reaches into her shoulder bag and fishes out a few pages of Konrad's film treatment. She fans her face.

'What's that you've brought?' Dominic leans forward, his expression alert.

'Just some reading for work.' She pulls the pages to her chest. Dominic frowns. He crosses one foot over his knee. A wave of nausea grips her as his odour fills the carriage, thick, warm and insistent. He knows that she has just told him a lie, a small one admittedly, but a lie all the same.

'You said you had come here to forget about work. You said the whole point of this trip was to find out more about the missing part of your family history.' His tone is petulant.

'That's true. I did. You're right.' Quickly she slips the pages back into the envelope and shoves it into her bag. Maybe she will get a chance to read them later, when he is not feeling so needy or wounded. 'I'm sorry.'

He glances across at her, the frown of irritation deepening across his forehead. He tries to smooth it over with a smile. 'What's wrong with you?' His tone is gentle.

A rush of tears threatens to overwhelm her. She glances out of her side of the window where a family of three are hurrying to catch the train before the guard slams the doors. 'I'm just tired.' She rests her head against the glass. She hears him sigh, but he says nothing. The glass window jumps, jolting her, as a few moments later the doors crunch shut. The train rocks and then lurches forward. Somewhere in the pit of her stomach she feels a low, heavy pull.

The late family elbow their way into the carriage, red-faced, dishevelled, rucksacks awry, apologizing as they look for seats together. A neat, elderly man soberly dressed in a three-piece suit stands to allow them room and then disappears further down the train, presumably in search of quiet. The family, two parents and a child of about nine, fluster with bags and books and snacks as they settle in their seats, talking in tense whispers through which she hears the flat tones of London. The little boy, who has strawberry-blond hair, patiently and wordlessly holds out a pair of skinny white arms for his mother to spread with suncream. When she's finished he doesn't thank her, but scrunches up in a corner with a book entitled: *Auschwitz: A Factual History*.

Dominic grumps around in his leather satchel – why does she find this endearing still, this scuffed relic from their life together? – and is soon safely engrossed in a Tom Clancy thriller. She reaches for a few pages from the package in her bag and begins to read. The train settles into a rhythmic hum. Other passengers are absorbed in magazines and subdued electronic music through earphones, which sounds like water chinking down a long metal well. After a while Dominic gives up on his book and sleeps with his hands protectively over his belly, which rises in a pregnant mound. She continues to turn the pages of the film treatment, wondering what it means to live courageously. Perhaps a life of courage is impossible without hardship, without something to pit yourself against. In ordinary living, by which she means the kind of living that she has settled for, so much has been taken care of; so much has been intricately constructed. To dismantle all this for the sake of courage seems foolish, cowardly even. It could be that she is simply tired. She recalls how during her teens and twenties she had wanted a life of courage, she had wanted to push frontiers, follow her Victorian heroines. It was part of the attraction of astronomy: she relished the company of the redoubtable women she read about: women with sensible tweed skirts, stout shoes and razor-sharp minds. In her first year at Cambridge she had been inspired by the tinkling wit and mirror-clear mind of a visiting professor of philosophy: a tiny woman in her seventies, dressed in a navy-blue suit, holding the lectern with fingers as delicate as a wren's claws, her face vivid, on fire with ideas. At the cocktail party afterwards Catherine could not take her eyes from the professor who stood near a French window, her narrow shoulders erect in the sunlight. She seemed to glow with possibility. That was the kind of woman she wanted to become.

Dominic's snoring breath fills the carriage, so familiar, so much part of Catherine's own bodily rhythms it is like listening to a recording of their intimate life together. There was grace in him once, too. She wouldn't have given herself to him so readily otherwise. There was that quality of brilliance about him, an expansiveness that she could not have found on her own.

Their closeness was immediate; she slept with him the first night after their walk to the Bridge of Sighs. Before that at dinner she remembers that they ate steak and drank red wine and he talked indiscreetly about various Cambridge professors, finding fault with all of them, presenting them as damaged, dysfunctional and, in the case of a certain colleague whom she subsequently came to call a friend, deranged. Instead of taking Dominic's drink-fuelled delight in condemnation as a warning that she should leave well alone, that one day she might be among the drunkenly damned, she'd felt privileged to be taken into his confidence. Dominic's lack of inhibition was refreshing, and, she had to admit it, wicked fun. He'd charmed her into bed and the next morning when they woke to the sound of pigeons ruffling romantically on the roof of his Georgian flat, a dusty sanctuary with floorboards that sloped and parped when you stepped on them in the middle of the night, he spoke of marrying her, but in a way that she could not take seriously at the time and thought of as a prelude. It worked, nonetheless. For the first five years of living together in their semi, she waited, daily, for him to ask her properly. But he never did. Marriage was the one subject Dominic had no opinion about.

Halfway through their first decade, Dominic began to lean more heavily on drink, and then, by the second half, he fully surrendered. She remembers the night well: a half-dozen bottles of wine shared with friends who departed after brandy, a half-bottle of whisky, then a drive to the twenty-four-hour supermarket for champagne and cake – he bought, by mistake, a birthday cake, and on his return lit the complimentary candles to cover his embarrassment. By this time they were alone. He took her into his heavy arms, soaking her with his sweaty exuberance, laughing, seeking her mouth, greedy, shaking, jabbering, out of control, and then she knew: he had found another. The long years of alcoholic seduction were complete. He had found matrimony.

Her friends told her to drag Dominic to AA. But he was not to be dragged. He remained stubbornly in situ in the semi, immovable as a stone god. As a way of coping she reached into her scientific understanding, her rationality. She read papers. She attended lectures. But she soon came to realize that this was an inadequate and utterly inappropriate response to the derailment she felt. In spite of her intellect, she discovered that she did not have resources that were deep enough. Her reserves had been called on time and time again and there was nothing left. She recalls the winter she was forced to take time off due to stress. Then she slunk into their spare room for a fortnight with a paper she was writing for the *New Scientist* on stellar infants 500,000 years old. After the paper was emailed to the editor she spent the next fortnight in Devon with her mother's Irish friend Doreen huddled by her Aga in a blanket, mourning a constellation of other infants that some instinctive part of her knew would remain unborn.

The train grinds to a halt, jerking Dominic awake. His first instinct is to look for her and his eyes when they find her appear startled, as if all her previous thoughts are written across her face. She wonders why it has become such a radical act for her to say what she thinks and feels. Maybe she lacks moral courage. Maybe it is history or convention that prevents her from saying quite simply: enough is enough. Maybe it is some deep-buried guilt. Maybe that is why she has hurriedly pushed the package deep into the recesses of her bag.

The train leaps forward again. Dominic yawns and pulls out a copy of the *Sunday Telegraph* from his satchel and makes a show of unfolding it and spreading its various components around on the seat. She glances over at the news section, which is dominated by the latest Downing Street turmoil about MPs' expenses claims, the European elections, Afghanistan. The train picks up speed. She presses her face to the window and lets her eyes slide over the medieval buildings, the honey-coloured stone radiant in the light. They leave the city and push through the suburbs, passing small red-tiled, sloping-roofed houses with washing on lines and neat rectangular fenced gardens, blazing with fire-coloured flowers. A field of horses takes off at the sight of the train, led by a grey and a chestnut galloping diagonally to the high point of a meadow, manes and tails flipping in the wind. At the top of the rise she watches the horses turn in unison and stare down the retreating enemy.

The boy opposite her reads his book of facts. His lips move with the words, and every now and then he dips his hand into a clear bag of Haribo. The sweets smell chemical and loud; they also make her feel hungry. She hadn't been able to eat breakfast at the hotel. On the other hand, Dominic had tucked into bacon and eggs and rounds of toast and jam, urging her to eat because it would be a 'difficult' day. She'd felt bullied by him; her sullen response to drink coffee and leave her bowl empty and plate untouched. Now with her stomach growling, embarrassing her in the silent stickiness of the carriage, she wonders whether she ought to go and find a restaurant car where she can have a quiet sandwich on her own. The boy opposite looks up at her sharply, as if she had just asked him a question. He has a pale, freckled face, with narrow eyes, framed by blue-rimmed glasses.

'I most want to see the death wall,' he tells her. His mother, a rounded woman in stretchy denim leggings and floral smock, smiles indulgently. His father, wearing combats and a creased black T-shirt, engrossed in listening to music, pays no attention. 'It's where they executed prisoners with a bullet in the back of the head,' the boy adds. 'They have punishment rooms, too, and ovens where they cremated all the bodies that you can still see.'

'You read about this in your book?' Catherine does not want to engage with him, but no one else in the carriage seems interested in taking responsibility.

'He loves reading,' his mother says proudly. 'We bought him as many books as we could about it.' Her expression falters a little and her next words sound uncertain. 'It's educational, isn't it?'

'They have all these exhibits.' The boy turns to the

relevant page in his book and reads out a list: 'More than eighty thousand shoes, three thousand eight hundred suitcases, forty thousand pots and pans, forty kilos of eyeglasses.' He glances up, puzzled, and asks his mother, 'What's eyeglasses?'

The father turns down the volume on his music for a second and yanks himself upright. 'Glasses, duh.' He reaches over and playfully cuffs the side of his son's head. 'Like you're wearing, duh.' Parental duties discharged, he slumps back into stereo.

The boy fingers his blue glasses, which have a little motif of tropical fish swimming at the sides. He gives his father a hostile look before returning to his grim list. 'Eight thousand letters and six thousand works of art.' He gulps down some air. 'That's an awful lot.' Now he appears innocent and slightly bewildered. He reaches into the bag next to him and pulls out a fistful of gummy sweets, lime and yellow and electric blue mirroring the luminous fish at his temples, and stuffs them into his mouth. He chews and stares out of the window.

Dominic stirs and yawns.

'I think I'll go and get some coffee,' she says. Dominic throws her a disgruntled look. 'Do you want me to bring one back for you?'

He grunts. 'Don't you think it's pushing it a bit expecting to find a decent restaurant car on a Polish train?'

The couple in the carriage laugh and even the little boy joins in. As Catherine gets up she feels the atmosphere settle into something familiar: an exasperated, we'll just have to grin and bear it tension that she recognizes from situations when certain English strangers meet and assume a common enemy.

'Dominic. It is the twenty-first century.' She shoves her way past his sandals, ignoring his aghast look.

'Really,' he calls after her, his voice heavy with irony. 'I hadn't noticed.' The other passengers laugh again. Now she can see in the reflection of the window Dominic leaning towards the boy, enquiring about his book. Feeling a sick lurch of a minor betrayal, she makes her way down the train, holding on to the sticky chrome door handles for support. At one point the train hurls itself around a corner and she falls against a window, jabbing her cheekbone on the glass. By the time she returns to the compartment with two coffees and a packet of biscuits for her queasy stomach, the hot drinks spilling on to a cardboard tray, soaking the little paper sugar tubes, she feels dishevelled, pushed and more perturbed than she ought to be.

Dominic grimaces as she hands him the soggy coffee carton. He takes a slurp and swears as he scalds his lips. He glares at her. 'What happened to your face?'

She touches her cheekbone. The bruise feels hot under her hand. 'I lost my balance.'

He shrugs, for some reason satisfied, and takes solace in his newspaper, folding himself into it as if he is the one who has just been injured and not she. Catherine sits down. Her cheek throbs. Openly she pulls the film treatment from her bag, wondering whether he really did believe her lie about reading for work. It would be too easy to lie to him, she realizes, because the truth is too shattering. He will not be able to comprehend what she has to tell him. Maybe, she thinks, a lie might even be the kindest thing.

They arrive at Oświęcim Station. The boy gets up first, spilling sweets on the floor, and as they leave, she treads on one, feeling it squirm underfoot. She hopes her sandals will be comfortable enough for a day on her feet. Dominic is red-faced as they step down from the train on to the platform. A hot breeze blows around her ankles. The boy stands on the platform between his parents, who seem bewildered. He turns and waves, his face chalk-white, but animated and much less afraid than his parents. They hover anxiously, fiddling with their rucksacks, pulling them higher up their backs.

'Have a great day,' the father calls out, wires from his headphones dangling round his neck, and then checks himself. 'We might see you later,' he adds in a lower, more sober voice.

Dominic nods and walks in the direction of the exit. Catherine wonders how he knows where to go, but then she sees that all the signs are in English as well as Polish.

Outside the station the heat slaps her face. She reaches into her bag for a hair tie and scrunches up her hair into a tight knot and pulls it back over her ears. Dominic observes her, his eyes hard with irritation.

'We need to take a bus now.' He reads from the guide-book. 'Or it's a twenty-minute walk.'

'Let's walk.' She knows that he will disagree, but she feels the need to announce her preference before it is dismissed. It feels important that he should not disregard her today.

He closes his eyes briefly and runs his hand across his heavy forehead. His pink shirt is dark with sweat. 'No, let's not. I'm too hot to do anything.'

She wonders for a moment whether she dares to walk away from him. He sees the hesitation in her face and it worries him. He throws her a rumpled smile. 'I'm just not fit enough. Sorry.'

On the bus they sit with their thighs pressed against each

other, both staring straight ahead, silent, absorbed in their own thoughts. Her bruised cheek aches. She wonders what mental preparations Dominic might be making, if any at all. All around them the other passengers are talking in quiet voices. Music from headphones is subdued and there is a palpable fear holding people still and tight. The family from the train are at the front. The boy refuses to sit back in his seat. He hunches forward with his hands clasped around his knees, white feet lifted clear of the dusty floor. The bus has double glass windows. Trapped inside the layers is a fly and she watches it hop up and down fizzing in irritation. The bus lurches to a halt and she is appalled to find that she does not want to leave her seat. Dominic stands up immediately and because she is still seated is forced to stand bent with the back of his thighs pressing into the seat as the other passengers get off. His face is livid as he turns on her. 'What are you waiting for? Come on.'

They file towards the entrance which has an artificial quality, like a film set. The boy from the train reaches the gate first and reads the inscription out loud. '*Arbeit Macht Frei.*' His father takes his arm and pulls him away. She watches them surge forward into the crowds. Every now and then she can hear the boy's voice cut through the silence with a string of bright questions.

'I've had enough of that precocious little bastard,' Dominic mutters as they step under the gate. So intent is he on avoiding the family of three that he collides with and almost knocks over a pair of painfully thin teenagers with rucksacks, a boy and a girl with the angel hair of Scandinavia, who hold hands as they walk through.

'Sorry.' Dominic offers an apology that is accepted with serene smiles. Next under the infamous arch is an elderly couple, in cropped trousers and strong walking shoes, faces protected from the sun by white cotton hats, who quote the inscription to each other in dogged American accents. Catherine's stomach jolts. She becomes aware that Dominic has gone on without her. Now she notices him a few paces on the other side. He lifts his camera from his satchel. 'No.' She tries to cover her face with her hands, but it is too late. He scowls as he puts the Canon around his neck.

'I don't think you should take photos.' Her voice is shaking

He throws her a flat smile. 'Why on earth not?'

She is taken aback by his vehemence. 'It doesn't seem appropriate.' She wants to add that she thinks it is disrespectful, but does not want to antagonize him further. The small rage that she had felt brewing on the train is now threatening to boil over.

He looks at her and the light in his eye is hard and bitter. 'This' – he points to the camera and then the gateway, his mouth curled into a sneer – 'is the whole point of being here.' His voice trembles with emotion and she feels a pulse of fear. She has never seen him so choked with outrage. 'You have no idea.'

'Perhaps I'm being over-sensitive,' she tries, noticing that other people are stopping to take photographs.

He shoves the lens cap on the camera. 'Perhaps,' he snaps, 'I shouldn't let your naivety ruin my day.'

The American couple glance at them. Now that his anger has surfaced she knows from experience that he needs time to let it find its own level. 'Please, Dominic, let's drop it,' she says, keeping her voice neutral, her heart thumping. 'Let's just go in.'

He exhales and pulls a white linen handkerchief out of

his trouser pocket and mops his beetroot-coloured face. He compresses his lips and then strides on towards the queue waiting for the cinema. Stunned, she watches his bulky figure push through the polite crowd.

The cinema is hot and crowded and smells of suncream and scented fabric conditioner, eye-wateringly sanitized. Catherine cannot help but compare the clean clothes billowing with overfed health surrounding her with the images of striped camp uniform, the filthy stick limbs, the stripped desperation flickering in black and white on the screen before her. The crowd watches dutifully. There is a sensation of being in church. Next to her is the old man who gave up his seat to the family on the train. He stands erect in his suit, his eyes weeping quiet tears. As the film ends, he bows his head. The crowd begins to disperse. A few people yawn and cover their mouths with their hands.

Dominic sidles over, takes her arm and whispers, 'Sorry I was tetchy earlier.' He deposits a kiss on her neck below her ear and she tries not to flinch. She tries to smile and forgive in return; it was something minor, a misunderstanding, but her respect for him is fading, and it frightens her, to feel how quickly her contempt is building, like very thin layers of ice.

They leave the darkness, and come out into the light blinking, teary and dazzled. The camp's surrounds now seem to her too bright: birds are singing and there are even butterflies flitting around the strimmed grass verges where gardeners are at work pulling weeds. There's a smell of cut grass on the hot breeze and the sweet note of someone's everyday perfume. Some children are walking around eating.

Dominic drapes a damp arm over her shoulder. He

looks into her face and brings his coarse thumb up to her cheekbone, as if checking a child for playground damage. 'How is it?'

His concern is worse than his anger. She shrugs him off. 'It's fine.' His question seems grotesque.

Dominic removes his arm and they walk separately along a path leading to a barrack, and again she has the feeling of being on some sort of stage. They hover in front of the wooden building. 'Are you all right about this? Shall we go in?' he asks, failing to disguise the hint of impatience in his voice.

She doesn't respond. She is looking at the dark entrance and feeling utterly numb. He grunts and moves on past her, bumping her with his shoulder, deliberately she thinks. The small flare of irritation unfreezes her and she follows him inside.

The barrack is packed with subdued tourists. Sandals and trainers scrape on invisible grit as they shuffle past grim tiered bunks, which remind her of farmyard stalls. After the blazing heat outside, the air feels damp and chill. People are coughing. Someone sneezes. There is a rustle of bags and pull of zips as people reach for fleeces. Catherine feels her head swim as a terrible tiredness sweeps through her, but naturally there is nowhere to sit down or rest. She and Dominic have separated. Every now and then she catches sight of his vigorous grey head, like a senior judge, seated above an obsequious crowd. His shirt is a pink egg and moves in that effortful way of his, as if he were pushing his body uphill from behind. His head whips round as he locates her.

Dominic comes over and brushes against her, bumping her body, needing to touch her, and then he moves off again to look at something else. She remembers the walk in the garden with Konrad. Its intimacy now seems stolen from another life. She wishes now that she had answered the phone the second time. The space around her squeezes shut. Her chest is tight. She staggers on through another airless cell and with each step feels her hope begin to crash.

Dominic stands looking at a collection of suitcases, all in various shades of brown, like different gradations of soil: some are scuffed and scratched, others stiff, almost new-looking with neat handles and gleaming brass corners. Some of them are marked with initials or names. She stands next to him. She can feel the swampy warmth of his body, the heave of his breath. He touches her arm. 'My God,' he says. 'I don't know how much more of this I can take.'

She now feels the weight of his disappointment in his own lack of courage, which, she realizes, has always manifested itself as a kind of grief. The part of her that is still connected to him feels a pulse of compassion; she recognizes that he is at the beginning of his mourning for her. She decides that she will be kind; her break with him will be clean. It will be quick. It will free them both.

She moves on past the terrible rubble of history, impatient now to return and begin the conversation they must have. At the same time it appals her that she should be so self-absorbed in such a place. Here deprivation occurred beyond anything she or Dominic could imagine, here human suffering reached its peak, here life as she and ordinary people know it was made void; here people were obliterated, stripped of identity, broken. Here people were refused humanity.

She tries to slow down and take in the mounds of shoes, the spectacles, clothing and human hair, but the volume of despair begins to press in on her. Swiftly she passes into the next area, aware that she has left Dominic behind. Now she pauses at the displays of art, drawn by the collection of letters, some ornamented with drawings: a pot of red tulips on a windowsill, in the background a view of snowy hills under a pointillist Milky Way. Pink and blue curtains, suggesting a little girl's bedroom. The image, more than anything she has seen so far, squeezes at her heart. She moves on to the next drawing: a haunting etching of a concert given by a skeletal pianist, his head a skull as he plays in a cell with bare floorboards, shadow fingers creeping up on him like some ghastly, monstrous hand. The only light in the drawing is the clear page of music. The next drawing is of two figures lying on a bunk titled: *Death of Hunger. Small feather, black ink 53 x 40 cm.* A plate carved in wood captures her attention next, its rose relief delicate and touching, trefoil leaves immaculate as pastry leaves on an apple pie. And then, a final drawing: *Flowers in the Snow. Small feather, Indian ink. Cardboard.* It shows two children, a boy and a girl, no more than two years old, slumped dead in the snowy cold. She stands transfixed before it. So absorbed is she by the drawing that she does not hear Dominic come up behind her. She jumps at the touch of his lips on her neck. 'Had enough?' he asks. His face is quiet and still, all anger spent. He does not notice that she is crying.

After lunch in a café some distance away from the camp they go for a walk. Down a quiet wooded lane they find a small lake set in a copse of swaying birch and elm, an emerald jewel, and for a moment they are both stunned by the ephemeral beauty of the place, as if it is an illusion that will soon be whipped away from them and replaced by something else, something terrible, brutal and crude. They sit down by the water's edge and wordlessly remove their sandals. When Catherine immerses her white foot she is shocked to find the water icy cold and gasps out loud. Dominic rolls his trousers up to his knees and wades into deeper water. He holds his trousers by the corners and looks at her with the first warmth she has seen since he arrived. 'I love this.'

She nods encouragement, hoping it will quiet the babble in her mind. They have never been the kind of couple who talk animatedly about their personal discoveries or epiphanies after visits to museums or galleries and so his recovery, if that is the right word, is unsurprising, but it still disturbs her to see him so ready to move on to the next part of the day. Without, it seems, acknowledgement of what happened to millions who died because they happened to be born Jewish. He had once speculated that his own family may have been Jewish, but he never pursued it. The past held no interest for him, perhaps, she now understands, because even the present is too much for him.

'I love it because it makes me feel eight years old again.' He lifts a foot and scoops water in a glistening arc to splash her. She obliges with an outraged shriek and pats at her spattered clothes. The river water smells of old caves. A pair of dragonflies, glamorous in slim-fitting jackets of malachite green and jet, glide across the water like a pair of tango dancers, joined in mid-mate. Dominic notes them fondly as if he had conjured them especially to make his point about rivers, which is, he tells her gleefully, that they are wedded to movement.

Wedded. She lets the word hang in the thick air un-remarked for a moment. He watches her, anticipating a response. This is the moment, she realizes. She sees Dominic push his hair out of his eyes with both hands, like a boy coming up after a long underwater swim, and then lightly get down on one knee. The green water swirls up around him soaking his trousers to the waist. 'Catherine . . .' His eyes are imploring. At the spectacle which seems to her both proposal and baptism she brings her hands up to her mouth in horror, and simultaneously sees his expression give way to alarm, pulling him upright again. A pair of ducks flashes past him with warning cackles. Unmoved, he stands in the water with his head down, staring at his own shattered reflection.

She retreats to the bank and pulls on her sandals. Her heart is beating so hard it feels it could injure itself on her ribs. Dominic remains in the water. She thinks he may be crying. She averts her eyes. If she looks at him, he will sense her betrayal, and she does not want to do this to him, not here, not now. Not yet.

She moves from the water's edge. Further along the bank is a bell-shaped tree and she is suddenly drawn to it, compelled to discover what is hidden beneath its skirts which hang ankle-length to the grass, fractionally longer than the other trees grouped with it in a dense hedge of green. It is slightly lopsided at its crown, fuller on the left side, its branches swaying. Some of the tips on the leaves have a yellow tinge of autumn, always the time of year when she feels most alive. She thinks of the photograph that had attracted Konrad. Perhaps if she hadn't been photographed by Dominic on that warm autumn day none of this would have happened. It might not have been this way.

Underneath the tree there is a chapel quiet. She stands

upright and drinks it in, feels her breathing slow; her mind still wanders, though, images and thoughts tugging her attention this way and that, like a scuttle of leaves along a pavement chasing each other. She gazes up. There never is enough time for proper noticing, not like this, not with Dominic, and that is what she most yearns for: time to see, time to observe, time to feel. She stretches her hand out to the tree. Its body feels warm and is a soft seal grey, growing steadily lighter as it flows upward, dividing into two arms just above her head. She notices the bark has age spots, discolorations, freckles, bruises and scars just like human skin. She imagines staying with the tree, bedding down under its dark bell to wait for the stars and then in the morning waking under its green, avid growth. She would like to come here again. But not like this.

'We've missed the last bus.' Dominic glances up from the guidebook open in the crook of his knees as she returns to the lake. 'We'll have to spend the night.' He catches the shock on her face. 'What's the matter? You look like you've seen a ghost.'

'Surely we can get a taxi back?' Her voice wobbles with fear.

He snaps the book shut and regards her through tight lips. His shoulders come up as he exhales his indignation. 'Oh, Catherine.'

The taxi driver overcharges them and Dominic argues with him, his body pressed against the side of the vehicle as if the driver were trying to make a break for it without paying. She hovers on the narrow kerb outside the hotel, unsure of how to deal with this, embarrassed at the way Dominic is raising his voice. The driver, a short Polish man in his fifties with a tight-skinned face and pointy razor-sharp teeth, spits his insistence in response to Dominic's huffy demands that he should take the złoty notes, limp, exhausted prayer flags, flapped in his face. She reads disbelief in the driver's eyes, and then resignation and then in a final flash a contemptuous pride as he yanks the car forward, causing Dominic to fall back on to the kerb. He picks himself up and whacks the back of his trousers, his top lip curled cartoonishly. 'Bastard.' He shoves the crumpled money into his pocket and throws another baleful glare in the direction of the retreating car. 'Cunt.'

'But you didn't have to pay him anything. That taxi ride cost you nothing.' The words fly out, almost stinging her. She is aghast at her lack of caution. This argument is for, what it is always for: the need for an antagonist. Her breath tightens; her chest feels made of hard wood. Now it will start.

He storms in to the hotel. His trousers are still wet and caked in dirt. It looks as if he has soiled himself. She knows that he cannot resist the claw of drink and leaves him slumped in his seat in the bar. Upstairs in the room she takes a hot shower. She recalls the morning. She stood here, in this exact spot, this square of plastic, but she was a different woman then. Now she feels . . . she doesn't know what she feels, there isn't a name for this feeling or this combination of feelings, but if she were to try to express it she would say that she is experiencing an extreme form of dread. It occurs to her that Dominic may even try to kill her.

She steps out of the shower and wraps herself in a towelling robe. She is shivering. She paces up and down and tries to compose her thoughts. She is being melodramatic. He may have drunk out his rage; it may not be as bad as she thinks. She goes to the minibar and drinks in quick succession, for courage, two little bottles of brandy.

He comes up two hours later. His breath is heavy, laboured, his body lathered in sweat as if he has been shifting furniture. The quick, hard light in his eyes frightens her. He brings his hand up as she opens the door to him and she flinches. He has never hit her and she wonders why she believes he is going to start now. His clammy fingers reach for her cheek and squeeze it. 'Are you feeling any better?' he asks and then falls against her chest. She pushes him upright.

'Come on, Dominic.'

'What do you mean, come on? I'm just trying to get in the fucking room. Just give me a bit of space, fat bastard that I am.' He laughs. Spittle flies into her face. 'Sorry,' he says, leering at her. 'Sorry for being such a bastard. No, sorry for being such a drunk fucking bastard who can't control himself.'

'Come on.'

'Why do you keep saying the same thing? *Come on, come on.*' His eyes glitter as he mimics her voice. 'Why are you so boring?' He parrots her laugh.

'I don't know, Dominic.' Hatred flares in her stomach. She is shocked to find herself wishing for a knife, a sharp knife. Maybe it is I who will kill him, she thinks.

'You know what, you do *know.*' He shoves her aside and almost falls into the room. 'You know what's going on, whereas I, I don't have a fucking clue.' He hovers by the mirror and looks at his huge blooming face. 'What an ugly bastard I am. What an old, used-up, ruined waste of time. I had it once,' he mocks himself. 'I was someone, once.'

'Dominic, please, don't do this.'

'Don't order me about. I'm sick of you ordering me about,' he continues, staring mournfully in the mirror. 'I don't care about you any more. I've had enough of this, you make me sick.' His shoulders slump as he leans forward and almost touches the glass with his lips. She realizes that it is himself he is addressing, not her.

She listens to him admonish himself and feels despair wash over her. She knows that whatever she says he will not hear; there is only the mad music in his head. She goes into the bathroom and slides the door closed. From the bedroom she can hear the sound of agonized sobs. She puts her hands over her ears and rocks herself back and forth.

She wonders as she walks in the Planty an hour or so later to calm her mind what it means to say that you are close to someone. When someone strips themselves bare, when they let you see what terrifies them – is that intimacy? Overhead, the trees shiver with birds in anxious, twittering preparations for sleep. In the sky she notes the semicircle of Corona Borealis and within it a star of sixth magnitude that shines steadily for months, sometimes years on end, but then disappears from view, as if it has dropped from the sky. Exactly why this happens has puzzled astronomers for years. All that she knows is that the star R CrB throws out a shawl of material when it fades that hides it from view. It does not really disappear. Over time the shawl dissolves and the star is revealed in its full brightness again.

The night air feels cool on her arms. She is glad not to have a cardigan or jacket with her, to be without encumbrance. She walks down the darkening avenues. There is no one around. She continues walking until she comes to the statue of Copernicus where she stands for a moment, pressing her head to the bronze, which still holds the day's warmth.

After ten minutes she arrives on Ulica Kopernika. Simply reading the street sign causes her stomach to roll over and her teeth to chatter. The street is deserted. She shivers and rubs her hands down her arms. No open cafés where she could order a hot coffee or brace herself for what she is about to do. She slows her pace and looks up at the apartments where curtains ripple and lights shine through open balcony doors. She hears voices and the sound of televisions. The air smells of rotting garbage and drains. The pavements are so narrow, she has to step into the road to avoid the parked cars that have been driven up over the kerbs and are packed close together. One rusted estate car has a cardboard coffin lying in the back, battered and unrealistic, like a stagey home-made prop. An old man out walking a dog lets his pet cock its leg against the hubcap in what seems like a nightly ritual. He glances at her and mutters some words in Polish that she does not understand.

She shudders and turns to go back to the hotel. She has already decided that she will ask the concierge for another room. The thought makes her hesitate. If she is not going to share a room with him, then she need not immediately return. She can keep going.

She walks briskly down the street, looking at the apartments, thinking that she will know by some instinct which one is his, but they flit past her in a blur. Then just near the end of the row, she finds what she is looking for. He doesn't notice her at first. He leans on the railing of a peeling wrought-iron balcony, right up in the corner, with his back stretched, one hand under his chin. His other hand dangles over the railing and inside his fingers she catches the glow of a cigarette. Her throat closes over as she watches him take a last smoke and then flick the still burning end down to the street where it lands a few paces to her left. She watches it burn itself out and then calls up to him.

Inside the apartment the smell of fresh coffee makes her head swim. He puts the tips of his fingers on her shoulders and looks at her, his face troubled as he notices the pulsing bruise on her cheek. 'I'm so glad you've come.' Then he goes to the kitchen where he pours her coffee into a white mug. He presses it into her hands and guides her to a sofa strewn with old velvet cushions. His socks lie on one of the cushions and he reaches over her and delicately peels them off and puts them on the floor. The wall behind the sofa is fitted with shelves lined with old books. She peers at the spines glowing in the lamplight in shades of sienna, russet and sand. 'Left over from the war,' Konrad tells her.

Cradling her coffee, she takes a closer look. Emily Brontë, Jane Austen, Charles Dickens, George Eliot. The familiar names surprise her. She looks up at him. 'I thought your aunt taught history. These are English novels.'

'Her history books are over there.' He indicates a dark bookcase packed with volumes in the far corner. 'But she was very proud of this collection.'

Catherine feels her stomach flip. It is beautiful the way he hasn't asked why she is there. 'I didn't know that she spoke English. She just seems so very Polish in your story.' She hesitates. 'I can call it a story, even though it is true?'

He takes her hand. 'Yes, you can call it a story.' Gently he leads her away from the sofa and over to the fireplace. There is a gilt mirror hanging over the mantelpiece. She looks at their reflections. Both tall. Both pale. Both handsome rather than attractive. We look sane, she thinks. At the same time an image of Dominic's broken hope superimposes itself on her thoughts. Shuddering slightly, she pulls her hand from Konrad's. His eyes remain mild, drawn to a photograph on the mantelpiece. It is clear that he wants her to look at it too.

'I took this just before Janek died.' He lifts the photograph from its place on the mantelpiece and hands it to her.

She stares at the glass. The man in the photograph stares back at her. He is thinner in the face than she remembered from the time she met him in Brighton, but he is still wearing the same loose gold watch. His hair has receded to two smudges on either side of his temples, but his eyes have a brightness and alertness. He looks into the camera as if there is something important he has to say. Behind him, a cobalt cloudless sky stretches into the distance.

'We went for a drive to the mountains that day.' Konrad pauses. 'Janek had been ill with a chest infection after Krystyna died and this was the first day he felt well enough to go out. On the drive over, he talked a little about the war and then he asked me to do something for him. He knew that he wasn't going to make it through another winter, and so he asked me to find you. He wanted me to tell you that he wished he had earned the right to call himself your father. He was sorry that it had never happened.'

She nods and glances at the photograph in her hands. 'He died two days later,' Konrad says. Her tears splash on to the glass. 'I'd like you to keep it.'

The apartment feels warm. She looks around at the elegant antique furniture, the dining table covered with papers and a laptop, the rugs heaped with boxes of old photographs and tins containing the relics of the past.

Konrad follows her gaze. 'I'm in the process of sorting it all out. I'm trying to put her things into one pile and his into another. I've found some things for you, like his airline ticket back to Poland in 1989 and a newspaper article about the visit of Pope John Paul II to Kraków.' He hesitates as he reaches into a box marked video and pulls out a cassette. He goes over to an old-fashioned television in the corner of the room and slots the film into the VCR.

The screen jumps with static and she hears the sound of a man speaking in Polish before the image clears. A tall elderly woman with long grey hair walks through an avenue of trees that Catherine recognizes immediately as the Planty. The woman is laughing and fanning the air with her hands as if lifting an invisible crinoline. The man behind the camera laughs. He says something to the woman who glides over to the nearest bench and sits down. Sunlight falls on to her face. The man says something very softly and the woman looks startled. She turns her head directly towards the camera; her eyes are clouded topaz. She smiles. A great peace seems to come over her. She folds her hands into her lap and once more lifts her chin to the sun. The film suddenly freezes and then it stops.

'That was my father talking to her, wasn't it?'

'He took that on her eightieth birthday,' Konrad says. He comes over to her and takes both her hands. His touch is warm and tender. 'You probably guessed that he told her that he loved her and should have married her. In another life he would have done so.'

Catherine's chest aches. She longs to get down on her knees and look through everything Konrad has gathered together, but the present is still there, holding her back, like a glass screen.

Konrad's grey eyes wash over her. 'I've missed you.'

'I've missed you, too.' They look at each other.

'Can you stay?'

'No.'

'Dominic?' The name drops from his lips.

'Yes.' There is nothing that she can add that will explain how she feels. It is as if Dominic's visit has posed a question. He is a riddle only she can solve.

'I could arrange a duel.' He smiles at her and then takes her arm and turns her towards the shelf of books. 'Why don't you choose one at random, see what comes up?'

She frowns, not really understanding. He turns his back while she scans the shelf, wondering which book to pick. 'I don't know that he would agree to a duel.' She pulls down a copy of *Northanger Abbey* and flicks through the tissue-thin pages with her thumb.

'Well, we could just have a brawl in the square.' He runs the tip of his finger down her bare arm then leans his head on her shoulder and looks down at the pages. 'Spot anything?'

'No, what am I supposed to be looking for?'

'A secret code.' His voice is lazy.

'You're joking?'

'No, I'm not. They used novels in the war to send messages to prisoners. I've always suspected there might be a code in this collection, but I've never looked.'

'I don't believe you. How could you resist?'

'Have you chosen your book yet?' His tone is mock severe.

'Anyway, he isn't fit enough to fight you.' She replaces

Northanger Abbey and pulls out a copy of *Great Expectations* and flicks through the pages, remembering when she had read the novel at school. 'I can't see anything. It's a no, I'm afraid.'

'You mean I'd win too easily.' Konrad breathes steadily at her shoulder.

Laughter bubbles in her throat. 'I mean: no code!'

'I could take him out for a beer then, explain the situation.'

She pauses, the copy of *Wuthering Heights* fluttering in her hand, for there on page forty-three are faint pencil dots over a dozen or more letters. She hears Konrad catch his breath.

'Oh, my God.'

His arm encircles her and together they carry the book to the sofa where they sit and write out the letters.

'S A B O T A G E.' He spells out the first word and looks at her, triumphant. 'You know it's given me an idea. Maybe I could find a way to trip Dominic up in the street, scare him in some way so that he has to go home.'

'Don't joke.' She pushes closer to him and peers down at the page. 'What's the next word?'

But he does not reply. Instead he kisses her full on the mouth and runs his fingers under the back of her hair and lifts it. She feels a tingling at the base of her neck and a softening down through her body.

He pulls away. She catches her breath. 'P R I N C I P L E D R E S I S T A N C E,' he says.

'You're joking.'

He grins at her. 'No, I'm not. Look. Read it for yourself.'

She studies the dots and leans forward to write down the letters on the paper on the low table. She ought to be making plans to leave. But the thought of returning to the hotel seems impossible. If she stayed, *if* she stayed, she could talk to Dominic in the morning when he was sober. She could explain. It need not be unpleasant. They were all three intelligent adults. Konrad's jokes of duels and sabotage were intended to ridicule the whole process of leaving someone for someone else, and rightly so. It was ridiculous, ludicrous to feel so bound to something that had long ago burned out. She turns to Konrad. 'I'm not going to go back to the hotel tonight.'

He holds her hand. 'Are you sure?'

'I have never been so sure of anything in my life.'

Now it is her turn to kiss him with laughter on her lips. When she pulls away she sees by the look in his eyes that she has made the right decision.

11

Kraków, March 1940

Krystyna arrived at Kraków Station just before dark. A chill fog billowed around the station lamps, sulphur light shrouding the passengers stepping off the train. They were mostly older Poles from the country who gathered on the platform in quiet, brown huddles, suitcases clamped close to their sides. They walked along the platform with their eyes averted. No one lingered to smoke or talk. They kept their mouths clamped; only the white breath pouring from their nostrils betrayed their fear.

Krystyna recalled how different it had been the last time she had visited Kraków. Then, she'd been intoxicated by the relaxed exuberance and grace, the women dressed in jackets with nipped-in waists, neat gloves, round heels; the smell of French perfume mingling with exotic, hot, oily fumes of the trains. As her father helped her down from the train, taking her hand in his and smiling up at her so that she felt like a proper lady, a flock of pigeons had flown around them almost in celebration of their arrival.

She was ten and the trip to Kraków was the first time she had travelled alone with her father. Irena had not wanted to come; there was gardening to be done at the dwór, an excuse that fooled neither Krystyna nor her father. They employed gardeners, of course. But there was something mistrustful in Irena's nature – her father called it highly strung – that compelled her, basket in hand, to spend afternoons clearing stone pathways under rose arches that gardeners had already made free of weeds.

It was with a sense of glee and abandon that Krystyna had anticipated this rare trip away from the censoring eyes of Irena. Prior to the visit to a renowned stud farm outside Kraków, her father had patiently listened to Irena's advice not to buy more horses, and then, equally patiently, disregarded it. By inviting Krystyna along he was making her his ally.

Back then it was coming into spring, but still cold, she remembered. After the business part of the trip was done and the deal over the two striking bay colts was finalized, her father took her to see the medieval city. He treated her like an adult, consulting with her on all the tiny decisions about where they should eat and what they should do. At her suggestion they had taken hot chocolate with tiny macaroons in a café with dark red walls and a black lacquered counter. She remembered the newspapers held in presses with little gold chains, the sound of the bell as new customers came in and greeted each other with kisses and exclamations of delight; some even brought flowers, little posies of violets or lily of the valley, filling the café with whispered confidences and a swooning scent. She remembered also the quiet way her father had looked at her, admiring her smart new blue wool dress, with the narrow leather belt, her pale hair washed and brushed flat and smooth, held back from her face with a pale blue satin band. She recalled, too, his words: 'Never be afraid of being beautiful, but more importantly never be afraid. Never. Never. Never.' She'd taken his hand and made a promise to him that she would always be brave and he'd turned away from her for a moment. He'd brought his hand up to his face and the sun had glinted off his signet ring. She'd looked at the embossed horse in the pose of a rear and felt a surge of conviction pass through her. Her father turned back to her. He caught her looking at the ring and, twisting it off his finger, pushed it across the table towards her. As he watched her try it on her thumb – it was of course too big for her little fingers – there was something else in his gaze, something much deeper than approval or satisfaction. It felt more like recognition. 'I want you to keep it,' he said. 'We will buy a ribbon so that you can wear it around your neck.'

She had spent the past two weeks sleeping in barns and sheds, stealing eggs and potatoes and wood from stores to stay alive, and now as she reached the city, she was able to look back and see that the feeling of strength she had gained from her father had kept some small spark of resilience aflame deep within her. Keeping her head down, merging with the downcast crowd at the station, she was saturated with weary relief.

Carrying her duffel bag, the ring concealed on a ribbon around her neck, she moved down the platform, drawn by the closeness of warm bodies, the simple ordinariness of being with people again. She realized that the secret strength she had inherited was present in these people too. In some, especially the younger men, it was held quite lightly, almost tauntingly in a form of bravado, but in others, especially in the older people, it was buried deep, occasionally revealing its presence in a gesture of reassurance: a light warning look, a softening of a hand, an erect set of the shoulders, a directness, once acknowledged rapidly concealed. As she followed the crowd, she felt some of her fright give way to relief.

She had made it. Even so, she had no plan. When she looked back over the past few weeks of travelling, sometimes alone, sometimes with others who had escaped the Russians, who shared their food, and helped her make her way into the General Government, she could not believe that she had left the deep snowy tracks of the forest, the silent white trees, the dark empty villages and travelled into the heart of a bustling city. It didn't seem possible. There had been a man on the train who had looked at her as she sat with her face pressed to the cool glass. He sat opposite her and arranged his legs sideways so that they would not brush against hers. He wore working clothes, a cap pulled down low over his eyes, but there was something in his glance that made her think he was not a worker. His hands were too white and fine and he had the lean length of thigh that comes only with hours of riding. It was hot on the train and she briefly opened the neck of her coat to let in some air. When she looked into the dense fog-filled night she saw his reflection in the window and saw that he was staring at her throat.

Now as she hovered near a queue of people waiting to board another train so that she would look as if she were part of something, he came up behind her and put his hand on her shoulder. She turned and he stooped to see her better in the diffuse, smoky light. 'I know a safe place if you need one.' His voice was calm, but his eyes were watchful. Over his shoulder she could see that the station was crawling with young Nazi soldiers, in polished black leather boots, the dazzling swagger of their uniforms commanding attention. She noticed that each time they moved the crowds parted, leaving an arena around them so it looked as if the soldiers were about to enact a performance of some sort, a pageant with elaborate props and rituals. She pulled her gaze away. The tall man bent towards her and spoke directly into her ear. She caught the rush of his warm breath and the urgency in his voice. 'We have an hour before curfew. Follow me.'

Something about his assured air of authority made her obey. She followed him out to the front of the station where flags heavy with black swastika symbols slumped on their icy poles. A pair of white horses pulling a plum-coloured carriage swished by, straight from a fairy tale, but the scent of cigar smoke on the air and the sight of two German soldiers in furs, one with a pair of gold-rimmed spectacles gleaming on the bridge of his nose, brought a reminder of the casual shooting of the German Shepherd dog. Her mind strayed back towards Benedykt, sprawled in the snow, one fist curled around a stone he had grabbed possibly in defence, his shirt padded with stolen oats. Guilty grief sluiced through her. She shouldn't have let him play the hero; she should have insisted on going with him. The mare would have waited in the forest. She hadn't thought things through clearly enough; she had been less than brave, and for that Benedykt had paid with his life. She felt hopelessness and despair snap at her heels as she hurried along the icy pavement, anxious not to lose sight of the stranger.

He turned down a narrow street. She followed, glancing over her shoulder to check that they were not being followed in turn. She had failed Benedykt; she had made a mistake and would have to try harder the next time. She needed to be more careful; she had to stay alive because she still needed to find Janek and his father. That was what she must do. A short distance ahead the man from the train slowed his pace and came to halt outside a narrow four-storey building, its windows lit with a dull yellow light. She saw that they had stopped outside a small hotel.

All hotels in Kraków were being supervised by the Gestapo, he told her, once they were inside the lobby which smelled of damp coats. A low-wattage light bulb illuminated walls the colour of river silt. There was no carpet on the stairs and their feet squeaked on bare boards as they climbed up to an attic room with a low vaulted ceiling. Once they were inside the man locked the door and instantly apologized for putting her in such a position. 'But I could see at the station that you did not have a plan and that made you a target. If you are going to stay in Kraków you will need some idea of how to survive without attracting attention and you will need identity papers.'

She wondered whether to tell him that she had just survived weeks alone in the forest, but the man didn't seem as if he would be impressed by her tales of derring-do. He was looking around the room with a pinched expression, as if he expected better.

The attic furniture consisted of a single bed and a low scuffed armchair. Under the leaded window was a cold-water sink and she went to it and washed her face, breathing in the smell of water that had been held in a rusty tank. A piece of black material was tacked at the top of the window and before the man rolled it down she caught sight of the two unevenly sized church towers of St Mary's rising up out of the fog, seeming to push against the thick sky.

Opposite the basilica was the Cloth Hall where she and her father had shopped for souvenirs all that time ago. Then she had been dazzled by the displays of silver and amber and they'd spent a long time choosing the perfect pendant for Irena, but now looking down, the long Gothic hall seemed smaller than she remembered. She yawned. A weary part of her wanted to crawl under the blankets on the narrow bed and sleep away her profound exhaustion, but she needed to question this tall man who had taken off his cap and was rubbing the vast pinkish dome of his bare head, marked around his forehead with a red line from the tightness of the wool cap.

He was a colonel in the Polish Army, he told her, when she had settled crossways on the bed, drawing up her knees, hugging them with her arms, her back flinching away from the clammy wall. He took the chair, and stretched out his long legs. He had taken off his boots and while he talked, he occasionally reached down and rubbed at his toes inside his wool socks. He winced. 'I have terrible chilblains,' he said. 'They start to itch when I get warm.' He shrugged and his tone lightened. 'Although it is not that warm.'

She agreed. 'It would be nice to have a fire in here.' He smiled at her and asked her name. She gave it to him and then she told him her story, beginning from the moment she had left the dwór. The colonel listened, his hands linked under his chin, as she spoke for what seemed like an hour, relieving herself of the burden of silence. As she spoke, she felt the tension ease in her back. Her stomach growled and she put her hand over it and laughed to cover her embarrassment. At one point he reached into his satchel and pulled out a brown paper bag which contained a greasy round of rye bread and a half-moon of salty cheese.

He split the bread evenly and pushed it towards her, looking away from her as he chewed; his blue water eyes reminded her of Izabela. She wondered whether Janek's mare had found her way back to the old woman's barn. Her spirits rose at the thought. If the horses were together and safe, she could rest knowing that at the very least she had done what she could for them.

The colonel finished his bread. He took from his trousers-pocket a handkerchief and wiped his hands with a deft movement. There was something economical about him; clearly he had grown used to making the most of what little he had. He cleared his throat and looked intently at her collarbone. 'I knew your father.' His voice was husky. 'We trained in the cavalry together.' He paused and swallowed. 'I am deeply sorry for what may have happened to him.'

Her hand came up and instinctively touched the signet ring. She gazed at him and remembered how he had looked at her on the train. 'You recognized this?'

He nodded. 'He always wore the ring. He used to joke that it made him indestructible. Whenever he was wearing it, he felt he could do anything.'

The colonel dabbed at his head with his handkerchief and then eyed his worn black leather boots pushed together under the bed. 'I've got to check something and I want you to promise me that you will not say what you have seen.' She felt her stomach lurch, wondering what he was about to do. As he reached down for a boot, his face brightened with anticipation, hinting at intrigue which made her lean forward and watch closely as his fingers prised off the sole from the base of his left boot. A rectangular oilskin package plopped out on the floor and deftly he unwrapped it to reveal a brown envelope bound with a thick rubber band. Inside was a thick wad of grey banknotes. He scooped them up and glanced at her, his eyes now swimming with merriment. He pulled more notes from the heel of this boot and still more from the other boot, and then he stood and discreetly turned his back so that he could reach down inside his clothes, pulling out more and more złoty notes, like a conjuror revealing playing cards. She watched wordlessly as the pile of notes grew into a mound of bleached leaves in the centre of the room. 'Will you help me to count them?' he asked her.

There was nearly forty thousand złoty, money he said would be used to fund the underground army, the growing network of people who were determined to fight the German occupation. The army, known as the Home Army or AK, operated from a network of secret addresses across Kraków, from shops to cellars to factories to railways and abandoned schoolrooms. One of its main aims, he told her, was to sabotage the Nazi infrastructure by slowing down production of essential parts in the factories that were staffed by thousands of workers intent on disrupting the efficient Nazi machine. Trains carrying goods and supplies were derailed on a daily basis, and foodstuffs intended for Germans siphoned off and redirected to the Polish workers.

'It is quite a sophisticated operation already.' The colonel's head gleamed in the low light. 'Now we are building our own press and printing works and communications centres so that we can inform as many people as possible of our operation.' His eyes glowed with pride.

As he sketched further the details of the resistance, his low, strong voice calmed her. He bent down and scratched his foot again. Despite days of travel, he had a good, clean smell, like new timber. 'We are only at the beginning,' he said.

'Could I . . .' She hesitated, suddenly shy, aware of her own lack of experience and slightness, her girlishness which crept into the room and seemed to mock her. She lowered her eyes. 'Be of any use?'

He chuckled, a low rumble in his throat, and looked at her fully for a moment, considering her request. His face was long with dished cheekbones, a shadow of stubble at his jaw. Under his eyes were pouches the colour of dark tea. His long neck seemed strangely vulnerable, rising from his shirt in a tentative stem that seemed too slender for the Adam's apple that bulged as he swallowed, a ripe nut trying to burst from its skin.

'A girl,' he said, 'is more than useful. We have a whole network of liaison girls sending messages back and forth across the city. But first, before we recruit you, you will need identity papers.' He eyed her pale hair. 'German papers.' When she looked shocked he said that changing her identity could potentially save her life but also that of many others who would be relying on her to pass information. He would find someone to teach her German. How was she at accents?

'I was always the lead in school plays.'

The colonel laughed. 'If you can pretend, then you can survive.' He swung his eyes around the small room as if hunting for spies.

She slipped from the bed and paced the attic room a few times, careful not to brush her ankle against the mound of money. The colonel pretended to be absorbed in his own thoughts and she felt grateful to him for giving her this moment alone to decide. She went to the window where she imagined the square outside, its great expanse barren and empty except for the Nazi occupiers prowling the perimeter. On their trip to Kraków her father had told her that the site of what would become a city to rival Venice or Rome in its architecture had first been recorded in the tenth century by an Arabian traveller, and that it had been surrounded by burial mounds suggesting a turbulent history even back then. She lifted the black curtain and peered out into the diffuse light. What gave the Germans the right to claim territory that was indisputably Polish? Kraków had witnessed the coronation of dynasties of Polish kings. In the darkness she could just make out the castle on Wawel Hill, which had been called the Polish Acropolis. She dropped the curtain and turned once more to the attic room. What the Germans and the Russians had done was a form of theft, she decided, the worst kind of violent theft imaginable. The Germans, and the Russians, who the colonel had said were now supporting Hitler, were united in their bid to obliterate Poland, to tear it to pieces, to annihilate its glorious past. But, and her heart soared at the thought, the occupying armies were not going to seize their prize without a fight. The colonel's account of the size and scale of the resistance made her tremble with excitement. Poland was silently, stealthily, steadily preparing for battle.

She glanced over at the mound of money. Hope lay in organized resistance. And here was its key: a soft, secret cache sent by a nun, no less, who had acted as a courier on behalf of an official from the President's office. After he lost touch with his head of department the official had sought out the colonel. He wanted the money – the last of Poland's public funds – to go to a member of the military. He'd recruited a young nun who had delivered the money to the Hungarian frontier, pulling packet after packet from under the folds of her habit, before slipping off into the night, crossing the border undetected, as silent as an owl. From there the money had been taken under the wing of the Home Army, flying from courier to courier until it reached the colonel in a field in a town outside the city one moonless night. He had taken cover under a great melting oak to hide the packages in his clothes and boots before boarding the train and eventually spotting her. She imagined all this as she paced the tiny attic room. She came to a stop near the pile of money. The colonel gave her an expectant look.

'I am ready to serve the resistance.' Her heart pounded as an image of her father leaning against the tree in the forest came into her mind. 'I want to fight for my country.'

The colonel chuckled and inclined his head towards her. 'My dear, I see that you've inherited your father's impatience. Tomorrow, you will join us, but tonight you must sleep.'

Relieved, she sat down on the bed. He unfolded his length from the squat armchair and scooped up the money from the floor, stuffing it back inside the boots and down into the corners of his satchel, which he pushed under the bed. She watched the top of his naked head duck down near her feet and had to resist a childish urge to brush him with her toes. Next, he urged her to sleep, to take full advantage of the bed.

'What about you?' she asked. 'What will you do?'

He smiled wryly. 'I'm not going to sleep. Not with the Gestapo swarming the hotel.' He paused and looked at her. 'Listen, if I cough loudly three times, then that is your signal to get up and be ready to run.' He caught the flare of alarm in her expression. 'Don't worry, I shouldn't think they could be bothered to climb all the way up here.' He chuckled. 'Most of them are lazy and unfit, that's why they're Gestapo and not army.' With nonchalant grace he eased his limbs down into the low seat and took up a book from the pocket of his jacket hanging over the back of the chair.

She left her clothes on as she peeled back the covers and settled on to surprisingly clean sheets. Her hair smelled of horses and the forest, familiar, comforting smells that she associated with home. The colonel was reading in the chair next to her, turning the pages of a paperback with a slight crackle. She felt a rush of warmth, the first in weeks, and allowed her sore muscles to relax into sleep.

In the morning they left the hotel early and crossed the city, keeping to the cobbled side streets to avoid the military police who patrolled the main square in threes or fours with bored expressions, stopping people at random and asking to see documents or check packages. In the back streets, some of the narrow shops had stars painted on the front doors and notices saying 'Nicht Arisch'. Against the skyline she could see the dreamy towers of Wawel Castle, the hilltop residence of Polish kings, now emblazoned with swastika flags flaring against a dull white sky. Many of the walls around the churches were covered with German notices and orders which she asked the colonel to translate.

'This is one way for you to learn German,' he said, keeping his hand near his mouth, his eyes scanning the street in case he was overheard.

All the posters were orders exhorting the 'inhabitants

of the General Government' to capitulate to German demands. The words 'strictly forbidden' and 'penalty of death' were emphasized in case anyone was in doubt.

One proclamation stuck on to an official noticeboard outside a church stopped the colonel in his tracks and caused his face to tighten. Gritting his teeth, he reached forward and ripped it from the board. Breathing hard through his nose, he folded it and pushed it inside his coat pocket. Later, when they had reached their destination – a large cellar under an elegant home belonging to a professor of history at the Jagiellonian University – he read the paper aloud to his new initiates, a group of young men and women, some university students, some factory workers, some post office clerks, who had gathered together.

'Inhabitants of the General Government. Victorious German arms have, once and for all, put an end to the Polish state. Behind you lies an episode in history you should forget forthwith. It belongs to the past and will never return.' She heard one or two of the students mutter and shuffle their feet. It was cold and clammy in the cellar and the collective breath of the group hung grey-white in the air, a damp cloud enfolding them. Only the colonel hovered above it, the dome of his head shining under a naked light bulb, as he continued to read.

'The General Government can become the refuge of the Polish people if they will submit loyally and completely to the orders of the German authorities and accomplish the tasks set them in the German war effort. Every attempt to oppose the new German order will be ruthlessly suppressed.' The group murmured their dissent and one or two young men called out their defiance, their voices raw and high with emotion.

The colonel lifted his head from the paper and waited for them to settle down. Krystyna felt a knot well up in her throat as she looked at him so composed, as if he had just read a weather bulletin, announcing a storm was on its way. He gave a tight smile. A young man standing next to Krystyna clenched his fist and huffed impatiently. He was a few years older than her, a stocky, healthy courier with a thick flap of gold hair and blazing blue eyes, crinkled at the corners as if he had spent too many long hours out in fields under sun. A space contracted in her lower belly as she thought of Janek. For the first time, she considered whether he might be dead.

'Signed by the governor general Hans Frank.' The colonel held the paper at arm's length.

'Who is he to tell us what to do?' the young man next to Krystyna called out.

There were mutters of approval from the group. Once more the colonel waited for the clamour to fade and then began to speak in a level voice. 'I am here to lead you, to gather you together as a united force, to offer you a way forward from this situation. The Polish nation is here under this roof. All of you have the right to fight for your own nation, for the soul of your good nation and for your identity. The identity of the Polish people belongs to no one but the Polish people. Believe in this. Trust in the strength of our blessed nation. Trust in the power of God to guide you by lighting your way in the darkness. There will be many trials ahead and many tragedies, many times when you will feel like giving up, but you must act at all times with courage, with good heart. Have courage in your own ability to resist, not only to survive, but to fight, for this is the Polish spirit, the immortal spirit of freedom which has been bred in us over a thousand years and which no invader may conquer.'

At the end of his speech there were cheers and people hugged each other and kissed. Krystyna felt her arm tugged by the young courier next to her. 'We are going to fight.' He grabbed her hand and kissed it vehemently, his fingers firm on her wrist, his lips dry against her skin. His hair brushed her bone and sent little electric shivers up her arm. His passion was magnetic and she felt an urge to kiss him full on the mouth. His eyes shone. 'We are not going to give in to them. We will resist.' He pulled her into his arms and she felt his heart beating hard against her chest. Afraid of what she might meet in him, she leaned her forehead into his shoulder to ward off the rapid, pulsing push of his body.

The next evening she was sworn in as a member of the Home Army. The power kept flickering on and off, causing an uneasy tension to filter through the cellar. Condensation streaked the gloss-painted walls and there was a smell of must and old furniture. The history professor and his wife used the cellar to store inherited pieces of furniture that they had no room for upstairs. The professor's wife who let them in from a low door at the side of the house, ingeniously painted so as to blend with the wall of the house, had not had time to sort through the items to give them away and her first concern was that there would not be enough space for the group to meet comfortably. The colonel assured her they would be able to navigate their way around the clutter of side tables, stacked with legs pointing upward like bear traps, a hall stand, brass hooks tarnished and dull, a blurred oval mirror rolling on its side at ankle height, a pair of dining chairs with faded velveteen seats, a rolled-up carpet, looming sentry-like in the corner, and a large round table, covered with a soft ivy-green chenille cloth, on which the colonel rested his file of recruits, a Bible and a heavy brass cross. Wooden crates, filled with books and papers, jutted against the sloping walls, providing seating for the group. Now they were silent as the colonel lifted the cross and Bible ready to begin.

She watched each member of the group stand before the colonel and, holding the cross in their hand, swear the oath. She was last in line. When it was her turn she felt her heart thud as she made her way to the front. The young courier touched her shoulder and whispered a word of encouragement as she approached the colonel. Recognizing that she was nervous, he looked at her and smiled warmly as if she were a favourite niece. She felt her fear give way to excitement as she took the cross from him. It felt warm and slightly greasy from the previous oaths. She wondered whether she would stumble over the words. There was such a lot to say. She closed her eyes once and then opened them to begin:

'Before God the Almighty, before the Holy Virgin Mary, Queen of the Crown of Poland, I put my hand on this Holy Cross, the symbol of martyrdom and salvation, and I swear that I will defend the honour of Poland with all my might, that I will fight with arms in hand to liberate her from slavery, notwithstanding the sacrifice of my own life, that I will be absolutely obedient to my superiors, that I will keep the secret whatever the cost may be.'

The colonel put his hand on her shoulder. His eyes were solemn. 'I receive thee among the soldiers of freedom. Victory will be thy reward.' He paused and swallowed thickly. 'Treason will be punished by death.'

He rested his hand on her head in confirmation and as she returned to her place in the group she felt the clean, clear joy she remembered experiencing after Communion in the dwór chapel, a tiny jewelled space with a blue starred ceiling and radiant painting of the Virgin. The group shifted around the furniture and made room for her, welcoming her with smiles. Then the electricity failed and someone lit candles in the sconces where they gave off a warm, quiet light. Everyone was talking and thumping each other on the back. She realized that this would be one of the rare times she would be able to talk freely about who she was. After this night, all her personal information would be strictly censored. At one point in the evening she noticed the colonel watching her and felt a glow of pride. She hadn't faltered over the oath. She'd spoken clearly and with conviction. Now she felt the thrill in her, a low thrumming in her lower belly, as she turned over the words of the oath in her mind, savouring them almost. The hardship and loneliness of the forest seemed to slip from her shoulders like a weighty cloak she had been carrying for someone else; she no longer needed its protection. Her new life was about to begin: her life as a soldier of freedom.

They celebrated late into the night. The young courier had smuggled in a bottle of vodka and there were toasts to the success of the resistance and songs and stories. The colonel was gracious, sharing out his time with his new army, being careful not to spend longer talking to one or another for fear of showing favouritism. When it came to her turn he seemed tired, his dark eyes dulled. But he spoke to her fully and said that he thought she would do well in her new role because she had the right temperament, the right spirit. 'You keep going when things get difficult and that persistence in you will serve you well.'

'My stepmother called it stubbornness.'

The colonel smiled and rested his hand on her shoulder. Now she wondered whether he had children of his own. He had not spoken of even a wife. 'I want my soldiers tough.' He faltered and brought his hand up to his forehead, as if he had forgotten what he was about to say. She wondered how much sleep he had allowed himself in the past few days 'I want my soldiers never to surrender.'

She remembered her father urging her never, never, never to lose heart. For a moment she felt his spirit in the underground room. She retreated to a cool space to collect her thoughts. After a moment, seeing her alone, the colonel came over and muttered in a low voice so the others would not hear and perhaps be envious: 'We can stay tonight in the apartment of a friend,' he told her. 'You'll have your own room, and there is even a bathroom.' The thought of sinking her tired body into warm water was tantalizing and made her wish now for the party to end.

It was almost midnight by the time the exhausted but still animated group began to put on coats and make their farewells. In the celebrations new friendships had been forged, and a couple of new romances, which she observed with wonder because the preliminaries had been so perfunctory. Some new couples were in full passionate embrace when the door to the cellar was flung open and the professor's wife stood hovering with the hall light behind her, illuminating the fibres of white in her hair. Krystyna's throat dried. The woman's face was so pale and rigid that she thought she was about to throw herself down

Leabharlanna Poibli Chathair Baile Átha Cliath
Dublin City Public Libraries

the stairs. The cheerful farewells faded and all the faces, the colonel's included, turned to look at the woman. She gave something like a cry and a sob and then lurched towards them. The new lovers looked at each other and a ripple of fear passed through the entire group. The colonel immediately took the woman's arm and guided her to a dining chair where she sat with her head bent to her bosom which rose rapidly as if there were too much air trapped in her lungs. Krystyna tried not to stare. The woman bent lower and crossed her arms in front of her stomach. She gave a low moan then lifted her head. Krystyna had never seen such an expression on anyone's face before. It was a look of utter bewilderment and abandonment.

At the colonel's encouragement she began to talk, her voice low and throbbing, occasionally fracturing into sobs as she tried to control herself. Her husband, the history professor, had returned from the Collegium Novum for his meal at midday. As they sat down to eat, the woman said, he had seemed agitated. He told her that the German authorities had invited all the professors, lecturers and assistants to a talk at the university; the title made him smile, she remembered, and hold up his soup spoon: 'The Attitude of the National Socialist Movement towards Science and Learning'. He'd turned the spoon over several times as if doubting its reality. 'They are lecturing us on *our* attitude towards learning.' He chuckled at that and finished his soup. He felt better, he said, for some hot food and sane company, but she felt uneasy. She had begged him not to go back to the university for the afternoon. She pulled her arms across her stomach. 'I was convinced it was a trap of some sort.' There was a silence. The professor's wife said she had waited all night

Leabharlanna Poiblí Chathair Baile Átha Cliath
Dublin City Public Libraries

for her husband to return. She was too frightened to leave the house in case he came home.

'Why didn't you come down sooner?' the colonel asked.

The professor's wife began to weep. The colonel put his arm across her shoulders. 'Because at every moment I expected him home,' the woman wailed. 'I thought that if I stopped waiting and came down then that would mean he would not come. As long as I was there, ready for him upstairs, sitting where I always sat in the evenings reading by the fire, he would step back in through the door as he had always done.' Her voice gave way once more to sobs. 'I was ready for him.'

Krystyna watched the colonel's reaction. His jaw tensed and his eyes bulged for a moment. She thought he was trying to contain his anger. He drew breath then rested his hand on the woman's shoulder again for a moment before he addressed the young courier.

'I need you to go to the Collegium Novum straight away and find out what happened.' The colonel swept his eye over his new recruits. 'Take someone with you.'

Krystyna was surprised to find her hand in the air. The colonel blinked when he saw that she had volunteered. Sweat pearled on his brow and he wiped it away with his handkerchief. He swallowed and she thought he was about to pass over her. Then he nodded. 'Pretend you are students. Find out what you can and return immediately. We will be waiting.' His voice was thick.

The courier stood by the door leading out of the cellar. He glanced over his shoulder as she took her place at his side. He smelled sharp, like a young dog. 'Let's go,' he said and bounded out through the door.

The cold air froze her cheeks. The fog had now lifted and

the narrow streets were empty, glittering frost trails, the shops and tall houses dusky, quietly hunched, as if they had moved a few inches closer for protection. There was no light; all windows were darkened. A flurry of stars gave out a casual light, too remote to touch the shuttered city which had withdrawn, gathered its strength inwards. They began to walk. Her companion strode along a few paces ahead of her, his chin muffled in his scarf. She realized that she did not know his name. Somehow they had missed talking to each other in the celebrations. She wondered whether she ought to introduce herself, but it seemed absurd, an irrelevance. He whispered to her that the college was not far. His breath streamed over her arm. His eyes were jay's-wing blue. 'We'll go down here, and then take a left over there; if we see soldiers keep your eyes down and do not speak. I'll talk to them in German.' She was surprised. She wanted to ask him where he had learned the language. Her impression was of a farm labourer, but he seemed comfortable in the city and clearly knew how to navigate the side streets and the park that held great snowy trees.

They came upon the university set in a wide clearing at the end of one of the park avenues. Its long stone windows and archways protected by black iron gates were in darkness. On the steps outside the red-brick façade a pair of Nazi soldiers stood like frozen statues. The courier told her to wait behind a tree. He would find out what had happened. She tried to protest, thinking that something would go wrong. She would end up losing him as she had lost Benedykt in the forest. She gripped his arm and he saw the fear in her eyes. 'Don't worry, you can see me from here. If they get heavy, run, but you won't need to. I promise you in a few minutes I will be here again.'

'What's your name?'

'My name?' He stared at her and knitted his brows. Then he tore his head away and his eyes strained towards the Germans. He didn't want to miss his opportunity, she saw, and now she regretted asking him.

'My name,' he said. 'My name is Janek.'

Blood thudded in her ears as she watched him stroll casually up to the soldiers and accept a cigarette from the taller of the two. Bored with their duty, the guards were open to distraction and their faces became animated as they talked, using their hands, pointing behind them to the college. If they weren't wearing uniform, they all could have been a group of students conversing after an evening lecture. She curled her fingers into fists and dug her nails into her palms. Janek.

He returned to the tree within minutes, breathing hard. He said nothing of what he had learned and she did not ask. Their flight back across the city was rapid and when they returned to the cellar it was almost as if no time at all had passed. A space was cleared for them in the centre of the low room. Someone lit another candle and placed it close to Janek. The lecture had begun on time, he said. Every row was filled. Nearly all the professors of the university came and they were quite relaxed as they took their places. When the hall was crowded and the doors locked the Gestapo marched in and announced to the chair of the meeting that as the university had always shown anti-German tendencies everybody in the hall was under arrest. One or two of the professors began to protest. The SS followed and began to prod and push the professors with rifle butts. There was chaos. No one knew whether they should stay or fight to leave. One elderly white-haired man, a renowned professor of mathematics, fell to the ground and suffered a heart attack. One of his colleagues went to help him and was beaten senseless by an SS soldier with a rifle butt. Janek bit down on his lip as he reported this.

'Were the soldiers there?' the colonel demanded. 'Did they witness this first hand? Why would they tell you this?'

Janek eyed the group. 'They were there and they seemed sorry about it. They felt guilty for what had happened and they wanted to talk about it, I think.' He glanced towards the professor's wife. 'One of them told me he was the son of a university professor.' He paused. 'I am sorry.'

There were mutters from the group. The professor's wife sat straight in the chair with one hand splayed over her mouth. Over the top of her fingers her eyes glistened in the candlelight.

'They rounded everyone up,' Janek added gently. 'They are in Kraków Prison.'

'In prison,' the wife said in a high, disbelieving voice. 'They have taken them away like criminals.' Tears sprang on to her pale cheeks, smearing her make-up. 'They surely cannot get away with this. It's barbaric. What harm is there in a group of elderly men?' Her eyes were wide.

Her words hung in the damp air. Krystyna looked towards the colonel. His face had an ashen look and a muscle in his neck was pulsing. 'We need to find out what they intend,' he said briskly. 'We'll disperse and meet again tomorrow evening at our usual time. We should have more information then.' He nodded a few times and licked his dry lips. 'Go to your safe places now.'

He waited until everyone had gone, in twos and threes at spaced intervals so as not to draw attention, and then they went upstairs with the professor's wife. They sat at the table where the professor had taken his midday meal. A few dry crumbs of bread nicked Krystyna's elbow. His soup bowl and spoon had been washed and returned to the table. There was a photograph of the professor above a dark wood dresser. He wore robes and carried a pile of papers under his arm, his expression faintly puzzled as if he had been caught off-guard. His wife, an elegant woman in her late fifties with oyster-grey pearls in her ears, noticed Krystyna looking and smiled before glancing down at her hands. She placed them on the table. They were bluish at the tips with cold. On the end of her nose a tiny soap bubble of mucus caught the light, but she did not seem to feel it and made no move to wipe it away. 'Thank you for staying with me,' she said. She spoke carefully, rolling her tongue around each word as if it might scald her.

The colonel reached over and patted her hand. She pushed back her chair and said she would fetch them some soup; there was a little left over from lunch. The silence grew thick, punctured only by the sound of ticking from a longcase clock that stood in one corner near the doorway, dropping the seconds with a heavy, hypnotic beat. Krystyna thought of her mission across the city to the university. She recalled Janek talking with the soldiers who had seemed so friendly and casual. It seemed impossible that young men such as this had helped to arrest an entire university; that young men such as this, sons of professors, had marched in and pushed over revered men and women, jabbing at them with rifle butts as if they were cattle. It was incomprehensible. She looked over at the professor's empty chair. Here he had taken lunch with his wife. The thought made a wave of nausea clench at her stomach and as the soup arrived she struggled to lift her spoon. She waited for a few moments, aware of the colonel's measuring eyes on her and, not wanting to disappoint him or cause the professor's wife any further distress, she gulped down the acid saliva burning her throat, picked up her spoon, dipped it into the grey bowl and began to eat.

12

Kraków, present day

The first thing Catherine notices is the brightness of the light and the hot pepper smell of geraniums drifting in from the window box on the balcony outside. A low hum of traffic tells her that the morning is well advanced. Beside her Konrad sleeps on his front, his face rumpled up against the pillow, his lower lip rubbing the white trim. The bed smells faintly chemical. Before they had slipped into it sometime in the early hours he had insisted on unpacking a new cardboard wrap of fine cotton sheets that he had brought with him from America. 'For some reason I thought they were too good to waste on myself,' he told her as they unfolded the new cotton and hoisted it like a pristine sail over the bed.

'Well, at least I know now that you don't make a habit of this,' she'd retorted as they eased new pillowcases from their cardboard arm bands and pulled them on to the two feather pillows at the head of the bed.

'Was this Krystyna's bed?' she had asked, looking at the freshly made bed.

He had smiled and reached for her hand. 'Does it make a difference? What if I tell you that it wasn't?'

She sat down on the bed and the springs pinged under her weight. 'It doesn't sound like a new bed. It seems to me as if it has had a history.'

He sat down next to her and took her face in his hands. 'Does it?'

'Yes, it does.' She rolled away from him and lay flat on her back looking up into his face. Her stomach was pulsing with joy. 'It feels incredibly solid. Heavy. I feel as if I'm lying in a boat. I could go anywhere, let the wind carry me.'

'It has held the weight of many dreams, you're right.' He stretched out beside her and looked down the length of their legs. 'Look at us, here.'

'Yes, look at us.' She got up on one elbow and gazed down into his face. She paused. Something in his expression seemed remote. 'Why do you look so sad?'

'I'm not sad, I'm moved.' His voice was thick. He swallowed before he spoke again. 'I'm where I dreamed to be.' He reached for her and kissed her.

They both sat up and she helped him lift off her dress, watching him unbutton his shirt while he ran his eyes over her body. 'Let's not rush this,' he said. 'Let's take our time, let it be how we want it to be rather than how we think it ought to be.' He slid his trousers down his hips and pulled them off. Still sitting, they rocked in each other's arms for a moment and then lay down on the bed.

His skin was cool. She rested her face in the crook of his neck and breathed in his clean smell. She could feel the rise of his chest against hers. Slowly, with long, sweeping movements he began to explore her body with his hands. She felt her breathing quicken. He kissed her shoulders, her breasts, her belly. His breath was warm; his fingers moved over her, seeking her. She felt as if he were peeling off layers of feeling. Piece by piece she came apart under his hands and then piece by piece he put her together again. She shuddered with voluptuous shock. Close to dawn, held in his arms, her head on his breast, he said, 'You know I feel that everything makes sense again.'

Now she leaves the bed and he reaches for her hand. His grip is warm and masculine. She feels the wiry hairs on his forearm and brings it up to her lips. It smells of her intimate scent. Desire for him pulls her back into the bed and they make love with slow intensity, feeling their way with each other; almost as if they are both acknowledging a debt or enacting a promise they made a long time ago.

They take a shower together in the tiny apartment bathroom and she is surprised to find him shy with her. He tenderly massages the shampoo into her hair with his strong fingers until she feels the warm pull of physical energy coursing through her, but there is a hesitancy to his moves, as if afraid that they have overstepped some kind of invisible mark. 'You have wonderful hair,' he says, taking a heavy wet strand of it and allowing it to coil round his arm. 'Strong and springy, and the colour is so rich. It's almost intoxicating.'

'Almost?' she teases him. Lifting her chin, he rinses the last of the shampoo off the back of her head. She feels the warm water seep down her back and buttocks. 'Actually it's the bane of my life,' she tells him. 'I've been so tempted to cut my hair short. You know, do away with any form of vanity.'

'I don't think enjoying your beauty is vanity.' He shuts off the shower and steps out of the cubicle and briskly towels the water from his body, using both his hands in a see-saw motion across his shoulders and his waist. The sight of his clean navel makes her stomach dip.

'Really?'

'Yes, really.' He moves closer to her. She feels the damp steam between their skins. He rests his hand on her buttock, his palm, warm and casual, causing a thrill to bubble in her throat. 'It's a duty. For someone as fine as you are.' He moves his hand. She likes the way he lingers on the word 'fine'.

After they have dressed, he apologizes. There is nothing in the small galley kitchen that he can offer her for breakfast, not even coffee. 'Everything's kind of provisional.' His eyes sweep across the kitchen which is not so much disordered as denuded; there's a single unwashed plate in the sink, a small saucepan on the gas cooker containing a forgotten boiled egg, globule of cooked white bearding the shell.

'It's all right, we'll go out.' She feels a spasm of hunger at the thought of fresh coffee and a warm bread roll, maybe some bacon and eggs. 'Can you get a decent breakfast round here?'

'Well, there's somewhere on the way back to your hotel.' He pauses and frowns. 'Are you okay?'

She feels weak and has to pull out one of the kitchen stools to sit down for a moment and gather her thoughts. She has been acting as if she were alone and free to spend the morning leisurely taking breakfast, flirtatiously drinking coffee, sealing what had taken place, but what she has forgotten, and this amazes her, is that she must face Dominic.

'I suppose I should go back.'

He pulls out another stool and sits opposite her. His eyes linger on the bruise on her cheek. 'Did he do that to you?'

'No.' She laughs. 'I fell into the window on the train to Auschwitz.'

Konrad frowns. She can tell that he's having trouble believing her. 'Should I come to the hotel with you?'

She leans forward and kisses him. 'No. It would just make everything worse.'

'I could wait downstairs, or somewhere close by.'

'Thank you for being so gallant, but it's really not necessary.' She brings her hand up to her head. 'I need to do this properly. It may take some time. It's a lifetime I'm dealing with here. An entire history.'

'I understand. But call me if it gets too hard. I'll come straight over.'

'Thank you.' She looks into his eyes. He holds her gaze intensely as if he's afraid he might never see her again. She touches his hand. 'Look, it's all right. I'm not going to disappear.'

'Are you sure about that?' His smile returns. He reaches over and pulls her off her stool and into his lap. 'You'd better come back.' He kisses her on the lips. 'Now, I guess you'd better be gone.'

'Look, I'll come over later, as soon as I can.' She stands up and glances around for her bag.

He's about to reply when the telephone rings in the other room. He goes to answer it, leaving her hovering in the kitchen. His voice sounds quiet, strained. He doesn't speak for long. She hears the creak of the sofa after he puts down the phone and a sound that is like a paper bag being crumpled. She becomes aware of the sound of a tap dripping on to the plate in the sink. Slowly she gets up and walks through to the other room. He is sitting with the telephone in his lap, his bare feet turned inward, right big toe overlapping the joint of the left. His nails look young. His damp hair has fallen over his eyes and when he looks at her he blinks rapidly. 'My father.' His voice is husky and filled with fear. 'My father has killed himself.' He brings his hand up to his temple and shades his eyes. 'I have to go home.'

A sob catches in her throat. All words now seem inappropriate and inadequate. She realizes with a sudden panicky feeling that she does not know him well enough for this. For something like this there needs to be a network, family ties, arrangements, routines; there needs to be some kind of safety and security, none of which they have; theirs is too tentative a beginning to withstand such a shock. Trembling, she sits down beside him and takes his hand. She holds it tight.

'Will you go back today?' Her voice sounds stronger than she feels.

'Tonight, there's a flight at nine tonight.' Already engaged with the practicalities, he does not look at her. Roused from his stupor, he stands up and flips the hair away from his eyes. 'My God,' he says, gazing about the apartment. He begins to pace, stepping over books on the floor, the coded novels that had only last night seemed like recovered treasure. 'The last time I spoke to Mom she said he was down, but that was nothing unusual. He was still reading his newspaper every day, still part of something.' He stops pacing and throws his head back. 'I just can't believe that he would do this to her. I can't believe it.' The anguish in his voice tears at her.

She feels torn. Should she make her break with Dominic and offer to travel with him?

'I'm going to go to the hotel now, briefly.' She can't use Dominic's name. 'And then I'll come straight back.'

He shakes his head vigorously. 'No, no, you must deal with Dominic in a fair way. It's important for you to get this right.' He rubs his face and she sees some of his colour return as he begins to make mental preparations to leave. 'We've got to do this properly.'

She feels afraid. What they shared seems to be evaporating. 'I don't want to leave you like this.' Her voice is dull.

He holds her. She buries her face in his neck and inhales his smell. Could it be that they have had their moment – their one night of bliss? She wants to sob at how unfair this feels. She almost wishes they had not met. To lose him so cruelly is almost too much for her to bear.

'Now, we both must go and face our pasts,' he says to her, holding her at arm's length.

She leaves him, too choked to speak.

Tears pour down her face as she walks back to the hotel alone through the Planty, taking the same route she had taken only a few hours before, passing the same trees and benches, the Collegium Novum, its red-brick façade glowing in the late morning sun. Last night she had been filled with hope and anticipation, and, yes, courage. She had braved her escape from Dominic. She had left him sleeping and crept away to her new love, and she had felt strong and almost valiant as she took the first steps towards her own freedom. But last night seems another time and place altogether, and she is different, too, irreversibly changed. Now she is returning to her past with a breaking heart.

Needing something to fortify her, she stops for a coffee at the café where she first met Konrad. The waiter there recognizes her and greets her with sympathetic eyes. She sits in the booth where they talked, aware that she is rubbing salt into the wound, but part of her doesn't care. She sips her coffee. She can't face breakfast; she is too distressed to eat. She needs to gather her thoughts because she is going to need all of her strength just to face Dominic. There will be questions and there will be accusations. She recalls his slumped figure staring self-pityingly into the hotel room mirror and her courage wavers. She lets out a long tight breath and catches the eye of the waiter watching her from the counter. He comes over immediately. 'You want a refill?' He hovers with the fragrant coffee pot.

'Thank you.' He touches her hand and she marvels again at the human decency of ordinary Poles. How different is Kraków: older, slower, less self-assured than many British cities with their brawl of traffic and mixed-up architecture, their noise and their bravado. Sometimes she loved the eclectic sprawl of modern-day Britain, the anything-goes mentality, but after a short while here in this medieval cloister, this city of deep and profound struggle, Britain seems in comparison unbearably arrogant. She feels a tug inside her at the thought that she will soon have to return. The waiter looks at her with his grave brown eyes. She gestures to him to bring the bill, which he does, carrying it solemnly on a white saucer as if it is a note summoning her to an event of some importance. She pays the bill and leaves a twenty złoty tip.

The hotel room is empty. She walks around cautiously inspecting the twin beds which have been made, covers smoothed flat, clothes tidied away behind the sliding wardrobe doors, fresh white towels folded in the bathroom, the floor dry and clean. The room could be awaiting new guests. She feels a prickle of fear, thinking now that Dominic might have guessed where she had gone, and simply left, packed his clothes and returned to Cambridge to lick his wounds. The shock of the call delivering the devastating news of Konrad's father reverberates and now she is struck by the thought that perhaps she has been abandoned a second time around, perhaps Dominic has left her without warning. It would be a fitting form of punishment for her betrayal.

Heart thudding in her ears, she continues to pace around the room. Sliding open the wardrobe door, she is almost sick with relief when she sees Dominic's shoes, his best shoes, the brown leather brogues he wears when they go out to dinner in good restaurants. Fine dining had been a feature of their early life together – Dominic adored Italian food, sumptuous, soft, generous food: warm hunks of ciabatta dipped into a green treacle of olive oil, seared fish, potatoes spiked with aromatic rosemary. He liked her to dress up for these occasions, twist her hair up from her neck, wear scent. On her fortieth birthday he bought her a pair of high heels in soft red leather. They were too glamorous for her, she had told him, without thinking that he would be insulted by her rejection of his gift. He had accused her of being unadventurous. She never wanted to try anything new. She was stuck. Boring, that word again. The shoes remained unworn, still wrapped in tissue in their stiff white box. She knew that she ought to throw them out, or at least give them to a charity shop, but somehow she couldn't even bring herself to open the box. It was as if all the insults he had pitched at her that night, and her comments about the red shoes had triggered some terrible unreason in him, some awful need to unpick her, strip her of her dignity, humiliate her so that she believed him, would come flying out and claw at her all over again. She slides the door shut and then tenses as she hears the hotel room door click open.

He stands in the space between the two beds breathing heavily, as if he has been running. His shirt is dark with sweat and one side of his face is red and sore. His nose is crooked, as if it has been taken off his face and stuck back on again in the wrong place. Konrad's ironic joke about a 'duel' suddenly springs into her mind. She imagines Dominic had somehow found his way to Kopernika and forced his way into the apartment, or maybe he waited and accosted Konrad on his way out to the airport. It would appeal to his sense of drama, his need to make their relationship central and messy and prolonged. Her chest thuds with fear.

Dominic sits down heavily on the bed. 'Bastard broke my nose.' He lifts his wounded eyes to her and she can tell by the slight slackness in his lower lip that he has already had a medicinal drink or three. 'Accosted me in the square.' He forms one hand into a fist. 'He just came at me from nowhere.' He looks rueful for a moment, but then a gleam of spite lifts him from self-pity. 'I split his fucking lip. Polish bastard. Then I smashed his windscreen.' He raises a fist, scored with red capillary lines, oozing sequins of blood. 'He drove away with it all crazed over.'

She feels a spasm of hatred for him then, for putting her through such agony. She turns from his glassy eyes and walks into the bathroom where she peels a towel from the clean bale and casually throws it to him. 'Clean yourself up. We are going out for lunch. We need to talk.'

His eyes flare and his colour slowly rises to her challenge. She expects him to start on her and her stomach flips at the thought. In brawling with the taxi driver, he has crossed an invisible line and she can tell that in spite of his injuries he is excited by the experience. His eyes are more alive now than she has seen in years. Her mouth goes dry. She remembers Konrad's disbelieving glance at the bruise on her cheekbone. Dominic has never touched her. His sort of violence is subtle, a slow wearing away at her soul, but now she wonders whether in knowing that he has nothing to lose he might change his tactics. He takes a step towards her and brings his face close to hers so that she can almost taste the alcohol on his breath. 'Yes, *ma'am*,' he says in a parody of an American accent. 'We certainly do need to talk. What the *fuck* have you been doing?'

'You know.' She is amazed at how calm she sounds. She closes her eyes. He will punch her, now.

She feels a breeze whip past her and flinches in anticipation. Instead he does as she asks and meekly goes to the bathroom and takes a shower. She closes her eyes and tries not to think of the shower of a few hours earlier; its tender innocence strikes her as naive in comparison to the ugly realities facing her now.

Outside, the square is busy and she has to concentrate to avoid the knots of people milling around in shorts and T-shirts. Puppet dragons dance on strings and the air is filled with a multitude of squeaks and squawks from other livid toys decorating the stalls. Dominic's face is set in a scowl of irritation that sets her stomach churning. Leaving the chattering square, they walk down Floriańska Street, not quite side by side. At the coffee shop she had left only half an hour ago he stops and suggests they go inside.

'Not here.' Her earlier confidence has drained away from her and she now feels shaky and light-headed.

Dominic thrusts out his bottom lip. 'Why not? It looks

good. Quiet, and that's what we need, isn't it?' There's a stain on the sleeve of his blue linen shirt that looks like dried blood. He is normally fastidious about changing his shirts, because of the copious amounts of sweat he produces, but this time he has chosen to remain in his battle clothes. His face is swollen, his left eye beginning to close into a puffy slit. His breathing comes out in a wheeze and now she wonders whether they ought to go directly to the nearest casualty.

'I think your nose is broken.'

He shrugs. 'The last thing I want to do is to spend the remaining hours of my holiday in some crappy Accident and Emergency department. I'll get it seen to at home.'

So he is intending to leave soon. She feels relief, but she is not able to relax fully. He won't let her off the hook this easily. He will bear his wounds with a certain self-justified pride in order to see this through, and he will need to win, to come away the victor. She will need to think of a way of allowing him that without compromising herself.

He is halfway inside the café and her waiter has already come over to greet him, but she hovers in the entrance, hoping her lack of enthusiasm will make him want to find another more suitable place further down the street. The brighter Italian would possibly ease the tension a little as they would be more exposed there. But then she wonders whether it matters; what difference does it make that Dominic has chosen the café where she first met Konrad? He can't change what has already been set in motion. So let them go in, let them sit in the same booth, nothing will be violated, nothing will be taken from her. If anything it is quite fitting that she should begin with one man and end with another in the same place. Dominic is, after all, part of the conversation she has been having with Konrad, part of the same history. She presses forward with what she hopes is a conciliatory smile.

Dominic whirls round and backs out of the café. 'Sorry, but I don't like the look of that waiter,' he says. 'He has insolent eyes. Let's go somewhere else.'

'How about the Italian?'

His lips soften. He touches her arm. 'Good idea.' His voice has lost its combative edge and for a moment it seems as if all is settled and ordinary between them, an odd feeling that makes her doubt herself.

They are careful with each other as they take their seats, shake out their spotless white napkins and place them in their laps. She watches Dominic make minute adjustments to the gleaming cutlery and glasses, moving them with a mathematical precision, his eyes absorbed, lost in the consolation of calculus. Not for the first time, she wonders whether he might be autistic.

The waiter, a young Italian with close-cropped monkish hair, brings them menus and retreats with a bow from his waist. From the direction of the kitchen, the front of which is open so that the heads of the chefs and cooks can be seen moving back and forth like a theatre puppet show, comes the sound of a soprano saturating an aria, the notes sinuously moving like a bright stream through the percussive sounds of metal on pans, chopping on wooden blocks, squeaks of trainers turning on laminated flooring, steam and running water.

Dominic orders clams for a starter; she chooses a goat's cheese and walnut salad largely because it sounds bland enough to calm the churning in her stomach. The clams arrive like a nest of fledglings and she watches Dominic dive into them with relish, moaning with pleasure, sucking their pale juices from his fingers. Her goat's cheese is cold and sour, the walnuts tough and bitter. She leaves most of it untouched on her plate.

'May I?' Dominic indicates her leftovers.

'Go ahead.' She pauses, aware now of the potency of her words. 'I'm not hungry.'

He looks at her with coolly assessing eyes. 'You've never been much of a gourmet, have you?'

'That's not true. I enjoy my food.'

'Yes, but in all the years I've known you, I wouldn't be able to say what exactly it is that you like. Your tastes aren't strong or defined. In fact, you've always followed my tastes.' He wipes his mouth on his napkin and sits back. His paunch protrudes against the edge of the table. She knows that she ought to concede and admit that he is right. For a long time she did allow him to choose for her in restaurants, but only because she thought he wanted her to do that. She did it *for* him, because that had seemed important to him at the time. He had needed her to be guileless, unsophisticated and doubtful because, naturally, it made him feel generous and secure in his own convictions. Instinctively she has always known this; she has always known that she needed to protect him and not the other way round. She should not be defensive, but something else is happening. Her rebellion is waking up.

'Your tastes.' She pushes away her plate. 'Are you really so sure of your tastes?'

He gives her an odd look. 'Well, yes, of course I am. I should think that I know who I am by now, Catherine.' He attempts a smile.

It is always dangerous when he uses the full version of

her name, but she ignores it and pushes on. 'Whereas I don't, is that what you're saying?'

'I'm not talking about now. You know what I'm saying. You didn't have much of a clue about food when I first met you; come on, you've admitted as much yourself, many times.'

This is true. It has been part of their game, their discourse for as long as they have been together: her hopelessness about food, wine, clothes; her unworldliness, her untutored self against his sophisticated one. It was good-natured opposition; all the couples they knew indulged in some form of one-upmanship. By refusing to play the game she is somehow breaking the rules that govern relationships; she is daring to challenge the very idea of coupledom as they have known it – as he has prescribed it. Why? Because she has something better, but this may not be true; she may be breaking free to endure a life alone. Would that be so bad, though, compared to this? 'True, you were my Socrates, my Svengali, my Professor Higgins.' She giggles in spite of herself. 'But now you're not; you're not in charge of my tastes.'

His eyes narrow and he hesitates before taking a hunk of ciabatta and dipping it into a pool of olive oil. 'You're leaving me, I know, but you don't have to insult me on your way out. We could make this civilized. You don't have to get petty or vindictive about it.'

She feels her stomach tie itself into knots. Their main course arrives. He slices off a piece of rare steak and brings it to his lips. She remembers the meal here with Konrad in the crumbling garden. If only they had known what was to come. She glances at Dominic. This is where she is, where she always is. He has already consumed half a bottle of red wine and she notices that his awareness is beginning to slip. He looks up as if she has just voiced her feelings. She remains silent and watches her fish dish slide into the space before her.

Her lack of response unnerves him and he eats his steak in quick sharp bites. The broken nose suits him in a way, makes him appear more sympathetic, although this is only an illusion. He will be calculating how he might intimidate and undermine her without really seeming to. It's his master strategy and she is now, she realizes, utterly tired of it.

'Would you like to know why I am leaving you?' she asks, putting her knife and fork down on her plate and leaning on her elbows.

He dabs his mouth with his napkin. 'For another man of course, a younger model, better looking, less fat, less . . .' His face reddens and he glances at her over the napkin, now stained with bloody steak juice. 'Of a challenge, I suppose. I've always suspected you would prefer an easier, more suburban life. Your taste in men is like your taste in food: pretty bland.'

She feels her teeth set. 'Now who is insulting whom?'

'Look' – he waves his fork at her and a fleck of meat spits across the table and lands on her cheek – 'you asked me why you were leaving and I'm telling you what I think.'

'You also said we should keep this civilized.' She feels a lump in her throat. His attempt to diminish her is pathetic and she sees that it is his only defence. He won't or can't put up a fight for her. He knows that he has already lost her and that makes her feel sad for them both.

He pushes away his plate. His knuckles are red and sore, as if he had dragged them across a stone wall after punching the glass windshield. 'What do you want to do about this, Catherine?'

The directness of his question takes her aback. She had thought they would spend the rest of the lunch sparring, circling each other with their hurt and their justifications. He opens his hands as if he is offering her the chance to explain herself, outline her new future, but it is too soon and she flounders. 'I don't know.' She hesitates, aware of sounding weak. 'I just need some time.'

He leans his chin on his hands and nods slowly. 'Of course, you need to consider whether you are doing the right thing. You hardly know him.' His eyes slip away from her.

She feels a pulse of sympathy for him then and reaches across the table for his hand. He moves it minutely out of reach and then, exhaling with irritation, calls the waiter over. 'Can I look at the dessert menu? And I want to see what liqueurs you have.'

The waiter bows his head, his expression deferential. 'I will bring it for you, sir.'

Dominic reaches for the wine bottle and pours himself another full glass of wine. His eyes are skittering across the table, trying to fix on some ordered pattern. His face is a mask of pain, its colour so high it makes her eyes water to look at him. The waiter returns with the menu and a list of liqueurs. Dominic orders zabaglione and grappa. 'For you, madam?' The waiter regards her with his head held to one side. Dominic huffs his impatience.

'Nothing more to eat.' She sits back, her mind calmer and clear. 'But I would like an espresso and another bottle of still water.' The waiter slips away. She looks at Dominic half turned in his seat, his legs twisted over each other. 'I'm sorry,' she says. 'I really am.'

There's a grating sound as he gets up from his wooden chair abruptly and bending low as if to avoid a fierce light, he makes his way out of the restaurant. Her hand moves up to her mouth where it hovers, fingers involuntarily picking at her lip. After a while her breathing calms and she is able to rest both her hands once more on the table in front of her. Discreetly the waiter appears with her single espresso and another bottle of water. She cancels the dessert and liqueur order.

Later she walks for a while around the city, winding her way down streets she has never visited before, catching glimpses of people talking and laughing in softly lit spaces. Some look at her and smile in acknowledgement, including her in the afternoon's proceedings, and she feels somehow part of something larger than her, some greater fabric. She drifts around the city for an hour or so longer, remembering her walk with Konrad when they had discovered all the churches and magical places, and the act of retracing those steps helps her; it reminds her that there is another life she could lead.

It is early evening when she arrives back at the room, tired and hungry again. The first thing she notices is that the wardrobe door has been left open and inside there is an empty space. As well as all his clothes, Dominic has packed hers. She checks the drawers and finds that he has gathered up everything: T-shirts, bras and knickers, cosmetics, even her toothbrush is gone from the holder in the bathroom. All she has is her shoulder bag. She puts it down on the carpet and sits on the bed and looks about the room. Why on earth has he taken her things?

The silence hums. She considers going downstairs and having a drink in the bar. It would be good to sit for a while with the concierge. He has probably witnessed a lot worse. To be left with only the clothes you are standing up in is really not anything to be distressed about. She lies back on the bed and kicks off her sandals. She listens to her breathing and feels the warmth of her own body. The silence clears around her. I am beginning, she thinks. I am beginning again.

A chink of light worming its way through a gap in the curtains wakes her. She is still lying on top of the bedclothes, her feet dangling over the edge, face down on the cover which oddly smells faintly of Konrad. She sits up, her head fuddled, not knowing for a moment where she is. She gets up and goes to the bathroom where she pees. Washing her hands, she looks at her face in the mirror over the sink. The downturn of her mouth is not so noticeable any more. Someone once told her that in repose, when she wasn't conscious of anyone looking at her, she looked grim. It wasn't meant unkindly. She had been complaining of someone else taking advantage of her at the time, but the comment had struck her deeply, and had made her aware that how she appeared on the outside must mirror how she felt on the inside, and that was: beleaguered. She wore a look of perpetual strain; she knew because she checked in windows and mirrors when she felt she could catch her unguarded self. But her face now looks as it used to, ten or fifteen years ago, when she was still curious about her future, when she was still open to new experiences. She lifts her hair off her face. She must have slept for around twelve hours. The whites of her eyes are very clear. A surge of energy courses through her as she lifts her arms and pulls off her rumpled linen dress, remembering to hang it on the hook on the bathroom door before she steps into the shower.

After breakfast she heads straight into the square, where the red and white striped stalls flap like tents in a hot breeze. Clouds bump across the oceanic sky, bold and rambunctious, swerving around the steeples of the many churches. Catherine's hair is fragrant from the coconut courtesy shampoo she found in a basket in the hotel room, along with a tiny folding toothbrush, nail scissors and small comb. She is naked under her dress, which is damp from the shower steam and flaps around her thighs. She passes a lingerie shop, lacy and satin confections displayed on Perspex busts in the antique window, and steps inside on to a deep pink carpet. A Polish woman in heavy make-up, eyebrows drawn in two fine arches, looks up from her magazine, puts it down in her lap and sighs with delight.

Fitted with an ivory silk bra and matching briefs that feel taut and cool against her skin, Catherine makes her way to a boutique recommended by the owner of the lingerie shop. 'It has exquisite things.' Her immaculate blue eyes had widened. 'There is so much there for a woman to love.'

Now inside the shop which is snug and fitted with white mirrors, sparkly ceiling lights and surprisingly spacious changing rooms, screened by blue velvet curtains with heavy pale blue ropes on gold hooks, Catherine looks at the pile of clothes draped over the back of a gold ballroom chair and feels a kind of girlish thrill at the thought of trying them on without worrying about time or critical comments. 'Every woman must love what she wears,' the lingerie lady had said, as if looking feminine were a kind of delicious duty. 'You have a clear, elegant look with your pale skin and rich hair. You should wear amber and gold and red, the colours of the forest.'

'I usually wear blue or green,' Catherine had said,

admiring the woman's palette, which was ivory and gold, like an Italian princess.

'I know, darling, time for a change.'

Now she lifts a black and gold sleeveless dress from its hanger. The material feels reassuringly heavy and when she tries it on she is pleased at the way the line of the cut hugs her bust and makes her waist seem smaller. She feels composed in this dress, poised for anything. Next is a skirt in black satin which smooths over her belly and flares around the hem in a little kick. She twists her head back over her shoulder and sees how the skirt accentuates the curve of her backside. Stepping out of it, she realizes that now she will have to buy shoes to compliment her new wardrobe.

As she pays for her new purchases with her credit card she feels no surge of guilt, more a feeling of bemused wonderment that she had not thought to update her clothes before. Over the years she has bought things, of course, but these were pieces she needed either for occasions, dinners, awards, formal meetings, everyday work and once worn seemed to take on the role of ambassador for whatever occasion they served. The clothes themselves seemed remote from her. When she looked in her wardrobe at home, kept in the spare room, she didn't see anything she liked, let alone loved: what she saw were events; entire evenings could be conjured by the sight of just one dark green velvet dress and matching jacket, evenings that were never amalgamated with others because each time she went out she had, on Dominic's insistence, to put on something new. He had bought her clothes which in the first few years of their relationship she had dutifully, and gratefully, worn. Some of the clothes were expensive and she wonders what he will do with them now.

Two pairs of shoes later she sits with her bags gathered around her and drinks a Coke under the shade of a yellow umbrella. Closing her eyes, she listens to the sound of the trumpeter playing from the steeple of St Mary's. Horses clop past on the cobbles and there is a sweet, hot smell of dung, mixed in with frying onions. Her calf brushes her crackling, expensive bags and she smiles to herself, thinking that anyone who saw her now would draw the conclusion that she is a frivolous tourist come to take advantage of the favourable exchange rate, not someone whose partner has left her without anything to wear for the rest of her stay. She considers this. She could have bought more practical things as well. A pair of jeans would be useful, as would some sensible walking shoes. She finishes her drink and stands up and just then catches sight of herself in the café window opposite and almost laughs out loud. I look like I'm planning something, she thinks, something I'm not even telling myself about.

13

Krystyna opened the novel. It was best to choose any chapter at random and work with the sentences in mid-flow. She was working in English with a copy of Emily Brontë's *Wuthering Heights*, moving rapidly with her pencil, composing her message by placing dots over the letters. She was on page seven.

She was faster now in English and proud of the progress she had made with her evening lessons with the colonel at his new lodgings: two small rooms with a cold tap, blank walls and blacked-out windows on the anonymous outskirts of the city.

It had become a routine that after curfew they settled down in two wooden chairs before the tiled stove and read to each other. *Wuthering Heights* was a favourite of the colonel's, the first entire novel he had read in English; the wildness of the Yorkshire landscape appealed to him and the spirit running through the novel like a stream of bright blood. The story was passionate; it was also brutal. The colonel said that it wasn't possible to read gentle art during a war. Reading was a form of protest, a way of reclaiming the soul from all that was happening around them. Members

253

of the underground were under constant threat from the Gestapo; many people had been arrested and tortured to reveal names of superiors. The evenings of quiet reading were a welcome respite.

Currently, the colonel was absorbed in Lord Acton's *History of Freedom*, and had read passages to her that she thought she would use in code when he passed the book on to her. The secret messages she composed in novels were sent to friends of the colonel, among them people who had worked for the Polish government before the war now held in German prisoner-of-war camps. For the Polish captives, saturated by German propaganda, the coded novels were the only source of real news. At first Krystyna doubted that the subtle messages were being noticed, but then a few weeks ago a cryptographer who had worked for the intelligence service managed to send out a message via a liaison girl that the English novels, permitted by the Germans, were much appreciated and made camp conditions so much easier to bear.

She turned another page. The number was in the top right-hand corner, which meant that the code would flow from left to right down the page. If the number were in the bottom right the code would flow upwards and back through the numbers in reverse order. The morning was hot and she wished she could open the small attic window to let in some air, but it had been sealed shut. She was working at the top of a narrow stationery shop that served as the unofficial headquarters of the resistance. Downstairs, the colonel, wearing thick-rimmed glasses and an ill-fitting suit, stood behind the counter and met with his chief of staff, section leaders and liaison officers who came and went under the cover of ordinary customers.

She worked swiftly for another half-hour and then pushed the novel into its sealed packet. She rubbed her eyes. Dust swam in the thick air. The attic's sloping wooden floors were so thick with it that it puffed out under the soles of her shoes like dry forest fungi whenever she moved, which was rarely. By now she had trained her mind to concentrate for long periods without needing to shift position. She was aware at all times that a sudden movement from her upstairs could betray them and put the entire operation at risk. She leaned her elbows on the table where she worked and rubbed her fingers against her sweating forehead. From downstairs in the shop she heard the sound of the ringing till.

Most of the customers were Polish people, but there were some young Germans who came in search of writing paper on which to compose letters to new wives or girlfriends, favouring smooth, neatly sized pages in a pale shade of violet. So eager were they to purchase paper of quality that they overlooked or chose not to notice the faint watermark of the Polish eagle wearing its defiant crown.

Every day plain-clothes Gestapo officers also came to the shop to turn over the produce, casually pressing the batches of envelopes with their fingers, as if testing fruit for ripeness. They demanded to know the strength of the lead in the unmarked pencils, the same pencils that were being used to compose secret messages above their heads. When she heard the colonel cough insistently three times, she knew they were downstairs, and kept all her movements to a minimum. One time she was about to relieve her bladder in the bucket pushed up against one of the small spaces under the eaves and had her trousers pulled down to her hips when she heard the cough. It had an anxious tone, a bark, or so it seemed to her as she hovered and tried desperately to control the urge to relieve herself. The pain made sweat spring on to her brow as she cupped herself, breathing deeply, waiting for the all-clear signal, a single cough, which did not come until her palm had grown warm and wet.

If the colonel were taken for questioning, she had to wait for an hour before leaving herself. This had not yet happened, but she anticipated it every day, and so did he, but he did not speak about it. The entrance to the back stairs leading up to the attic was hidden by a heavy filing cabinet covered with books and papers, piled up in a haphazard way, sheaves of pages bending under the weight of heavy volumes, tobacco-stained paperbacks, old creased city maps and postcard collections. On the chairs, tea trays and glass jars were stuck with sharpened pencils. The blinds were kept drawn and the shop had a stuffy, packed, unwholesome atmosphere, deliberately contrived to prevent lingering. When they were seen arriving together, he introduced her to customers as his daughter.

Nothing was left in the attic room for fear of raids by the Gestapo. She carried everything she needed in her customized vanity case: books for code making, pencils, notebooks, a torch for when the electricity failed, which was often, some hard bread to keep her going through the long hours. In Kraków there were plenty of shops selling food to the Germans, shops which Poles were forbidden to enter, but there were German-speaking Poles who acted as couriers, including her now that her German had improved; in this way she ensured that she did not go hungry. She usually worked until four when the colonel shut up shop, warning her by jangling the shop bell four times.

In the event that the colonel was unable to warn her she had been given a capsule of cyanide that she knew she would have to take the moment the Gestapo entered the attic. She kept it in a small velvet purse hung on a silk cord around her neck. Her father's signet ring was stitched into a separate part of the purse. When she bent forward to write she could feel the material brush against her skin. Often when she was working on her codes her fingers would stray to her throat and feel for the capsule snug in the seam of the purse. It was preciously fragile; the mere act of swallowing it would fracture the glass. In seconds her throat would be pierced and the poison would enter her blood. Sometimes the urge to take it from its velvet pouch and put it into her mouth was almost irresistible. She imagined the taste of it, the forbidden feelings it would offer up, secret feelings, feelings that were unbearable. Some days she was so afraid that she did not have the strength to resist the temptation of the glass pearl, she considered crushing it underfoot. But to do so would have put the resistance at risk, for if she were caught in the attic she would almost certainly have been tortured.

Last night she'd broached the subject with her team-worker Janek while they were at the wireless station. Did he think about it? Didn't he want to know how it felt to take poison?

He paused to consider, his eyes glossy in the lamplight. 'No and neither should you. Forget about it. It's too dangerous even to imagine.'

He turned away and fiddled with one of the dials on the radio set. There was no reception. Strange disconnected bird calls of broken sound filled the store cupboard where they worked, wedged on tiny stools, knee to knee. A hot prickly smell caught the back of her throat. She became aware of the heat from her belly and her arms, the smell of her own sweat, the dampness of the hair on the back of her neck. His rusty scent. He looked at her and his glance caused a shudder to run like a jolt of electricity right through her body.

The radio hissed and then cleared. A single word. A fragment of news from London. Indistinct. The word 'grave' which she jotted on her pad, the rest indecipherable, the words stretched and distorted, as if spoken through wool. Janek scrabbled at the dials to find the announcement, but it spooled away from him. For a moment he sat in silence.

She leaned forward and twisted the dial. The sombre, yet clear tones of Churchill pushing through the matted noise surprised them and they giggled and looked at each other wide-eyed. 'BBC,' Janek breathed, his eyes heavy with joy. 'It's the BBC, from London.'

'The news from France is very bad.' Churchill's words caught her across the bridge of her nose, almost as if she had been slapped. Janek's back stiffened. She scribbled down the words. 'We shall not forget the gallant French people. As the only champion now in arms, we will do our best to defend our island and we will fight until the curse of Hitler is lifted from the brows of men.' Janek's knee jiggered. His breathing was heavy. Her pen felt like a hard bead between her fingers as she wrote out the bulletin on two pages with a carbon sheet between them, taking care over the words, knowing that the colonel would need this message to be accurate.

A tap at the door from their lookout indicated that it was safe to leave. She folded the bulletin into a tiny square and slid it behind the mirror in her vanity case. She snapped the small brass lock shut.

Janek glanced at her from under his thick fringe. 'I could deliver it.' His eyes were steady.

'No.' She lifted the case. 'You have the copy. You know where to go if I don't make it?'

He nodded. 'The coffee house,' which was the code name for the meeting place. From here one of the colonel's staff would arrive to take the message and the news that she had been captured. Honorata, as she was now known, was one of the few liaison girls, perhaps the only girl, for they did not communicate with each other or know each other's real names, allowed direct access. She lifted her vanity case. Janek met her eyes. 'See you tomorrow.' He shifted off his stool and went down on his knees under a shelf. He began to prise up the floorboards ready to hide the radio sets and equipment in their hollow space.

She stepped out into the street. It was early evening and still light. Many workers, bags and satchels slung over shoulders, were travelling home from offices and shops. With any luck she could reach the colonel before curfew. She would have to stay the night there, of course. It was too dangerous to cross the city alone at night. She walked briskly, her case held close to her thigh. She wore a grey dress and jacket and smart blue shoes with a stout heel. Her hair was now styled into a short bob. Often she wore different-coloured scarves. Her heels tapped along the pavement. She crossed the road and passed a row of shuttered shops. There was a sulphurous smell coming from the drain outside. She increased her pace and then became aware of the sound of someone behind her matching his steps – she knew it was a man by the heavy footfall – to hers. She slowed. It was important that she should not give any signs of fear or make any obvious turns or moves that would corner her. She had plenty of time. The street ahead was busy; a stream of workers was coming towards her, faces pallid in the low evening light. She gathered her thoughts. If she walked to the end of the street and then turned left she would be close to the entrance of the park. It might be dangerous to walk under the trees in the growing darkness. She would have to find a way round to the station.

She reached the end of the street and paused, pretending to watch the traffic. German cars hummed down the road, ignoring the streams of people who leapt out of the way. A tram shook down a track. She became aware of someone standing behind her so close she could feel his breath on the back of her neck. Her hand rose to her throat. Her heart hammered against her ribs. She stepped out into the road and then felt a hand on the collar of her jacket as she was jerked back, away from the wheels of a glossy black car that rolled past smoothly. She whirled round, lips trembling, and she came face to face with her shadow.

'Careful,' he said, and dropped his hold on her jacket. He was in his late thirties with a sallow complexion; tired, brown eyes with all the kindness drained out of them. 'You nearly got yourself killed.' His eyes strayed to her vanity case.

'Thank you.' She addressed him in flawless German and his eyes faltered for a moment. Her heart lurched in her chest. She held his gaze. His eyes swept away almost in apology. He took a step back and inclined his head. She moved away smartly on her heels. She would take the river route.

Halfway down the path, with the water lapping in the

breeze, she sensed that she was being followed again, this time by two men. The young Gestapo agent had possibly had second thoughts and sent them after her. On their hit lists, they had photographs of some of the underground army personnel. Being so close to the colonel she was undoubtedly a prize. She knew they stripped women for questioning, pushed them into windowless cells, beat them and wore them down by forcing them to stand for hours without sleep, or food, or water to drink. The Gestapo interrogators crawled through your mind. They were as tough as parasites, impervious to human weeping or suffering, immune to pain, intent only on extracting information.

She moved closer to the river. If they grabbed her she would throw the case in first and then jump in, drown, before they caught her alive. She heard them say something to one another. Something about the curfew. She had forgotten. Now she was almost certainly about to be stopped.

She came to a long boat berthed against the shoreline, its wooden figurehead carved into the shape of a dragon. An old man with legs like two bent hinges came up on deck with a bucket and paused for a few moments. Something in her face made him smile at her in greeting as if he had really come out to see whether she were coming as she said she would. He called out a name: 'Basia,' his eyes narrowing as he registered the two dark figures coming towards her on the tow path.

'Yes, Uncle,' she called back, her voice cracking with relief. 'It's me, Basia, come to check that you are all right.' She watched the old man unfold a worn rope ladder and throw it across to her. His eyes were beady.

She stepped on to the ladder. The rope was so rotted it almost gave way under her. She balanced her weight and then called out: 'Stand back, Uncle, I need to throw my case on board first.' The old man hesitated. The boat was narrow. It would have been too easy for her to miss and hurl it across the other side. Instead of moving as she had asked, he stood firm and caught the case in both hands like a sack of flour. He held it to his chest and scanned the path, while she scrabbled up the rope. She pulled it away and the boat rocked back into position in the scummy water, out of reach.

Under the glow of a lamp she saw two men lighting cigarettes, blowing streams of smoke into the sultry air. One of them, the shorter of the two with a face like a smudged moon, began to cough. The other, taller, fiercer, his face as hard as a shard of glass, smoked in strong pulls and then flicked the end into the river where it extinguished with a soft fizz and swirled into the current. The old man put her case down on the deck and nodded. Around his mouth there was a trace of a smile. The agents moved on along the path.

After resting at the old man's insistence in a tiny bunk on the boat, rocked by the river, while he kept watch on the prow outside, she was able to leave and complete her mission. When she reached the colonel's lodgings and showed him the bulletin he pretended for a few moments to be surprised, but she knew that he already had the news. He patted her on the shoulder and looked at her creased and rumpled clothes which smelled of the river. He told her that he was on his way to a meeting at the monastery with his senior staff. She should rest. He would see her at the shop in the morning. His face was the colour of wax and she knew from the deep pouches under his eyes that he'd had little sleep. As Churchill had indicated, the news from France was indeed grave. The Polish government-in-exile operated from Paris. The collapse of the country under the Germans meant that the entire resistance organization was under threat. It seemed impossible that funds from Paris could get through, not now. Not only that, but there had been plans to begin a general uprising, based on the assumption that the Germans would soon be beaten on the Western Front. Now all hope of a German defeat had dissolved. Hovering behind the colonel's pale weariness, she had thought she saw the first clouds of doubt.

Now she turned over a page of *Hard Times*. Sometimes the code worked flawlessly, a neat set of pencil prints like a pricked-out dress pattern, but today she could not settle. It was partly lack of sleep — dawn had seeped into the sky while she lay awake worrying about what would happen now that France had been captured — but mostly the heat. It sucked on her energy like a big soft mouth. She put her hand on the back of her neck where her skin felt cool. She was pleased at least that she no longer had to bear the full weight of her hair. She looked entirely different with shorter hair: sharper and more self-contained. Few people from her old life would recognize her now. She wondered whether Janek, the other Janek, would know her. She still thought of him as *her* Janek. Sometimes as she worked in the attic she imagined that he was searching the country for her, driven by the desire to know that she was safe, and this fantasy somehow kept him alive. But there were also days when she did not think of him at all and when she did, it was with a jolt, a reminder that her priorities were changing and that she had in place a new family and a job, a way of being that was so different to what she had known it was almost as if she had become someone entirely new.

From outside came the sound of church bells. She stopped work and lifted her head. The bells were not usually rung during the day as the Germans wanted to keep the Poles out of the churches for fear that mass was being used to transfer secrets or plot sabotage. The Führer had ordered the Germans to destroy the Polish spirit by especially targeting the Catholic faith. SS officers in black swept on people as they left mass, beating them with batons. Some graves and gravestones had been desecrated. But in spite of the brutality the Germans failed to shut down the churches completely, mostly due to the defiance of the priests who stood their ground and ordinary people who continued to attend church, as she did whenever she could, for a few minutes to kneel with brow pressed against the altar rail or to light a candle, to affirm that the Church was still part of them and mattered deeply. 'They can take our lives and twist them whichever way they like, but they cannot twist our hearts; our unshakeable hearts,' she'd heard a priest say in church in the presence of German soldiers who did not understand Polish.

The bells gathered force. It sounded as if all the churches across Kraków were calling in great strident hammer strokes. The ringing reverberated in her chest. She went to the window and knelt on the floorboards. Peering through the glass, she saw that the sky was a creamy blue. She could see church spires, dappled grey in the morning light, and tiled roofs in terracotta and green. The clamour increased so strongly it vibrated the whole building and caused the floorboards to shake. She heard a noise downstairs and realized that the colonel had arrived. The bells hurled out their sound. If he coughed now she would not be able to hear him. Fear jumped in her throat and her fingers automatically moved towards the purse around her neck. When it came to it, would she really have the courage to do it?

The noise of the church bells was so intense she could not concentrate on her work. She stayed crouched by the window, the glass steaming from the heat of her skin. The urge to break it open to let in some air was strong. She heard the shop door opening downstairs. It sounded as if someone had gone out to the street. She strained to see what was happening on the pavement below, but the sealed window revealed nothing, only the taunting blue sky.

She dusted off her knees and returned to her desk and picked up the copy of *Hard Times*. If she couldn't work on codes, at least she could try to read. The bells would have to stop some time; they couldn't go on ringing all morning, or could they? She didn't know. The city was different every day. The buildings and streets looked the same as when she first arrived, but there was a new feeling every morning; she could almost taste it. The changes were small; sometimes just an addition of a new order or notice taped to a lamp post or tree or nailed to one of the noticeboards that once had been used for prayers outside the churches. The orders mostly took the form of lists of new offences together with punishments that could be expected for breaking the rules. Gradually the occupation was turning into a slow annihilation. Rights were demolished, people were being degraded, forced to become servile and subordinate. It was forbidden for Poles to travel in certain carriages on trams or trains, or enter particular restaurants or shops. Those were reserved for Germans alone. No Pole had a right to own property; no Pole had a right to take part in any sort of cultural activity; there was no right to study. Radio sets were no longer permitted in Polish homes and discovery was punished by death. Executions for small infringements had become almost commonplace. She had learned, like everyone else, to turn away from the bodies slumped against blood-splashed walls, but not in coldness, not indifferently. Every shooting of every innocent Pole, whether peasant or professor, fuelled the resistance; with every outrage the invisible passion grew stronger.

Some of the younger underground members made it their business to take revenge on the Germans even though it was against the rules. No one was supposed to act alone. No one was to commit vandalism. No one was to become an outlaw. The colonel reminded them often that they were part of a principled resistance.

Nonetheless, some of the more hot-headed and impulsive young men, Janek among them, found total obedience impossible. Janek told her that one night he had followed a German officer home and waited for him to go up to his city apartment in one of the older, established blocks where most of the high-ranking officers lived in a state of grace. Downstairs in the elegant lobby, Janek took his pocket knife and cut a slash across his own arm. He let blood gather in a thick seam. This he smeared on the stone steps leading up to the apartments, on the balustrade, and daringly on the brass door handle of the apartment the German officer had entered only minutes previously. He cleaned off the rest of the blood on the stone steps outside. This incident was shortly after they had discovered that the university professors, many of whom had homes in the apartments now so casually occupied, had been transferred from Kraków Prison to the Sachsenhausen Oranienburg concentration camp.

The church bells stopped abruptly. She waited, her ears anticipating another pounding. Downstairs she heard a chair scrape across the floor and then, hours ahead of closing time, the signal. At first she thought the colonel had made a mistake. Perhaps the ferocity of the bells had fuddled his mind and made him think it was later than it was. She hovered by her desk, the coded novel in her hands. The shop bell jangled again and this time there was the unmistakable sound of the filing cabinet being pushed away from the door at the foot of the stairs. But still she could not move until she heard the colonel call out in an over-loud voice to a customer that they were closing early today.

'What was all that about?' she asked, stepping into the shop which looked even more disordered than usual.

'Celebration.' The colonel's voice was terse. 'Now that they have France, they want us to think they've won.'

She didn't know what to make of this. War seemed nothing to do with winning or losing; toppling countries like lines of dominoes. That was just how it appeared on the surface. But underneath the game there was something more sinister and mean, a dark seam of contempt that felt personal. She couldn't think of how to express what she truly felt to the colonel. In a way she was embarrassed. 'They're crazy, what about England?' she offered in reply.

The colonel peered at her over his glasses and then real-ized that he could take them off. He placed them in the top pocket of his suit and blinked. A few weeks ago he said he would make some enquiries about her father on her behalf. She wanted to ask him now whether he had heard anything, but his weariness stopped her from voicing the thought. He would tell her when he was ready. Now he put his hand on her shoulder. There was no weight to it. 'They are saying that England no longer matters. England has no army left. It will be finished in ten days.'

She thought of the posters that had been taped around the city showing a wounded soldier in the rubble of Warsaw, his fist drawn against an image of Neville Chamberlain, the British Prime Minister who had led the country into war before Churchill. Below the image was the caption: 'England, this is your work.'

'But that can't be true, can it? England won't give up.'

'We hope not.' The colonel rubbed his eyes and smiled faintly. 'It may get unpleasant here in the city. We ought to leave soon.'

She moved towards the boxes. 'I'll help you to clear up.' She pushed the boxes into a corner. The colonel locked the cash drawer on the counter and stacked a few envelopes in a pile, arranging them so that they fell into line. She could tell that it gave him satisfaction. What discipline it must have taken for him to keep the shop so untidy and chaotic, to override his natural disposition daily.

The colonel came out from behind the counter. There was a slight hump between his shoulder blades, and the stoop meant that when he moved he pushed the air first with his forehead. 'Do you enjoy your work here?' His eyes were downcast.

'Yes, of course. I like it very much.' She paused. He had never directly asked her how she felt, and his interest confused her. 'I'm learning something. I'm learning a lot.'

She could see that he was relieved. 'You don't feel that you're missing your education?'

'No. I have the books we read together and my work – it's more than enough.' She tried to sound bright and hopeful, but the penetrating quality of his stare unnerved her. 'Why? Why do you ask?'

He lifted the shop key from its hook by the door. 'I sometimes wonder whether I have done the right thing.' His eyes swept the shop as if he were looking at it for the last time. 'What sort of life is this for you, for any young woman?'

The uncertainty in his voice shook her. 'It's a perfectly good life,' she offered. 'I don't want any other, not now. And if you asked any of the others they would say the same thing. This work is what we live for.'

He sighed. 'But at such a price. Such a terrible price.'

She went up to him and touched her fingers to his elbow. Rarely had she seen him so filled with doubt and she understood that it had been triggered by the news of the defeat of France. Did he feel now that it was only a matter of time before England, their one remaining ally and friend, also fell?

'My life is my choice,' she said, meeting his eyes. 'I have sworn an oath.'

He took a deep breath and then cleared his throat. 'Krystyna.' His voice was strained.

She stared at him, surprised to hear him use her real name.

He continued: 'This is the last time you will work here. I'm assigning you to other duties.'

She inhaled. She wanted to protest, but it seemed as if this was something he had decided a long time ago and had just been waiting for her to stop and look at him so that he could tell her. Still, the thought of losing the privilege of working every day with him made her panic. 'I'll work harder,' she blurted out. 'I'll be quieter, too. You don't need to worry about me.'

His eyes were horrified. 'You must know that in making you my assistant, I have put your life at risk, unforgivably.'

'I forgive you!'

He smiled at her desperation. 'Two Gestapo agents came here this morning asking for a girl who matched your description.'

She felt her mouth go dry. So the men from the river had somehow tracked her down. It was she who had put the colonel at risk. 'I was careful this morning; I know I've not led anyone here.' But even as she spoke she knew that she could not be sure.

'I'm not suggesting you have blown our cover. I simply want to protect you.'

She grasped then that her quiet days of coding in the attic room were about to end. Clearly the colonel had other duties in mind for her and it was her duty now to accept. She swallowed. It was difficult not to cry, but if he saw how weak she was, he might take her off liaison duties altogether.

'Honorata.' Now he used her code name, carefully, as if he wanted her to listen with more attention than usual. 'I want you to go to the vestry and stay there until I come later. We have to work on a new sermon.'

She understood. He was sending her to the newspaper office in the basement of an unremarkable house tucked away in the suburbs. Getting there would take a couple of hours by two trains. She lifted her chin and her eyes moved towards the filing cabinet and the floor above it where she had spent some of her happiest hours. 'You won't be working with anyone else?'

He looked startled at her question. 'No, I won't be working here at all. I'm closing down this operation.'

She felt foolish. How could she think that she knew better than her commanding officer? He had been trying to let her down gently and she had not listened. She'd allowed her will to stand in her way and shame her again. When faced with decisions she disagreed with she became rebellious. In Irena's words: stubborn as wood. 'If you follow no one but yourself, you will end up alone,' she had told her when she refused to comply once too often. Her mind lingered on an image of the kitchen table at the dwór and with difficulty she pulled her thoughts back to the present. 'Thank you,' she said to the colonel. 'I have been happy here.'

He nodded and touched his face with his hand for a moment. Leaving him to lock up the shop, she went out into the street, scanning the building entrances for signs that she was being shadowed. The cobbles were hot and slippery under her feet. She took her usual circuitous route to the station through the narrow back streets where people lived with shutters pulled and blinds drawn day and night. Today the houses seemed even more tightly closed than usual.

She came out on to Kopernika and here the heavy mood lifted. Many apartments and houses had their doors and windows open for a change, and glancing up she caught sight of winged chairs and bookcases, rugs, desks, the wink of a chandelier, and felt an ache in her chest for the familiar contours of a room in a place she could call home. For so long, she had lived according to necessity: sleeping in stale beds that gave her no comfort, dressing in small, cold corners, sharing bathrooms with girls she could not talk to. Her duffel bag accompanied her whenever she moved and had become her protective shell. The bright, homely rooms overlooking the street made her feel as if she had been cut off from the world of ordinary human existence for too long.

There was no one in sight. No one leaning on a balcony, looking down at the life in the street below; no one calling across a greeting to a neighbour; no one laughing or arguing; instead there were sounds of intense musical preoccupation. At first the tentative notes of a violin, then a piano, chords piercing the thick summer air and growing in fullness until the vibrations swelled in passionate wavelets all along the length of the street to be answered next by a cello, and then a bright flute and then, a few floors up, an oboe, the sound reminding her of the peacocks at home who had chosen as their autumn roost the wide ledge under the eaves of the barn where they called to one another in major notes, shaking the misty rain from their inky oil-painted throats. She remembered watching them with her father, marvelling at their tiny dancing headdresses and the deep darkness of their swivelling eyes, highlighted by arrows of white, and a sob escaped her.

The music reached a crescendo above her head. She stood listening, half in fear, half in delight, as the impromptu orchestra continued to perform its invisible concert. Then anxiety gripped her as she realized that she would now have to hurry to the station or she would miss the last train.

It wasn't until she had boarded the train and settled in a German carriage that she understood what the music in the street had been for. It had been a spontaneous response to the bells orchestrated by the Germans. Forced to listen to the insulting peals of celebration, the musicians of Kopernika had retaliated in the best way they knew. It made her smile and helped to ease her mind from the

colonel's decision to close the shop. The colonel had
boarded the train and sat a few seats away from her. She
looked at him, his spine straight in his seat, his head resting on the grubby grey pillow between the winged seat
dividers, nodding in time to the pull of the train. He
wore the thick black-framed glasses he used as disguise,
with real glass in the lenses in case someone looked too
closely. People had been beaten up for wearing empty
frames. His skin glowed in the soft yellow lamp of the
carriage and she wondered what it would be like to rest
her cheek against his.

At the next stop he opened his eyes and looked at her
over the top of his glasses. She thought she saw a trace of
worry in his expression, but he quickly concealed it as he
stood to retrieve her duffel bag and vanity case from the
luggage rack. He put her luggage down between their feet
and momentarily glanced away. Trembling, she offered
him her hand. 'Goodbye.'

He took her hand in both of his and squeezed it. He
closed his eyes, unable to speak. She saw his Adam's apple
pulse in his throat. She realized that it was now too dangerous for him to stay in Kraków. She wondered where he
kept his poison and hoped it was somewhere he could
reach in seconds. She disentangled her hands from his and
then felt him pull her roughly to his chest. His breathing
was damp over the top of her head.

She stepped out on to the platform without looking
back and made her way across a bridge to the single line
where she would wait for the slow train to take her to the
vestry where she would be making her home in a new
room in a new safe house.

When she arrived at the newspaper office Janek was

already there. The room was lit by a low lamp and smelled strongly of new chemical print. Newspapers on flimsy paper were stacked awaiting dispatch. All over the country illegal presses had been set up and networks of couriers, using specially designed bags and hollow bicycles, made sure that news of the resistance got through. Janek was already at work on the laborious process of folding or rolling the papers so that they could be disguised.

'You didn't wait for me?' Her reproach came out before she could stop it.

He glanced at her, his eyes puzzled, the gold gleam of his hair piercing the darkness. His hands shook as he folded a newspaper into the size of a small envelope. She could tell that he was biting back words that could wound her.

'I'm sorry.'

He lifted a page up to the light. It was almost transparent. She read some of the messages and news items. The main story, of course, was the impact of the German assault on France. The Poles were being urged not to lose hope, but to keep up all their efforts of resistance. She moved closer to him and he made room for her, sighing as he did so. She reached for the next paper and they worked silently for a while, folding and smoothing. She slipped into a dreamy mood, remembering the bells and the music from the street and the colonel's arms around her in the carriage, his wet eyes as he had pulled away and then swiftly brought his hand down her cheek in one move. She could still feel the gentle pressure of his touch; as if extracting some kind of promise from her. She wondered whether she ought to tell Janek that the shop had closed down, but looking at him with his bottom lip thrust out as he rolled a paper, she felt that she could not. 'We're ready.' His voice startled her.

They hid the news bulletins under a blanket. In a few minutes the couriers would start to arrive, some by bicycle, others on foot, and the process of distribution would begin. Each courier took only a few copies to sow around like seeds. Copies were read many times and passed on, secreted under mats in apartment blocks, pushed into hidden cracks inside old churches where they would be retrieved later, smoothed and read sometimes by magnifying glass; when the pages became too soft and limp they were used as rags to clean windows or mirrors, all traces of ink vanished by this time, the words digested and absorbed.

The couriers came in ones and twos, some needing to talk about what they had witnessed, acts of violence or brutality they had not been able to prevent or avert. It was this exposure to harm that tore into them, especially the younger ones, whose faces had a white, fixed look, all expression wrung from their features, their eyes tight and dry as they related their tales, not for sympathy, but because they were too filled up with horror already and anything extra could not fail but to spill out. Some of them wanted the stories to be written down so that the world would know. One boy had seen soldiers knock into a gutter an old Jewish man who failed to bow. The Germans had kicked him in the kidneys until he stopped groaning. A girl had watched a group of soldiers terrorize a deaf woman by holding a pistol to her head and pretending to shoot. A boy of eleven had found a dead child hidden inside a suitcase, its face so bloated and crawling with blue flies it no longer appeared human. He had taken the grotesque case to the river rather than leave it in the street. He had vomited after he told the story. Krystyna had cleaned up the mess and wondered just how much more of this they could all take.

The last courier, a boy of thirteen named Marek, who they liked because he never complained of being tired or hungry, failed to show up. Midnight passed and they grew restless in their small room, needing to stretch their cramped limbs. After half an hour of squirming and sighing and twisting to get comfortable, Janek stood up and announced that he had to get out for some air. 'Perhaps I'll see him coming down the street.'

'I expect so.' She agreed too readily, but she knew this was dangerous. She kept very still as he left, shouldering his way out of the room as if it were somehow in his way. Marek usually travelled by bicycle from another suburb not too far away. He was frequently late because although he didn't like to talk about himself, others, usually older people, would want to stop and talk to him. For many, he was their messenger, their sole contact with the outside world, and they often accosted him and asked him what was happening before even he could possibly know.

She smelled Janek's fear as soon as he returned, seconds, it seemed, after he had gone out, panting as he locked the door and pushed the filing cabinet against it. 'Get down under the table. Get down.' His eyes glared at her. His cheeks were livid with a high flush. 'Round-up. The Germans are piling people into trucks.' He switched off the light. She went down under the table and felt his hand, surprisingly cool, on the back of her neck. Her skin prickled. She crouched on her knees, her nose almost touching the floor. Janek was behind her. His heat was heavy, pressing against her. She smelled the sharp, high note of his sweat and her legs went slack. Out of the darkness his hand reached towards her and rested on her hip. She twisted her body round and looked at him. 'Did you see Marek?' she whispered.

He shook his head and she saw shame in his eyes and something else that she recognized. He drew himself up on all fours, moving like a cat, his expression full of a deep softness that made her want to rise to meet it. He lowered his head. His hair had a hot metallic smell. His mouth was close to hers. 'No.' She turned her head to one side and he eased back from her, his eyes clouding, and she felt a pang for him. Outside a truck pulled away up the street, grinding its gears as it began to climb the hill towards the forest. Janek waited a few moments longer and then sat up, cracking his head on the underside of the table, shifting his legs pointedly away from hers. His expression was distant, detached. A soft four-beat knock on the door propelled him on to his feet. She let him get the door and then stood up, brushing down her skirt which suddenly felt too thin for her.

Marek tumbled inside. His eyes immediately darted to their faces as if they had important news for him. Krystyna dropped her gaze. Marek told them that the Gestapo knew there was an illegal operation in one of the houses. 'They were close,' he said. 'They went next door.' She felt nausea rise in her stomach. If they had been discovered they almost certainly would have been tortured. There was a good chance that the Gestapo would return the next night. They would need to stay away for a while.

Janek gave Marek his copies of the bulletin, helping the boy to push the thin papers into the various hiding places on his body, down his boots and inside the hollow tubular frame of his bicycle. After he was packed up, he stood before them for a moment, his eyes brimming with light. 'You two are the luckiest people on the street tonight. Why they didn't come here, I don't know. They were on their way, but something stopped them.' He looked at Krystyna. 'Maybe you were born under a lucky star.'

'Maybe.' She patted him gently on the shoulder. 'Be careful on the way out, Marek.' A part of her yearned to go with him, to walk in step with him as he wheeled his bicycle back along the dark street, talking of what had happened in the way that children talk, as if there is nothing else to consider other than the mission. The colonel had said that children made good soldiers because they didn't question their orders and she knew that those like Marek were particularly valued because they wanted to succeed at all costs. She wanted to succeed, too, but now working so close to Janek she felt compromised. She wondered whether she could ask her supervisor if she could be taken off the vestry operation. The trouble was, it was known that she and Janek worked well together. After their first mission to the Collegium Novum, they had been treated as a pair, and it had been tempting to think of him as the person she could most rely on when things got hot, but after what had happened tonight she knew that she did not want to see him again. The ache she felt around him did not belong to him; her feelings were with Janek, the other Janek. The fact that they had the same name had made her feel that there was some connection between them, some emotional bond that also included the remote Janek. Out of her need for him she was able to capture a feeling, a mood that she remembered from the long afternoons lying in the hay loft at home. He was not Janek and yet he was. Through him she could feel something of that time when she was free, when her world was safe. And it made her lonely; it made her realize what she missed.

Wordlessly they packed the few remaining newspapers

into false-bottomed suitcases, locked them and pushed them under the floorboards. Janek went outside to check the street was clear. She pulled a tablecloth over the top of the filing cabinet that hid their cache of suitcases and then added a pewter-framed photograph of the woman who had once lived in the house, eyes as luminous as a film star's, the shadows of the photograph illuminating her fine bone structure. Krystyna had no idea who she was. Her photograph was all that had been left in the house. She remembered Marek's comment that she was born under a lucky star and she wondered whether that meant that she would be somehow safe. But it was naive to think like that. Her need for freedom must not make her foolish.

A half-hour passed and Janek did not return. She realized that she did not know Janek's family name or anything about his history. He had not spoken to her of his past. For him the immediate present was too filled with possibility and danger. His restless energy propelled him towards a future that he and other young men like him imagined so fiercely and so intensely the past was overridden. The past was to men like Janek, she understood, almost an irrelevance. It would be recovered after victory, though. It would be mourned when the threat had gone. But there were many who wondered whether there would be enough people left to make a future. All the struggle and sacrifice might be in vain. But Janek had never expressed doubt. Indeed, he had told her not to listen to the pessimists who claimed that the Germans had already won. 'Everyone should shut up; we won't lose our nerve.'

Another half-hour passed. Her stomach felt tight with hunger. In her mind she saw Janek's eyes searching hers for the answer she had not been able to give. Now she wished she had surrendered. It confused her how quickly her feelings could change. It would be simple to be with him, she knew; the longing to end her loneliness was a powerful urge that pulled at her like a tide. Next time she would not resist. A light tapping at the door interrupted her flow of thoughts. A young voice gave the password: 'Tea with jam.' With a dry mouth she got up.

An ashen-faced Marek stood outside, his thin body trembling from head to toe. At his hip, his bicycle was crumpled, as if a giant had squeezed it in his fist. His clothes were shredded and there was a wide grit-studded gash down the length of his arm. His knuckles oozed blood. He dragged the bicycle down the basement steps. His eyes were fixed with fear. She asked him about the bulletins and he said they were still inside the bicycle frame.

She glanced at his arm glinting with blood: 'That looks very sore, let me see if I can find the First Aid box and put some antiseptic on it.'

He stared after her, his thin chest heaving. She found the box on a high shelf and brought it down and held it in front of her. Marek stared at her again. Then he spoke, his words coming out in short gasps. 'The Gestapo chased after me in a black car.' He struggled for breath and then continued: 'They tried to knock me down. They put the lights on full and tried to blind me. I swerved and the bumper caught my bike. I fell into the road. They got out. There were two men and a woman. It was a woman who had been driving. One of the men had a gun. I lay as still as I could. I thought that if I pretended to be dead, they would leave me alone.' He pulled his sleeve across his eyes and took a deep breath.

She put the First Aid box down on the filing cabinet

next to the film star photograph. She gestured to Marek to sit, but he remained standing, caught in the glare of the basement lamp, his eyes two huge, dark pools. 'They came up to me and they started to argue about what to do. One of them said they should run over me, just in case. I heard them go back to the car. I waited for the engine to start and then I got up and ran. I didn't look where I was going, I just ran. A woman who must have been watching let me into the front porch of her house. She bolted the door. The next thing we heard was the screaming of brakes and then shots. I looked through a crack in the door. I saw one of the Gestapo men fall down dead. Then I saw Janek firing with his revolver.' Marek hesitated and took a long, ragged breath. Krystyna's heart began to hammer as she understood.

'They got him and beat him around the head with his gun and then they tied his hands and pushed him in the car.' He looked up at her. Tears rolled down his cheeks, all his young soldier's defences dissolving. 'I am sorry.'

She took the boy's battered body into her arms and comforted him, feeling his tears soak the front of her dress. She was grateful to him for the release, for her own feelings were dry as she imagined the journey Janek would now be making to the Gestapo headquarters where they would torture him to reveal names of his superiors before shooting him. She gently prised Marek from her and sat him down on a stool. She gave him her handkerchief and watched him wipe the tears from his face and then she reached behind her for the First Aid box. Taking it into her lap she opened it and there found antiseptic and tweezers and cotton wool.

'Give me your arm.' Marek did as she asked. He was

quiet now, his narrow face shut down, and she was able to clean his wound in silence. When she had picked out the last bead of grit, she paused for a moment and her fingers went to her neck where her purse nestled in its warm hollow. She opened it and fished out the glass capsule, as delicate as a raindrop rolling in her palm. Marek's eyes were now alert. 'You know what this is?'

He nodded at her, his eyes silent with awe. 'I want you to take it,' she said.

He picked the capsule from her palm and held it between his thumb and forefinger.

'Careful, don't pierce it,' she said. 'Have you somewhere safe to conceal it?'

Marek patted his shirt pocket.

'No, better put it inside, if you can,' she said.

He undid his shirt, turning away from her in embarrassment. Underneath he was wearing a grubby white vest and over his breast she saw a crude kind of pocket made from a small patch of pale gold material like curtain fabric. Biting down on his lip he dropped the glass capsule into the seam of the home-made pocket. She did not ask what was inside the pocket and he did not offer to show her. He turned away again as she retied the ribbon around her own neck, her fingers feeling for the ring, still held securely inside the purse.

Marek drew his hand across his face. His eyes strayed to his crushed bicycle leaning up against the filing cabinet. 'We need a hacksaw,' he said. 'To get the papers out.'

14

Jasna Góra, present day

Catherine stands before the ebony altar. She would like to kneel but there is not enough room. She is aware of the breathing of people behind her, the quiet shuffling and murmurs, the heat of bodies pressed close together. One old man with a military badge pinned to the lapel of his suit mutters a stream of prayerful Polish. Next to her a tiny woman with a deeply seamed heart-shaped face lifts a pair of hazelnut bright eyes up to the Black Madonna and makes the sign of the cross.

Earlier Catherine had taken one of the wide tree-lined avenues leading up to the imposing baroque monastery of Jasna Góra, the crown of the Bright Mountain, capped at its summit by a soaring bell tower that shimmered in the searing midday heat. Outside on the ramparts various groups of pilgrims, mostly older Polish people wearing metal badges showing the name of their town and labels denoting the number of times they had visited the shrine, paused for a moment to look up at the sky. A few were silent. Some spoke words of comfort or encouragement, and there were the sad, sweet, dignified smiles she had grown to recognize among the older generation, smiles that spoke of lives from another darker time. The pilgrims wiped the sweat from their faces. They adjusted clothing and sipped water from plastic bottles. Revived, they progressed in single file through the jewel-box interior of the basilica to the iron gateway guarding the Chapel of the Black Madonna known as Our Lady of Częstochowa.

As the icon is revealed the hush is broken by a ripple of anticipation and excited whispers. People press forward from the back to take a closer look and Catherine's foot is trodden on across her instep. She bites her lip to stop from calling out. An old man with a military medal, a silver cross, silently offers up his space. His eyes are clouded, blind. She moves to one side. He shuffles forward.

Her height allows her a good view of the famous work, reputedly painted by St Luke on a tabletop made by Jesus when he was still earning his living as a carpenter. The painting was peacefully enshrined in Constantinople for five centuries. Its turbulent history began when it was shot by a Tartar arrow. It was rescued by Polish cavalry only to be stolen in 1430. According to legend, the Hussite thieves were unable to carry the icon because it mysteriously increased in weight. Frustrated, the thieves slashed at the Madonna's face with swords. Almost immediately she started to bleed and the terrified thieves dropped the painting, leaving it to drown in a pool of mud and blood. Sharp-eyed monks later pulled the painting clear, washing the disfigured face in a fountain of clean water that miraculously appeared where the Madonna fell. News of her powers of recovery spread across the land; she became a source of national strength. During the Second World War, pilgrimages to the chapel were forbidden. But after the war ended, half a million Poles flocked to the Bright Mountain to pay their respects to their lady who had witnessed so many years of sorrow.

The hooded eyes, the black robes covered with gold lilies, the strange crude paw of a hand lend the painting a melancholy air. The Madonna looks no more than fifteen. Something about her reminds Catherine of photographs of strong, wistful Afghani girls with their dark skin and translucent eyes, a younger brother bundled in their arms. The Christ child is tiny and seems oddly disconnected from the Virgin mother, his attention drawn to something happening in the distance. A Bible nestles in his lap, cradled by his left hand. His right hand reaches up to touch his mother's robe at the neck. It is the only point of tenderness in the painting, which is not beautiful; she would even call it clumsy. Despite its awkwardness, or even perhaps because of it, there is something alluring about the image. The icon feels ancient, elemental: hewn from rock or mined from the earth. She cannot take her eyes from it. The Virgin's long, sorrowful gaze seems to pull at something deep within her, something beyond words, beyond observation. She looks around her at the faces in the chapel and sees that no one is unmoved.

The pilgrims leave the chapel and make their way to the treasury which is filled with votive offerings. On display are swords and jewels, but also rosaries fashioned from beads of dried bread saved from rations in the concentration camps. An old woman stares at one such rosary, her breath misting the glass. Her fingers quiver as if clicking off each hard pearl. Another cabinet displays the tear-gas cylinders used against Solidarity protesters in the 1980s and the Nobel Peace Prize awarded to Lech Wałęsa.

Outside in blaring daylight the pilgrims disperse. Catherine watches a mother wipe the traces of a spilled sticky drink from the chrome arches of her son's wheelchair while he, caught in spasm, writhes in his seat, his mouth darkly open, his eyes fixed on the miraculous sky. She settles down under the shade of a beech tree to a simple lunch of bread, cheese and a heavy sweet apple. Over in the sun a couple of pilgrim teenagers fling a ball, lobbing insults and banter in a language with too many hard edges to be Polish. Nearby, under a cascading weeping birch, a girl with artificial legs lies down and reads a book, her hair glinting copper in the sunlight, her lips curving into a smile of complicity as words work their magic.

Catherine finishes her lunch and stretches out on the grass. She can feel the sun burning the skin on her feet and pulls them back into the shade. She closes her eyes. It's been so long since she spent time on her own – she cannot remember when she did not have appointments, either professional or personal. In ordinary living she is always with people: colleagues, and of course Dominic, even when she was not with him she felt that he was there with her; he was always somehow within reach, a constant, inviolable presence.

A full week has passed since he left. A complete circle. She had needed to put some more distance between them and so had stayed on. Dominic hadn't returned to the hotel before he caught his flight. He'd left, as he said he would, on the nine o'clock flight, confirmed by a terse phone call when he arrived back in Cambridge. She realizes now, with a tight feeling of wonder, that Konrad had taken a flight at the same time on his way out of Europe to America. It was possible that their paths had even crossed. They might have noted one another in the check-in queues, maybe even brushed shoulders. In her mind they are inextricably linked. She imagines them sitting together, waiting, lost in reading, but drawn together somehow by some invisible, potent energy.

She shifts position under her tree and opens her eyes to the blue of the sky. What she is thinking is nonsense; it is superstitious thinking, a relic from her ancient brain, her reflexive reptilian mind; this is how her mind thinks when it has not had enough sleep or time to rest. There is no link between Dominic and Konrad. They travelled separately; they moved in opposite directions.

She lifts up on to her elbows and bites into her apple, savouring the clean white flesh. Why has she never tasted an apple before? How puzzling. And how strange it is too that she has not had time to reflect properly on her life until now. She finishes the apple and throws away the core. Nearly thirty years have gone by, perhaps a third of her life, and she has not understood this simple thing. It is this: while she was waiting for something better to happen outside her life, there was another life going on inside, a life she chose not to inhabit, a life that fitted her completely and perfectly: her own true life.

She lies back on the grass. The sky is a luminous bowl. She breathes deeply. Her body feels warm and light, composed of sand. She thinks of the Madonna's gravely beautiful face. A few days ago Catherine had made another pilgrimage. She'd hesitated about going to the church − she was still in shock, unable to sleep as she turned over the events of the past few days − but she was glad she went. The cemetery at the Holy Cross Church was small and well tended. She arrived early before the sun became too hot. Women in headscarves knelt at the gravestones, weeding, or arranging flowers. Catherine carried peonies, a creamy bunch, the most extravagant she could find. Their graves were in a shady corner under a stone wall: two smooth, well-worn mounds. She divided the peonies between them, refusing a jar of water offered by one of the Polish grave-tenders, instead laying the flowers down on the warm earth. She closed her eyes. An image of a boy and a girl lying side by side in a barn filled with light came into her mind. She smelled the sweetness of the hay, felt the prickle of straw under her back, heard the quiet breathing of horses in the stalls below. She stood up, brushing the Kraków soil from her clothes. A gust of wind snatched the petals from one of the peony heads and flung them into the air. She watched them fly: touching and separating, touching and separating until they were no more and then she left.

A shout from a tree now catches her attention. Halfway down the hill a girl calls out for her father. She watches the man, neat, fair, dressed in a blue cotton shirt, pause and turn to wait for his daughter to catch him up. She comes up the hill, huffing, and then leans her elbows on her knee for a moment to catch her breath. She is around eight years old with a halo of fine, white-blonde hair. When she lifts her head ready to continue her journey, Catherine notices that one side of her face is disfigured by a maze of scar tissue. She looks as if she has been in a car accident or fallen through a glass window. She hurries forward and then trips on a tussock of grass and falls. Too far away to come to her rescue, her father brings his hand up to his mouth. The girl gets up, dusts off her knees and gives him a wobbly grin. In her hand she holds a tooth knocked out in the fall. Her face breaks into a full gap-toothed smile. It is one of her front teeth. She rushes forward with cries of joy. Her father receives her; he lifts her up into the air like a conquering hero and swings her up on to his shoulder. Bearing his daughter and her proud tooth, he continues on up the hill.

It is late afternoon. Catherine makes her way down into the Old Town. The stone walls of the houses are stoked with heat, interior blinds drawn against the sun. There are few local inhabitants. The town seems to have given itself up entirely to pilgrims who flock around the trinket shops chattering over rosary beads and small wooden replicas of the Madonna. She buys one, a perfect painted oval, which fits comfortably in her palm. After paying the shopkeeper, she wonders where she will put her icon. She cannot imagine taking it home to Cambridge.

Light-headed with hunger, she finds a small restaurant in a cool stone courtyard where she slips off her sandals to soothe her swollen feet. She orders salad with potatoes and a tall glass of iced lemon cordial. She is the only person eating alone and for the first time she feels a stab of loneliness. Most of the other people are Polish couples, or middle-aged women talking in low confessional voices. One woman shows her friend a painted wooden rosary and something passes between the two women, some understanding that feels exclusive. Catherine wonders what people offer in confession, whether they enter with sorrowful shameful stories already prepared for the patient priest, or whether they wait until they are inside the chamber, and there, unseen in the dark, they allow the truth to emerge.

She knows a priest in Cambridge, a professor of theology. He helped her once. He received her in a quiet private room. There were no screens. He held her hand while she talked and sobbed and the simple warmth of his touch made her feel healed. She has never forgotten him. He was Polish. He asked her to come and see him again, but she never did. Her shame felt too great. She remembers what he told her as she wept: 'Don't be ashamed. To confess all, to lay yourself bare is a beautiful truth.'

She carried this with her like an unvoiced promise. In their early years Dominic sang with choral groups. She had dutifully attended his concerts and had been moved, sometimes to tears, by the great masses of Handel, Bach and Mozart, works that soared and trembled and made her feel somehow transformed for the time she was there, but at the parties afterwards, surrounded by singers cramming down sausage rolls and cold triangles of pizza, she would become quickly sloshed with warm wine as Dominic's red face and booming voice circulated the room, and the quiet feeling of joy would dissolve.

She wonders what Dominic will do. He has always been a creature of habit and the transition will be difficult. He will find it almost impossible to believe that after twenty-eight years of being coupled to her, she is no longer there. She can hardly believe it herself. She almost wants to go back and check that she has truly left and is not still there waiting for her to return. It's odd to think of her divided, in two minds, two places at once.

At some point she will have to face the actual process of separation, and all the heartache and accusations that will entail, but perhaps she can allow herself a little time. She wants to understand what has happened to her. People separate and meet other people constantly, but her single encounter, or more precisely a series of encounters – she is not sure she would yet describe it as a relationship – has made her reconsider everything. She thought she knew her own life. She thought that she could no longer be surprised. She never expected that she would have to reassess what mattered most.

Dominic will tell his friends and colleagues that she has betrayed him. He won't be able to resist circulating his own rumours, and it will save him; the intrigue and the gossip will fuel him through many a lonely, drunken evening. As long as someone listens, and he won't mind who – the first sympathetic female colleague no doubt – he will be fine. He might even recover.

Or, he might go under. He might, and she grips the edge of the table at the thought, fall into despair. She orders vodka and takes a sip from the shot glass, running her tongue around the sweet, oily rim. The two middle-aged women linger over coffee, their talk still conspiratorial. Neither woman seems aware of Catherine, but she is grateful to them for shielding her from scrutiny. If she were the only customer, she would have to read.

Not so long ago Dominic told her that he thought suicide was rational. It was, he argued, the best solution to a life of extreme disappointment: for perpetual anguish was by its very nature undesirable. When she tried to argue that anguish need not persist, that it was a chosen state, he looked her in the eye and said calmly, 'So why are you so anxious all the time? Is it because you choose to be?'

She had wanted to retort that she was happy, but could not because his words had stunned her. She'd gone and stood in the garden. It was summer and the night was velvet around her. She had watched the stars until she grew cold and before she went back inside she had made a quick, calm vow that she would leave him as soon as she could.

So she has kept her promise. She wonders what will happen next. Inevitably, Dominic's colleagues will take him out for drinks, one or two might invite him to supper and let him fume and grieve, but there will also be those who will be secretly relieved that they have parted: not for her sake, but their own. Knowing how young she was when she first met Dominic, friends of his had acted as unofficial guardians. Part of their self-appointed duty was to watch out for her and warn Dominic to curb his excesses when he plunged into his narcissistic play pool where the games and rules were known only to him. It was a good system. For the first few years, it saved her from drowning. There were people she could call at any time of night. Bill. Tony. Michael. They kept Dominic on the straight and narrow, stopped him from imploding; prevented iniquity and injury. The Holy Trinity, he called them. She was more inclined to think of a triad of superheroes, smashing their way feet first into their kitchen, bringing sanity, common sense and clean towels.

The Three Graces: they were regular visitors in the early days, and she enjoyed having them around. It was like having three brothers. They were lively and teasing, but always courteous, keen to respect Dominic's claim on her. Even so, she suspected that Tony would have made a move given half a chance. During one of their late-night conversations in which they compared each other to fairground attractions or animals or musical instruments – such were the games they played when drink made sequential conversation impossible – Tony said that she made him think of a hall of mirrors.

'Go on, don't stop there: what's her animal?' This from Michael, an engineer whose role was to stop everyone falling over and who one day would be instrumental in building the world's most beautiful bridge.

Tony looked at her. Involuntarily she lifted her hair from her face and flicked it back over her shoulder. His gaze made her heart beat faster.

'A flying fox.'

A burst of derisive laughter from Dominic made them all whirl round to face him. He was slumped in his dining chair. In those days his belly was not quite as rotund as it became in later years, but it was beginning to develop a pot. He patted it. 'She's too plump to be a fox: her arse is too big.'

'Dom.' The warning came from Bill, softly insistent. 'Don't start.'

It worked. She remembers how Dominic deflated and poured himself another drink, while Michael changed the subject. She remembers also how Tony continued to look at the spot on her left shoulder where her hair had been until she flung it away. She'd fallen a little in love with Tony then and believed he was her protector. When they saw each other after the incident they both found it awkward. Sometimes she thought of calling him and asking him to meet her alone. But she never did. It just felt too risky. In the end Bill, Tony and Michael stopped coming round. Nothing was said. Nothing happened. There was no great, defining Dominic drama that decided them. Their withdrawal of support was discreet, but it was definite. All three had had enough. They had grown tired of being witnesses to Dominic's self-destruction, and had reached the point, she realized, when they felt that she ought to know better.

She stayed. Every time the line was crossed – the

drinking she could manage, but the bullying and verbal abuse she could not – she made plans to go, but these plans were temporary solutions. She had offers of places to stay: safe houses, quiet spare rooms, under-used studies. There were promises that she would not be disturbed, that she could work and continue her life as normal, but of course there was nothing normal about having to escape from the person with whom she shared her life: it was utterly abnormal and it made her feel as if she had failed, as if she were truly to blame for the way it was. She wondered whether there was some deficiency in her that made him react to her differently, some inherent weakness in her that he could not resist exploiting.

She coped by doing what many people in emotional upheaval do: she removed herself from the source of strain. She spent longer periods away from home, sometimes driving out to the Fens where she would sit in her small hatchback with the radio on and watch the light curving along the water. Sometimes she took her binoculars with her and watched the stars, not with her analytical professional self, but with a feeling of anticipation and excitement she had not felt since she was a child. On nights like these, the stars were exclusively hers. Ophiuchus, Alpha Serpentis, Antares, Scorpius, with its twin guardians: Sigma and Tau Scorpii. She swung her binoculars across the sky. When she returned home she felt full of light.

But these were brief interludes. Mostly the bleak weather of their relationship continued unbroken. She remembers coming home one afternoon – she had a migraine and needed to lie down somewhere dark and cool – and finding Dominic in his study with a bottle of wine at his elbow. Her knock startled him. He had whirled round in his swivel chair and she saw that his trousers were open and that he had been feeling himself while he worked or drank or whatever it was he did and the sight of his red face, his rumpled clothes, his thick member, standing querulously in its nest of black hair, caused her to gasp in shock.

'Oh, you've surprised me,' he said. He looked down at himself. 'I haven't finished yet, perhaps you'd like to join us?'

The study reeked of booze, sadness and frustration. Nausea threatened to overwhelm her. She started to back out of the door. 'I'm sorry,' she said. 'I need to lie down.'

Laughter accompanied her to the bedroom where she pulled the curtains and lay on the bed. Her head pounded. Lights fizzed and sizzled behind her eyes. Although it was still early afternoon the mirror in the room became strangely luminous as if reflecting the light of the moon. She wished she had felt well enough to drive to the Fens. She could have sat in her car and waited for this to pass. From the study she could hear music, a great choral mass, and it made her want to sob. Grief swelled in her. She felt close to surrender. Now it has happened, she thought. I am no longer in control; he has reduced us both, diminished us, drunk and abused the best of us. Tears soaked her face. Her chest was tight with misery. She thought of the Polish priest's kind face. I can tell no one about this, she thought. There is no one I will embarrass as much as I embarrass myself.

They shared a home. It was practical to remain. To leave meant to dissemble and that felt too destructive. There had already been too many breakings. She stayed because she needed things to remain intact. She needed a structure even if it was a contorted one. Some part of her feared that if she broke away, she would end up with nothing. Then came the night when she made her vow, and it didn't matter any more.

Still her prediction had come true, in a way. She did end up with nothing, at least for a while: he had taken her clothes. He had even taken her toothbrush. Back in Cambridge she would not have coped. In order to free herself, she needed distance. She thinks now about how each type of star, and there are hundreds, represents a temporary phase in a life cycle. Many will stay on their main sequence for billions of years, but for each there comes a time when the hydrogen runs out and the star must evolve. Every star must become something new.

She trusts the night sky. It is the face she understands most intimately. When people fret about storms or unpredictable weather, she feels no reciprocal twinge of anxiety – more a relief that the world still operates according to natural laws. On her trips out to the Fens she tracked the weather, followed its swells and rhythms with growing love. In the weeks before she left Cambridge she drove out there at least once a week. On windy nights she wrapped herself up in her car, holding close her wild, contained freedom, her sense that there would come a time when she would move towards her new life.

She has no guarantee that Konrad will return. The business of death is complicated. There will be obligations, practical and emotional. There will be little time to think beyond the immediate. Of this she is acutely aware, and it doesn't make it any easier to deal with. She won't pursue him. She won't even contact him. Perhaps a trip to the mountains would do her good. She has read the guidebook and studied the photographs of snow-covered peaks, lakes and deep forests. The pull of fresh air is strong. It will be cooler in the mountains.

Over a spiky espresso she considers other options. She could perhaps book a flight to another country somewhere in Europe, somewhere close: Hungary or Romania, or Germany. She has always wanted to visit Italy. She ought to make the most of this time because it will not come again; she can't imagine there will be many other periods in her life when she will be stranded in central Europe between lives. But the thought of leaving Poland panics her. The idea of going elsewhere is unthinkable.

She could imagine working and living in Kraków. It's not so different from Cambridge; its cloisters and narrow streets remind her of the city. She finishes her coffee and asks for the bill. The waitress, stylish in a crisp black and white uniform, brings it on a white saucer. Catherine ignores the universal mint imperial sweets and leaves a large tip.

It is dusk by the time her train reaches the city. She decides against going straight to the hotel and heads to the Planty where the great planes and chestnuts ripple with birds making their night-time preparations. But tonight the park feels different. She walks to the end of one avenue and shudders as the breeze lifts the hairs on her arms. Now her cool decisive mood has worn off and she feels vulnerable. Now she is afraid that everything she hopes for will be taken from her. She has been abandoned, not once, but twice. She is fooling herself to think that she can simply cast off one life and start another.

In the thick silence of her room at the Europolski, Catherine sits cross-legged on the bed and tries to calm her nerves. Now she feels overwhelmed and out of her depth.

It's not possible to demolish in one afternoon what has been built up over nearly thirty years. As her father understood, there's a price to pay. She is not sure that she has the courage to endure a life of uncertainty. She doesn't have the guts to live without the known, the orderly, the familiar. Now, she realizes with chilled horror that she misses Dominic. Her need for him is real and ugly. Her hand hovers towards the phone. She will call him just to hear his voice. She dials the number and waits. The phone is wet with her breath. She hears it ring. Normally he picks up straight away, but there is no answer. Feeling somehow cheated, she replaces the receiver.

She raids the minibar and drinks a brandy miniature, feeling the alcohol caress her stomach. She understands its seductive pull, its sweet embrace. For so long she has watched its wanton charms beguile like poison, it is no wonder she is tempted. It would have been easier perhaps if she had got drunk, or had let herself slide into insanity, but she had remained, on the surface at least, in control. Cold. Dominic always accused her of that: there was no heat to her, nothing at her core: she had no nucleus. She was empty. 'Well, you made me that way.' She'd hurled a counter-accusation at him once: 'You took the best of me and made me your own. You stole me because you were too frightened of yourself.'

'You were nothing until you met me. You were no one. You were void.'

She finishes the brandy and reaches for another small bottle. She unscrews the cap and pours the contents down her throat, gagging at the taste of whisky. Fear overcomes her and feeling shivery and sick and weepy, she pulls a quilt around her shoulders and burrows down into the bed.

She comes round an hour or so later, her mouth claggy with thirst. She drinks an entire bottle of mineral water standing up. Her hair hangs lank over her breasts and her stomach burns with tension. Dominic always had trouble being alone. It floored him like an illness. Perhaps she is more like him than she thinks. After so many years together this is not surprising. Her plan to strike out now seems foolish, a delirium brought on by her first taste of freedom. *She doesn't know Konrad.* But Dominic knows her. He understands her. He lets her have as much space as she needs. Their life together has been awful in the past, but now it is not nearly so bad. If she thinks about it rationally, *coldly*, she has a lot of freedom, more so than many other couples she knows. They don't even sleep together any longer – only on the rare occasions he needs sex – and there is a wonderful, voluptuous ease in having her own room; she can read or listen to the radio or simply lie in bed and dream. She would have all this if she returned.

Dominic would forgive her. He would understand; after all it is her first lapse. He once said that he thought she ought to have an affair. It would make him feel less guilt, let him off the hook for his bad behaviour. She suspected that there had been other women, of course there were. Why else would he let her live alongside him like a student lodger? She never contemplated being unfaithful to spite him or even match him despite the temptation of Tony. She didn't think she was brave enough for an affair.

But there was more. There was always the possibility that she might change her life. There was always the possibility that she might reclaim her soul. I am the gardener, she thinks. I am responsible for what I plant, for what I weed out, for what I tend to. I am responsible for what I reap. If I go back to Dominic, I must be prepared never to see Konrad again, but if I leave Dominic I must be prepared to feel that I have dug up my life and raked it bare. I must be prepared to take the risk that nothing new will flourish. That my garden will stay dry.

What supports does she have? Her colleagues have complications of their own. She had disappointed the Holy Trinity. There's no one else she would consider, certainly no one she might invite to fly to Kraków and keep her company, like a trusty female companion from a Henry James novel. Her friends are his friends. Not one person she knows will be disinterested.

She is alone. Reaching for the padded envelope containing Konrad's notes, she thinks of Janek and wonders how he survived those first years on his own after he left Poland. She wonders what it must have cost him simultaneously to turn his back on his country and to give up the woman he most loved. What reserves of strength kept him going? She wonders also why he left it so long to return, why he lived invisibly, his past a secret known only to him. She pulls the quilt around her shoulders and begins to read from notes Konrad made after a conversation with her father.

After an hour or so she puts the notes down on the bed. She now knows that in the years after his escape her father tried to make a new life. After making his way to Britain in the fifties with help from the Polish Red Cross, he drifted through a succession of hotel kitchens in London. He sank his arms in grimy sinks. He put up with abuse that for him seemed like banter. He lived in single rooms in Palmers Green alongside other Polish men, many of them ex-soldiers evacuated after the war, who were also looking for a way to avoid the slippery grip of the past. The English kept their distance. There were signs in windows: 'No Irish. No blacks. No Poles.' One landlady told him that if he were a good Pole he would be back in his own country. The gift of silence that he had received in prison kept him intact through those early years.

One night in Enfield he met a beautiful young nurse out with her friend. The nurse had long dark hair, blue eyes and white skin, and she let him buy her a Dubonnet and lemonade. After their first night he walked her to her small room and she put her cool hand on his arm and said that she wanted to see him again. He had nice manners like most of the Polish men. She giggled and wondered if he had a friend for her companion. They began seeing each other, once, twice, three times a week. She became familiar. He knew the touch of her, the smell of her skin. Many other Polish men were marrying English or Irish or Welsh women. He listened to their bright talk in the bars. Some came from eastern Poland and their family homes were now part of the Soviet Union. They had no desire to go back to a communist Poland. They would build new lives through hard work. Sometimes they shared with each other letters from Poland that urged them to stay in England.

Each time Janek left the nurse at her lodgings, he felt he knew her a little less. Her frivolous confidence alarmed him and made him wonder whether he was making a mistake. One night he tried to talk to her about it, but she dismissed his doubts. He was too sensitive, she said. He would have to become a stronger man to put up with her. He read in the local newspaper about a young Polish man whose body had been found slumped in the kitchen of his small rented room. The gas oven was turned on. The verdict was that the man had taken his own life while the balance of his mind had been disturbed. Someone said that he had been a political prisoner in Warsaw.

In the days before he was married in January 1958 at Enfield Register Office, Janek walked in the park at Palmers Green where there was an old stone wall with a deep flower border that was always warm and light even in winter. By then he had accepted that he would have to live the rest of his life without being known. There was no going back. His new fresh young wife was waiting for him. He had no choice but to become someone new. In some ways, it was a relief.

Catherine gets up from the bed and goes to the window. She lifts the curtain and looks into a violet dusk, the skyline lit by the glow of illuminated churches. A horse and carriage clops across the cobbles. She opens the window and from the church closest to the hotel she can hear voices at Evensong. A warm breeze fans her face. She closes her eyes. Konrad will return, not to her perhaps, she has already relieved him of that obligation, but to the city itself. He has a flat, a project, a life to take up once more and continue. He has every reason to come back. She can't imagine that he will abandon his film. She turns from the window and looks at the padded envelope lying on the bed. Konrad will surely return whereas she may not, at least not until she has separated from Dominic and come out the other side. The breeze from the window is cool on her neck. She turns once again to face the sky. Leaning her elbows on the windowsill, she watches the stars become visible within their constellations, faint at first and then growing in magnitude as the night darkens and deepens around them.

15

Kraków, April 1943

Spring brought a nervy restlessness that crackled through the city. The sky lightened from grey to blue and bird-song pierced the early morning air. In the Planty, sharp green spears thrust up from the ground, little questing buds beneath the bereft trees. There were days of sun. Clear starlit nights. But despite the change, or perhaps because of it, the Germans were perpetually disgruntled and stood about in anxious knots on the steps of their appropriated buildings. Offences such as forgetting to show deference before senior officers were overlooked one moment, punished severely the next, the violence compensating for the inexcusable lapse in concentration.

Scores of well-dressed German women now inhabited the city, parading in twos or threes, their perfume lingering in the streets and on the trains and trams. Perceived dis-obedience or even close proximity brought contempt from these women who considered the Poles *untermenschen*, or sub-human. Travelling to work one morning, Krystyna happened to brush past a well-built woman who stood blocking the tram doorway. Before the metal doors closed behind the passengers, the woman had remarked, 'When are they going to put a stop to this disgrace of still letting Poles travel by tram?' There were mutters of approval from the other Germans in the carriage. Struggling to move down the tram, the Poles remained implacable. The German woman planted her feet and held on to the strap above her with the force of someone pulling on a church bell. She had a heavy, square face, offset by a smooth pelmet of hair that did not quite disguise her over-large ears. Shoved in the small of her back by an elderly man impatient not to be left behind, Krystyna had no other option than to squeeze past.

The blow from a hand cluttered with rings caught her across the eye. Head bowed, Krystyna inched forward, momentarily blinded by stinging tears. She found a space in the middle of the carriage between two slim Polish women who held their breath as she joined them. It was too tight to reach up for the strap. Krystyna braced her feet and tried to keep her head up. The sour scent of unwashed wool was strong. Her caught eye flickered. She could still feel the cold of the German woman's ring grazing her eyelid, the lashes turning inward. Opposite her the old man who had pushed her forward on to the tram was staring at her from his seat. When she met his eyes, he looked away down the carriage as if searching for someone he knew. She willed him to turn back to her, but he did not.

A soldier who unknown to Krystyna had watched the exchange got off at her stop and followed her. Halfway down Russia Street, he tapped her on the shoulder. Her heart froze as she saw the black uniform, the red band with the swastika on his left arm. She began to apologize, but the SS officer interrupted her. He was young, tall with fair hair and clear blue eyes that searched her face which was still moist with tears. He spoke to her in broken Polish. Then he pulled from his pocket a pressed white handkerchief and offered it to her. She tried to refuse by smiling, indicating to him that her eye was no longer streaming so much. She thanked him in German, but he insisted that she take the handkerchief. 'Please,' he kept saying in Polish. 'Please.' She lifted the handkerchief to her face. The smell of new linen caught the back of her throat. Tentatively she dabbed her eye, careful not to stain the immaculate cloth, and went to return it to him. 'Keep it,' he said. His eyes met hers for a second. Then he bowed. The sun glinted on the glossy peak of his cap which bore a delicate grey metal insignia of a skull. When he lifted his head she saw that his skin was flushed. To cover up his embarrassment he clicked his heels, his body jerking to attention. Then he strode away towards the tram stop. She watched him go, twisting the handkerchief over and over in her hands.

After she had recovered her composure she walked on, looking behind her every now and then to check that he was not following. The Germans were known to trap people with kindness. One SS officer had stopped a woman on her way home with her young daughter who was crying with hunger. He offered the woman a loaf of bread. She accepted gratefully and thanked the officer. He allowed her to pass and then after a moment drew out his pistol, aimed and shot the child through the head. Such casual cruelty was engineered to break people, to make them cowed and afraid, but the Germans had little understanding of national character; they were not aware of the extent to which they were fuelling a powerful and passionate rebellion against all that they represented. Seen in this way their attempts to subjugate people were almost pathetic, but they still had to be watched. Even German children enjoyed taunting and teasing Poles.

The soldier on the tram confused her. His politeness, the way he had approached her, so aware and so curious and so anxious not to give offence, was puzzling, because he had no reason to act decently. For days afterwards she found that she was looking out for him when she travelled to work on the tram and once or twice she received sharp glances from other SS officers unsettled by her scrutiny. After a while she trained herself to concentrate instead on the sky which trembled with planes heading east.

The feeling in Kraków was that the Germans would overpower the Russians, but that the battle would be long and hard. The Germans would lose much of their power and in their weakened state would easily be finished off by the Allies. Once the Allies stepped in to help there would be the chance of freedom. But there were other darker feelings that, given the increase in brutality, the round-ups and public executions, there would not be enough people left to form a proper country. In defeat the Germans would undoubtedly unleash more barbarism against the hated Poles. The church porches fluttered with death notices. Many of the dead were young people in their twenties or thirties. Dates of funeral masses were given, but often no burial followed. The bodies had been extinguished elsewhere, as everyone knew, but few spoke openly about, inside the concentration camps.

Poland was dying daily. It was diminishing, like a carcass fought over between a pack of dogs. Now, only shreds of the former life remained. It was enough to keep the younger population fighting. Scraps were better than nothing, after all. The older people, those who had seen more, and had the benefit of hindsight, were watchful and cautious, less optimistic about German defeat. History had taught them about Russian violence, more quietly insidious than German thuggery. Russian methods went in deep under the surface. There were no grim execution parades, no blood on the streets of the occupied towns. Instead people simply disappeared; they sank into a bottomless lake, leaving not a trace. Efforts to find the vanished were blocked so effectively it was as if the person had never existed.

Krystyna tried not to let fear of the future overcome her as she set off to work each morning. It was important that she remain detached in order to do her job properly. The colonel had recommended her as a liaison girl and researcher to the Press and Propaganda Office. Now she worked for one of the many underground newspapers, monitoring radio bulletins, typing messages, running errands for the editor, a rather dry, laconic, intimidating man in his late forties named Lech who had worked as a lawyer, and who she suspected would have preferred a young man as his assistant. On her first morning he had looked her up and down in silence for a few moments before asking her how old she was.

'Nineteen.'

His eyes tightened as he blew smoke towards the low ceiling. 'Have you done this sort of work before?'

'Yes.' She went to elaborate, but he held up a hand to stop her.

'How about some coffee?' His fish-eyes scrolled across her face.

'Oh, that would be nice, thank you.'

Lech stared at her. Krystyna felt her face grow hot. She glanced down at the shoes she had borrowed that morning.

They were smart brown and cream, but a little too tight across the instep. She had high arches. When she stood up she felt as if she were about to topple forward.

Lech's brow was furrowed with disbelief. He shot a look at one of the reporters, a man named Piotr, who was in his late twenties and wore a leather waistcoat with his shirt-sleeves rolled up to show muscled forearms thickly covered with fine brown hair. The office smelled powerfully male.

'Leave her alone, Lech,' Piotr said. 'She's obviously a better class than you are.' He moved towards her and gently took her arm and pointed her to the office door as if he were steering a young child across a busy road. From a shelf he took down a Thermos flask and pushed it into her hands. 'If you smile with your beautiful blue eyes they will fill this for us in the café across the road. Tell them that the laundry is in need of more soap today. Have you got that?'

She nodded. Then with flaring cheeks she went across to the café to complete her first assignment.

Lech and the other reporters preferred to work through the hours of the night and her hours were nine until five so she often arrived in the morning to find the office empty. It was a former laundry room in the basement of an old three-storey house of grey stone. Outside the street was always cold.

Worn stone steps led down to the office which despite the addition of brown carpet and metal filing cabinets still smelled of damp laundry, cold water and carbolic soap. There were no windows, just a metal grille through which she could see the street outside, empty save for the stagger-ing, wrinkled pink legs of pigeons. Lech's desk was closest to the air vent. One day she'd finished her work by dinner time. There was still no sign of Lech or Piotr. It was airless in the room and so she went over to the big desk and sat in his chair. There was a clean sheet of paper in his typewriter. She placed her fingers on the keys and at that moment she heard two people come down the stairs, talking in low voices. Lech entered first and his eyes registered surprise, but he made no comment. His hair was sticking up at the back and she knew that he had just got out of bed by the smell of milk that hung about his clothes. Piotr had washed and shaved. He greeted her, but she was unable to answer him. Lech snorted down his nose as she relinquished his warm chair.

As she got up she said, 'Your typewriter doesn't stick like mine. It's much faster.' Lech stared at her and then lit a cigarette. Her mouth went dry. She could barely believe that she'd spoken such words to him. He threw her a bulletin transcript from a wire tray. 'Four hundred words, think you can do that in twenty minutes?'

She looked at the bulletin. 'You want me to write it up properly?'

He shrugged. 'Every minute you spend looking at the paper is wasted time.'

After that she was allowed to write some of the stories for the army staff bulletin. She took care over her sentences, cutting all excess until she had the crisp, professional effect she wanted. She hoped that Lech would comment on her style but he never did. He treated her as he treated all the other reporters, with brusque respect, leaving them to get on with their job. Sometimes as she typed through the smog of tobacco, the radio buzzing, the lights swinging as the electric power surged, she longed for company of another kind. Piotr was friendly and offered her cigarettes, which she refused, but he was not really that interested in what she had to say. He had a wife and two children, a boy of five and a girl of three. He showed her their photographs which he kept folded up in his wallet.

Her working routine helped to provide a sense that she was making progress towards an end. But some days an aching emptiness settled in her and she was unable to write her reports. She would sit at her desk and her mind would block. Lech usually sent her out on some errand when she became like this. She went then to another secret office in the cellar of a house nearby that was processing identity papers of the dead, creating fake documents for Home Army personnel and other Poles at risk. Under the glare of a bare light bulb swinging from the cellar ceiling, she ran her finger down lists of names, turned over photographs, scrutinized papers, and then left when she found what she had come looking for, and that was the absence of names she spoke now only in her heart. After these missions, returning to her own office she found the scent of spring unbearable.

As summer approached the Germans began losing to the Russians on the Eastern Front. When the news filtered through to the Germans in Kraków, some acted confused, even chastened, like the SS officer who had followed her that day, but many others behaved like spoiled princes clinging greedily to the last vestiges of their stolen empire.

One day while on her way to deliver a message to a pick-up box in the city centre, she saw the emperor. Alerted by the shouts of SS officers outside the Nazi Party Headquarters, she crossed the road and joined a knot of people, mostly Germans, who had sensed someone of importance was about to arrive. The SS officers' faces were stretched with tension as they scanned the street. She soon saw why. A procession of five black cars flanked by motor-cycle outriders streamed down Franciszkańska Street. At the party headquarters the procession came to a halt and out of the cars poured dozens of SS soldiers with hand-held machine guns that twitched as they formed a double cordon along the pavement.

A man in a heavily decorated uniform stepped out of a car in the middle of the convoy. Under his cap, his hair shone a startling blue-black. He turned. His gaze seemed to sweep the entire street before it came to rest on the huddled group of observers watching him. A German woman whispered in an excitable voice to her friend that it was the governor general Hans Frank. Krystyna kept quiet. She had read about the actions of the despot Nazi emperor, who had appropriated many treasures from his new kingdom. Paintings and artworks stolen from mu-seums and collections had appeared in his own residence, including a famous painting by Leonardo da Vinci of a lady with an ermine, which it was said hung in his bedroom.

The governor general turned stiffly to his aides. His body appeared rigid and out of alignment as if he had slipped a disc or damaged his neck. An aide offered him an arm and the crowd watched him sullenly refuse assistance. His face darkened. He scuttled towards the party head-quarters, but just before he went inside he halted for a moment and turned again towards the onlookers. The crowd held its breath. The German woman who had recognized him gasped as she saw first what they then all noticed: the terrible white fear in his face.

A few more weeks passed. The underground army stepped up their railway and factory sabotage efforts and the Germans grew ever more nervous of defeat. A whole branch of the Press and Propaganda Office was dedicated to lowering the German morale. This was done in various ingenious ways including the compilation of fake reports from non-existent German resistance organizations claiming that Hitler and his crew were finished. Around the city the anchor-sign of the resistance – a P and W combined – began to appear more frequently on factory walls, chalked there by Boy Scouts gleefully declaring that Poland was fighting. Reports came through from Warsaw that engineers had tapped German megaphones and broadcast the Polish national anthem. At the sound many pedestrians had stood still in the streets and took off their hats. Some of them openly wept.

On her way to work now Krystyna noticed a renewed sense of purpose in the posture of the pale, slight young women on the trams who, like her, risked their lives daily to work as liaison girls. Young factory workers, many of whom were part of the various sabotage units, had a spring in their step as they streamed along the streets. It was thrilling to think that almost the entire Polish population was part of the insurrection in some form, if only in sheltering someone fully affiliated to the underground. Even loose membership filled people with a sense of purpose and pride; it revived the spirited good humour that she remembered from before the war when people were witty and teasing and vital with one another; it resurrected small acts of kindness and courage and love.

She lived now with Halina, a professor of art history who had known the colonel. After a period in hiding on a remote estate outside Kraków, the colonel had transferred to Warsaw. Krystyna had written to him and he had replied with necessarily short messages that told her little except that he was well and thought of her often and hoped that she was keeping up with her reading. Krystyna was now attending secret lectures at the flying university organized by Halina for half a dozen students at her elegant flat on Venice Street. Sitting in the candlelit room crammed with paintings and valuables from Halina's family estate in eastern Poland, listening to the professor speak passionately about the Italian Renaissance or the Romantics or the Greeks, the realities of the brutal occupation would fade for an hour or so. After formal lectures Halina's assistant Lidia served tea and cake. The professor would relax then and talk to them more freely about Polish history, her voice softly insistent. She would address each of her young protégés by name, as if she wanted to impress on them personal memories of previous subjugations under Russia, Prussia and Austria during the partitions which banished even the name of Poland and forced five generations to live under the yoke of foreign rule. She not only wanted them to know the facts, but to build a bigger picture in their minds, to feel the shape of Europe, to understand the forces that created it. Halina was thirty-two, but her intelligence and intensity made her appear at least ten years older. With her rolled dark hair, strong jaw and sinewy frame, she was saved from severity by the gold warmth in her dark brown eyes that darted with fire as she read from the Romantic poets.

The other students – there were four young woman, and two older men – attended erratically. Most weeks one or another would not show up. Halina would wait for a few minutes for them to arrive, seated at her desk which was covered with books and papers, its frank scholarly disorder seeming to suggest a sense of normality; and after she was sure that no one would be coming breathlessly pounding up the stairs, apologizing for their lateness, she would say in her quiet fine voice, 'Well, shall we begin?'

When it was just the two of them, Halina received her with cries of delight, clasping her hands, her strong, broad face radiant in the dim light. She led Krystyna into her cluttered room and let her sit down by herself for a few minutes to compose her thoughts. Then she would bring tea or share her own supper of tomatoes with eggs or vegetables with noodles if it was late and she had already begun to eat.

Sometimes they talked of eastern Poland, of the estates, the lakes, the soft nights, as if to confirm to each other that such a place had once existed. One night Krystyna told Halina of how she had escaped the dwór and travelled alone across the forest with her horse searching for Janek and his father. She told her, too, of her frequent errands to the house close to the newspaper office and her dread of what she might discover in the documents of the dead. 'Sometimes I think it would be better not to know,' she told Halina. 'But I keep going there, even when I try to stop myself.'

Halina listened, her restless eyes stilled in the candle-light. When Krystyna had finished speaking she reached out and took her hand. It was a while before she could speak and then she said simply that her own father, a Polish general, had been taken by the Russians to a prisoner-of-war camp. She had been receiving letters, but now they had stopped. 'When I cannot bear not knowing what has happened, I try to think of Keats's admonition to live in negative capability. I try to hold on to the thought that I can still live in doubt, that I can make a valuable life in the midst of all this uncertainty.'

It was comfortable in Halina's flat. The cluttered rooms spoke of another kind of life and some days as Krystyna helped Lidia with the chores she felt that she could begin to understand what Halina meant by living with doubt. The three of them created a life that sustained them and sometimes felt full. They ate their meagre meals in the dining room from porcelain plates and drank from fine glass goblets with a silver band around their rim. There was wine. At night she slept under a faded linen quilt and the old, creaky feel of the bed and smell of cedar in the room made her feel fortunate to have found such a shelter when so many people had been taken from their beds and transported to frozen places from which they would never return.

One morning at breakfast Halina seemed unusually pensive. She barely glanced up as Krystyna came into the dining room having slept and dreamed of home. Janek had appeared in the dream and he had held her face in both his hands. He said that he wanted something from her, but when she woke she could not remember what it was. Sometimes she shared her dreams with Halina, who was interested in psychoanalysis, but this morning the professor's eyes were dull and her hair, normally neatly groomed, had been pulled back hastily.

Krystyna sat down and Lidia poured tea. Halina's hand shook as she lifted her tea cup to her lips. She smiled tightly at the younger women and then gestured to stop Lidia lifting the teapot to replenish it in the small kitchen off the dining room. 'Please, Lidia, sit down. Eat something with us.'

Lidia put down the teapot and glanced at Krystyna. As she sat down, she swung her gleaming golden plait over her shoulder. She reached forward and from a basket in the centre of the dining table took a small piece of bread which she broke in half.

'I have something to tell you.' The professor spoke in a husky voice. 'This morning I received a visit from a neighbour, a musician; he plays sometimes in piano bars. Late last night he heard some drunk Nazis talking about a massacre. They mentioned an announcement that would be made later on today. According to these Nazis, mass graves have been found in Katýn Forest near Smolensk.' Her voice wavered. 'They contain the bodies of thousands of Polish Army officers.' There was a silence as she looked at them across the table. 'Thousands of our army officers shot on Stalin's orders.'

Lidia gasped and brought her hands up to her face. Krystyna stared, unable to believe what she was hearing.

Halina continued in a dry voice: 'Not only officers, but engineers, priests, teachers, doctors . . .'

'Doctors?' Lidia called out. Her father was a doctor. Since the start of the war he had been working at the Lazarus Hospital treating tuberculosis patients.

'Landowners.' Halina's eyes now rested on Krystyna, who waited for Halina to continue, but the professor was too shaken. Eventually she was able to whisper, 'There is a list that will be published by the Nazis who have recovered some papers of the dead.' She cast her eyes about the room. 'I will go out later.' Her right hand came up and rested on her chest as if she needed physically to move her breastbone so that she could take her next breath to speak. 'Then I will at least know.'

There was a silence. Lidia's glance was horrified.

Krystyna put her hand over her eyes. Halina waited for a moment and when she had recovered her composure she said that the Russians were trying to cover up the crime by blaming the Nazis. The Russians wanted to put across the message that the Red Army was the only hope for the Polish people who had suffered enough under the brutal regime of the Nazis. The bodies slumped in the pit were evidence of Nazi atrocity.

'Perhaps it was really the Nazis,' Lidia said.

'No.' Halina's voice was flat. 'It is the Russians.'

Krystyna thought back to her time in the forest. She pictured Benedykt standing in the snow in his Russian Army coat, his boots rubbing sores on his small white feet. Now she wondered what cruel soldier had given him that coat, the coat that would keep him alive just long enough to be killed by the other side.

'When will we know?' she asked.

'I am sure it will be soon.' Halina's voice was dry. 'The Nazis will want to make the most of this opportunity.'

Krystyna imagined the pit in the forest. She would not now be able to sleep until the Germans had announced the terrible list.

Halina tried to finish her breakfast, but her hands were trembling too much. She laid down the remains of her bread and pushed her plate to one side. Her lips were pale and in her eyes there was a strange, ghastly look. Lidia dropped her gaze, but Krystyna could not. She kept her glance fixed on Halina and willed her to find her courage. She needed more than anything to see that the professor was not afraid. Eventually the professor looked at Lidia. 'I think we could perhaps have some more tea.' Her voice was quiet, but it was poised.

Afterwards while Krystyna and Lidia cleared away the breakfast things, Halina went to her room. When she returned she had changed into a neat grey suit and her face was freshly made up with a pale foundation and lipstick; her hair was smoothed. Lidia pulled out a dining chair for Halina to sit down. 'They may think that they are reducing us to a land of peasants,' Halina said after a moment. 'But, what they don't realize is that there are enough of us who have clean minds.' She looked directly at Krystyna and then at Lidia, fixing her eyes on theirs in turn. 'You are both young. You are the future. You won't forget. You know the truth is incontrovertible. Mr Churchill is right.'

She got up from the table and went over to the gilt mirror where she adjusted her hair, smoothing a few unruly strands. When she was satisfied, she turned to the two of them who still sat transfixed at the dining table. 'I'm going out now, and when I come back we shall begin. In the meantime, you could do some private reading. I think it is a good morning for poetry.'

A few days later Krystyna was at work when news came through on the radio from London that Russia had refused permission for the Katýn graves to be examined by the International Red Cross. At the announcement she looked up from her typewriter. Piotr, who had been checking the Reuter wires, stopped what he was doing. Lech stared at the radio. He looked over at her and for a moment their eyes locked. A muscle twitched at his temple. His face was grey and unshaven and she knew that he had been working all night without sleep. He swivelled abruptly in his chair and then returned to the piece he'd been writing. Without saying anything he yanked out the page from the typewriter and ground it into a ball in his fist. He leaned back and flung it across the office like a dirty snowball. Krystyna watched it land on the thin carpet. Piotr stood by the

Reuter machine, the air around him tight with cigarette smoke. She sat for a moment looking at the report folded into her typewriter. It was almost complete, a few words needed, that was all, but she followed Lech's example and ripped it from the roll.

Shortly after the announcement the Soviet Union broke off diplomatic relations with Poland. For Halina it was a clear admission of guilt. Every morning now before work Krystyna queued in offices to try to find out more information from the Germans. But names of the dead remained sealed. Then a message came through from Warsaw. The colonel had sent his own observer to one of the sites. Seven mass graves had been dug side by side on sloping, sandy ground near to a rest house that had been used by the NKVD before the war. Young trees planted at the grave site were judged to be three years old. The bodies lay in rows several layers deep. The men's hands were tied with cord around their backs. All of them had been shot in the back of the head at the base of the skull. German bullets, but the Germans admitted they had supplied ammunition of that calibre to the Russians. Some of the corpses had broken jaws. Some had army greatcoats filled with sawdust wound over their heads. Krystyna asked Lech why this was and he said that it was to suffocate those who struggled to live.

A few days later a brown paper package arrived at the flat from the colonel. Krystyna took it to the kitchen. It felt weightless, as if there were nothing inside. Unable to open it immediately, she put it down on the table near to the breakfast things and went to get her coat ready to go out to work. She returned to the kitchen. A weak light showed up the creases in the brown paper which looked as if it had been used many times over. Her hair prickled on the back of her neck and she felt sweat break out on her upper lip.

Inside the package there was a letter from the colonel. He apologized for not writing more often. His new position in Warsaw was demanding as conditions there were so much worse than they had been in Kraków. He was sending her the package because the observer he had sent to Katýn had been able to take away some personal effects from the mass grave. He was sorry to have to tell her that among those things there was a notebook that had been kept by her father . . . She was unable to read any further. Reaching into the nest of brown paper, she lifted out the notebook and then sinking down on to her knees she held it pressed against her chest. For a long while she remained on her knees on the floor trying to breathe against what felt like a hard iron bar clamped across her chest.

All day she remained in the kitchen with the notebook. At first she simply held it in her lap unable to open it. A few grains of sand slipped out from between the stiff pages when she did eventually begin to read. Some of the entries were so water-stained it was impossible to decipher them, but there were others when her father's handwriting struck out across the page with a shocking force. He had used the notebook as a diary to record impressions of his life at a prisoner-of-war camp. There were also drawings. One showed a vast barn with no windows, surrounded by a high fence topped with rolls of barbed wire. There were also drawings of men, some wearing uniform, writing letters, talking in small groups or sleeping on rough wooden bunks that stretched in tiers up to the wooden rafters.

When Halina came home she found Krystyna sitting in

the dark. She turned on the light and Krystyna saw the strain in her face. She said that she had found no news. Her father's name was not on any list. After reading the colonel's letter she gently suggested that Krystyna take a bath. The water was tepid, but soothing and took some of the tension from her body. Towelling herself dry, Krystyna thought of her father living in such close quarters with other men and realized that at least he had been with people he respected and, recalling his tender drawings, even loved at the end. She was glad that he had not been alone.

After hanging up the towel to dry she went to her room and lay on her bed. Halina had put the notebook in its paper package on the bedside table. The colonel's letter was folded on the top. Krystyna turned off the light and lay in the dark. Images of her father's life in the camp flickered across her mind. They — he had not once written the name of his captors and now she wondered whether the notebook had been censored: were those blurred pages really the result of being buried underground? — had kept the men alive on rations of herring and boiled water over the months that they were held. Her father had written the names of people who had died from illness brought on by the inhuman conditions and drawn a cross next to each one. The entries described a routine of early morning inspections and roll-call. There were frequent searches. The dreariness was broken by lectures sometimes given by professors; her father had written of a talk on anatomy by a surgeon and another memorable lecture had been given by an architect on the use of light in buildings. Priests took mass daily and at Christmas the men of her father's unit had gathered together and sung carols. But there were also fights and disagreements, especially among the younger men, who felt the frustrations of incarceration more acutely than those of a mature age. Her father had written of intervening in disputes. 'Discipline is the first weapon of survival I tell them, but some do not believe me.' He had also written of missing being able to walk freely across open land with the wolfhounds, whose loyalty he recalled right to the end of their lives when they jumped to save him and were shot on the spot. The last image he had of his home was of their bodies slumped together in the moonlit snow.

Krystyna lay on her bed with her hands clasped against her chest. The pain across her chest was less suffocating now, more of a dull ache. She almost felt detached from it, as if she were floating outside her body. She listened to the sounds outside the building. A German motor car rolled down the street, the hum of its engorged engine fat and sweet. Kids were fascinated by the polished cars, drawn to them like pneumatic fairground rides, and she had seen young German officers lift up ragged boys and put them behind steering wheels. She wondered whether the boys would remember this after the war ended. What images would they carry with them? She heard hurried footsteps, the quick, light steps of a woman in heels on the pavement outside and guessed that it was coming up to curfew time. Most people went in well before the deadline. Now she could smell onions cooking in the flat upstairs. A door opened and the quick footsteps from outside echoed on the tiled hall. There were more than twenty people living in the block, mostly middle-aged women, who were brisk, always in a hurry, but sometimes one would stop and look at her searchingly, pausing on the stairs or at the table in the hallway where messages were left. It was how it was: people showed who they were by omission. They didn't volunteer information or ask questions. Real life was lived under the surface.

She got up from her bed and peered out under the blackout curtain. The moon shone in a dull disc. She went to the shell of brown paper curled on the bedside table and brushed it with her fingers. She looked around the room with its shrouded light. Her senses now felt alert, sharpened by her father's revelations. His voice was so clear he could have been speaking to her in this room. She sat down on the bed again and drew the notebook into her lap. From the pages there came a smell of damp earth. She clicked on the bedside lamp and once more began to read. The last entry was dated Sunday, 7 April 1940. Kozielsk Camp. Her father had written:

A letter to my daughter.
What can a father say to his daughter when he does not know whether she is alive? He can say only that he loves her. He can say only that he dreams of her and that sometimes he wakes convinced that she is calling out his name. He can say that he remembers each year of her life and that the girl who accompanied him across the fields and through the forests and down to the lakes is with him still. He can say that he tried to teach her about strength and courage and he can say that he hopes that something of those lessons might have helped her to survive.

We are leaving the camp today and have already packed our things. They won't tell us where we are going, of course, but over the past few days they have moved out large numbers of officers. Many suspect that we will be transported to a hard labour camp. I suspect that being older and lame I will not survive longer than a few weeks, especially in the depths of winter.

Some news has reached us in the months that we have been here. We are able to write letters and the priests send through whatever information they have and that way we have built up something of a communications network. But the news I am afraid to tell you, my dearest daughter, is not good. Irena has gone. She was transported to work on a collective farm and I received one precious letter from her at New Year, but heard nothing for weeks after. The winter was severe and many of us feared that we had lost wives and loved ones and now we have had it confirmed. We try to comfort each other, but each man is alone in his grief. The hand of despair claims some. It is difficult to remain active.

You will of course want to know what has happened to your brother and for weeks I have been trying to discover whether he is alive by making enquiries through the priests who have patiently sent messages on my behalf. I have heard a rumour that Anastazia and Henryk may be living in a Lithuanian convent. I cannot tell you what hope even this scant news gives me. Sometimes it seems as if the darkness parts for a brief moment and there is light.

They are asking us now to line up and soon we will be making our way out of here and so this is my last opportunity to say to you that you are in my thoughts. But more importantly, you are in my heart. Whatever this day brings, you should know that your spirit has sustained me through this time and will continue to remain close to me when we depart to wherever we are going next.

I am your loving father, Aleksander

Tears rolled down her face as she closed the notebook and put it back on the bedside table. She brushed them away but more came, heavy soaking tears that she had not cried before. She turned her face into the pillow and let herself weep. She thought back to the time in the forest when they had buried the old mare in the snow. She remembered taking the shovel from her father and the look in his eyes that had made her push down her questions. She remembered the feel of the shovel as she dug into the snow and the quiet way her father had watched her, the faint, sad smile on his lips as she glanced at him when she had finished, and the voice he used when he began to urge her that she must leave the dwór. She remembered also the walk home, following the tracks made by the sleigh that had carried the mare.

She drifted through the following days and Lech was kind to her and said she could take compassionate leave, but she decided to go into work. It broke up the days and gave her a focus outside her own concerns. Halina continued with her enquiries about the fate of her father and came home too exhausted to speak. Lidia cooked their meals and because Halina had suspended her teaching they spent the evenings reading, absorbed in private study, and retired to bed soon after curfew.

When several weeks later Krystyna heard through Lech that the colonel was looking for more staff in Warsaw, she applied for a transfer, not thinking she would be taken seriously. Then the colonel sent a communiqué asking her to travel to Warsaw with one of his advisers who was leaving Kraków the next morning. She was back at the flat and packed in less than an hour. Halina took her into her room and opened her wardrobe. 'You must choose something pretty to take with you.' Her face was drawn, but she tried to cover this by speaking brightly.

Krystyna ran her fingers through the dresses. There were

dozens in pale violet, lavender and haze, colours of mist and smoke. 'Take them,' Halina said. 'Take as many as you can carry.'

'But I'm going to Warsaw.'

Halina looked down at the sandals Krystyna wore. 'You will need something better for your feet.' She pulled out a stout pair of walking shoes. 'Not very elegant, but the heels won't slip.'

Under the two grey dresses in the small suitcase, Halina tucked in a cotton pillowcase, a nightgown, some bars of soap and three English novels, which felt suspiciously heavy, writing paper, envelopes and a fine pen. In a borrowed leather satchel Krystyna carried her passport and identity papers and a small amount of money. Halina walked her through the Planty to the station, but left without hugging her goodbye in case they were being shadowed. A gentleman in his late fifties raised his hat as the train arrived. Krystyna got into the carriage next to his and spent the journey reading a German newspaper.

The next morning Jerzy Kaminiski, shot in Warsaw at the start of the war, went for a walk with his niece Honorata Nowicki, who had disappeared in eastern Poland, to the palace on the water. The uncle talked to his niece of Marie Curie, who had been born in Warsaw, and Chopin and English literature and the muscled mermaid who appeared on the city's coat of arms. At one point he stopped talking and looked at her closely. Then he told her that she had turned into a beautiful young woman. He was proud of her work and pleased she had made progress with her studies in history and art. The niece thought her uncle looked tired and much thinner than when she had seen him last. His head was now rubbed almost completely clean of hair, except at the back where a few grey patches remained, the nakedness of his skull making his ears seem longer and more pointed. There were deep pouches under his eyes and when he spoke a vein on his temple throbbed with tension.

They stopped by the lake. The water was surprisingly clear and fresh. The park around the lake smelled of spring. There were even crocus hearts in the grass. But over the city the sky was dark, the clouds filled with smoke that poured from the ghetto where she now learned that the terrible final liquidation was taking place. Over the past year tens of thousands of Jews had been obliterated. Trains from Treblinka had passed through Warsaw. They were filled with the clothes of those the Germans had exterminated, clothes that had been worn by mothers, fathers, sons, daughters, grandparents, uncles, aunts, fabrics that still bore the shape and smell of living people, fabrics that were destined for the German textile mills where they would be mashed to a pulp. Some Polish railway workers had discovered three wagons of human hair. The colonel told her that the ghetto had been under siege since Easter Monday. German artillery had been shelling houses from the attics of which a few brave Jewish militant fighters continued their struggle. The colonel looked into the water. 'They are fighting now with bottles of petrol.' His voice was flat with exhaustion. 'We have been doing what we can to help them, but it is not enough. Most of them are too starved and worn down to be able to make the escape journey through the sewers.' He said that the Germans were now forcing the last of the inhabitants out by burning down the buildings of the ghetto one by one. He closed his eyes momentarily at the thought. She reached over and placed her hand on his upper arm. His hand came up and clasped hers. His fingers were cold.

After a moment he continued: 'A Polish woman, a mother, came to see us last week. She had taken in a Jewish baby from a family who lived in the same block of flats as her. They had pleaded with her to look after the baby as they could not take him to the ghetto. She brought him up with her own children, a boy of six and a girl of five. She kept it secret for a long time, but then last week the Gestapo paid her a visit. Two men arrived at her flat and asked to see the children. The mother told them they were at school; there was only the little one at home. They said they would wait. They sat down in her flat and watched the baby play on the floor with his toys. Then when the door opened and the two other children ran to greet their mother they took out their revolvers and shot them dead. At the door they turned to her and said, "Now you may bring up your Jewish brat," and then they walked out leaving her there with her dead children at her feet.'

Krystyna looked across the water where a white duck with a clutch of golden ducklings glided in a wide circle, their webbed feet beating frantically under their still bodies. She watched them for a while. Each time the ducklings eased away, the mother nudged them back. The colonel watched them too, his face half turned from her so that she could not see his expression. When she finally spoke her voice sounded fierce. 'My father said to me once that we honour the dead when we determine to live. When we fight on, we fight in their name.'

He glanced at her and then nodded his head slowly. 'You are right, my dear,' he said. 'We will fight on.' His eyes strayed once more towards the pall of smoke the colour of thunder that hung over the ghetto. An acrid smell now filled the air. 'We will never give in.' His eyes were brimming with emotion now. 'I am so glad to see you.' He took her arm and guided her away from the water and then across the park, switching automatically into German as a group of SS officers approached and stopped to throw bread to the mother and her ducklings. The officers gave them a brief glance before turning away, oblivious, reaching into their pockets for more bread as if this were an ordinary cloudless spring morning.

16

Kraków, present day

It is close to dawn when he calls. She reaches for the phone and cradles it in the groove of her neck.

'I'm sorry for waking you.' He sounds thin, distant, strained.

'That's all right. It's good to hear your voice. How are you?'

A long pause. 'The funeral was yesterday.'

'How did it go?' The question sounds odd, as if she's enquiring about an ordinary event, a trip out somewhere.

'A few people came, around a dozen in all. My father didn't really have friends, but my mother's friends . . . they came; they wanted to be there for her.'

'At least she has support.' She hopes she doesn't sound as if she's referring to her own situation. 'That will help her to come to terms with it.'

'She's been amazing . . .' Another pause, she hears a catch in his voice. 'So controlled that I'm concerned about her. She doesn't seem to have stopped to reflect on it at all and I'm worried that soon she's going to crash. When the friends stop coming round, when she's left on her own, she's going to realize that the person who sat in the conservatory in his reading chair for all those years is no longer there.'

'It may take her a while.' Catherine's voice is gentle. 'She may just need that time alone. She may just need to feel it in her own way.'

Konrad sighs. 'I hope so. But at the moment she's acting. I just wish she could let go a little. I just wish she could stop pretending that everything is all right.'

'Could it be that this is the only way she can deal with it?'

A silence.

She wonders whether she has offended him. 'And how are you . . . how is it affecting you?' she asks.

He exhales. 'Mostly I'm angry. I'm furious with him for leaving my mother. I can't forgive him for not being able to cope, for giving up, for refusing life. For . . . oh, Jesus, there's a whole list of things that I'm angry with him about.'

A flicker of fear touches her. 'That doesn't sound good.'

'No. I'm actually finding this a lot harder than I expected. I'm just trying to get a grip on the fact that my father died of unhappiness.'

'You couldn't have done anything for him.'

'No. There was nothing anyone could do. Towards the end of his life everything became mute, nothing touched him. All he did was read his damn paper and stockpile pills. He was just biding his time, waiting until most of the family were out of the country: his grandchildren, his daughter . . .' He breaks off.

'And you, of course.'

'We were all safely out of the way. We weren't going to come round unexpectedly and save him. You know I can't get it out of my head that what he has done is criminal;

that he has actually committed a crime. In my head it feels as if he's committed murder.'

The anger in his voice jolts her. She realizes how little she knows of him.

Konrad continues: 'I keep remembering that last time we talked. I tried to interest him in my film, but he didn't want to hear about it. I think he even asked me what it had to do with him and when I said it had everything to do with him, it was his *sister* I'd been going to see in Kraków, he looked at me as if I'd betrayed him, as if I'd violated something deep and private . . .' He breaks off again. She hears him get up from a bed or a chair and go over to a door which creaks on its hinges, blowing in the wind. He closes it firmly, as if he wants to make sure that he is alone. He comes back, breathing thickly as he speaks again into the phone: 'I told him that I didn't understand him. I didn't know why he had chosen to live such a half life . . .' He falters.

'What was his response?' She tries to sound neutral.

'He said that he wished he had gone to Poland to honour his father's death. He said he wished he had gone while he was still well.' He takes a deep ragged breath. 'He realized that he had left it too late. He was very sorry about that. I said that he could still go. He could make the trip with me. But I saw that it really was too late for him. He couldn't have made it. He just wasn't strong enough in himself, and he knew it. Now I understand that it was easier for him to take his own life than face his regrets.'

Catherine does not know how to respond. The terrible bleakness of Henryk's life is unanswerable. She sighs. 'I'm so sorry. For him, for you, for your family. But I understand. I know how you feel. I never properly spoke to

Janek. For years it was as if he didn't exist. It's only through you that I have come to know him at all.'

Konrad is silent. When he speaks again his voice is even lower than before. 'I'm wondering whether my decision to go ahead and make my film may have made it worse for my father. It presented him with a challenge to face a past he had so carefully tried to forget, just like your father. He was frightened of what he would find. Maybe I unwittingly pushed him in deeper. Maybe I should have done what you did and left well alone.' Catherine now hears doubt in his voice.

'Of course, he would have been frightened, but is that a reason not to challenge?' She is surprised at how calm and rational she sounds. 'The past belongs to all of us, surely? We must be free to interpret it in our own way and not allow others to narrate the scripts for us. Your father chose silence. My father did too, but *we* can choose to speak.'

A long hesitation. 'We can choose, yes, you're right, but what if in choosing we dishonour those we love?'

'I don't know, Konrad. I don't know.' She hears the frustration in her voice. 'I think you're in the middle of all this and I think it's too soon for answers. I think you must live for a while longer with the questions.' She feels him almost reel from her. Another long pause.

'You know, I can't come back, Catherine.'

She hears the words as if they are being spoken from a distance, as if he has gone to the end of a long tunnel and is whispering to her from his cupped hands. She can't even be sure of what he has just said.

'I don't understand,' she says.

Konrad speaks again. All warmth has drained from his voice, leaving only a flat residue. 'I can't leave . . .' There's another pause in which she hears him breathe in tight bolts. She thinks he will ask her now for a little time, but there is nothing, only a thick silence sealing the distance between them.

She sits up in the bed. Her hair falls in hot tangled ropes around her shoulders. She's wearing the new silk nightdress with the satin straps she bought for when he returned. She has imagined him touching the fine slippery fabric, his hands floating under it. Opposite the bed she can see her reflection in the mirror over the chest of drawers. Her face is red and creased, like a newborn's, but her eyes are dark and old and staring into space.

'I'm sorry.'

The walls of the hotel room seem to collapse inwards. She looks up at the ceiling half expecting a shower of white plaster dust to rain down on top of her. The overhead light swings innocently on its slightly yellowed cord. A breeze flips the curtains. A smell wedges its way through the window and into the room: sickly exhaust fumes combined with heated metal and the off odour of blocked drain. She can't think of anything to say.

After another long pause in which she thinks he might have gone away and returned to the phone he adds, 'This isn't easy for me either.' She wonders what he means. It can't be that he wants her to *console* him, or to give him permission to tear her life into pieces, wreck her hopes, pull up her dreams and fling them away, as if they mean nothing. Maybe he wants her to apologize, too; to tell him that she's sorry that he can't make it because she never expected it anyway. She has been a fool. She was right to worry that he would betray her because he just has.

'Well,' she says in a controlled voice that surprises her.

'Obviously, you've made your decision.' She thinks of putting down the phone right there and then, but it feels too heavy and too slippery in her hands.

'Catherine, this doesn't mean that I don't want to.' She hears him reach for another breath. 'There is no place I would rather be than with you.'

The pleading note in his voice enrages her. She considers cutting him off. She wants to swear and shout and cry. She wants to hurt him and the violence of her feelings jolts her fully awake. 'Look, please don't do this – you've let me know what the situation is, please don't insult us any further.'

'I'm sorry you feel that way, Catherine.' His voice has taken on an edge of irritation.

Panic rises in her. He will go soon and she won't have said how she truly feels. Her chest is so tight, she can barely breathe. 'What about your film?' she manages to ask.

She hears him draw breath sharply. 'I have to abandon it now. Everything has changed.' He clears his throat and she thinks he is going to continue, but something has distracted him: a voice in the background, a woman's voice, confident, full, familiar. She feels ice trickle through her blood. Everything slows for a moment. Her mind clouds and then in the next instant becomes clear.

'You had better go.'

'Yes.'

She feels sick at the note of relief in his voice.

'I'll try to call you again.' His words sound hollow as if he is talking to someone else.

'All right,' she says. She puts down the phone. For a while she sits upright in bed with her reflected image staring across at her from the mirror with appalled concern.

She hears the click of the bedside clock radio and the faint groaning of the water pipes in the bathroom. Somewhere deeper into the hotel a door slams shut. She shoves back the quilt and swings her legs over the side of the bed. Her feet touch the bare floor. She peels off the nightdress and lets it drown in its own creamy voluptuousness on the bathroom floor. All the sleep in her body has evaporated. She feels viciously alert. She slides the cold shower screen behind her and steps under the head, bringing it down a few notches from where Dominic had screwed it so that it is closer to her own height. She turns the water temperature up and presses full power.

After towelling herself dry she dresses in one of her new outfits because she cannot bear to put on the clothes she wore the day before, which seem to her to smell of her own gullibility. Only yesterday, she had believed in love, but yesterday now feels like a contradiction and love now feels as if it is personally mocking her, standing observing her with its hands on its hips, rocking back and forth because it managed to ensnare her and take from her a delicious secret desire. Love has feasted on her, gorged on her need and her hope and now it has gone, flown like an over-stuffed bird: awkward, waddling and grotesque. She would shoot it in the heart if she could. She would wring its neck.

The mirror accuses. It tells her she is guilty. To silence it, she combs oil through her hair, she ritualizes, she dots foundation into her scorched cheeks, pats it smooth, spreads it up to her ears and down around her nose which is crisp around the nostrils from the crying she must have done in her sleep. Now she remembers that she woke at 3 a.m. in tears, full heavy tears as if a catastrophe had occurred, and she had used up most of the tissues in the box. Shaken, she had put on the light and read to the end of the film treatment until she began to doze. Konrad's call was her second waking.

She pulls mascara through her eyelashes and the effect makes her eyes seem older and more hostile. She wonders whether she is going to become ugly, a woman coarsened by disappointment. She doubts anyone will ever want her again. Her wounds will show. From now on her work will have to be enough. Her perfume bottle is still almost full. She picks it up and sprays a fine mist down her arms and then is almost floored by a wave of longing for him as she remembers how he kissed her neck and breathed in the scent. She will have to find a new scent with no reminders.

Finishing her make-up with a slick of pale rose lipstick, she goes down to the lobby where the concierge glances at her as if he somehow understands all that she has just gone through. He smiles and makes a flowing gesture with his hands in the direction of the dining room which is still surprisingly dark, the tables immaculate pools of silver, linen and glass, as if set up on a theatre stage.

She takes her seat at a table for two near a window. A waitress, whose black skirt is zipped up only halfway down the small of her back, pulls open the heavy yellow drapes revealing a sky the colour of smoke. She whisks off the other setting and asks Catherine whether she would like tea or coffee. She orders coffee and then as the waitress leaves she calls her over again and changes her mind.

'Tea, please, I'm sorry.'

The waitress nods and takes the order to the kitchen. Watching her go, zipping up her skirt with a swift, graceful movement, Catherine feels a stab of envy for the young woman's simplicity, her innocent beauty, her honesty. She wonders whether this is the beginning of a new life of pretence, a life in which she will go through the motions and appear to be all right when really she feels as if a strip of her soul has been torn away, exposing all of her inadequacy, a dark gap, something vital missing. Some lack in her that will need covering up. She glances around the dining room at the frozen white tables and wonders why the other guests have not come down to breakfast. Now she looks at her watch, puzzled – why had she not checked the time before she left her room? – and sees that it is only 6 a.m.

Her first thought is to leave the table and return upstairs, but the waitress has already taken her order and it would appear odd not to wait, perhaps more odd than arriving on her own in the dining room at this hour. She wishes she had brought something down with her to read, not that she would be able to concentrate. Konrad's decision has not surprised her. It was perhaps naive of her to think he could return to America and bury his father and then seamlessly come back to Poland to pick up the tentative threads he had started with her. Such momentous events need ropes, not threads; long-term security, not fragile hope. She had meant it when she said that she understood, but what surprises her is how unprepared she is. All her real plans were to be made on his return; they were plans she wanted to share with him, offer to him not as consolation for his loss, but in the belief that something new might emerge for them both. She is not prepared to meet grief itself. She is not prepared for its solitary shock.

After breakfast she goes up to her room and stands before the window, looking down on the street. Most of the shops are still closed, but a few stall-holders are setting up. She watches a woman in a blue apron unload a plastic crate of flowers from the back of a white van which is parked so that Catherine can see the interior fitted out with wooden slats on which rest more crates of cut flowers. The woman has a rounded back and scuttles rather than walks between the van and her patch which she has made into a shady arbour with large yellow sun umbrellas, slightly overlapping one another, like parasols on a crowded beach. In a beaker she arranges a cluster of anemones, the colours of which have the polished soft beauty of sea glass. She stands back from the arrangement, admiring the flowers as if she has just painted them. Catherine's eyes are drawn to a perfect bunch of cream roses which she longs for with a desperation that takes her aback. The thought of these flowers being bought by someone else makes her rush from her window and run down the stairs and out of the hotel. When she reaches the stall and breathlessly claims the roses, holding them to her nose, inhaling their fragile perfume, drinking them in, she realizes that she has forgotten to bring money.

The woman does not understand English. As Catherine apologizes, telling her she intends to go back to the hotel at once and bring down some money, and please would she keep the roses and not sell them to anyone else, she leans her head to one side and nods. She takes a step backward indicating that she is not interested in payment and wants to get on with her day. Catherine remains rooted to the spot, holding her flowers, all her limbs filled with a sudden dull pain. She wonders whether some disease that she had not known about has just become manifest in her body. This is the moment, she thinks, when I acknowledge my own death. An image of Henryk releasing with ardent concentration from the palm of his hand a stream of tiny white antidepressant pearls one by one into his morning tea comes into her mind. The little boy who had never known his mother and father, who had been raised by nuns for the first three years of his life in a convent in Lithuania until he was adopted and taken to America, had died of unhappiness as an old man. She looks down at her flowers. A feeling of despair washes over her as she moves away from the stall.

Clutching her roses, she wanders around the square. She has always believed that unhappiness is not an illness, but a chosen state. Even in her worst times she had refused chemical assistance; instead of medication she had chosen to feel her own sadness, to work and live through it, or perhaps alongside it. She'd even grown used to it in a way. It was her way of separating her own feelings from those of others. In her sadness, she was fully herself. She feels a glimmer of understanding as she thinks of her father and of all the years he kept himself safe inside his own sadness. She doubted he ever sought treatment. He was not ill. He was not to be cured except through time. It had taken him years to come through his silence; no one cajoled or coaxed him, no one said to him that it was time he came to terms with his past: he had no time frame other than that he set for himself. She sees now that there was dignity in her father's choice. He returned home, to his country and ultimately to himself when he was ready.

A carriage drawn by a pair of dove-grey horses glides up to the pavement. A young coachwoman in white shirt, dark waistcoat, loose trousers and pert hat with a spotted veil climbs down from her driving seat and polishes a lamp.

She looks relaxed, at ease in her own body which has the supple, well-defined lines of someone in their twenties. The coachwoman lights a cigarette and blows out a luxuriant plume of smoke. The horses each rest a hind hoof and lower their heads, eyelids flickering against the sun. The rich smell of their sweat reminds Catherine of the last warm days of autumn. Dropping her cigarette and extinguishing it with the toe of a polished shoe, the coachwoman raises her eyebrows to enquire whether she would like a ride. Catherine shakes her head. 'Sorry, I have no money.'

Catherine walks across the square, holding herself carefully because of a sudden twinge in her back which feels as if a cold rusty poker is being pushed between her ribs. It feels odd to be without a bag. This is how it must be for a man to walk, she thinks, unencumbered. She wonders how Konrad is feeling right now. Did he put down the phone and go back into the room from where his wife called him? She imagines a woman of her own age sitting on a low chair near a window. The woman, pale with dark hair, slender, immaculately dressed, glances up at him as he comes back, her expression a mixture of compassion, pride and complicity. She will hold his eyes. Catherine imagines his look in return; it is the look that she associates most completely with him: thoughtful, open, hopeful, as if the person he is looking at has just asked him the most important question of his life. Through that look flowed a raw, gentle masculinity. She had felt amazed by it, and shy and grateful and moved. He had made her feel her own deep womanliness; there was nothing she held in reserve, she realized, nothing she would not have given him. And now she is never going to feel this again. She has been jilted. The thought causes the poker to jab and twist sharply against her upper ribs. She wonders without any sense of drama whether one of her lungs has collapsed. She decides to walk on some more and if the pain has not gone, then she might find a taxi.

She reaches the river. The wide sweep of water is a dark and rich olive green. In the distance the Gothic towers of the castle and cathedral rise against a restless sky. Suspended above the castle in a single island of blue is a silver air balloon. She watches it for a few moments. Clouds race behind it, but the balloon itself remains utterly still. She wonders how many people are up in the basket looking down on the water and across the city and whether their lives are balanced as precipitously as hers seems to be right now. The balloon has an eerie, lunar beauty, a presence as if somehow it were watching her, absorbing all sound, all motion, all thought. She moves on down the path, keeping her eyes on the balloon, compelled by its magnetic pull.

The water smells of silt. In the grassy verges along the river bank she can see white heads of clover vibrating with bees. A short distance along the river there is a wooden jetty with a narrow boat tied to a hitching ring. She walks towards it. The pain in her back eases a little. The clouds begin to disperse. She looks at the boat rocking in the water. Perhaps I will be all right, she thinks. She doesn't quite trust this feeling, but it stays with her as she passes the boat which is painted down its sides with colourful dragons. A young man falls in step beside her. He is in his late twenties or early thirties, tanned, good-looking with lustrous dark hair that smells of the smoky river. 'Hey beautiful, where are you going?'

She ignores him and continues walking, her eyes now fixed on the hilltop castle. She knows that the young man is following her and then she becomes aware of the cream roses in her hand. They make her look conspicuous. She considers dropping them into the river so that she can walk unhindered, but she can't bring herself to ditch them so soon after securing them. She holds them by her side with their ruffled heads pointing downwards. The young man speeds up his pace and gets ahead of her and then walks backward so that he can appraise her. Now she wants to laugh. His blatant assessment would be quite comical if she allowed it to be. Instead she tries to affect a look of polite disinterest as she walks towards him down the wide river path.

'Are you Polish?' he asks.

'Yes.'

For some reason this satisfies him and he backs away from her, but not before he has given a respectful bow as if she were his Polish mother, his eyes darkly serious and puzzlingly grateful.

She walks for a good hour, passing cyclists and tourists and people walking dogs. Afterwards she returns to the hotel thinking she will collect her bag and then go out again to have lunch. But the quietness of her room calms her and she lies down for a moment on the bed. She falls into a deep and dream-filled sleep and is still dreaming of her grandmother's house when the phone calls her back to awareness. She sits up. In the mirror opposite her face looks smoother and younger. She lifts the phone and her heartbeat suddenly hammers in her ears.

'Hello.'

'Hi, it's me.'

'Hi . . .'

'Are you okay?'

'Yes, I'm all right. I went out for a while down to the river.'

'I'm sorry about earlier. I couldn't really talk.'

'That's all right. I understand. I'm not expecting anything. I'm sorry if I sounded abrupt.'

She hears him sigh and her stomach turns over. She wants now to sob, to turn her face into the pillow and heave her disappointment into it.

'I can't do this.' There is a catch in his voice. 'I can't leave everything on hold like this.'

'But you need to be there. You said everything had changed.'

'Everything *has* changed, except how I feel about you. Yes, I need to be here, but I also need to be with you. This is tearing me into pieces, Catherine.'

'What do you want me to do?'

'I can't ask you to do anything. I can't ask you to wait because I don't know how long I will have to be here. I just want you to know that it isn't the end.'

'It feels like the end.' Her face in the mirror is white. She draws a blanket across her feet.

He tries to speak but his voice thickens.

She realizes that he is crying. She holds back her own tears and manages to say, 'It's all right.'

He blows his nose. 'Listen,' he says, still choked. 'How about we make some sort of plan? We could arrange to meet in Poland in a couple of months or so. What do you think?'

'I don't know.' She is aware that she needs to trust him again.

'Then come here.'

'What? You can't be serious.'

'I've been thinking about what you said about choices. Catherine, I'm choosing. I'm choosing you. I don't care where we are. I'll even come and get you.'

She laughs, delicious laughter. 'You really would, you really mean it?'

'Listen, I'm serious. Can you get back to Poland in a couple of months? Would you be able to take some time off?'

She considers his idea. Her heart beats wildly. 'How do I know that things won't change in the next couple of months?'

He sighs. 'You don't. Neither do I, but all we can do is to mean what we say now.'

'I'm sorry to have to ask you this, but did you mean what you said earlier – about abandoning your film?'

A pause in which she hears him exhale a long ragged breath. 'I was upset, I'm not using that as an excuse, but I went for a walk too and I know that I have to make this film. Of course I have to make this film. I really have no other choice.'

'You do. You can walk away from it. You don't have to follow it through.'

'I've chosen, Catherine. Can I make it any plainer?'

Now she is crying. She pushes her hair from her face. 'All right,' she says. 'Okay.'

'Right, it's the end of June now,' he says. 'We could meet at the end of August.'

'Would that give you enough time?' She is amazed to hear how precise and like her professional self she sounds, as if she is organizing a meeting with a colleague.

'I think so.'

But she can't ignore the quiver of doubt in his voice.

And so she offers him another chance. 'The end of September might be better for me.'

'Really?' The slight strain in his voice dissolves. 'You could come back to Poland then?'

'Yes. I'll come back at the end of September. Before I leave I'll book a room in the same hotel.' She understands that she needs confirmation from him and it makes her feel uncomfortable.

'You could stay in the apartment.' She hears the note of hope in his voice and then the tension in her body relaxes as she understands that he has wondered, too, whether he ought to follow something so unformed and new. Why had she not considered this? She glances towards the mirror where the roses sit in a water jug; their soft cream faces have bloomed in the heat while she was asleep. The crawling sense of fear lifts from her and seems to take with it some accumulated layers of the past.

'Yes, I'd like that,' she says and hears him smile in reply. 'I'd love that, in fact.' Buoyed by confidence she continues: 'But let's not call in the meantime, let's not be sad and awkward and difficult to reach, let's just do what we both need to do and then meet when we are ready.'

'Okay. It's a deal.' He laughs and then sighs. 'Catherine, you are beautiful.'

She is about to quip a smart reply in return. Something like: I know – I've already been told that once today – but instead she says his name – *Konrad* – and it feels amazing on her lips. It is the loveliest feeling to know that she can trust this man and it is incredible to her because only an hour ago she felt that he had betrayed her utterly. She knows that they will meet in three months and the thought is wonderful, intoxicating and yet also sobering because she will have used the time to make the right kind of preparations. She doesn't know yet what that will entail, but it will be difficult and it will be lonely.

They talk for a little while longer and he tells her more about his father. After putting down the phone she goes over to the window. Her father took years to make his choice to return. It could not have been easy to come back after all that had happened. She wonders whether he felt free when he died, whether he finally escaped his memories. Her thoughts turn to Henryk. In the end, he had chosen his own way to die. He had researched on the Internet how many tablets were needed, Konrad had told her, and had taken exactly a dozen more; he'd remained precise until the end. Indeed, he was experiencing a lift in his depression, a window of brightness, and it energized him; it enabled him to make a decision: the first important decision in years. And then he acted without fear. She now understands. One man chose life, the other death. One chose to return, the other chose to leave; but both men made a decision they would not reverse and because they decided irrevocably, because they saw through their decision until the end, they were not to blame.

She thinks now of her own decisions. All her life so far has been tightly bound to another person. All her decisions have been made with that other person in mind. Now she feels that she has been given an opportunity, a chance to do things well, to make the rest of her life more like the life she has always wished for herself.

She considers her options. She could go back to Cambridge, take time off work and find somewhere else to live, perhaps a cottage on the Fens. The thought makes her mind race. She could go to Welney and live by the water, watch the sky and the gathering birds. She has always wanted to write her own book on astronomy, but has lacked the time and space. Welney would give her what she needed and there were people at the institute who would encourage her to take a sabbatical. It wouldn't be difficult to arrange. She could hand over her research to her deputy who would be delighted at the opportunity.

Or she could leave Cambridge altogether and find somewhere in London where she had friends, or used to have friends, highly successful people who were at Cambridge with her and now worked for financial corporations or the Foreign Office or the BBC. She wonders whether they would recognize her.

The other choice is to move to Devon near her grandparents' old home by the sea. She could find a cottage to rent until September and work on her book there. But the thought of three months seems too short to encompass a move and resettlement and the beginnings of a book as well. There is also the question of Dominic.

She will have to face him and tell him that their life together is over. She must not leave him dangling with expectations and anticipation. She can't fully inhabit her new life until she has shed the other. She picks up the phone and this time checks the clock. It is nine, a Wednesday. Dominic has no lectures on a Wednesday. He usually works from home in his small hot office which she can now smell as she waits for him to pick up the phone.

'Hello.' He sounds brisk, annoyed, self-important.

'It's me. Catherine.' She feels her mouth go dry and wishes that she had prepared what she was going to say. The air in the hotel room feels suddenly charged and dangerous.

'Hi.' His voice softens a notch. 'Where are you?'

She wonders why he has to ask. 'Still here, in Kraków.'

'And how are you?'

She is surprised. She expected recriminations, a cata-logue of his preoccupations and feelings. She expected him to sound desperate. She expected to have to console him.

'I'm all right, I think.' She pauses; normally at this point in a conversation he will interrupt, but he stays listening.

'You think?'

'I'm coming back, Dominic. We need to talk.'

He draws in breath sharply and she realizes that he has not expected this. She has a sense of him trying to control his feelings and not say too much. 'Call me before you leave for the airport.' He sounds slightly out of breath. 'Give me some warning.'

After she puts down the phone she wonders why he needs warning. She imagines at first that it must be the state of the house. He will need some time to clear up the signs of his latest binge, put things in order for her return, but that has never been something he has worried about before. He has perversely taken pride in the careless way he lived because it demonstrated his distress. It showed her that he needed her. The thought of stepping back into the hot disorder of their home suddenly depresses her and she wonders whether she ought to call him again and say that they should meet instead at her office. But there are things she needs, things she would like to collect and have with her. She will try to book a flight for the next day and then call him as he requested. She will do this gently and kindly and without reproach. She will remain composed when she steps back inside the house.

She spends the rest of the day in a small café on the

square. She takes the envelope with her and reads to the end of Konrad's notes and film treatment slowly, resisting the temptation to rush through it to find out what she needs to know. She grasps that the story of her father's early life, his hidden and unknown life, is more painful than she expected it to be, but it is still a most precious gift. Now she remembers that Konrad had said that there was more and that he would tell her when they met; what he had written was only a fragment to help him shape the first draft of his film. She runs her mind over the first telephone call of that morning. How strained he had sounded; she understands that she had been speaking to his American self. The Polish part of him called the second time and she was able to give him another chance.

After she has finished the final part of the story, she drinks vodka and with her mind still afloat with the impact of what she has just read she walks around the square looking up at the two uneven towers of St Mary's outlined against the sky. She waits for a few moments and then hears the bugle call soar into the shimmering night sky in echoing warning of a long-ago attack and she waits for the brave plaintive interruption before returning to the hotel.

She takes a taxi from Cambridge Station. It is raining when the car pulls up at the house. The windows are steamed up and she cannot see out. While the driver works out the fare, she watches the wipers flick back and forth over the windscreen. One rubber blade catches and drags across the glass. Just as she is about to get out, she hears the sound of her own front door open and then she sees Dominic come down the path and glance at the taxi. She thinks he might come over to the car, but his attention is distracted by someone else: a young woman, slim-hipped in tight jeans with short dark hair, who holds up a set of keys, indicating her car, a black Mini Cooper parked across the road. She watches Dominic squeeze his bulk into the Mini, laughing at his own ridiculousness, and she feels a pulse of tenderness towards him. The young woman gets into the driver's seat and pulls away smartly, spraying water from her tyres.

'Are you ready, or what?'

Now she remembers the taxi fare. 'Sorry.' She hands over a ten-pound note to the driver, a young man with diamanté earrings and hair shaved up at the sides. 'Keep the change.' She opens the car door and steps out in the rain.

The driver pulls her suitcase out of the boot. He grimaces at the weather. 'Another brilliant summer,' he says.

'Yes,' she says. 'Another extraordinary year.'

He glances at her before he climbs into the cab and drives off. She reaches into her bag, but cannot find her house key so she opens the front door with the spare key kept under a terracotta tile. It feels strange, as if she is breaking back into her own life. The hallway smells of Chinese food and she drops the key on the hall table and looks at her post. Fewer letters than she would have expected have come for her, mostly bills and subscription notices. She pushes the letters into her bag and walks on towards the kitchen, her heart beginning to thud so that she can hear her own blood pulsing in her ears. The kitchen is tidy. Takeaway food cartons have been pushed down into the bin – she opens it to check – and dishes and cutlery have been washed and put in their correct places. There is a new J-cloth folded over the taps on the sink. Feeling like an investigator at a crime scene, she opens all the cupboards and then inspects the fridge which is stocked with cheese, ham, supermarket salads, tomatoes, olives and the remains of some fried rice. A half-full bottle of Sauvignon Blanc juts out of the door.

She goes upstairs. She walks into the spare room first. Her books are still there, on the bedside table. She finds another bag and begins to pack more books, her files and laptop. Sitting on the top of the bookshelf are the binoculars in their heavy box. She picks them up last. She opens the case and lifts them out. They smell of old churches. She puts them over her neck and feels their reassuring weight for a few moments. Then she takes them off and puts them back in their box.

Stepping into the main bedroom she sees that the bed is unmade; the curtains are closed against the dull day. There is a stale, sweet smell. The bedside light is still on. She switches it off. As she does so she notices a tiny pearl earring caught in the fibres of the carpet. She picks it up and leaves it beside the lamp. She pulls down a large suitcase from the top of the wardrobe and returns to the spare room to pack her clothes and shoes. Folding her favourite cardigans and dresses, she feels a sense of release, as if every tiny closed door inside her has swung open delicately on oyster hinges. Tears spring down her face. She goes over to the bedroom mirror and then after a moment or two she is able to smile, at first with disbelief and then soft delight as if she were welcoming home someone she has not seen in years.

Her car starts the first time. With her suitcases and bags pushed on to the back seat, she pulls away from the house. Misted rain blurs the churches and colleges in her rear-view mirror as she drives away from the city, taking the road to Welney. When she reaches the water she stops and sits for a moment, listening to the honking clamour of swans, geese, ducks and wild waterfowl criss-crossing a sky alive with wings. A fan of sunlight opens slowly behind the clouds, irradiating the scene with an intense saturated light. Catherine reaches over to the passenger seat for her binoculars and then she gets out.

17

Warsaw, January 1944

'We have two choices.' The colonel paused and observed his staff of twelve seated around a trestle table, illuminated by a single low-wattage light bulb. He rubbed the space between his eyes. The meeting had been going on for several hours at the Home Army headquarters in the basement of a paint factory. In the dim light many of the delegates appeared tired and pallid. 'The first is that we hold our battle plans against the Germans and wait to see whether the Russians renew diplomatic relations.' He swallowed. Krystyna, seated at his left, noticed beads of sweat clinging to the surface of his skin. He wiped his dome and went on: 'The second is that we continue our fight alone.' He glanced at the men seated at the table.

There was a short silence. Krystyna felt the tension vibrate around the room. She ran her eyes over the delegates, who in their drab coats and worn shirts looked more like a collection of exhausted shopkeepers than top army commanders and home government representatives. Lack of sleep due to weeks of living in cramped, underground basements under constant artillery fire had given them a remote, shut-down look. A fine coating of plaster dust clung to their clothes and hair and eyelashes, accentuating the impression that they were no longer vibrant men of flesh and blood; instead they had become walking automata composed solely of bone and ash. They lifted their heads. One or two locked eyes, their tiredness leaking away for a moment just long enough for the colonel to understand that every one of them knew exactly what was at stake.

The quartermaster-general, a trim, efficient man in his mid fifties with a shock of iron-grey hair flipping over his forehead, leaned forward and rested his wrists on the table. 'We all know the Russians are using every means they can to discredit us. We've seen the articles in the Soviet press declaring that the Home Army is nothing but a bunch of Gestapo agents.' His expression was filled with contempt. 'We know very well what the Russian attitude is towards Poland.'

There were fierce nods of agreement from those seated around the table. Krystyna remembered the pressure of the Russian soldier's boot on her hand in her bedroom at the dwór, the way he had twisted his foot for maximum impact, the way his eyes had changed, going cold like an extinguished match.

The chief of staff, a tall, intense man with a long white face, spoke next. 'I think we can fairly assume that there will be no resumption of diplomatic relations with the Russians.'

The quartermaster-general nodded tightly. 'Indeed. If we stop all our efforts against the Germans we will only hand Russia the evidence it craves to prove to the world that we are one of the enemy. That could mean losing the trust of the Allies.'

The chief of staff pressed his glasses more firmly against his nose. 'The question is whether we remain underground, or come out into the open.'

The colonel nodded slowly. 'To emerge for battle with the Germans and then retreat into hiding once the Russians have entered Poland would be' – he paused, a muscle twitching high on his temple – 'unfeasible.'

There was stirring in the room. Mouths broke into smiles. The colonel drew back his shoulders. His eyes were two fixed points of light in the gloom. His unwavering gaze reminded her of the way the wolfhounds at home had looked when they scented a rat. The colonel continued: 'We must stand firm. We must show the world that we are the first defenders of our own territories. The Home Army is evidence of the existence of the Republic of Poland,' he finished to murmurs of approval from the delegates.

It was close to curfew time when the meeting broke up and the delegates dispersed at short intervals from the factory building, wrapping faces in scarves against the bitter cold. Krystyna pulled on her coat and walked with the colonel to Stare Miasto where they had taken rooms in an old schoolhouse. As they approached their building she looked up at the needle-thin ancient houses and churches huddled in the darkness and then looked over her shoulder to check that they had not been followed.

Inside the stone porch of the schoolhouse, the colonel put his hand on her shoulder and looked down into her face. 'Get some sleep, my dear.' Between his brows there was a deep mark in the shape of an M. She recalled how during the meeting he had repeatedly pinched that spot and wondered whether he was again being plagued by

sinus trouble. On rare occasions he slept for a few hours
in the morning to make up for the long sleepless nights
and that was the only concession he made for the efforts
he demanded of his body. Sometimes he seemed on the
point of collapse, and then he would stop and bring his
palms up to his eyes for a few moments, his head bent.
Her heart would falter at the sight of him. The thought
that he might not be able to continue was more of a
worry to her than her own exhaustion which came over
her in waves, numbing her to most familiar sensations.
She had grown used to being hungry and thirsty and cold
and frightened, and had learned to lean on these depriva-
tions, like a rope support in a long, dark tunnel. The light
at the end was in sight. She could stumble towards it as
long as she knew that the colonel was ahead, showing
them the way out. 'Goodnight,' she said and made her
way up to her room.

In the weeks that followed, reports began to come
through of disappearances of Home Army soldiers, invited
for meetings with the Soviets, in these cases, never to
return. Bodies of Home Army soldiers were found buried
in shallow snow graves at a Soviet camp. There were more
grim dispatches, and each seemed to strengthen the colonel's resolve not to enter into a war of nerves with the
Soviets but to show the world that his army was on the side
of the Allies. The army had intensified sabotage activities
against the Germans under Operation Tempest that mobilized all soldiers in the eastern provinces, supplying them
from a vast network of secret workshops that mushroomed
across the entire country. The colonel, pinched thin from
a monotonous diet of appropriated German tongue and
wine, forced himself to remain steady at the helm. Once as

Krystyna worked on typing up radio bulletins, she caught the colonel staring at her with incredulity as if she had disappeared, too, and had returned without him being aware of it.

In February, the bombshell dropped. The British and American governments had met with the Soviets who demanded in exchange for assisting Poland against the German occupation large sections of Polish territory in the east, including the ancient cities of Lwów and Wilno. In return for this sacrifice, Poland would gain land in the west from the Germans, pushing the frontier through East Prussia, Danzig and Upper Silesia. Krystyna heard the announcement on the radio and summoned the colonel. He listened and then went to his desk to compose a message in return. Krystyna sat at the typewriter and pulled a fresh sheet of paper into the machine. The colonel then began to dictate in a dry, confident tone. She typed quickly, her heart racing as his words resounded around the room. 'If violence and brute force should win instead of right and justice, there will be no peace in Europe, and the Polish nation will never submit to force. We shall not give in or bend; on the contrary, there will be a breakdown and anarchy in the Polish nation if there should be submission to Soviet demands.'

Throughout the spring the German troops, anticipating the Soviet advance, intensified their efforts to keep their grip on the city and by summer the German civilian population began to leave Warsaw. Fleets of cars bumped through the rubble-strewn streets, skirting the steaming ruins. Inside the heavily laden cars German children pressed their faces to the windows and watched the procession of canvas-strapped wagons bring up the rear. Those without transport walked, some leading stolen cows or goats, determined to milk the last drop from the country they had occupied for nearly five years. Poles came out and jeered at the departing Germans. The need for revenge was tacit; sometimes now as Krystyna walked to the factory she could almost smell it in the air.

The colonel and his men were tightly engaged in plans to start a rising throughout Warsaw. There were long arguments, heated discussions, debates that sparked through the night. Daily they radioed appeals to London for assistance. They urgently needed weapons, food, medical supplies. Sometimes there were promises and they prepared spaces for air drops, risking their lives to wait for planes that never arrived. Radios, constantly hammered under the aerial and tank bombardments, stopped working. Days went by with no communication at all. Gaunt from exhaustion, the colonel ordered the quartermaster-general to count the weapons and ammunition supplies and then count them again. 'Ten days,' he told them, late one night, his eyes glazed, his head gleaming in a strip of moonlight that streamed in from a gap in the curtains. 'We can hold out for ten days.'

Zero hour drew closer. It preoccupied them all. The whole of Warsaw felt bound by secret invisible wires that hummed with tension. The late summer skies were restless, brooding, unpredictable. Some mornings it rained; in the evenings it was too hot to sleep. In her tiny attic room at the top of the schoolhouse, Krystyna rolled and turned in her narrow bed, trying to find a cool point of relief. Sometimes she simply sat up in the dark and listened for the sound of tanks that would signal the end. The Russians had advanced as far as Praga. They were on the other side of the Vistula opposite the Old Town. The curved oak beams of the ancient house shook from the thud of artillery fire. At any point it was expected the Russian tanks would roll across and the Home Army would no longer be alone in their fight against the Germans.

When the morning came she dressed immediately without bothering to turn on the light; all she needed was within arm's reach. She carried her shoes and walked down the gritty stairwell in her bare feet, navigating her way by feel. In the porch she slipped on her shoes, holding on to a crooked iron banister for support, and then used her shoulder to push open the heavy front door. Outside a light rain was falling, smattering against the thin lead roof of a church.

Although she did not need to hurry she walked briskly, her stomach fluttering with anticipation and nervous tension. The streets seemed to rise up around her with a kind of knowingness and awareness. It was unsettling. Now that the moment was finally near, it felt strange as if it were not the anticipated time itself, but a rehearsal. She headed towards the factory. Overhead the sky rolled with grey clouds. A few people were walking to work with knapsacks that seemed more tightly packed than usual. Excitement lapped her belly as she pushed on faster. No one, she noticed, was bothering to protect themselves from the rain.

She reached the factory building. It faced two narrow, parallel roads, both dead-ends, bricked in by the dark and terrible wall of the ghetto, scorched and riddled with bullet holes from machine-gun fire. That rising had ended in defeat. The Germans had continued their bombardments until they had annihilated everyone inside. Along the length of the wall at regular intervals there were blood-stains, blackened patches that had dried as stiff as tar. There was an acrid charred smell in the air and the entire area had an eerie tightness to it that never broke.

Next to the paint factory was a tobacco factory, a German garrison guarded by two pillboxes. She came within fifteen yards of the nearest pillbox and noticed the barrel of a machine gun trained on the street. If she were stopped she would pretend that she was a factory worker who had come to work early. She would say that she was the personal assistant of the factory owner, who would vouch for her when she arrived. What the Germans didn't know was that the factory owner had built his own garrison of young men and women ready to fight. They arrived for work in factory clothes, paint-spattered trousers or overalls, heavy boots, shirts with rolled sleeves and caps; they carried bags and had an air of purpose about them. By now some of them recognized her as she fell into their morning and evening slipstream, although they assumed that she was not one of them, but a secretary or an office worker by the quality of her clothes. She still wore the dresses given to her by Halina and she washed them every few days in cold water, hanging them up to dry on a nail stuck in the bowed beam in her room.

One of the sealed-off narrow streets contained a large sash window that was always kept open and through which she could climb into the basement of the factory. She checked that she was not being followed and then pulled up the window. It was rotting in its frame and rattled alarmingly. She looked back over her shoulder before she went through. The street was deserted apart from a thin black cat picking its way along the cracked paving slabs as if walking on thin wire, its whiskers dewy fresh in the smoky light. It hesitated and fixed her with a pair of luminous green eyes before dipping its dainty jet head to snuffle at a discarded wrapper that she saw had once contained German cheese. A grocery store had stood on the corner of the street, but the German shopkeeper had weeks ago shut up his business.

Her feet touched the floor. She pulled her dress straight and brushed off a few flakes of peeling paint and damp wood clinging to the material. Stumbling to find the light switch she stabbed her hip on the edge of an old filing cabinet and bit her lip to stop from calling out. The caged bulb fizzed and she thought it was about to blow, but then it glowed brighter and she was able to make her way up the stairs through the levels of the factory, passing waist-high vats slicked with lakes of oil, the paint seething underneath, thick and unctuous as cold cream. The machines fitted with paint-encrusted paddles and ploughs were awkwardly stilled, as if caught by surprise. The rich chemical vapour had a swooning, sweet quality that made her eyes swim and her heart race.

She reached the largest top room, flanked on one side by long clouded windows. The basement was too cramped to accommodate all twelve members of the Home Army and government delegates who would meet here to make their final decisions before zero hour. The trestle table from the smaller meeting room downstairs had already been carried up, along with a stack of chairs which she now began to arrange round it. In the far corner was a deep sink encrusted with paint in many different colours like an artist's dried-up palette. She turned on the tap and to her surprise it sputtered and then gave out a shuddering gout of rust-coloured water. She went to turn it off but then saw to her amazement that the water had run clear. A jug and glasses were kept under the sink. She rinsed them and filled a glass and smelled it. There was a tang of metal as if the water had sat for a long time in a tank. She drank a glass and then another, wiping her mouth on the back of her hand, her eyes smarting.

Through the milky windows Krystyna could see the red clot of the sun emerging from a bed of thick cloud. She went over, rubbed a pane clear, and looked out across the city. From up here she could see the whole of Warsaw stretched out like a dark island. The Prudential Tower dominated, its sixteen storeys forming a solid pillar against the skyline. From here she could see Stare Miasto and the tower of the Town Hall and further to the west the Western Station. The rain had cleared and spears of sunlight were trying to push through bolts of cloud that were now rimmed with gold. She glanced at her watch. In exactly fifteen minutes the first of the delegates would arrive.

She took another look around the room. On a small table under the window stood a portable gramophone with two pistols concealed inside. The wireless set was contained in a brown suitcase under the floorboards. She would wait until most people had arrived before she set it up. There was always a chance that one of the team had been followed by the Gestapo. Since the colonel's decision, tension had been brewing in the suburbs among groups of restless young men and she knew that he feared for the secrecy of the zero hour. The strain was pushing them to start their own insurrection, and it was taking all his powers of delicate leadership to insist they listen to their commanders.

She glanced at her watch again. Seven minutes. All seemed to be in order. She could hear that the factory had started up downstairs and knew that workers were arriving and, hidden among them, the first of the delegates. But she hovered at the door unable to leave immediately, a prickling feeling at the back of her neck suggesting that she had forgotten something vital. She whirled around and stared into the room. She must control her nerves. Now would not be a good time to succumb to stage fright. She took a few deep breaths and made her way downstairs.

At the main entrance a tall, stooped young man was posted. He nodded as he saw her. Annoyed that the other guard had not yet arrived, she stepped out on to the street. The grainy light made her blink. On the pavement opposite the factory building another young man in working clothes slowed and made brief eye contact and then made two holes with each of his forefingers and thumbs to show that he had seen her and was acting as a spotter should the Germans decide to storm the factory. Krystyna made the sign back to him and wondered where the other guard was. To calm her nerves and buy a few minutes of time, she decided to take a short stroll around the factory.

Stepping away from the front of the building she caught sight of a young man, short and wiry, running down the street, his yellow knapsack flying up and down on his back. At one point he lost his cap and had to dart across the street to retrieve it. As he came close to the factory he slowed and she realized that it was the missing guard. Irritated, she ignored him and turned down the dead-end street directly opposite the factory building. She was halfway down when a piercing whistle stopped her in her tracks. The hairs on the back of her neck brushed her collar. She swung round.

He stood three paces away from her, cap in hand. His feet were firm and level on the ground as if he were planting himself before her. He looked into her face and his eyes flared a gentle, marvelling green. They held each other's gaze for a long moment. Neither spoke. They let their eyes roam across each other and gradually took in faces and bodies, still intimately familiar and yet incredulously and impossibly changed. Everything around them was held in the fragility of a moment that might in a breath slip away.

She was shaking when she returned to the meeting room, appalled to find that the first of the delegates had arrived and was pouring a glass of water from the jug she had placed on the table.

The quartermaster-general eyed her as he lifted the glass to his lips. '*Sto lat.*' One hundred years. His smile was ironic. 'Would you believe that today is my name day?' He strode over to the window and looked out across the city and she could see him thinking about the days ahead.

She knew that he had lost his twenty-year-old son. He had been executed by the Nazis, shot with a dozen others suspected of being members of the resistance as a warning to the people not to fight. His son had been rounded up and taken to prison. Weeks later, an SS officer had ordered him out of his cell and tied his hands behind his back. Just before he led him out to the street where he would be shot with his comrades, the SS officer had taken from his pocket a wedge of hard plaster of Paris which he forced into the young man's mouth, breaking one of his teeth in the process. The others faced the firing squad with the same blind white mouths, but she knew, because the quartermaster had watched his own son's execution through binoculars from the bell tower of a church, that the SS had failed to silence the defiance in the young man's eyes. Every one of them died calling out their loyalty to their subjugated country, not through their forcibly closed mouths, but through their hearts.

Now he turned away from the window and caught her looking at him. His smile was wistful and she wondered, hoped, that he had a daughter. With hands fluttery from shock she found the screwdriver hidden under the sink and used it to prise up the floorboards and pull out the suitcase with the radio inside. The quartermaster helped her and by the time they had got the radio working another two delegates had arrived.

The colonel came up the stairs last, wiping his domed head clean of sweat as he strode into the room, beaming broadly at the other delegates, shaking hands and exchanging greetings and banter as if this were an ordinary meeting on an ordinary day. When it was her turn, he held his head to one side for a moment and scrutinized her, narrowing his eyes slightly as he asked her how she was feeling. 'We'll take some time to talk later,' he whispered before he was swept up into greeting his chief of staff.

The meeting got under way and Krystyna settled in her usual place at the colonel's right and took notes. Zero hour had been set for five o'clock the next day. All previous operations had taken place at dawn or dusk and the timing of the final insurrection was designed to catch the Germans unaware. It would seem like an ordinary day. Home Army soldiers would mingle with civilians coming home from work and make their way to their assigned houses in small groups. The buildings had been chosen with care and were mostly corner houses situated at important crossroads or facing railway stations, German barracks, stores, offices, public works departments and factories. Before five o'clock the soldiers would take over flats and buildings; residents would be shown papers signed by the leaders of the resistance which gave authority for the new occupation. It was anticipated, the colonel said, that most people would leave quietly, mingling with the crowds, so as not to draw attention. It was essential that all the units observed the utmost secrecy. The colonel looked around the table and met the eye of each of the delegates in turn. A deep silence swelled in the room, filling every space. The colonel continued in a soft voice: 'I wish every one of you strength, courage and determination for the battle ahead.' He stood up. The meeting had lasted four hours. He nodded as the other delegates got to their feet. They stood around the table and the colonel led them in prayer.

When they eventually lifted their heads Krystyna glanced up at the high factory window. She could see that the rain had cleared and the sky was a fresh blue. One of the delegates had brought a vodka bottle with twelve small glasses. Each glass was filled to the brim with the clear liquid, and she was given a glass to lift in toast. 'To freedom,' the colonel said and tossed his vodka into his open throat and swallowed it down quickly. The other delegates followed, some with tears in their eyes, including the quartermaster who stared at his glass for a moment before taking it less vigorously than the others, slowly and with a reverent care he might have reserved for the sacrament itself. 'Long live Poland.'

A short while later, taking the stairs down to the ground floor, her head swimming with the effects of the intense meeting and the vodka, she wondered whether he would still be there. Maybe the guards would have changed shifts and he would have disappeared again, absorbed into the feverish crowds. Somehow she had convinced herself that what had occurred earlier had been an illusion she had invented in the nervousness of preparing for battle. Maybe it was not Janek after all, but someone who had looked like him, someone else who had played along with recognizing her because she had reminded him of someone, his sister perhaps, or a school friend. She pressed on down the stairs. But of course it had been him. She would have known his whistle anywhere, the call he used for the wolfhounds when they lived on the dwór.

He was still there. He didn't speak when he saw her. His face was pale and she saw that he was shivering in spite of the heat pouring through the grimy glass at the top of the main door. He had been leaning against a wall to support himself and now that he saw her he straightened up. She took in the waxy look of the starving, sunken eyes, the growth of fine downy red hair on his arms and along the line of his jaw. She needed to begin her round of messages to various strategic places in the city to confirm the zero hour, but she did not think that she could ask him to wait for her for another two hours without food. He glanced up at her and she saw the same mixture of hope, shyness, doubt and weariness in his expression that she remembered and in that moment she understood that he had really returned to her. She met his eyes. 'Come on, I'll find you something to eat.'

He followed her out of the building, letting her go on some way so as not to draw attention. She lifted her head; her anxiety and shock had cleared now, and she felt light and confident, buoyant even as she walked down the street towards Stare Miasto. There might be some potato soup left; sometimes when she returned from meetings the schoolmistress, a middle-aged woman with a fierce temper, would have brewed up a pot of thin gruel. It tasted bland, but it was better than nothing. She glanced over her shoulder and felt a burst of joy at the sight of him walking with the slight bow-legged steps she had unconsciously looked for in every young man she had encountered over the past few years.

They crossed the city centre. A German Tiger tank was shoving its way forward, its long barrel gun flicking back and forth like the twitch of a thick tail. Not so long ago the sight of such a tank would have caused havoc on the streets, but now people stood by and openly sneered. 'Hurry up, the firm are leaving,' one conductor called out from the step of his tram. 'Get your goods while you can before they go out of business.' He had a tray hung about his neck on which was displayed a collection of cigarettes, cosmetics and matches, and which he now indicated gleefully. A young woman passer-by threw him a coin and he graciously gave her a lipstick from his tray. 'For you, darling.' She pushed it into her pocket. She wore strong boots with thick army socks and Krystyna knew that when zero hour came she would be heading towards her unit. The feeling of release and good-humoured spirit was infectious. She looked at the faces surrounding the tank. Some mothers stood holding the hands of young children; there were older women in headscarves, carrying willow baskets; men bent and braced from years of toil, one or two thin younger men, and all of them had the pale starved look of hospital patients resigned to a long period of institutionalization. On this day they were startled to have been given a reprieve, a brief and healing moment of sunlight. She saw Janek watching the crowd, too, but he hung further back, half hidden in the shade.

There was enough soup left for one bowl, the schoolmistress said, watching them with folded arms as they sat down in the narrow kitchen. She poured the soup for Janek and ignored his complaint that Krystyna should eat too.

'I'll have something later,' she said. 'Stay and rest for a while. I have to go out again.' She glanced at the schoolmistress, who gave a sigh and then picked up a basket from under the sink.

'I'm off, too,' she said. She looked at Janek. 'Will you be staying?'

His eyes were two huge pools. 'I have quarters, at the factory.'

Satisfied, the woman nodded at him and then went out.

Janek bent over his soup and finished it. After a moment his head came up. He swallowed and placed his hands on the table. His skin was very white. 'My father came to warn you,' he said, glancing down at his empty bowl. His voice was husky, much deeper than she remembered. 'He knew the Russians were coming, but your father refused to go. He would rather die fighting, he said. He gave my father money and told us to leave. We went quickly in the afternoon while it was still light.'

She stared at him while she took in this information. His face was bowed in shame over his soup bowl. His guilt was plain, as if he had only just now received the order from his father that they were to go and take their chances, leave everything they loved and cared about behind.

'What happened to your father?' she asked. 'Did he survive?'

He ran his hand across his fine eyebrows. 'You remember that he was not strong. When we were captured by the Russians in the forest, I managed to escape, but my father – they took him.' He lifted his eyes towards her. 'I don't know what happened to him. They took him away.' He spoke without bitterness.

'Why aren't you angry?' She couldn't believe that she had just asked him this and wished that she could have taken the question back unasked. His eyes were two green wounds.

'I don't know. I joined the partisans and lived with them in the forest and for a time I was fighting alongside the Russians. Some of them became my friends.' He glanced up at her, expecting, she saw, for her to judge him, perhaps even disown him. His fragility and vulnerability moved just under his skin, like clouds moving across the moon. 'They wanted me to join them and become part of the Red Army, but I refused and came out of the forest and made my way to Warsaw where I met some people who thought that I would be useful in the underground because I know Russian.'

She stared at him. He turned his eyes away from her again and glanced down at his spoon sticking out of the soup bowl. There were obviously things he had experienced that she could not ask about, not immediately; she understood that she needed to leave him with some form of protection. She had no right to expect confession, or even explanation. Her feeling of exhilaration at finding him now shifted into something else, a new feeling that was deeper and harsher, more painful. She understood then that she was freer than Janek, but that had always been true. She had always known that she was the leader and that he would be condemned to follow; defiance was not part of his nature, he was too wild and sensitive, too acute and open. His courage was of a different order to hers; his courage required that he overcome his deep and profound gentleness, his far-reaching kindness and generosity. His innate decency. She could imagine him making friends with Russian soldiers in the forest, sharing jokes with them and meals and being grateful to them for their humanity, their kindness in return, and that would have consoled him. It would have helped him to feel not so alone. She knew then that she could not tell him that the Russians had murdered her father.

She understood as she left him to sleep in her attic room that she had carried with her all these years a kernel of anger that had taken her through the forest. It had kept her alive. Her rage at the injustice of the occupation of her country, her passionate patriotism, her faith had been tempered by those she met like Halina and the colonel who had helped her to find her core of certainty. 'You make me proud. Your strength shines through you,' the colonel had said to her after the meeting. He had patted her shoulder before he turned away to the important business of military strategy, his face already alive with the prospect of bringing the underground out into the open at last. The colonel had been her constant, her most reassuring figure, her armoury against loss, her light in the dark.

Janek had gone from her room by the time she arrived back from her duties. Of course he had to prepare with his unit at the paint factory, but returning to find the place empty she felt bereft and lay on her bed. The scent of him – warm and sharp, more manly than she remembered

– lingered on her blanket. She pulled it around her and sobbed inconsolably. Her tears shocked her with their intensity; people sometimes went for months being able to cope with extreme, almost unbelievable loss and tragedy and then broke down at something small and insignificant and now perhaps it was her turn, perhaps she would crack up when she most needed to be clear and prepared.

She woke early having slept through the night. As she dressed in her dove-grey dress and pushed the red and white armband into her duffel bag, she felt calm. Her anxiety had been replaced by a sense of curiosity about how the day would unfold. Before she left her room she wrote down her thoughts in her journal. She went to put the journal back in the drawer with her father's notebook, but hesitated. There would be no other day in history like this one. She picked up both books and slipped them into her bag.

The meeting was set at the factory for four to go over the last-minute details before zero hour. She entered the top room to find the colonel in a state of agitation, pacing up and down by the high factory windows. All the other delegates were seated around the long table, some smoking with tension, and the air was hot and tight with talk. The situation in the tobacco factory next door was not good. During the night the Germans had increased their garrison by fifty men.

'They have two machine guns,' the factory owner told the meeting.

'How many of our men are downstairs?' the colonel asked.

'Thirty-three.' The factory owner licked his lips. His eyes darted about the room. She knew that Janek was among them and a beat of fear hammered in her chest.

'What arms do you have?' the colonel asked.

'Fifteen rifles, maybe forty grenades and a few filipinki,' the factory owner replied. The other delegates stopped talking and stared at him. The colonel moved back to the window and paced up and down, his eyes raking the afternoon sky. He wore a smarter suit than usual, made of soft brown linen, which was a little large for him and sloped from his shoulders. Around his arm was a red and white band stitched up from two pieces of cloth, one of which was a clean white handkerchief. Eventually after a long pause he turned back to the factory owner.

'Can you hold on for an hour until the battalion arrive?'

The factory owner blew out his cheeks. He was a large, powerfully built man with huge hands. He thought for a moment and then nodded before making his way down to the factory floor. The meeting began, but they had reached only the second item on the agenda when the sound of a lorry outside caused the colonel to move swiftly to the window. It was followed by the sound of two rifle shots. The entire meeting rose and moved towards the window. Down in the factory yard, revolver in hand, the factory owner was running for cover with two of his men. A German lorry was jammed up against the entrance gate. They could see the driver slumped backwards, his hands still raised to defend himself from the bullet that had passed through the windscreen and shattered his temple. There was a burst of machine-gun fire as the German pillbox guarding the tobacco factory ripped into action, spraying the street with pellets in sharp, juddering belts. The colonel reached for his revolver.

Taking the steps two at a time, he ran down the stairs. Close behind, Krystyna followed. They reached the second level. The factory owner had come back inside and was now shouting orders to his men. The Germans from the garrison would soon arrive on the scene and they needed to be ready to defend the factory at the windows and gates. She tried to spot Janek but there was too much motion, too many heads bending, pulling rifles from bags and hiding places, pushing filipinki grenades into pockets, the expression on each of the young faces of such intense and strict absorption it made her think of prayer. After a hurried word with the factory owner, the colonel raced back up through the stairwells, grabbing her arm as she came down, almost dragging her with him.

Breathing heavily, they went to the windows. Machine-gun fire pelted the narrow street in a dense hail that at one point broke through the window where they stood, sending them all scurrying for safety against the walls. There they watched the bullets fly in an arc across the room and pepper a line of holes in the wall over the door. A fine shower of plaster dust floated into the room. Coughing, the delegates yanked out handkerchiefs and pulled them across their noses and mouths. Krystyna moved to the next window, her feet crunching on shattered glass, and peered outside. She could see German soldiers in full equipment occupying the house opposite, flexing their knees as they aimed their machine guns at the factory.

'Go to safety now!' the colonel ordered. 'Go downstairs!' She was the only woman in the room and she knew that his order was directed at her. She met his eyes and then she shook her head. If this was to be her last moment, she wanted to remain with him.

'For God's sake,' said the quartermaster. 'We can't let them force their way in. We'll never get them out again.'

The Germans were now within close range and at any minute could storm the building. Down in the yard she could see the factory owner with a great plank of wood in his hands directing his men to pile barricades up against the factory gates. A glint of copper caught her attention. There in the midst, carrying a paint barrel in his arms, was Janek, his long slim neck visible like a fine white rope. She watched his narrow shoulders release the barrel, a light movement as if he were pitching a forkful of hay. For a moment he was still and then he pivoted back towards the group of men and boys dragging more drums and barrels across the yard. His gaze floated upward for a second before he dived into the mêlée.

Bullets were now showering the top room and they were forced to shelter beneath the table. It jerked and shuddered under the onslaught. At one point in the attack the table lifted clear above their heads, and she gasped before it came down again. Krystyna tasted metal in her mouth and realized that she had bitten down on her own tongue. After another belt of fire, the colonel ordered them to run for the door and make for the second floor. She closed her eyes and prayed – a short, sharp appeal – and was amazed when she opened her eyes to find that she had emerged on the landing, her fingers clutching at the hem of her dove-coloured dress in which she saw a small smoking hole.

The sound of machine-gun fire was now a hard wall with no break. The colonel and his chief of staff were at a window and they were smashing at it with a long iron pipe. Then the colonel called to the group of young men below: 'Which of you is the best grenade thrower?' and she saw a red head jerk in his direction. Janek came up to their floor.

She stood a few paces away from him. His chest rose and fell as he caught his breath. His eyes were as calm as the cold waters of a lake.

He raised his arm. She had watched this movement many times. His fingers were curled around a filipinka, but in her mind it was a big knotted spruce cone, and instead of factory workers watching him, there were wolfhounds with their tails held high and a bright, expectant look in their eyes. He drew his arm back and the hounds strained and looked across the snowy meadow. The cone flew in a high clear arc and she felt the whistle of cold air against her cheek. His back tensed and then released. The dogs sprang after the cone, snow flying under their feathered legs as they skidded around it. He watched the scuffle for a moment and turned back to her and there it was: the look, not of victory, but of complicity, and it was as if that time and this moment had melted into one.

After the explosion the machine gun was silenced. They watched the Germans below pull two dead soldiers away by their legs. Their expressions were stark. They knew there would be further retaliation. She saw the colonel and his chief of staff huddled in earnest talk with the factory owner. The young men posted at the windows were firing indiscriminately from Tommy guns. The factory owner was shouting at them not to waste ammunition, but they continued to fire. Every now and then one of them would glance over to where Janek had once more taken up position with his gun.

Two hours later they were back up in the top room with six soldiers from the platoon of thirty-three, many of whom were bleeding from wounds, but still determined to hold the factory until the battalion arrived. Zero hour had passed and the whole city was now enclosed in the hard fist of battle, fighting street by street, house by house, bullet by bullet. The storm had broken.

It was just after seven when the battalion finally broke through to cheers from the six soldiers who climbed out on the roof. Janek led them out there after the spotter was injured and with his precise aim lobbed another filipinka into a lorry filled with German police armed with guns and grenades. The explosion caused the lorry to swerve and burst into flames. She watched him standing on the roof with his gun at his side. From down below came screams as the men in the lorry burned alive and she knew that this time there would be no light in his eyes.

The battalion took the rest of the German garrison and by eight o'clock there was a shout of joy from the new spotter posted on the chimney. Janek turned to her from his post at the window and then using the butt of his rifle he cleared away the shattered panes of glass. He put down his gun and reached for her hand, pulling her up on to the sill. She felt the night air blow hot on her face. He jumped down and then reached for her, lifting her on to the tiles which stretched in a broken jigsaw across the roof. She felt his hands on her waist. His face was grimy with sweat and a bullet had grazed the fine lip of his ear. There was a stream of dried blood on his neck. His smell reminded her of that of a wild deer. 'The flag! The Polish flag,' the spotter shouted. 'Our flag, right in the middle of the city.'

She walked to the edge of the roof with Janek and they stood together looking out on a sky that boiled with an intense orange fire towards a flutter of white that vanished and reappeared, vanished and reappeared, like the pale hull of a boat trying to right itself in a wind–whipped lake. The wind chased a bolt of black smoke across the sky and then they saw it. Janek squeezed her hand. It was the Polish flag, its white and now red colours sailing from the mast of the Prudential Building. Now they could see a flotilla of other flags lifting up out of the burning seas; one flew from the cupola of the Post Office Savings Bank and another from the Town Hall. She turned to him. Tears were pouring down her face and she saw that his cheeks were wet too. When he pulled her to him she tasted grit and salt and smoke. Close to him now, she felt the fragile bones of his ribcage and heard the strong sound beat of his heart.

A blast flung them both face down on the roof. They lay for a second, fingers touching, breathing heavily. Through a tangle of hair, she could see blood on the side of Janek's face. Her heart hammered. Her legs felt heavy as if something were pushing down on her from above. She tried to move her neck and back, but she was pinned to the ground. She watched a procession of boots thud past her eyes. Everything would be all right; as long as she could still feel the fingers flexing in the hand that now gripped hers, she would survive.

'The roof's been hit by a shell. The chimney's collapsed.' Janek got up on to his knees and bent his head to look at her. In the firestorm, his eyes were aquamarine, lashed with gold, impossibly clear. 'Lie still for a bit; they're pulling the rubble off your legs.'

She squeezed his hand. 'Is your face all right?'

He brought his fingers up to his ear which was pouring with blood. Feeling the wetness he tensed and then smiled as he realized that his ear was still attached. 'It's fine.' He stared down at her. 'Can you feel your legs?'

A cool sensation fluttered along her dress as shards of

broken bricks were lifted off her. She looked down. Her legs had been cut to pieces. 'Bend your knee,' Janek ordered. She did as he asked. Her leg felt as if it no longer belonged to her; the toes were numb.

'Could you take off my shoes?' she asked.

He bent at her feet and removed both shoes. She smiled, wondering what Halina would say if she saw what had happened to these, her best shoes. Her feet were grimy. He took her feet into his lap and rubbed them. 'Can you feel anything now?'

She grinned at him. 'Everything seems to be working again.' She stood up in her bare feet and dusted down her dress. Now Janek turned his head away, suddenly embarrassed. He still held her shoes.

Back inside the factory building, they found the colonel on his knees under the table with an engineer. The blast from the German shell had torn up part of the floor where the radio was hidden. She could see that it was dented down one side. Small components were spread out on the engineer's jacket. He held a tiny screwdriver between his teeth and talked to the colonel as he worked. 'I'm going to need another part, sir. I'm afraid I won't be able to get it working tonight.'

The colonel nodded and slowly climbed to his feet. Seeing Krystyna's dishevelled state his eyes widened with alarm. With his gaze still on her he said to the engineer, 'The world will just have to wait.' He addressed Janek next: 'Take her downstairs and see that she gets some treatment for those cuts.'

After seeing the nurse in a hot basement room she was shown one of the resting stations, a bare office with curtains put down on the floor over plastic wrappers. Once he had ensured that she was safe, Janek returned to the battle. All through the rest of the night she was aware of the thud of German artillery beyond the walls a few hundred yards away, and the crackle of machine-gun fire, but the sounds, close as they were, did not worry her, and eventually merged into her dreams. For the first time in five years, she woke without a feeling of dread.

Over the next ten days the whole city mobilized to repel the Germans. Posters declaring 'To Arms!' appeared on fire-blackened and bullet-drilled walls; improvised red and white flags, made from tablecloths, curtains or bedsheets, hung at the windows of houses. Householders besieged the passing soldiers, offering them precious conserved jars of food, blankets, petrol, torches and, miraculously, flowers. The feeling of elation was infectious, the tension from years of secret underground existence bursting into a passion for bold, open resistance. Tentative at first, people soon overcame their exhaustion and were revitalized by the new feeling in the air. It made them fearless. Scrawny little boys, armed with bottles of petrol, fought alongside grizzled old men. One boy of twelve succeeded in blowing up a German Tiger tank and became an instant hero. The soldiers who carried him aloft through the streets on their shoulders later stuffed his pockets with filipinki and he made several more direct hits. Women emerged from cellars with brooms and fire spades, determined to fight. At the Deaf and Dumb Institute, situated on the front line, the deaf-mutes joined in the battle; led by a bearded, old chaplain, they fought with Tommy guns and when their ammunition ran out they hurled rags soaked in petrol at German tanks.

In those first feverish days, the Home Army took

command of the post office, the gas works, the water and electricity plants and the railway station. Some battles lasted for twenty-four hours and fiercely contested strategic positions changed hands several times in the course of the fighting. When Krystyna had recovered she returned to duty at HQ. One of her first tasks was to write a bulletin to be circulated among all the Home Army districts. She sat down in front of the typewriter, wincing as she arranged her bruised legs. She had barely seen Janek since the first night. He had rejoined his unit which was defending the railway station. The colonel paced the length of the windows, his face stark in the pale morning light. But in spite of his weariness there was a bounce in his stride as he detailed the battles of the rising. 'Our struggle has only just begun and there will be many long and difficult days ahead, but for now I report that we have recaptured significant parts of Warsaw. The spirit of justice has wings. We are taking back Poland.'

She stopped typing. The colonel was standing motionless at the window with his back turned. She saw his shoulders heave slightly. He dabbed his eyes. Each time he returned his handkerchief to his pocket, he had to retrieve it again after a few moments.

They were interrupted by the chief of staff. He walked in carrying a folder and went directly to the colonel at the window. Heads bent in the watery light, they looked at aerial maps marked out with positions still held by the Germans. 'We have them surrounded,' the chief of staff said, his eyes blinking rapidly behind his glasses. 'The men are firing day and night.'

The colonel shoved his hands deep into his pockets and resumed his pacing, keeping his head turned towards the long milky windows. 'We will again radio the Allies for ammunition and food supplies.' He paused. A vein pulsed on his temple. He looked out across the city. Drunk on oxygen, palls of smoke streamed in vertical columns up the sky.

'We may be able to compensate for the enthusiasm with captured booty,' the chief of staff said. 'But the men will have to learn restraint. I'll try to have a word with the sergeants.' His smile was rueful. He brought his hand up to his head for a moment, as if the weight of it were too much for him, then he straightened, pushed his folder under his arm and left.

The colonel remained by the window, his left arm folded across his body, his right hand cupping his face. It seemed as if he had forgotten that she was there. She made a minute sound with the typewriter and it pulled the colonel from his thoughts; he resumed his pacing, more vigorously now. 'Start another bulletin: to the Allies. This time we hold nothing back. We tell them we are risking everything to keep our hold on the capital. They must understand how serious this situation is.' He began to compose, directing words to her so quickly that she struggled to keep up.

Later, Krystyna returned to the old schoolhouse. The sky over the medieval town was clear; the evening star shone out from the quiet twilight. She splashed water on her face and neck in the narrow bathroom. Some of the little basins were cracked. She wondered how children were coping with the incessant bombardment that caused buildings to shake like freight trains. The Germans had sent Luftwaffe bombers to strafe the city with fire-bombs. The factory district had come under persistent attack, the Junkers flying low in formation, skimming rooftops, engines screaming as they jerked away. The Germans were using fire as a form of revenge; people had been forced down into the labyrinth of cellars and narrow passageways where they were burned alive. She couldn't imagine how sensitive children were being protected from the know-ledge of what was happening around them. How could anyone explain a campaign of terror to a child? Krystyna realized how she had grown used to couching terrible events in sober sentences. Her bulletins were models of restraint, sometimes even breezy in their tone: the aim, of course, was to keep up morale, not to let people fall victim to the fear that clawed at them all. Everyone pretended that they were unafraid. Typing her reports gave Krystyna the feeling that the situation was not out of control. She thought of her last bulletin and wondered whether this time it would be heard.

A few days later Janek, ordered by his commander to rest, arrived at the schoolhouse. His eyes were two red spots in his filthy face. Krystyna was shocked. He seemed to have aged; he was a dry husk, a forlorn figure who stumbled into the kitchen unable to speak. She thought it was exhaustion. She told him he could have her room for a few days. She would sleep in a storeroom downstairs. Too weak to protest, he followed her upstairs and took off his boots. He hesitated, too shy to undress in front of her, and instead he dusted off his clothes. His hair hung in lank strands down the front of his face. Bristles of beard studded his chin.

'Thank you.' His voice was cracked with tiredness. She put her hand on his shoulder and felt something in him rise up to meet her. He glanced at her face, as if to check some-thing. He looked down at the bed and hesitated.

'Sleep for as long as you like,' she said. 'I'm going to work soon. I'll bring home something for you to eat.'

His eyes flared. 'You have always been so good to me.'

'Of course. I love you – you are my family.' She felt her face flush. She hadn't intended to sound so emphatic, but the words now spoken could not be taken back.

He rubbed at his face and one of his fingers strayed up to his damaged ear, the rim of which was crusted with dried blood. He brought his hand down. 'I don't know if I can go back.' His face was now stricken.

Was he trying to tell her that their closeness was finished? She understood that his years of fighting underground had changed him; maybe the person that she had loved like the best part of herself was someone that she had invented. The thought of Janek had kept her going through the long frozen nights in the forest. Now he seemed shaken and almost afraid of her. He sank down to the bed and put his head in his hands. After a moment she joined him and reached over and took his cold hand. In a low voice he began to tell her what he had seen the previous day.

The Germans had started using civilians as human shields to protect their barricades. To prevent the Home Army from using grenades, they were strapping women and children to the front of German tanks, nosing up to the Polish units, almost taunting them to fire. Janek had watched one child wrestle free from the ropes that bound him to the tank and fall to the ground only to be crushed by the tank's caterpillar wheels. His young mother, still pinned to the tank, had been forced to watch. She'd been unable to cry out and had twisted her head to one side and there Janek, acting as a sniper on the second floor of a building across the street, had caught her eye. She had looked at him, helplessly, imploringly, an animal trapped in its dying moments. He had watched the tank shove its way past until it reached the end of the street where there was a barricade made up of heavy furniture: tables, wardrobes, cabinets, bed posts, all piled up, legs sticking out like horns. There was a shudder and then a wumph as someone, not aware of what the tank was carrying, threw a bottle and the machine burst into flames.

Janek was silent for a moment. Sensing there was more, she touched his arm. He started to speak again. 'Soon after that I was joined by my commander. He needed me to man the barricade opposite the German police station. We went down and he handed me a machine gun. We could see the police station about six hundred yards away. There was a sentry outside covering the street. He fired towards us and at first we held off to save on ammunition, but then we came under heavier attack and my commander told us to answer them back. We got the sentry and a few other hits.' He brought his fingertips to his temples and shuddered.

'Then the Germans sent out a ladder.' He hesitated.

'A ladder?' She frowned, not understanding. She touched his arm. 'Go on.'

'They had roped people to the ladder; they pushed it out across the street and all I could see was a line of people: some old, some women and children, all very still and almost unreal, they made me think of scarecrows.' He drew his hand across his forehead. 'We could see the military police behind them, but there was no way we could fire through the people to reach them. They were advancing quite fast and we had to make a decision. I put down my gun. My commander asked me to pick it up again and fire.

If I didn't, he said, there would be ladders appearing all over the place. We had to let them know that we couldn't be broken. It was *they* who were forcing us to shoot.' He dropped his eyes into his lap.

'What happened?'

'I fired until the ladder was flat on the ground.' He lifted his face and bit down hard on his lip, drawing blood. 'We took out the line of police.' He closed his eyes, pushing away the memory.

For a moment they were both silent. She heard the dry rasping of his breath, the slight clogging of air in his nose. 'You had no choice. You did what you had to. Anyone in your position would have done the same.'

He lifted his head and regarded her with worn eyes. He swallowed thickly and then he dropped his gaze down into his lap while he sobbed in long, heaving, silent gusts. She rose from the bed and went out of the room and down into the small kitchen; there was nothing more she could do, no comfort that she could give him; all she could do was to leave him to find release.

The Polish positions began to crumble. Over the next few days she typed up more appeals to London for ammunition and medical supplies. The colonel paced and fretted, the contours of his face twitching as he dictated increasingly desperate messages. A report came through from London that Stalin was prepared to come to the aid of Warsaw on the condition that all the Home Army leaders should be placed under immediate arrest. Reports began to circulate accusing the colonel of leading a suicidal mission against the Germans. One report damned him as a war criminal. His response was to order his commanders to intensify the attack, using ingenuity and cunning. Fake signs warning of mines were placed in several no-go areas and the soldiers fought on, resorting to sticks and bricks when the ammunition finally ran dry.

The factory district fell to the Germans; the colonel moved their headquarters to the Ministry of Justice building in Stare Miasto. Polish units fought on the stairs and landings for control of individual buildings, but the ceaseless artillery battering flattened whole streets, knocking out fine old buildings like loose teeth. Ancient churches, convents and rows of houses collapsed into dust, the schoolhouse among them. On their last night in Stare Miasto, Krystyna stood with the colonel looking down from the ministry building at a broken landscape. Craggy mounds of rubble stretched as far as the horizon. The skies were blood-red from fires, the air acrid with smoke that poured in a constant stream from the devastation. Across the ruined expanse stumps of towers, amputated turrets and chimneys stuck up out of the smoking mounds. It had become a wilderness, a lost city, a mass grave.

The colonel put his hand on her shoulder. It felt as dry as paper. The strain of the past eleven days and an attack of dysentery had left him with little strength. In silence he stared out of the window, hung with shredded brocade drapes. His eyes flickered and she could see him thinking ahead. Earlier, he had said that they would probably have to evacuate through the sewers. 'Have all the cuts healed on your legs?' he asked. 'Make sure you change into trousers; any slight scratch could be dangerous.'

She nodded. 'We are going tonight, then?'

His eyes roamed across the remains of the Old Town. 'It is finished,' he said.

In the basement of the ministry she packed her duffel

bag, shoving her dresses, shoes, the journals and a few books down into the base. The red wool cap she left on the top. She pulled on a warm flannel shirt and a pair of men's army trousers, tying the cuffs tight around her ankles with string. She put on thick socks and shoved her feet into a pair of army boots. They slopped around her ankles as she walked, but the thick soles were a better grip than ordinary shoes. The sewer basins were notoriously difficult to navigate. One slip could mean being swept to death in the strong current, and because they were going to be moving in convoy, if she fell it was likely that she would take other people with her.

The colonel had set their departure time for 11 p.m. The twelve members of his team would use the manhole in Krasinski Square, just a couple of hundred yards from the German positions. She pulled on a dark sweater and slung the duffel bag over her back. Her stomach growled with hunger and she used her hand to try to silence it. The journey from the Old Town to the centre of the city was only a mile and a half, but to reach it through the sewer would take at least five hours. She knew about the dangers from messenger girls who volunteered as *kanalarki*, carrying information across the underground network, ducking through foetid tunnels three feet high. The worst, a young *kanalarki* had told her, was not the waist-high sludge or the sickening smell, or the creepy, echoey shouts and moans of men who had lost their nerve that rippled down the tunnels for miles: all that was bad enough, but not as bad as the fear of being gassed or burned alive. Canisters, grenades, smoke bombs and petrol were thrown down into the passages by the Germans in an attempt to cut off the routes. There was also another form of gas given off by the decomposing corpses floating in the slime, a gas so toxic it could make you go blind. But as the hour for departure drew closer, Krystyna tried to push all this horror to the back of her mind. At ten minutes to eleven, she slipped out of the ministry building and, bending her head low, ran as swiftly and quietly as she could in her slopping army boots to the square.

The colonel was already there, lined up against a wall with his chief of staff and all the government delegates. One elderly man looked over as she took her place in line, his hair flaring white in the Very lights that swung at intervals across the red sky. Close by, a church was burning, flames shooting into the night. A burst water main had created a lake across the street and it acted as a mirror, reflecting the ruins they were about to leave behind. The Germans were so close she could hear them talking. She felt a hand on her shoulder and almost jumped out of her skin.

'I came to say goodbye.' Janek's face shone in the darkness. 'I didn't want to miss you this time.'

'Come with us,' she whispered.

He glanced towards the entrance of the manhole lined by sandbags. 'I can't,' he whispered back. 'I'm needed here. I have to stay with my unit.'

There was a movement at the top of the line and she saw the colonel break away from the wall and come down towards them. His face softened when he saw Janek. 'I've heard good reports about your conduct,' he said. 'I'm awarding you military honours, but not yet. First you have to escort us down through the sewer. You know the route?'

'I do, sir, but I'm not at liberty to leave. I have orders to stay with my unit.' Janek spoke calmly.

'I'm ordering you to escort us, do you understand?' The colonel's voice was curt.

Janek hesitated. His rifle was slung over his shoulder and he carried a belt of German ammunition. 'One moment,' he said. Then, crouching low, he ran across the street. The colonel watched him go, a faint smile twitching at the corner of his mouth.

It took an hour to assemble everyone in the tunnel. She stood with her boots braced against the curved bottom of the sewer, up to her thighs in the foul tide. The stench rose up in putrid waves that brought tears to her eyes and made her immediately start to gag. Up ahead she heard the stifled moans of those who were also trying to hold down their own gorge. Her left hand held on to a rope that was passed along the tunnel by their guide who would lead the way with two soldiers carrying Tommy guns, one of whom was Janek.

'Listen, everyone,' the guide whispered. 'We leave in a few minutes. There will be no lights, no torches must be used except by those leading the way at the front. There will be no talking at all. If you feel too bad to go on, give three tugs on the rope, and we will stop. There will be a break every hour. Remember, absolute silence.'

The guide swung his torchlight back to the front, plunging the tunnel into a thick blackness. She felt panic squeeze her chest as the line began to lurch forward. Her boots were slipping against the pipe, like stones skimmed on ice. She tightened her grip on the rope and placed her right hand on the shoulder of the old man in front of her. She could just make out the outline of his white hair, a flicker of moon behind a dense cloud, and she kept her eyes trained on it as she shuffled forward one step at a time.

After a while of slow progress the guide reminded every-one to keep quiet as they were approaching directly under the German positions. She thought of Janek up ahead, leading the way, alert for grenades or obstacles. The Germans threw cement sacks down into the tunnels and if they came across one of those and tried to remove it, the build-up of water behind it could rush out and drown them all. Already she was soaked to the skin and shivering from cold from water that streamed down from the roof. Her cuts, which had barely healed, would be drenched in the noxious liquid. She tried not to think about the possi-bility of septic infection. It was pointless when she could die with her next step. The old man in front of her grunted and then suddenly slipped. He fell face down, his hands flailing, grappling at air. She was yanked forward and almost toppled on to him, but managed to keep her balance. She reached down into the filth and her fingers closed on his belt. She gripped it and yanked him clear. He came up gasping, spitting and gagging, the whites of his eyes bright with panic. She got him on his feet again and pulled three times on the rope. The line came to a stop.

After a short rest they plunged forward once more. Her leg and back muscles now ached and she saw green spots dancing before her eyes. Shaken by his fall, the old man in front of her was unable to keep silent any longer and moaned with each step. She worried that he was about to lose his mind and wondered what she should do if he started shouting. She knew from the *kanalarki* that some-times people who really cracked up and started hallucinating needed to be gagged from behind. She was carrying her duffel bag over her shoulders. If it came to it, she would tear off a strip of material from one of her dresses. Now she remembered the red cap sitting on the top of the bag and realized that she had forgotten to give it to Janek.

They came to a manhole and halted. She lifted her face and drank in some air. The sky at the top of the hole was dark and pricked with stars and she guessed that they were getting closer to the city centre. The old man in front of her was now shivering with cold. She could hear his teeth chattering. She glanced down and saw something floating in the water. The needles of fur clumped together made her think that it was a giant rat. She brought her hand up to her mouth. Choking down her fear, she gripped tighter on the rope. Sensing her distress, the old man in front brought round his hand and momentarily squeezed hers. She breathed out as the body of what she now recognized as a cat brushed past her thigh and floated downstream.

The guide whispered that they had five hundred yards to go. Up in the distance she could see the glow of a blue signal lamp, flickering like a candle flame. The old man grunted as he heaved himself forward and she became aware that they were now trudging uphill. She held tight to the rope and hauled her body after him. The sewer narrowed. The tantalizing blue light grew brighter and steadier and she realized that they were close. They were nearing the end. They were coming out into clean air.

Ropes were thrown down into the manhole. She burned her hands climbing up. At the first touch of solid ground, her legs gave way. She collapsed on to a street which miraculously was composed of houses still intact against a glittering night sky. The first gulps of ice-cold clean air made her dizzy. She lifted her head. Stars swam in loops of light. She felt her limbs turn liquid and she would have melted into black unconsciousness had she not felt someone behind her, bringing her back into the light, a pair of strong arms holding her up. 'Look, there, can you see Pegasus?' he said, his voice warm and close to her neck. She took another breath of air and looked up.

18

Warsaw, present day

It's late September, still warm enough to take breakfast outside. Catherine watches Konrad break open a fresh bread roll and dip the crust into his milky coffee. He smiles across the table at her before he begins to eat. He is paler than when she saw him last and there are new lines fanning around his eyes. His hair has become thinner and there are flecks of grey just below his ears. Now he reaches over and takes her hand. He turns it over and looks down at her palm.

'So, what do you see? What does my future hold?' she asks him.

He traces the lines across her palm. His voice deepens into a croak. 'Ah, much trouble ahead. Many forked paths, many difficulties.' He folds her fingers down and then brings them up to his lips. 'But you will meet a man, not particularly dark, not particularly handsome, who will love you.'

'How interesting.' She takes back her palm. He lifts his head and laughs, his expression boyish, with a lightness that sends a ripple through her body, echoing sensations from earlier when they had woken together in their large clean, bright room at the top of a new Warsaw hotel. She leans her head back and glances up at the roofs of the buildings where doves sit under shady eaves preening pink-green feathers in the morning sun. There are a few other couples drinking coffee at the outdoor cafés and their quiet conversation mingles with the crooning of the birds. The fronts of the narrow three-storey houses surrounding the square, every one slightly different, have a washed-out watercolour beauty. Immaculately reconstructed from photographs and paintings after the war, they are less than a hundred years old, but already have a patina of age and feel as if they have existed for centuries.

Konrad follows her gaze. 'The rebuilding began soon after the war ended,' he says. 'Krystyna remembered seeing Boy Scouts, barefoot, working in lines clearing the rubble with their hands and buckets.' He wipes his mouth on his napkin. 'She and Janek joined the salvage operation. There was a tremendous determination to reclaim the fabric of the city. To do something active after years of living underground.'

'It must have been like clearing up after an earthquake.'

'Hitler ordered the city to be destroyed. Afterwards, there was nothing left, virtually every building was destroyed, every street smashed, every cobblestone torn up. Entire streets were set alight.'

Catherine looks at the sunlit buildings, clearly outlined against the sky. 'It's strange, there's no residue. I can't believe that all this emerged from such destruction. This square feels so peaceful.'

'I think that has something to do with the spirit of survival that's unique to Poles. The Germans couldn't crush that. They were astonished that the rising lasted as long as it did. The colonel and his army held on for sixty-three days, and they had ammunition for only ten. They fought with their guts and lived on willpower. The Germans tried to obliterate an entire city, but people adapted; they carried on living in dens under the ruins. After the Germans left, they emerged starving – but victorious – from cellars and pigsties. They were dancing and hugging each other in the streets. Krystyna said that within a short time there were stalls selling bread, old women standing in the smoking ruins trying to make a little money by selling lace tablecloths folded over their arms; there were even flower stalls.'

'What happened to the colonel?'

'He gave himself up as a prisoner of war and was taken to a concentration camp in Germany. But one of his final acts was to find Janek and Krystyna who were hiding in a church with other soldiers. In a secret ceremony, he awarded them the Virtuti Militari, Poland's highest decoration for gallantry.' He pauses and takes a gulp of coffee, wiping his mouth on a napkin before he continues.

'More than six million Polish citizens, eighty per cent of the population living in cities, died under the Nazi occupation. Four hundred thousand citizens died within Warsaw alone.'

Catherine tries to take in the scale of the loss, but it is like imagining light years. She looks across the square where an old man is pulling up the metal blinds on a tiny antique shop. 'I wonder what happened to my father's medal.'

Konrad reaches across the table and takes her hand. She notices that he is no longer wearing a wedding ring. 'Janek remained with Krystyna in Warsaw for four years after the war and they tried to keep their identity unknown as it was dangerous for people connected with the AK. Krystyna told me that soon after the Soviets began their campaign against former soldiers, she collected anything incriminating, including the medals, sealed them in a metal box and bricked it up behind a wall. When the UB came for Janek in 1949, she didn't have time to take the box with her when she left. She knew it was only a matter of time before they came for her.

'She was forced to escape yet again.'

'She made it to Kraków. People she had worked with at the press and propaganda office took her in. When they tried to find out what had happened to Janek they were told by the UB that he had been executed for political crimes against the state. More than twenty thousand former soldiers died in communist jails and concentration camps. For years Krystyna believed that Janek was among them.'

'How did she discover the truth?'

'One of Krystyna's former students from Kraków, who became a professor herself, came to London and gave a talk about life under communism. Janek went along. He was struck by the young professor's vivacity. He said something about her reminded him of Krystyna.'

'Was this before he was married to my mother or after?'

'Not long after. She was newly pregnant with you.' He searches her face.

'It's all right, go on.'

'After the lecture Janek stayed behind and talked to the professor about Poland, and it was then that he found out that she had been a student of Krystyna's. He asked for her address, but it was years before he could find the courage to write.'

'And so, he continued to be dead?'

'He was trying to do the right thing.' He smiles at her. 'Isn't that what we all do? We try to do the right thing for others and in so doing we forget that the only right thing is to be true.'

He glances at his watch. 'There's more to say, but do you mind waiting here while I go and collect the car?'

Catherine shakes her head. She has been listening to him so intently she hasn't touched her breakfast. Now suddenly hungry, she reaches for a bread roll. He puts his hand on her shoulder as he leaves and she watches his lean frame cross the square and cut through one of the narrow passageways to the small car hire office they'd found yesterday shortly after they arrived. It was his idea to meet in Warsaw rather than Kraków. He has something he wants to show her. She knows what this is, but they haven't talked about it, yet. They will save their talk for the long drive across the country to the east.

Drinking her coffee, she sits and watches smartly dressed people crossing the Old Town square on their way to work. An old woman sets up a bread stall, settling down patiently under an umbrella. A group of children, carrying violin cases, pass on their way to school. A man walks his dog. She finishes her breakfast and sits for a few moments with her eyes closed against the sun. Some of the tension from the past few months lifts from her mind. She releases a long, held breath. She imagines Janek and Krystyna reunited after their years apart, long nights of restoring talk, the delight they must have felt in finding one another, and the fear. Now she understands what courage it must have taken for her father to leave his life in Britain and return to a country he no longer recognized. When she opens her eyes again she sees Konrad coming towards her, holding aloft a set of car keys, smiling nervously. Swallowing down her own apprehension, she stands up and crosses the square to join him.

It is close to dusk when they arrive. They get out of the car and stretch their limbs, too exhausted for more talking. She sees that she is still holding the hand-drawn map he gave her at the start of the journey. The map is so detailed it is more of an architect's impression than a set of directions. These are written in Polish on the back of the paper which is crisp and yellowed from age and has been stuck on to stiff cardboard to keep it intact. On the front is a drawing. It shows a large gabled house with a cobbled yard and a long, low stable block in front of the house which is surrounded by fields. A stream runs through one field that is lined with an avenue of precisely drawn oak trees. In the bottom right-hand corner of the drawing made with feather and Indian ink are the initials of her father. He had made the drawing while he was recovering in the new territories of Poland after his release from prison. It was his way of recapturing memories of an early life that he had thought had been obliterated. Catherine recalls what she had learned from Konrad on their long drive. The UB had gone to arrest Krystyna in Warsaw. They hadn't found her – she was already on her way to Kraków – but they ransacked her flat. They took photographs and books. At the next interrogation, the UB presented these things to Janek, laying them out on the desk as evidence of the life he had tried to conceal, and they told him that they no longer needed him to tell them any more lies because they had found what they wanted. They had her. She would be executed the next day. They convinced him that he had betrayed her; they broke into his mind; they planted doubt and fear. Afterwards, Janek drew what he could remember and then he sealed shut his heart.

Owls hoot through the trees as they walk down a long, sandy path towards a large new farmhouse surrounded by a white post and rail fence. Amber lights glow in the upper and lower windows and from the stable block, too. There is a horse lorry in the yard with the name of the Arabian stud farm on a sign on the side. The owners, a Polish couple in their mid forties with three teenage children, are expecting them and have agreed to put them up for a few days. The children are very excited to be involved in helping with a film made by an American.

A low sound attracts their attention and they pause. In the twilight they can see the outlines of horses moving slowly across a field towards them. Catherine's heart catches in her throat as she watches them, nosing the air, scenting something new. The younger horses stay close to their mothers, but as they come up to the fence, one young horse breaks away and pushes forward. It's a chestnut filly with a fine, chiselled head, nostrils pulsing with exquisite curiosity. She comes up to Catherine and presses her muzzle right into her palm. Catherine strokes her white blaze. Next to her she can see that Konrad has been claimed by a young grey horse who nuzzles his shoulder, her liquid eyes dreamy in the half-light. It's cooler here than it is in Warsaw. She can smell trees and earth and crushed grass. She can smell the sky. The stars are falling into place now. She glances up and sees that Konrad has leaned his head back to do the same. They lock eyes for a moment and he nods slowly at her in acknowledgement of the long miles they have travelled and the distance yet to come. Sensing a

Leabharlanna Poiblí Chathair Baile Átha Cliath

Dublin City Public Libraries

shift in the visitors, the horses drift away from the fence, and the couple watch them begin to cross the meadow which stretches all the way to a line of oak trees that Catherine can see are turning; their outlines are edged all around with the gold tinge of autumn.

Leabharlanna Poiblí Chathair Baile Átha Cliath
Dublin City Public Libraries

Acknowledgements

The Beautiful Truth is a work of fiction, but writing it would have been impossible without drawing on many memoirs and accounts of wartime Poland. The books I read were all fascinating and helped to enlarge my understanding of the Polish struggle to gain independence. For the story of the Polish Underground Movement I am indebted to *The Secret Army*, a memoir written by T. Bor-Komorowski, Commander of the Home Army, published by Victor Gollancz in 1950. I took the liberty of including the colonel as a character and using some of his observations, but most of his story, including his personal history and relationship with Krystyna, is entirely fictional. For anyone who wants to learn more about the heroic struggle of the underground resistance, his memoir is vivid, essential reading. While researching this novel, I delved into a range of sources and have changed some facts, timings and places for dramatic reasons. Any omissions or liberties, therefore, are entirely mine. Other sources which provided inspiration and invaluable material include:

Books

Wesley Adamczyk, *When God Looked the Other Way: An Odyssey of War, Exile and Redemption*, University of Chicago Press, 2004

Neal Ascherson, *The Struggles for Poland*, Michael Joseph, 1987

Emily Brontë, *Wuthering Heights*, Everyman Edition, 1991

Norman Davies, *God's Playground: A History of Poland*, Oxford University Press, 1981

Norman Davies, *Heart of Europe: A Short History of Poland*, Oxford University Press, 1984

Zbigniew Iwanski, *The Legends of Kraków*, Poland, 2005

Ted Kazmierski, *Then Nothing Will Fail: An Autobiographical Account of Survival in Poland Under Nazi and Soviet Occupation*, Verand Press, Australia, 1998

Countess Karolina Lanckorońska, *Michelangelo in Ravensbruck: One Woman's War Against the Nazis*, Da Capo Press, 2007

Michael Moran, *A Country in the Moon: Travels in Search of the Heart of Poland*, Granta, 2008

Voyage through the Universe, Time-Life Books, 1988

William Woods, *Poland: Phoenix in the East*, Pelican Books, 1972

Adam Zamoyski, *Poland: A History*, HarperPress, 2009

Websites

www.doomedsoldiers.com – Polish underground soldiers 1944–63. An all volunteer, non-political project which includes testimonies about the persecution of resistance soldiers after the war.

Film

Florian Henckel von Donnersmarck, *The Lives of Others*
Oliver Hirschbiegel, *Downfall*
Roman Polanski, *The Pianist*
Andrzej Wajda, *Katýn*
The Andrzej Wajda *War Trilogy*
The War File, *Europe's Secret Armies: The Polish Resistance*

Music

Hildegard von Bingen, *Heavenly Revelations*
Górecki, *Miserere*
Zbigniew Preisner, *Requiem for my Friend*
Vivaldi, *Stabat Mater*

For unfailing generosity and enduring friendship thanks are due to Michael and Tryphena Huntingford without whose financial support this book would not have been written; for enlivening conversation and many books on Poland thanks to Adam Krasnopolski; for the use of a great apartment in Kraków and many tips on Poland thanks to Andi and Kris Kosmaczewski; to my sister Emma thanks for joining me in Poland and for your superb street-nav skills; to my family and friends thanks for your love and patient understanding of my absence over the past two and a half years.

I thank my editor Kate Parkin for her highly sensitive touch in shaping this book and for subtly challenging me to become a better writer; Morag Lyall for her meticulous and perceptive copy-editing and my agent Maggie McKernan for her unwavering support and encouragement.

I also wish to acknowledge Joanna Kaliszewska for her careful reading of the proof and pointing out anomalies in the Polish. Dr Luc Vaillancourt's critical reading and comments on points of Polish and Russian culture and history were invaluable. Luc's ice hockey expertise also saved me from the embarrassment of skates slipping on ice.

I am also hugely grateful to the Royal Literary Fund and the Society of Authors' Foundation for grants which helped to support the writing of this book.

Read more . . .

Beatrice Colin

THE LUMINOUS LIFE OF LILLY APHRODITE

Decadent, tantalizing Berlin in a Germany torn apart by war at the turn of the twentieth century

The illegitimate, orphaned daughter of a cabaret dancer, Lilly Nelly Aphrodite's early life is one of reinvention. Transformed from maid to war bride via tingle-tangle nightclub girl, she lands in the heart of the glamorous motion picture world and quickly becomes one of Germany's leading silent film stars.

But when she falls in love with a Russian director, she has no idea that the affair will span decades, cross continents and may ultimately cost her everything.

'The storytelling is masterful and the language magical . . . a rich book, in both its prose and in the strength of its characters' *Sunday Times*

'Full of suspense, this is an all-feeling novel, seductively and dramatically told' *Daily Mail*

'An exceptional novel' *Sunday Herald*

Order your copy now by calling Bookpoint on 01235 827716 or visit your local bookshop quoting ISBN 978-1-84854-031-6 www.johnmurray.co.uk

From Byron, Austen and Darwin

to some of the most acclaimed and original contemporary writing, John Murray takes pride in bringing you powerful, prizewinning, absorbing and provocative books that will entertain you today and become the classics of tomorrow.

We put a lot of time and passion into what we publish and how we publish it, and we'd like to hear what you think.

Be part of John Murray – share your views with us at:

www.johnmurray.co.uk
 johnmurraybooks
@johnmurrays
johnmurraybooks